Out of Darkness

~

Book Three of

The Patriot's Warning

A Novel by

C. C. Carroll

Out of Darkness is Book Three of *The Patriot's Warning* trilogy.

Book One:
Edge of Darkness

Book Two:
Plunged Into Darkness

Book Three:
Out of Darkness

<u>Future releases</u>
Book Four:
The Power of Darkness

Also:
Elliot's Secrets and Other Short Stories

Cover photo by:
Mila, Jesse Herzog Light bulb Glance Blonde Girl
1zoom. me

Cover design by Cibyl C. Lane
Clane7420@gmail.com

Acknowledgements

I'd like to give special thanks to a reader, Kelly Slaven.

Kelly contacted me via Facebook after reading *Edge of Darkness* and *Plunged into Darkness* to ask when I would be releasing Book 3. I was so pleased with her reviews on Amazon that I asked if she'd like to be my beta reader for *Out of Darkness*.

All I expected was her opinion, but Kelly went ten steps further. She re-read books 1 & 2 to be sure nothing was out of place in book 3!

Kelly was literally my second pair of eyes.

Though we've never met or spoken to each other, I consider Kelly my new best friend!

Thank you, Kelly!

Slaven4U
So I don't have 2

"The only easy day was yesterday."

Navy Seals Motto

CHAPTER 1

Seventeen-year-old Emma flipped the shredded potatoes while she thought about all she had to do. There was no telling how far behind she'd end up thanks to her little sister's lack of judgment. Gayla banged the heels of her worn leather boots on the rung of her chair. Emma scowled but didn't let her sister see how irritated she was. Instead, she returned her attention to preparing breakfast while making mental notes of what she needed to take care of before she left. Emma seldom smiled, especially during winter. Why should she? What was there to be happy about? Complete isolation and grueling eighteen-hour days—that was her life.

Hardship was nothing new to Emma Harding. It was all she'd ever known. Her parents had homesteaded a farm in the middle of nowhere, Wyoming when she was seven. At fourteen, she became the sole provider for her two-year-old sister.

Her mother had died within hours of giving birth to Gayla. Two years later, as he taught Emma to use the horses to till the garden, their father had clutched his chest and fallen to his knees. Emma assumed it was a heart attack but often wondered if he had succumbed to a broken heart. Her father had worshiped their mother and was never the same after her death.

"I'm hungry," Gayla whined.

"Breakfast is almost ready." Emma turned and forced a smile for Gayla's benefit, as she often did. "It would be a lot better with a big glass of fresh milk." Emma felt a pang of guilt. There were several dozen jars of milk stored in the stream. Still, Gayla needed to understand that bad decisions carried consequences. The milk wouldn't remain fresh for long. Soon, it would become butter or some other dairy product.

Gayla pouted and rubbed her boots together. "I'm sorry. I thought she'd be happier if she wasn't penned up all night."

"Well, I hope you learned a lesson." Emma dumped eggs and potatoes on the worn white plates and plopped them on the table her dad had built for her mother a few years before the lights went out. Her hand caressed

1

the lacquered oak. How she wished her parents were sitting in their cane-backed chairs, enjoying breakfast with them. She'd give anything to have her father by her side as she hunted for the missing cow. He had always made her feel safe. But he was gone. Emma let out a slow puff of air. This wasn't something she was looking forward to. But she had no choice. They needed the cow.

"Eat!" She slid a plate to Gayla. "As soon as the sun comes up, I'm going to try to find Sally."

Emma wanted to be harsh. Very harsh. Even though Gayla was just a little kid and had no idea what she'd done, or how dire the situation was, it was time she grew up. Another cow would be giving birth in a few months, but until then, they'd have no dairy products without Sally.

They ate in silence. Gayla kept her eyes down and chewed slowly. Emma struggled with a way to punish Gayla without making her feel responsible for what the future held without the old milk cow.

Sally was not a free-ranger. She was much too valuable. For the most part, she was like a family pet. She'd follow Emma and Gayla around the farm as they did their chores, then obediently follow them to her pen in the evening. Emma was horrified to find Sally's gate open and the cow missing when she went to milk her the night before. Her little sister admitted to leaving it open deliberately.

Searching for her in the dark wasn't an option. Emma had barely slept and made several trips to the barn during the night, praying to find the cow in her pen munching hay or sleeping. Each time, she was met with disappointment.

The daily routine on the farm began at four a.m. On this morning, Emma was feeding and watering the animals at three a.m. She had to be ready to leave by daybreak.

***

After breakfast, Emma slipped into her mother's silk long johns and slid into the old ski pants. She layered the insulated top with a fleece and wool sweater. The ski clothes had proved to be a blessing during Wyoming's bitter winters, and Emma took extra care in handling them. They couldn't be replaced now, and she relied on them every winter. After putting on a pair of wool socks, she pulled on the suede, fur-lined boots and stretched her legs out. "Ah. Nice and toasty." She'd hoped for a smile from Gayla but received none.

Gayla sighed as she handed her sister a neck gaiter and ear warmer/headband.

Emma squeezed her small hand. "Thank you, Jellybean." Every time Emma called Gayla Jellybean, it brought back the memory of her father. It was his nickname for her. He said it was because she was sweet on the inside and tough on the outside. Emma had passed the moniker on to her little sister.

Gayla's lips tightened into a frightened frown, and she nodded.

Emma had the urge to make light of things. She had to go, but Gayla was terrified. She couldn't leave her that way.

Emma grabbed the sides of her head and fell to the ground. "Oh, no!" she wailed. "I can't see! The snow has blinded me!" She rocked back and forth on her knees. "Why didn't I remember the snow goggles?"

Gayla's eyes widened in panic. She took a deep breath, cupped her mouth, and stepped back. Emma watched as her sister's eyes shifted and landed on the table. She ran toward it, snatched up the goggles, and placed them on Emma's head.

The two chuckled as they rolled on the floor, laughing and hugging each other.

***

As Emma made sure she'd dressed appropriately for the bitter cold, she paused. She couldn't look at the ski outfits without remembering how they'd brought her parents together. Emma's mom was an avid skier. Her dad, not so much. But a chance meeting at Jackson Hole while they were in college had sealed their fate. Emma zipped the jacket and thanked her mom for the warm clothes.

"Wait!" Gayla begged. "Don't go yet. Wait a while. Maybe Sally will come home."

Emma tugged at her neck gaiter. The warmth from the fireplace was making her itchy. "I hope so, but we can't risk it. Sally's used to being cared for. Sort of like this little girl I know." Emma ruffled her sister's hair. "Left alone, she may freeze to death."

Gayla began to sob. "I didn't mean to hurt her. I swear!"

Emma cursed herself, bent, and held Gayla. "I know. And Sally knows too. She loves you. I'm sure she's fine. She's probably already headed home. I just need to hurry her along."

Emma stood and glanced around the cabin. What else did she need to do before leaving? She went to the large wooden pantry in the kitchen. Her fingers traced the panel of one of the doors. One more thing her dad had built. Memories of him surrounded her. She leaned against the wooden structure. "Please, Dad. Be with me. I'm scared this time. To be honest, I'm terrified." She straightened, shook the fear away, opened the doors, and checked the contents. Why hadn't she thought of it earlier? Now she'd lose even more precious daylight.

"Gayla, I have to leave soon. Put on your jacket and come with me."

If she didn't make it back, what would Gayla do? No! She couldn't think like that. She'd be home before nightfall. But just in case, Gayla would need extra food inside. The pantry needed to be re-stocked.

While Gayla put on her coat, Emma walked to a window over the porch and looked outside. A bad storm was coming. She'd seen the signs too many times before to ignore them, and she could feel it in her bones. Emma turned to Gayla. "While you get dressed, I'm going to get the snowshoes dad built for mom."

Using the snowshoes would consume a considerable amount of energy. She'd eaten a hearty breakfast and had packed plenty of food for a couple of days. The extra effort would be worth it. If they got a few feet of snow, Emma could easily step off into a three-foot ditch and snap her leg. If that happened, it could be the end. She needed the snowshoes.

She went to her closet, took them from the top shelf, and shivered. Not from the cold, but from the realization that her trek to find the cow could end in disaster. Maybe she should reconsider. They could make it without dairy products for a while. Emma covered her mouth and let out a gust of air. No. Their life was hard enough *with* the dairy products. She didn't want to think about how different it would be without them.

Emma walked out of her bedroom. Gayla stood beside the front door in her coat and slipped on her mittens. "Okay. So, what are we doing?"

Emma reached for her hand and led Gayla across the frozen yard to the cellar about twenty yards away. "I think we should fill the pantry before I leave. I've meant to do it for weeks."

Once they stocked the pantry, they walked back outside. Emma pointed to one of the rockers on the front porch. "Sit. It will be daylight soon."

As they rocked and waited for the sun, Emma ventured to go a bit further. "Gayla. Do you remember what I said we would do if we ran low on feed for the animals during the winter?"

Gayla nodded. "I think so. You said we should let the goats and cows forage. And we keep one *big* pig and a smaller male and female. We let the others out and hope they find food."

"That's right. What else?"

"Hmm." Gayla tapped her lips with her glove. "Oh, we keep all of the chickens, horses, and milk cows. The chickens and milk cows get food first."

Emma raised her hand for a high-five. "Good." Emma smiled and squeezed Gayla's small hand. "Good."

As the sun began to cast its light on the farm, Emma walked down the steps. She stood a few feet from the porch, stared up at the light falling snow, and shivered. She brushed the crystals from her eyelashes before embracing her little sister and issuing last-minute orders. "Go inside. Lock the door, and don't come out unless you need to use the outhouse, get firewood, or feed the animals. I left the wind-up clock on the kitchen counter. Make sure you wind it in the morning! I don't want to have to rely on the sun to tell the time when I get back." Emma scrunched her nose and smiled. "Got it?"

"Okay, Emma." Gayla's pupils seemed to darken, and her lips trembled.

Gayla was young, but Emma knew she would never admit that she was terrified. Was that a good thing or a bad thing? Emma's hand instinctively massaged her throat. She wasn't sure now. But they needed Sally. Should she take Gayla with her? Emma's breathing became labored. No. Gayla would slow her down, and she didn't have the clothes to withstand the bitter cold for long. Plus, she could get hurt.

"One more thing. If anyone comes, don't even *think* about asking them to come inside! Hide in the little room under the bed and be quiet."

Gayla began to cry and begged her to stay. Emma shook her. "Listen to me, Gayla. I've got to find Sally. We need her." She stood and wagged her finger. "Remember our lessons. Don't put more than one log in the fireplace at a time—and do it gently. Do *not* let the fire burn out. I put several loads of firewood on the porch this morning." She smiled, got on her knees, and squeezed Gayla's shoulder. But you know how to get more if you need it. Right?"

"Sure." Gayla glanced at the front porch lined with firewood, and a tear slid down her cheek. "Looks like you think you may be gone for a while."

Emma gripped her sister's shoulder tighter. "No. Silly. It just may get extra cold, and I want you to stay warm." Emma's gloves wiped across her

5

already chapped lips. "Gayla. If I don't find Sally by tomorrow, I'll head home." She gave Gayla a final hug, kissed her cheek, then gently eased her back. "I know I said I left extra feed for the cow, chickens, goats, and pigs. But maybe you should give them a bit of corn while I'm gone."

"But you said not to go outside."

Emma exhaled. "Well, not unless you have to."

Gayla's eyes filled with tears. She flung herself into Emma's arms. "This is all my fault! I may never see you again!"

Emma held her back. "Stop it! I'll be back! Like I said. If I don't find Sally by tomorrow afternoon, I'll come home." Emma twisted her mouth and put her hands on her hips. "What's our rule when things get tough?"

Gayla wiped her eyes and inhaled. "I know. I know. Be strong. Cowgirl-up." Gayla sniffled and took a step back. "Aren't you going to take one of the horses?"

"No. I don't want to worry about feed and water. Plus, if the snow gets too deep, they could break a leg. We can't afford to lose one." She rubbed Gayla's shoulder. "I know I'm leaving them in good hands."

Emma hoisted her pack, bow, and rifle on her back and stared at the cabin. "If it starts snowing hard, it could slow me down." She peered down her nose and shoved her fists into her hips. "I know I said not to leave the cabin unless you had to, but if for some reason I'm not back by tomorrow, you need to make sure the animals are fed. Got it?"

"Okay."

"No! Not okay. Promise!"

"Geez." Gayla's head dipped. She sniffled and clutched her coat. "Okay. I promise."

"Remember. Keep the fire going."

Gayla nodded and yelled as she ran into the house. "I love you, Emma!"

Emma headed toward the forest and fought the urge to look back. She wanted to run back, but that couldn't happen. Instead, she yelled, "I love you too!"

Soon, the snow would completely cover the tracks she'd found with the flashlight the night before. The faster she found Sally, the quicker she could return home to Gayla.

About a hundred yards from the cabin, Emma stopped and allowed her eyes to follow the tracks into the forest. She never went out there when she knew the weather might turn nasty. It was something her father had not only taught her but had warned her to avoid. He'd pointed to the forest. "Even a compass can fail you out there if the snow gets too deep to maneuver. Small dips and gullies can fill with snow and snap a leg like a twig. That would most likely mean death." He gripped her shoulder and gave her a stern look. "If you go out there during or after a heavy snow, never go alone!" His words haunted and terrified her, but she had no choice.

Emma turned and stared at the small two-bedroom cabin. The backdrop of the distant snow-covered mountains outlining the smoke billowing from the chimney brought a smile to her face. It looked like a picture. Maybe she could paint it one day. She looked down at the fading tracks, took a deep breath, and glanced at the sky. Gayla wasn't afraid of the dark. Emma had made sure of that. But she'd never been completely alone, and the fear of not returning home before nightfall troubled Emma. Both for her and her little sister.

"Please, let me find Sally," she whispered as she trudged into the timbers. "Gayla needs me. She's just a baby."

***

It was past noon. The tracks had vanished about two hours earlier, and there was no sign of the cow. Old Sally had been heading west, so Emma decided to keep going in that direction. The sun was overhead now. She'd take a break and wait for it to make a move instead of digging out her compass.

Emma's stomach rumbled. She sat beneath a tree, opened her pack, and pulled out a tin filled with jerky. As she nibbled on a piece, she thought about Gayla and felt herself tremble. It wasn't from the cold. Her mother's skiing outfit and gloves were keeping her warm. What if something happened and she couldn't return home? Even with all the food, there was no way Gayla could handle being all alone. Her eyes closed as she tried to quell the tears that threatened to form. She thought of her life and the loneliness. No. There was no way Gayla could handle that.

Josh Elliot and his wife, Lorna, had been their neighbors and her parents' best friends. They shared everything and helped each other through rough times. The Elliots had been preparing to move to one of the new ports on the East Coast when Emma's mother died. Josh had begged her father to go with them, but he declined. He swore he'd send Emma to them one day so she could go to school and live a normal life. For several reasons, that day never came.

7

Emma held no grudge for his decision. In hindsight, it was probably a blessing. She both loved and loathed her life. Her biggest struggles were the lack of companionship and worrying about Gayla. The closest she came to having a boyfriend had been during her brief visit to the Hudson Ranch. She was seven when she first met Jason Alvise. Emma smiled. She could still picture his boyish face. Their first encounter was brief, but Emma had never outgrown her infatuation with the handsome young boy.

Her heart raced. She thought of Jason often and fancied herself in love with him. How silly. Who falls in love at the age of seven? The memory of Jason lingered because he'd been so adorable running after the wagon as they drove away and because she'd never laid eyes on another little boy since. But, ten years later, his shouts of, "Bye, Emma! Bye!" still woke her night after night.

"Maybe it's time we left." Emma gazed at the hazy, dark horizon for a minute and clutched her temples. No. Stop it. You're just lonely. And this is your home.

***

The snow fell harder, and Emma glanced at the sky. She was hoping it would quit soon. She guessed it was around four p.m. Hope of returning home before nightfall vanished quickly. Instead, shelter and fire became her top priority.

While gathering branches, images of Gayla, alone and afraid, caused Emma to make a difficult decision. Not one to give up, she'd head back the next afternoon, with or without Sally. No way she would let Gayla spend another night alone. Emma thought about how different life would be for the next few months without the old cow and her precious liquid.

Sally had become their only milk cow when the other died a few months back, and it would be spring before her other cow's calf was born and she'd produce milk. They loathed goat's milk and cheese, but from now on, Emma vowed to keep one as a milker. At least the pigs and chickens would like it. The thought of the extra work didn't thrill her, but Emma would do what she had to.

After starting a fire, she built a shelter with her tarp. The night sounds were intimidating, but it was her concern for Gayla that kept her awake. Gripping her rifle, she stoked the fire for much of the evening before falling asleep.

***

Emma sat up and blinked her eyes. After a second of collecting herself, she blinked and looked again. No. No. No. No. No! She spun and took in her surroundings. Not yet! It couldn't be! She had awoken to an unrecognizable landscape. What was a green forest with a light dusting of snow when she fell asleep was now a white blanket of powder. Every tree, every path, appeared identical. The dark, overcast sky, filled with thick, ominous clouds, erased all hints of guidance.

If she went home, they would have no dairy products. She wasn't concerned about getting lost; she had her compass. But if she continued and broke a leg in the deepening snow, she'd most likely never make it home. She quivered. No good choices. She made the gut-wrenching decision to return home now instead of waiting until the afternoon.

Without Mother Nature to guide her, she opened her backpack and rummaged through the contents. The compass? Where was her compass? Panic set in. Without it, she had no idea where "home" was. She spun, unsure of the direction she should travel. "What have I done? What have I done?" She fell to her knees. Her screams echoed through the forest.

She needed to head southeast, but the dark skies gave no hint of direction. Leaning against a large oak, she took a few deep breaths and tried to calm her panic. "I think I need to go that way." Emma trembled with every step, wondering if she was, indeed, headed home. She rubbed her mouth with the back of her gloves and pulled her thick wool neck gaiter over her nose. Move Emma, move. How will Gayla survive if you don't make it back?

Emma trudged through the seemingly endless snow hoping to find some sign to lead her home. A chunk of moss on a tree would at least hint of which way was north. Soon, faith in finding her way home dimmed.

Emma's energy was fading. She needed to rest. She needed food. She leaned her rifle against a tree, shrugged out of her backpack, and pulled out the tin of jerky. Frozen. She snapped several chunks free, filled the inside pocket of her jacket, then tossed a brittle piece into her mouth. A ruckus in the distance startled her. Not a bear. Please don't let it be a bear! She spit the chunk of thawing meat from her mouth, grabbed her rifle, and ducked behind a tree. She raised the AR-15, peeked around the side of the big pine, then lowered the gun and rested it against the tree.

Emma's heart raced. "Sally!" Emma ran toward the cow. "I'm so happy to see you." She nuzzled Sally and brushed her icy face. "I can't believe I found you." Emma laughed. "Or did you find me?" She unzipped her jacket and pulled out the canteen of water she was protecting from the freezing temperatures. She squatted, emptied the water, and began filling the container with Sally's precious white liquid, stopping long enough to take several long gulps. The fresh warm milk renewed her strength and hope.

Emma had no idea which way was home. Maybe Sally knew. At this point, what could it hurt? Perhaps the longing of her warm stable would lead Sally home. She gathered her belongings, pulled the rope from her pack, and wrapped it around Sally's neck. "Let's go home, girl. Let's eat. Let's eat."

Sally let out a loud "moo" and moseyed along.

As they trudged through the snow, Emma thought about how foolish it was to forget her compass. The compass brought back the memory of one of her early hunting expeditions when she was ten years old. Who had learned more that day? Her or Dad? She smiled at the recollection.

***

"I wanna go home. We're gonna get lost."

"No way! We'll find our way home. Got my compass right here." Her dad patted his coat pocket. "I never leave home without it." He knelt and gripped Emma's shoulders. "I know trudging through all this snow is tough, honey, but can you go a little further? Maybe we can make it to the tree over there?"

"Okay, Dad," Emma whimpered.

They made it to the tree. "Can we stop now? Can we go home?"

"Shhh. I think I saw something." Her dad pointed to yet another tree.

After a few hours of slogging through the powdery forest, making it from one tree to another, Emma raised her rifle, fired, and brought down a ten-point buck.

She sighed and dropped her shoulders. "Can we go home now?"

"Uh, yeah."

Her father dragged her kill and repeatedly muttered, "Holy smokes, you never cease to amaze me."

***

Emma smiled every time she pictured the shock on her dad's face. Years later, she understood why her father had encouraged her to continue that day. It would have been easier to take their neighbor, Josh, to hunt for game, but *she* needed to learn.

10

Her dad and Josh kept the bull away from the heifers. The extra work to feed more livestock than they used was taxing on the two families. With a steady supply of pigs, goats, and chickens, they kept the cattle down to two milk cows, a bull, four for butchering each year, and a couple of extras. Anything could happen. Hunting supplied security and variety. If an illness hit their livestock, they'd likely starve without the skill.

The railroads had opened in their area when Emma was eleven. Her father and Josh bartered their extra livestock, smoked meats, produce, and canned goods. A short time later, Emma's life had taken a dramatic turn. Their only neighbors were gone, and she not only lost her mother but her father as well.

"Thanks for teaching me to cowgirl-up, Dad." Emma wiped the crystals forming on her cheeks and urged the old milk cow to hurry home.

***

Emma gasped. The rope around Sally's neck slipped from her hands. What she saw filled her with emotion and gratitude. She pulled the heavy snow-laden wool neck warmer below her chin and fell to her knees. "Look, Sally. That's not a campfire in the woods. That's smoke from a chimney! Dad said there weren't any houses in either direction for over a hundred miles! That's gotta be home!"

Emma felt it was best to let her emotions out now. No way Gayla could ever see her crying! Even crying tears of joy showed weakness. And, she had to be strong for Gayla. She tightly gripped the old cow and allowed the tears of relief to escape for several seconds. How many times had she done that over the years? Not many. There was no time for mourning, only time for survival. She took off her gloves, scooped a handful of snow, and washed her face. She'd leave no trace of fear or sadness. No. Gayla could never know Emma was afraid.

She kissed the cow below the ear and rubbed her neck. "You did good, Sally. You did good." She nodded toward the smoke. "Let's go home, girl."

As they neared the clearing in front of the house, her excitement ebbed. Emma stiffened. Her eyes squinted, her jaw tightened, and her mind reeled. No. Not one visitor since the census takers last year. Then she leaves Gayla alone one lousy time, and people show up? She pulled out her binoculars and watched three men lead four horses to the barn. Four horses meant four men. She could handle that. Emma inhaled. Stay calm. Think of Gayla. "Sorry, old girl, but I need to see what's going on."

Emma tied Sally to a tree and slinked toward the cabin.

CHAPTER 2

When the ex-President, Chris Alvise, received word that his old friend had died a few years earlier, he decided to send three of his security details on a rescue mission. His oldest son, Jason, insisted on going along. If they found Harding's children, Emma and Gayla, Jason and the others were to bring them home to Hudson Ranch.

The Harding homestead was about two hundred miles from Hudson Ranch, and not as easy to navigate as it once was. While some repairs had been made to the main highways and bridges, most of the less used roads had vanished beneath years of growth, and only a handful of bridges remained safe to cross. There weren't many vehicles anyway. Most people relied on trains and horses for transportation.

Chris Alvise stood outside the horse barn at Hudson Ranch. He grabbed his eldest son, pulled him close, and slapped him on the back. "Son, I know you want to do this, but I'd rather you let my men go alone."

Jason tightened his hold on his father. "Dad," he whispered. "I'm not a kid anymore. I want to find Emma."

His father released his grip and took a step back. "I know." His head bobbed, and a twisted grin appeared. "It should take about two days for you to reach their cabin. But this time of year, there's no telling what stunt Mother Nature might deliver. I hope to see you back in a week."

Jason frowned. "The snow's coming down pretty good. How about we make that three weeks. I'd kind of like to get away for a while if you don't mind."

His father chuckled. "Three weeks it is. You've been itching for some freedom since I was elected."

Jason threw his arms around his father and thanked him.

"What about me?" his mother asked.

Jason bent to hug her and kissed her cheek. "Thanks for sticking up for me when I asked to go."

She pulled back and held his face. "You're a grown man, just like you said." She flapped her hand for him to shoo. "Go. Go find Emma and her sister." Her mouth dipped into a tight, worried frown. "Jason, the Census your Uncle Frank found Emma on was taken several years ago. You need to be prepared…"

Jason cut her off. His jaw tightened. "Emma is okay. I can feel it."

His mother nodded, turned, and walked quickly through the snow toward their house. Jason knew she wanted to leave before he saw her cry. He yelled, "I love you, Mom."

She didn't look back as she raised her hand and waved.

***

Jason had hoped to make the trip in two days, but the sudden snowstorm slowed him and his father's men considerably. It was three days before they reached the Harding homestead and found Gayla alone.

Jason questioned the little girl. "How old are you?"

"Almost six, but I'm tougher than most seven-year-olds."

"No, kidding. I knew it the minute you threatened to shoot me with your slingshot."

Gayla scowled. "You better be glad you weren't a rabbit, Mister."

"I am. I am." Jason exhaled, patted his chest in exaggerated relief, then reached out and massaged her small hand. "So, how long have you been alone?"

"Since yesterday." Gayla lowered her head and tapped her toes together. "I set our milk cow free. Poor Sally. Emma went to find her."

"Emma?" Jason tried to disguise his pleasure at hearing the name.

"Yeah, my sister."

"Where are your parents?"

"Dead." Gayla shrugged. "Never met my momma. My daddy died when I was two. It's just me and Emma."

"I'm sorry." Jason hated to bring it up. His father had shown him the census report. Still, he had to be sure the family living on the property was the Harding family. Too often, they found homesteads occupied by people posing as owners after they murdered the lawful residents. The girl's answers gave him confidence that they were, indeed, Emma and Gayla Harding. Jason felt an overpowering sensation of relief.

Gayla breathed on the foggy windowpane, rubbed it with her sleeve, and stared outside at the falling snow. "Emma's going to be *really* mad that I let you in. I imagine she won't even make up a new bedtime story for me."

Jason scanned the hundreds of books lining the shelves. How sad what the EMP stole. He was fortunate to receive an education when so many did not. He noticed the hardcover on the coffee table and opened it. Page after page of masterpieces by The Highwaymen. Jason knew their work well. His mother owned several of their paintings. She said they were a group of African American landscape artists from Florida. You don't need to be able to read to appreciate beauty.

He closed the book and pulled up a chair beside Gayla. "If your sister isn't home by morning, we'll find her." He brushed her hair with his fingers. "If she's not back tonight, I'll read to you from one of your storybooks."

Gayla sighed. "Thanks, but Emma's read them to me so many times I can't stand it. Now she makes up stories. She says the other books are not age-appropriate." She glared at Jason, and her eyes thinned. "Trust me. You do *not* want to ask her what she means. She'll make you pull out the dictionary." Gayla shook her head and let out a puff of air. "Drives me crazy. All Emma does is read when she's not working." She shot Jason a smile. "I can read, too, you know. She makes me do it all the time."

"Really?" Jason took a breath and brushed his hair back. "What else does Emma do?"

Gayla huffed, shrugged, and stared back out the window. "What everybody does. Chops wood, mends fences, takes care of the animals, and grows food." Gayla swung around and ran for the pantry. "Are you and the others hungry? It's already past my lunchtime." She opened the doors and handed him a jar of stew. "Emma makes a lot of this when she butchers a cow or pig or kills a deer or other game. We have more in the hiding place under the bed, and the cellar is full."

Jason stared in disbelief at the jar and took in the contents of the pantry. Row upon row of canned meats, vegetables, soups, and stews lined the shelves. "Emma does all this—alone?"

Gayla raised her chin. "I help her."

"I'll bet you do."

Gayla returned to the window. Jason lifted the jars, examined them, and scanned the cabin. His eyes landed on Gayla, and he rubbed his chest. It felt full and weighty—as if his heart had outgrown the room provided. How in the world could Emma manage this by herself? Either this was a joke, or he was about to meet Super Woman.

Jason's men rushed inside, and one pulled him aside while the others took positions by the windows.

"We may be in trouble, sir. More people live here than just the two girls."

"How do you know? What's going on?"

"The barn is stocked and immaculate, and we found a cellar filled with homemade canned foods and vegetables. There's a good-sized greenhouse to the west of us. And that smell of smoking meat! Well, about a hundred yards from here, there's a smokehouse loaded with curing meat. No way a seventeen-year-old girl and her baby sister do this alone."

"But, Gayla says it's only the two of them."

"No way, sir. There's no telling how many live here. They may be watching. We should ask Gayla to call out and tell them who we are."

Jason hesitated and rubbed his chin. Little kids don't lie well if you catch them off guard. "Gayla, how many people help take care of this place?"

"Geez. I told you. Just been me and Emma since our dad died." She returned her gaze out the window.

Jason smirked and lifted his brows.

The soldier lowered his rifle and rubbed his chin. "What the hell? This is nuts."

Jason huffed and bobbed his head. "I agree."

Gayla rubbed her sleeve across the foggy window again. "Hey. Look. Over there. It's Sally. She's standing in those trees." Gayla held the windowsill, jumped up and down, and giggled. "Emma is trying to find her, and there she is. She was right here the whole time."

Jason pulled out his binoculars. Sally was *not* standing in the trees. She was tethered to one. He smiled and lowered his binoculars. "Gayla, I think your sister's home. She might think we're bad guys. Would you let her know Jason Alvise, son of President Alvise, has come to visit?"

Gayla ran to the door and stood on the porch. She waved her arms. "Emma, guess what?" she yelled. "The President's son is here. Jason said you met him a long time ago at his ranch."

Jason joined Gayla and shouted. "Emma. My Uncle Frank saw the census report. When Mom and Dad found out about your father, they sent me to check on you."

Jason's men readied their rifles.

"What the hell are you doing? Lower your guns," Jason barked.

"Not happening, sir. Our orders are to protect you at all costs."

15

Jason scowled and called out again. "Emma. Remember me? I'm Jason. President Alvise's son. I'm walking out. My men's orders are to shoot first and ask questions later. Please, I know you're armed. Lay down your weapon or…"

"Or what?" came the cold response.

Jason and his men turned and stared down the barrel of Emma's AR-15 as she lay atop the roof of the shed about twenty feet from the front porch.

"I would advise *you,* gentlemen, to lower *your* weapons."

Jason's hands crossed his chest as he leaned forward and chuckled. "It's you. It's really you. I knew the first time I saw you that you were going to be a hellion. I was about seven years old. I tried to chase down your wagon when you left. Do you remember?"

Emma kept her rifle leveled. "If you're Jason Alvise, you should remember what you told me at the barn."

"I, um." He shot a nervous glance at his men. "I think I said I was going to marry you one day," he said softly as his face burned. His men snickered and lowered their guns.

Emma lowered her rifle, put it on safety, and slid from the roof. Her landing was less than graceful. "Ouch." She stood and limped toward Jason. "That was easier a few years ago. I should have used the ladder."

Emma held out her hand as Jason rushed to her aid.

"Nice to see you again, Jason Alvise."

***

Jason's men took care of Sally while Emma warmed up by the fireplace and sipped a cup of hot tea. When the men returned, Emma and Gayla showed them around her property.

Emma pointed to the shed and laughed. "You've already seen the shed. There's a cellar door behind it. I try to keep it well stocked."

Jason smiled. "The men found it. They were impressed."

"Oh, then I guess there's no need showing it to you," Emma said softly.

"Are you kidding? I'd love to see it."

Emma felt her face warm. She wanted Jason to see it but didn't want him to think she was bragging. Her heartbeat increased as they went down the steps. When she lit the lantern hanging by the door, Jason's mouth opened, and his eyes widened.

"How do you do this by yourself?" Jason asked as he took in the contents of the small room.

16

Emma fought to disguise her pleasure at his reaction.

Gayla put her hands on her hips and tapped her foot. "I *told* you, I help."

Jason and the men looked amused, and Emma squeezed her shoulder. "Yes, you do."

"Do you want to check out the barn?" she asked Jason. "I know the others saw it. I watched them putting the horses up."

"I'm right behind you," he said and followed her up the steps.

When they reached it, Emma swung open the door to the barn. "The chicken coup is in here at the back. My dad said it would help with the wild animals having them for dinner. He and Mr. Josh put glass over the coops so the hens would lay better."

"Yeah," Gayla said. "Chickens like sunlight. Make them lay more eggs."

"You're pretty smart for a five-year-old," Jason said.

Gayla scowled. "Mister. How many times do I have to tell you I'm almost six?"

Jason threw his hands in the air in surrender. "I swear! I won't forget again."

Emma and the other men chuckled.

Emma nodded for them to go inside. "I keep the goats, horses, and mommy cows and calves in there at night and when the weather's bad. I bet they're starving."

"We took care of them, ma'am," one of the men said.

"That wasn't necessary," Emma blurted.

"Emma. You told me not to go outside unless I had to. I hadn't fed them yet, and they were hungry," Gayla pouted.

Emma glanced at the men, then lowered her head. "Thank you. That was very generous of you."

Jason pointed out into the field. "I take it that's a pole barn for the other cows."

"Yep."

Jason nodded toward the pigpen. "I see you keep them as far away as possible."

Emma pinched her nose and giggled. "Absolutely."

He looked at the garden about a hundred feet from the house. "Do you think anything survived in this snow?"

Emma shrugged. "Pretty sure. At least the beets, kale, and other greens. And the carrots. I mulched them good."

"Can I see the greenhouse?" he asked. "And the wonderful smell from the smokehouse has been driving me crazy."

"Sure." Emma would never admit it, but she was thrilled to show off her little farm.

***

Emma's heart had not stopped racing since she laid eyes on him. She knew it was Jason the instant she saw him. She couldn't believe he was there—and he wasn't a little boy anymore. She thought of the pictures of men in the old magazines her parents brought with them. Those men had nothing on Jason. He was tall, muscular, and much more handsome.

"Are you planning on staying the night?" her face burned as she asked.

"If you don't mind. We'll sleep in the barn."

"Why? So you can freeze to death? Gayla can sleep with me, and you can all stay in the house."

"Are you're sure."

"Don't be silly. Let's grab some meat from the smokehouse. It's way past lunchtime, and I'm starving."

Emma offered everyone a slice of ham and bread to tide them over until dinner was ready. Jason's men took theirs and went to check out the stream with Gayla.

"Tomorrow I'll show you the Elliot's old house. It's three times as big as this one and a lot nicer."

Jason seemed confused. "Why didn't you move there?"

Emma paused, then shook her head. "Several reasons. Too far from the stream. That's why we built the garden, barn, and smokehouse here. If something happened to the well at the Elliot's, we'd have to tote water from here."

"Makes sense."

"I keep it in good shape and stocked with clothes and supplies." Emma turned the slab of dough and kneaded it. "If something happens to this place, we'll have somewhere to move. But I hope we never have to."

"That's smart, Emma."

Emma looked down at the loaf of bread. "I can't take credit for something that wasn't my idea. It was Dad's," she said softly.

While Emma heated vegetables and panned the loaf of bread, Jason told her why he was there. "Dad wants me to bring you and Gayla back to our ranch. You'll be safe there."

Emma paused. Her heart raced. She and Gayla could leave and have a new life. Gayla could meet other kids, and she could be close to the boy she'd dreamed of for years. She walked to a window over the front porch and stared. As torn as she was, she quickly made her decision. Emma turned toward Jason. "We're safe here."

"What? Are you kidding? You're killing yourself."

Emma went back to the kitchen, lifted the Dutch oven, and slid it into the hot coals of the fireplace. She brushed her hands on her apron and exhaled.

"Jason, this is the only home I've ever really known." She took his hand, led him to the front porch, and pointed toward the majestic tree on the hill that enveloped two crosses under its umbrella of limbs. "My parents are there," she nodded, "watching over us. They died trying to secure our future. I can't let them down."

"Emma, please, reconsider. How long will Gayla last if something happens to you? We even have electricity and running water at the ranch. Well, most of the time." He shrugged his shoulders. "Seriously. How long can you keep on going like this?"

Emma wondered the same thing every day of her life. She looked back at the crosses. "Courage. That's what Dad said it took. He was always quoting people." She grinned. "Courage is not about having the strength to go on; it's going on when you don't have the strength. Theodore Roosevelt."

Gayla and the men headed their way, and the conversation ended.

CHAPTER 3

Jason and his men stayed on for several days, and he begged Emma to move to Hudson Ranch at every opportunity.

"Who'll take care of Gayla if something happens to you? At least, let us take her back to the ranch."

Appreciative, but torn, Emma struggled with her decision. Gayla *would* be better off at the Hudson Ranch. Complete isolation was no life for a child. Heck, it was all *she* could do to handle it.

Her throat knotted as she tried to explain things to her sister. "Gayla, we can visit. It's not right for you to live this way, and Jason promised to bring you back often."

Gayla jumped from the couch. "No. I'm not leaving. I'll run away. Please, Emma. Please don't send me away."

"There are a lot of children at the ranch. We're all alone here. You've never even met another kid. What if something happens to me? Who'll take care of you? You're only five."

"I'm almost six," she wailed. "You taught me to take care of myself. I can milk, make bread, start a fire, and fish. Just because I can't use the plow doesn't mean I can't use a hoe and grow food. You can teach me to preserve it. I can already clean fish and chickens. I can do it. I promise!" Gayla lunged at Emma. Her arms tightened around her like a chain. "Please! Please! Don't send me away!"

Emma's constricted throat was suffocating. She whispered into Gayla's ear. "I made Dad a promise. I said I'd take care of you. Being alone isn't good for either of us. But I feel like I'm obligated to make the farm work. I'm not sure what to do. Maybe we should both leave. Maybe you should go with Jason and have a normal life." She eased herself from Gayla's grip. "I need to think. It's going to be dark soon. Can you milk Sally and call in the goats and chickens?"

Gayla wiped her eyes and nodded her head. "I'll check on the smokehouse and greenhouse, too."

Jason walked up beside Gayla and squeezed her shoulder. "We'll help her, Emma. You take your time."

Emma's lips clenched. She nodded, walked out the front door, and took a deep breath of the frosty air. Then she walked alone through the falling snow.

***

Sitting on the fallen log beside the stream was always comforting. It was Emma's favorite, seldom used, retreat. The one place she could think and clear her mind. The peaceful trickling of water as it lapped over the rocks could mesmerize her for hours.

Jason was wrong. Gayla *could* survive without her. Perhaps she couldn't endure the hardship for years, but she was tougher than Jason realized. Maybe a test was in order. Emma tapped her boots together to remove the fresh powder covering her ankles and wiggled her tingling toes. The sky was turning dark, and the snow was falling harder. She stared at her boots as she knocked the frost away. Who was she kidding? This wasn't just about Gayla. It was about her. Emma had to be honest. She was tired. Part of her would love to leave and go with Jason. Then what? She didn't actually know him. She'd only met him once when she was seven years old. For all she knew, they'd end up hating each other, and she and Gayla would spend their lives working the fields at Hudson Ranch. No. No. No. No. Her little ranch meant freedom. She was going nowhere. But what about Gayla? Before she returned home, she stopped by the crosses beneath the tree. She needed to ask her parents for guidance.

***

"Gayla." Emma burst through the door, ran to the fireplace, and shook the chill away. "Bring in two loads of firewood. The temperature is dropping fast."

"We'll get it," one of Jason's men offered.

"No. Gayla can do it."

"Yeah. I can do it." Gayla sniffed. "But thank you."

"Wait," Emma stopped her. "Put two more loads on the porch. If this snow doesn't let up, we'll need it close by and dry."

"Four loads?" Gayla scoffed as she slipped into her oversized down jacket. "You tryin' to kill me?"

"Are you saying you can't handle it?" Emma's hands went to her hips. "What if no one was here to do it for you?"

Gayla bristled and crossed her arms. "Oh, I can do it. I just don't want to. I'm not dumb. I know what you're doing." She rolled her eyes, snatched on her gloves, and slammed the door behind her.

Jason scowled. "Emma, what *are* you doing? Good grief. She's a little kid."

"I need to see if she has what it takes to make it without me if something happens. There's enough food canned to last her years, and you promised to come back and check on us if we didn't leave. I assume you're a man of your word. She squinted. "Gayla's right about all she said she could do. If she has firewood and is willing to haul it, she'll be okay if something happens to me. I'll make sure there's always plenty chopped. One day she'll be strong enough to cut her own."

"I give up." Jason threw his hands in the air and scowled. "And yes, I'm a man of my word. Just don't shoot me when I come back."

The soldiers stared at the floor. One coughed and cleared his throat. "Ma'am, if word gets out that a seventeen-year-old girl outsmarted us and held us at gunpoint, we're doomed."

"Who am I gonna tell?" Emma spread her arms and smirked.

***

The men had been at Emma's for over a week and were preparing to leave. "I wish we could stay longer," Jason said, "but my dad gave me three weeks. If I'm not home by then, he'll send out a search party." He chuckled.

His tough laugh sounded hollow. Emma was sure she sensed a touch of sadness in his voice and expression.

"I understand," she said. Jason was leaving. The ache in her heart made it hard to communicate. She'd waited for him her entire life. Telling Jason goodbye would be heart-wrenching. But she couldn't let a ten-year-old encounter dictate her life.

Emma's heart raced as she strolled along the barn and let her hand stroke the extra season of neatly stacked firewood and kindling. She found it uncomfortable accepting help but had to admit that the burden they removed was overwhelming. She glanced at the new shed around the hand pump that Jason's men had built. The small pump at the kitchen sink only put out a fraction of the water. How many times had she been chilled to the bone while filling the buckets in the blistering cold? One winter, her fingers and toes turned blue, and she feared frostbite and the possibility of losing them. The shelter was an enormous blessing. The new outhouse alone had saved her countless days of hard labor. She glanced at the proud men. The thought of them leaving made her stomach twinge. She'd miss their companionship. She would miss Jason. The thought of him leaving made her nauseous.

Emma averted her eyes and looked at the ground. "I don't know how to thank you. Is there some way I can repay you?"

"Repay us?" a soldier scoffed. "Easy. The next time we're here, you can teach us to make hash browns. In the meantime, a few jars of your stew for the trip would be appreciated."

Secretly dreaming of someone your entire life and watching him ride away proved to be agonizing. Cowgirl-up. No time for sadness. Besides, Jason promised to return.

CHAPTER 4

The rooster hadn't even begun his cocky proclamation that a new day had arrived, yet Emma had already been working for two hours. She stared at the window. Dark panes stared back. Sunrise was taking its time. What a way to spend the morning of her nineteenth birthday.

Her little sister sipped a glass of warm milk while hand-grinding a batch of wheat. Emma cracked an egg on the side of the cast-iron skillet, ready to plop it into the simmering bacon grease. "Over easy, I presume?"

Gayla lowered the glass, revealing the half-moon of thick buttery cream attached to her upper lip. "Yes, please."

Who could look at such a sweet face and not smile? Gayla's cream-covered lips brought memories of Emma's hunt for their milk cow and her reunion with Jason Alvise two years earlier. One by one, she dropped four eggs into the simmering grease and waited a moment before flipping them. After a few seconds, she slid them onto a plate. Her forehead grew warm and clammy, and she wiped the sweat with her apron cuff. Jason might show up any day. Her tummy fluttered, and her face warmed again. Now she understood what her mom meant when she claimed butterflies filled her stomach when she first met Emma's dad.

Standing over the harsh wood-burning stove and preparing breakfast was Emma's favorite part of their morning ritual. The aroma of sizzling bacon and grilling hash browns with grated onion always made her salivate, often transforming the bottom of her apron into a napkin. The mouthwatering smells not only brought drooling but also conjured up memories of her mother. The crunchy potato concoction had been one of her favorites. How many failed attempts before Emma mastered the art of cooking them to perfection as her mom had?

Her mother had dreaded the long hours it took to run the small farm and complained that starting chores at four a.m., seven days a week, and working until ten each night could wear down even the hardiest soul. Ain't that the truth? Emma smirked. An entire day spent thumbing through books and magazines would be heavenly. Had her parents really taken

24

weekends off before the lights went out? And what was a week-long vacation like? The concept of a day off, much less a whole week, was unimaginable.

Not even severe weather afforded Emma a break, but those *were* her lazy days. After she milked the cows and goats, gathered eggs, and fed the livestock, she spent the rest of the day canning foods, making a variety of dairy products, sewing, and cleaning. Sometimes Emma prayed for harsh weather so she could relax. How much easier her life would be if she had accepted Jason's offer to move to Hudson Ranch two winters ago.

***

Emma was six months old when the global war had occurred. Her parents had explained that missiles armed to create an electromagnetic pulse (EMP) exploded around the world and ravaged the electrical grids. The planet plunged into darkness. Most devices and engines using electronic chips ceased to function, and within days, the population had realized the impact. There would be no food or medical deliveries, no running water, no electricity.

Her parents often talked about the fear and desperation and how millions had died within weeks from lack of medicine, food, and clean water. Emma never understood how people could have died because they had no electricity or cars.

Her mom and dad also told Emma tales of life before the EMP: cities with towering buildings and millions of residents, cars fighting their way through traffic jams, and families gathered around the television to watch a movie. Now that they were gone, Emma and Gayla had to rely on books and magazines to envision the world back then.

***

Gayla banged the worn heel of her leather boots on the rung of the chair.

"Gosh. Why do you always do that?" Emma scolded her little sister.

Gayla beamed. "Because it irritates you."

"Precocious brat," she muttered.

"Hey. What does that mean?" Gayla scrunched her eyes. "Darn. You got me again."

"Look it up," Emma said as her little sister mouthed the words and mocked her.

Gayla rapidly tapped the rungs and shouted. "I *hate* when you do that."

"Tough. That's how you learn."

25

Gayla snatched the worn dictionary as Emma spelled out the odd word. "P...r...e..."

The pursuit of survival left little time for Emma or Gayla to be kids. Most children were forced to grow up much too fast. Emma watched as Gayla struggled to read the definition. Perhaps concentrating on survival skills was more important than education. Then again, her parents had managed to do both for her.

CHAPTER 5

While sitting on a stump and taking a break from hoeing the weeds around the last of her summer crops, Emma sipped water from an old canteen and let out a heavy breath. She took in her surroundings. Years of hard labor. Not just by her, but her parents and the Elliot's. And how could she forget about all the help Jason and his men had given over the last couple of years? Was it worth it? Sometimes she questioned her decision to stay. She'd be twenty soon. How had she managed to keep everything going for more than six years? She smiled. Gayla. That's what kept her going. Things were easier now that she was eight, but, thankfully, her little sister had never been afraid of a hard day's work.

And Jason. Emma's heart often ran wild as she scanned the horizon and envisioned him galloping toward her. The effort to maintain the small ranch was exhausting. How many nights had she spent tossing and turning over the fear of not making it through another day? Years of nothing to smile about, other than Gayla's antics, had vanished after Jason re-entered her life. Smiles were frequent now that she knew he would continue to return. How she looked forward to seeing him. She missed him more than she wanted to admit.

A stately buck strolled into the clearing, searching for the scanty patches of grass. "Eat all you can, friend. It won't be here long."

The steely sky warned of an unusually frigid winter. Soon, a blanket of white powder would smother the amber landscape. Jason might show up any day. He and a couple of his friends always came before the snow. They would stay for a week or so, help chop wood for the winter, and check on the fences, barns, sheds, and roofs. She'd stopped arguing. Her protests always received rolling eyes and shaking heads. Then the men would go about their business. She felt a mixture of guilt and relief each time they came.

This time, Emma decided to let go of some of her hardheadedness when they came. Jason always asked if she needed anything. Her response was that she and Gayla needed nothing. That wasn't true. Taking a little charity for Gayla's sake was okay. Except for Christmas, when Jason brought gifts that Emma could not refuse, Gayla's only clothing had been hand-me-downs since their father died. How selfish. Gayla needed clothes and shoes. And the truth was, they were running low on several essentials.

Emma grinned. Why was she so afraid to ask for help? Perhaps it wasn't fear, but her pride and independence that got in the way. After all, she'd been accepting help for a couple of years. She couldn't believe Jason thought she was so naïve.

Did he honestly think she wouldn't find the extra hay he was bringing for the cows? And how could she not notice the corn that seemed to mysteriously fill the bin in the barn several times during the winter? Part of her wanted to tell him she was on to him, but another part wanted him to enjoy believing he was so clever. One day she would let him know how thankful she was.

Emma stood, twisted the cap on the canteen, and placed it on the stump. After she stretched for a few seconds, she tugged on the hoe and winced. Rough, calloused hands from chopping wood, plowing, and mending fences not only made her self-conscious, sometimes they caused excruciating pain. She'd love to shake Jason's hand without being embarrassed. But Emma learned the hard way to be selective when removing the thick pieces of skin. Once, she made the mistake of scrubbing away the toughened chunks. She wouldn't make that error again. The newly exposed flesh was bloody and blistered for weeks.

Emma rested the wooden handle of the hoe in the crook of her arm and grimaced as she flexed her stiff fingers.

A distant clatter broke her trance. Her heart pounded at the sound of squeaking wagons in the distance and faint laughter. Jason and his men. She envisioned them unloading bales of hay, hiding the carts, and snickering at their cleverness as they headed for her house. Emma was beginning to love winter. She knew she'd see Jason at least three or four more times before spring. Her hands flew to her mouth.

"I'm filthy!" She bolted for home.

***

Jason's heart raced at the thought of returning to Emma. He hadn't seen her since late February and didn't think April would ever arrive. He could not stop thinking about her.

His visit a few months earlier as she was harvesting her final summer crop brought a hearty laugh. Emma would have a fit if she knew he'd watched through his binoculars as she examined herself and rushed from the garden to clean up before he arrived. She could pretend all she wanted. Jason was sure Emma cared for him more than she let on. His heart pumped faster. He burst into laughter and nudged his horse to go faster.

Jason no longer tried to convince Emma to move to Hudson Ranch. It was a waste of time. She was determined to make her small ranch a success. Was it her parents that held her there? Perhaps it was merely her stubborn nature. It didn't matter now.

When his father's presidency ended, the Alvise family returned home to Hudson Ranch. President Cully was everything his father hoped for in a new president. The struggle to restore power continued, but many small towns now had enough electricity to bring in hordes of newcomers. The outlying areas, like Emma's ranch, would not see full power for years, if ever. There was no power there before the EMP, and it was doubtful the area would be populated enough to see it any time soon.

Jason turned and stared at the caravan behind him. He usually came with two or three men. This time, there were several wagons loaded with goods. How would Emma react to so many people at one time? Then, he'd have to explain why they were there. He shivered at the thought and imagined Emma's angst as he and his men installed turbines on her property. Randy, the power man, as he was called at Hudson Ranch, would be bringing the appliances and wiring necessary to provide Emma and Gayla with lighting, a gas stove, a refrigerator, fans, and other useful items. One day, they would build a large walk-in cooler and freezer. Imagining their reaction the first time they filled a real tub with warm water brought a smile to his face.

Jason squirmed as he envisioned how angry Emma would be when she learned the property adjoining her ranch had been fenced. His parents had known for years that he wanted to be close to Emma. So as a gift for his twentieth birthday, they had secured and fenced eight thousand acres next to her parcel. Beads of sweat formed as he considered the possibility that she might already know.

Thanks to his parent's substantial investment in gold and silver before the EMP, the Alvise family was one of the wealthiest in the country. As older ranchers nearby decided it was time to call it quits, the Alvise family bought their property. Later, they expanded and bought more across the state. Hudson Ranch had grown from forty-five-hundred acres to several hundred thousand. Some said the Alvise family owned Wyoming. Eventually, they began buying farmland across the country.

The Alvise's interest in buying more property wasn't about gaining more wealth or power; it was about empowering, growing, and feeding the country. Thousands of men and women worked the land, and many more found jobs building homes for the workers. Small towns sprung up near the ranches and farms, and trading posts lined the streets. Buying merchandise with gold, silver, and precious stones became more common, however, bartering continued to be a way of life.

Jason's parents had made an enormous impact on the country. He couldn't be any prouder to be called their son.

***

After the EMP, government officials were housed at the North American Aerospace Defense Command (NORAD) in the Cheyenne mountains. Though the Alvise's were wealthy, and their father had become president, it did not afford their children any slack. The entire family had helped work the fields and taken care of the livestock.

While his parents bestowed property upon him, it would be Jason's responsibility to turn it into a profitable ranch, and his parents expected reimbursement for the livestock and supplies. The property would always belong to Jason, but those helping set up the plantation would live on the farm and receive a percentage of the profits, as they did at Hudson Ranch. Jason and his father had scoped out the newly acquired land and had chosen specific spots for each new structure. A dozen or more homes would soon dot the landscape, forming a small community. But first, the pavilion, walk-in cooler, and freezer would be built. Jason was thankful for his parents' help but knew years of hard work lay ahead.

Emma owned five-hundred acres but used the adjacent land, which now belonged to Jason, as grazing grounds for her small herd. Now, they could combine their herds and move them as needed.

Jason wiped the sweat from his forehead. The *last* thing he wanted was to face the wrath of Emma Harding. He had struggled with his stubborn friend for almost three years. She had always refused his offers to send help. She couldn't afford to pay and would not accept charity. She would never admit she *needed* help.

"How the heck will you *ever* be able to afford it?" he'd fumed on one occasion. "You can't grow enough feed to enlarge the herd, and you can't drive the cattle to auction by yourself." He gritted his teeth. "You are the most hardheaded woman I've ever met."

"Let me tell you something, Jason Alvise," she growled. "We started with a milk cow and a calf. As soon as I can raise enough to trade payment for herding, I'll tell you!"

Jason smiled. Everyone knew he adored her. Everyone but Emma. He would give anything to tell her, but the truth was, she was somewhat intimidating. He couldn't believe how he cowered to a hundred and fifteen-pound woman. Then he pictured her on the roof of the shed, her rifle leveled on him and his unsuspecting escort of soldiers. Jason threw his head back and laughed.

She'd have a fit if she knew he'd been bringing hay and feed during the winter. Several times a year, some of the men from Hudson Ranch volunteered to make deliveries. Jason's mother organized those secret trips and hinted at how she'd love to go along with Jason one day and meet Emma and Gayla.

Chris, Jason's father, had scowled at the idea. "Sierra. Jason only gets to see Emma a few times a year. Do you seriously think he wants his mommy tagging along?"

His mother's face had reddened. "Sorry, Jason. I don't know what I was thinking."

Jason had kissed his mother's cheek. "Soon, I hope, Mom. Soon."

He knew his mother would fall in love with Emma and Gayla. He didn't want to break her heart if Emma didn't have the same feelings for him that he had for her. He hoped to find out this trip. The thought of rejection terrified him.

***

As they neared Emma's ranch, Jason raised his hand, and the caravan halted.

Almost three years earlier, Emma had been ready to shoot him and his men when she felt her sister was threatened. He didn't care for a repeat.

"Emma may have a problem seeing so many wagons and people headed her way. I'm not sure how she'll react." He rubbed his chin and thought a minute. "We need to ease our presence on her. This is where we part ways. Matthew, would you lead the caravan to the spot where we chose to build the new barn? You can set up camp there."

31

"Will do boss. The camp will be set up in no time. Right now, I'm ready to take a dip in the stream." He whipped his team into gear, and the caravan followed.

The thought of seeing Emma and Gayla sent a rush of blood to Jason's head, and his temples pounded. He glanced at the back of his wagon. Every ranch needed an entrance sign. Tomorrow they would install the posts and hang the wooden banner—unless Emma skinned him alive first.

CHAPTER 6

Jason stopped his wagon at the barn and called out. His ears buzzed from the ride. He massaged them and called out again. No one answered. After dismantling the horse from the wagon, he led him and his stallion, Guss, to the barn before heading to the house.

As he approached the cabin, he noticed the small covered wagons and lifted the tarps. "Sweet." He brushed the dry earth from a carrot and snapped a piece off. Emma knew her stuff. Still harvesting from the winter crop and already gathering spring veggies.

He grabbed a handful of green beans and munched as he knocked on the door. The chewing unclogged his ears, and they filled with the pleasing sound of giggles echoing from the stream.

He froze as he neared the brook. The worn cotton dress clung to Emma's body, and he caught his breath. He watched Gayla squeal in delight while Emma repeatedly splashed her.

Emma reached down and pulled something from the stream. She swooned as she raised a man's shirt in the air. "Quick, Gayla, run to the house. Someone is downstream!"

Jason winced and slapped the side of his head. One of the men who came with him must have lost his shirt when he rinsed off, and it had drifted downstream. He had to think fast. "Sorry, Emma. Guess I lost it when I stopped a while back."

The vision of her running toward him was paralyzing.

"Jason. I'm so glad you're here." She embraced him with her wet arms.

Before he realized it, Jason kissed her. It was several moments before she pulled away.

Jason took a step back. "I, I'm sorry. I don't know what came over me."

Gayla gave a lighthearted, goofy laugh, and then paused. "Oh, no." She covered her mouth. "Now Emma's gonna have a baby."

Her childish comment rescued Jason from his embarrassment.

"I guess I need to teach her about the birds and the bees." Emma flushed and chuckled. "Come on." She waved him toward the stream. Looks like you could use a bath, too. Wear your clothes."

Her comment shocked Jason. "I would never get naked in front of Gayla."

"No, silly," she snorted and slapped his arm. "I don't want to wash clothes. Let the stream do it."

They frolicked in the cool water until Gayla decided she was ready to go home. "Emma, I know we have a lot of work to do, but would you mind if I took a nap? I'm tired."

"Sure. But hang your clothes out to dry," she yelled to Gayla as she skipped home.

"Funny. Gayla doesn't look tired," Jason commented.

Emma grinned. "Yeah, funny. I think we should head to the house soon. You can keep me company while I prep the vegetables."

"I'm not going to sit by and watch. I'll help."

"If you insist. I was going to can the vegetables tonight, but it can wait until tomorrow."

"Nonsense. I'd love to help."

"Actually, canning is rather boring."

"Nothing could be boring with you around."

Emma tried to hide her smile. "Let's go inside."

As they finished prepping the vegetables, Gayla came out of her room. "I'm going to feed the animals. You two relax. I'll check the fire in the smokehouse too."

Emma scrunched her brows. "I think I need to take her temperature."

"She's a terrific kid. You did a fine job. I don't know how you did it, Emma." He spread his hands in awe. "I don't understand how you did any of this."

"Determination? Necessity? I do what I have to."

"I want to show you something." Jason clasped elbows with Emma and led her to his wagon.

"Your ranch needs a name. I took the liberty. I hope you don't mind." He pulled back the tarp, exposing the carved ranch entrance sign.

Emma gasped. In big letters were the words "Emma's Place." On the left was a woman on a rearing horse, on the right, a proud bull.

Her mouth quivered for several seconds. Two fists covered her lips. "How beautiful," she mumbled.

"I take it you approve?"

Just as Gayla wandered out of the barn, Emma flung her arms around Jason's neck, pulled him closer, and kissed him.

Gayla threw her arms in the air. "Great. Just what we need. *Twins.* You guys need to be more careful!" she snapped and stomped off.

"Yeah, I think it's time we talked," Emma giggled as she rested her head on Jason's shoulder.

***

Jason couldn't believe Emma had kissed him. They often hugged or held hands as they strolled around the property, much the same as good friends would do. But in only a few hours, they'd kissed twice. Jason was giddy and couldn't stop smiling. Then he felt the beads pop out on his forehead as he thought about what he had to do. How was he going to tell her he owned eight thousand acres surrounding her ranch? She would be thrilled—or furious. He wrestled for a way to bring it up while helping her prep green beans in the kitchen. An ounce of courage surfaced as she lowered the canning jars into the pot to be sterilized.

"Can you imagine how wonderful it would be to have several people helping can all of these vegetables?"

"Huh. Boy, can I." She sighed. "I spend several hours a night doing this when the crops are coming in. Between canning meat and vegetables, the canner is going pretty much year-round." She shrugged. "Things are what they are, Jason. I do what I have to so we eat well."

"Emma," Jason hesitated, "I sure wish I lived close by."

She blushed and tossed a handful of beans in a hot jar. "I'd love that. Heck, I think I could tolerate having you come by every day." Her face flushed deeper.

"I have a proposition for you." Jason took a deep breath and cleared his throat. Mustering his bravery, he went for it. "What if I can obtain the land around your property, and we share grazing, herding, and farming? We could make a killing if we worked together."

Emma stiffened, tossed a handful of beans into another jar, and ignored him until she filled them all and lowered the batch into the hot water. Then she turned and glared.

"Well, that explains the loaded wagon. How long have you owned the land?"

Jason sucked air and looked down. "About six months." After a moment, he exhaled deeply and stared her in the eyes. He had to appear in control. He refused to allow her to make him cower. What a joke. Simply gazing into her steely eyes made him sweat. "Not much slips past you, does it?"

Emma stomped to the door and flung it open. "Gayla. I feel like having fish for dinner. Go to the shed and grab a few poles."

Gayla came running. "A few?"

"Yep. And take plenty of worms and crickets." She glared at Jason. "How many do we need to feed?"

"Uh, with me, seven adults and two children." Jason's face burned with humiliating heat.

"Gayla, the stream's been brimming with brook trout. We'll need at least a dozen, but more would be better."

Gayla's eyes were huge. "Are you serious? Two kids are coming for dinner?" She covered her mouth, then threw her fists into the air. "This is the most exciting day of my life!" Gayla rushed toward the shed.

Emma watched her little sister sprint away, lowered herself into a rocker on the porch, and stared into the distance.

"I'm sorry, Emma," Jason said from the doorway. "I only wanted to help. The truth is, I wanted to be close to you." He walked over and knelt in front of her. "Please, forgive me."

"How old are the children?" She threw her arms around him. "Gayla's never had another child to play with."

He rubbed her back for a few seconds before letting her go and standing. "Matthew and Laura have a ten-year-old boy, Marcus. John and Iva's eight-year-old daughter is Shelley. They're wonderful children."

Emma stood and brushed her dress. Then she cocked her head. "How long did you plan on hiding them?"

Jason focused on his boots. "Uh. Until I got the courage to tell you."

"Go. Bring them here. They'll need somewhere to sleep. We'll make room." The look she sent Jason was both loathing and admiration. "I'm not sure how I feel about this. I feel like I've been deceived. But Gayla deserves some happiness." She was about to walk inside when she swung around. "I'm warning you! If she gets hurt, so help me, you'll pay!" The screen door slammed behind her.

***

Gayla stared at her string of fish and raced from pole to pole. "Come on. At least four more. Please. We have company coming." Her brows pinched, and for a minute, she thought she would cry. "Two of them are kids," she choked. "I never had kids visit before. I'm not sure what a kid is." Gayla sat on the bank and allowed tears of happiness and nervousness to run down her cheeks. One of the poles bobbed. Gayla wiped her nose and jumped up to grab it. A young man's voice broke the air.

"Cool, Gayla. Looks like you caught a nice one."

She froze and stared at the young boy and the girl standing behind him.

The boy ran to the pole and pulled in the fish while Gayla stood, paralyzed.

He held the fish high in the air. "Wow. Look at the beauty you caught, Gayla."

Everything was swirling and foggy. Gayla eased down on a log by the stream and found it difficult to speak. "I didn't catch him. You did," she whispered. She stared at the boy while he added the fish to the stringer. "What's your name?" she managed to ask.

"I'm Marcus." He nodded toward the girl. "That's my friend, Shelley."

It was Gayla's first experience with such young faces, and she sat, motionless for a moment. When she stood, her knees were shaky, but she forced herself to approach the girl and timidly reached out to touch her cheek.

Shelley stiffened and took a step back.

Gayla inhaled and snatched her hand back. "I'm sorry. I didn't mean to scare you."

"Mom and Dad said you never met any kids before. That sounds silly. They said I should be nice and let you learn to be a kid." Shelley scrunched her eyes. "Do you know what they were talking about?"

Marcus rolled his eyes and placed his head in his hands. "Shelley, you weren't supposed to tell her that."

Gayla chewed her thumbnail. "Hmm, I guess they figured it would take me a while to get used to being around kids." She glanced from kid to kid. "They probably didn't want you to be scared if I acted weird."

Marcus broke the solemn moment. "Whoa, Gayla! Look at the poles. This place is loaded. Whoo-hoo!"

Gayla and Marcus pulled in three more, fulfilling Emma's requirement. Gayla grinned. "Emma said more would be better."

"Fine with me," Marcus said as he lowered his bait into the stream. "Heck. I could fish all night."

Gayla fought her grin. "Me, too!" She baited her hook and tossed it in the stream. "Shelley, hold my pole, and I'll bait yours."

CHAPTER 7

Jason introduced the families: Matthew and Laura Wright, John and Iva Strong, and Eric and Leslie Brown.

Emma was hesitant about greeting her guests. Seeing so many new people at one time was overwhelming. "Excuse me if I seem nervous, but I have to admit..." Her eyes darted from person to person. "We went years without a single visitor. The census takers were the largest group to visit before Jason and his men showed up. And they were only here for an hour or so. Well, after I finally realized they didn't mean to harm us." She grinned. "I sort of kept a rifle on them for a few days while they camped in the yard."

"I can't imagine," Laura said. "The last thing we want is to make you uncomfortable. We'll do our best not to push you."

"That will be a first," Emma chuckled. "I've been pushing myself eighteen, twenty hours a day for years."

"What?" Iva asked. "Surely you don't mean you put in that many hours a day?"

The comment shocked Emma. "Sure. That's what it takes to keep things going. To be honest, even that isn't enough."

The scrunched brows confused Emma. She stuttered. "Can we sit on the porch and have some tea? I made a pot when Jason told me you were here."

They gathered on the porch with a cup of herbal tea and honey. Emma sat on the railing. She felt more comfortable there. She insisted her guests use the rockers and the chairs from the dining table. The men balked, but Emma assured them she spent more time on the railing than in the chairs.

"This tea is wonderful," Leslie said.

"Thank you. My mother's recipe. She had to come up with something before she ran out of coffee." Emma glanced toward the tree where her parents lay. "She was very creative."

They allowed a moment of silence.

"Would you mind telling us what your normal day is like?" Leslie asked. "It's been a long time since we set up at Hudson Ranch, and it was already running when we arrived. I'm trying to imagine how you do something like this on your own." Leslie's eyes scanned her surroundings.

"Well, let's see. I'm up by four to milk the cows and goats, collect eggs, feed the pigs and horses, and let the chickens and goats out to forage. During the winter, even the chickens and goats need extra feed. By then, it's time to make sure Gayla is up. We filter the milk and bottle it. During warmer months, we take it straight to the stream." Emma stopped long enough to take a sip of tea. Once she felt they wanted her to go on, she continued. "While I cook breakfast, Gayla churns butter, grinds wheat, or preps vegetables. After we clean up, I make a list of the things we need to do for the day. We usually head for the garden to harvest, till, or plant. When the weather is nice, we save gardening for later and bathe in the stream when we're done."

No one spoke. Emma's hands shook as she took another sip of tea.

"How do you keep the animals fed in the winter?" Laura asked.

Emma lowered her cup. "You'd be surprised at how resourceful the animals can be. But we plant as much hay and corn as we can and raise earthworms for the chickens. The pigs love milk. They usually get what we harvest at night. I plant lots of winter squash because they store well. Don't usually have much luck because of the short growing season. But sometimes I get lucky and have hundreds of pounds for the pigs." She took another sip of tea. "Pigs eat anything. Every winter, I feed them my oldest jars of canned meat and stuff. A few times, winter was so rough, I fed them almost my entire stash from the cellar."

Emma glanced at her new neighbor's blank stares, and an embarrassing heat filled her cheeks. "I'm sorry. I'm boring you with my ramblings."

Matthew Wright broke the long silence. "No. You're not boring us. We didn't understand how you managed. To be honest, we thought Jason was exaggerating."

"He's right," Laura said. "I want to hear more. I'm ten years your senior, but I swear, I want to be you when I grow up."

Emma couldn't help noticing Jason's smile.

"This is a new way of living for us. We need to know," Iva prodded.

Jason interrupted. "Emma, we had a lot of help at the ranch. Your chores and long days make ours look like a breeze. Please, go on."

Emma nervously rubbed the back of her neck, glanced at her audience, and continued. "Well, we mend fences and move the cattle around. Gayla is getting good at helping with that." She let out a slow whistle. "Harvesting hay for winter feed? That's brutal. We start early, while dew's still on the grass. We use the scythe and cut down as much as we can every day and spread it out to dry. Then we bundle it and take it to the barn. It takes us weeks. Luckily, there's plenty of food out there for the animals to forage."

Emma chuckled. "During one of those horrible winters, I learned the hard way not to let the pigs forage." She slapped her thigh and wiped the tears of laughter from her eyes. "Gayla and I must have been a sight! We ran around for hours with a rope and tried to grab the pigs and pen them." She sighed and wrapped her arm around the porch post. "I don't know how many times I tried to tackle them. I'd grab one, and they'd squirm out of my grasp. What I remember most is smelling like, well, a pig." Everyone laughed, and Emma felt herself relax.

"Once I got a sow in the pen and filled a trough with goat milk, they all went home."

Emma shook her head and grinned. "We have a double fence around the garden. The outside is four feet tall. A couple of feet in, we have a six-footer. The deer and goats won't jump because they're afraid they'll get trapped. The darned pigs just shoved the fence over and helped themselves to our veggies." The back of Emma's hand flew to her mouth, and she burst into laughter. "I know our parents watch over us. I bet they watched us all day and thought it was hysterical!"

Everyone was laughing, and Emma felt herself relax more. Being surrounded by laughter felt normal. It felt good. Emma looked at Jason. He wore a tight smile.

"Guess I never told you that story."

Jason shook his head and chuckled. "No."

Emma's grin widened. "Probably because I didn't want you to picture me covered in pig poop!"

The laughter grew, and Emma felt a strange warmness in her chest.

After a few moments, Jason wanted Emma to finish her story. "Okay, now tell us the rest of your day."

Emma shrugged. "There's not much more to tell. Now that Gayla is older, she cleans the sty, coop, and barn. We have to keep them clean. We can't afford the animals getting sick."

Emma felt a twinge of shame. "Even though we grow fields of corn, since the herd has grown so much, we fall short on feed every year no matter how hard we try. I, uh, I ration feed before winter is over and always lose several head of cattle." She glanced around, expecting to see at least a hint of scorn, but saw none. "I do my herd thinning then. I can't stand to know they're starving, and we need the protein. I smoke and can the meat."

Her lip curled. "For some reason, we haven't been losing livestock for the past couple of winters. It seems the hay and corn last much longer." She smiled at Jason and raised her brows. Jason scratched his forehead.

"Emma, before we had dozens of field hands to grow feed, we thinned the herd like crazy in the winter. It was either that, or like you said, they'd have starved," Matthew said.

Emma was shocked. "Really?"

Nodding heads surrounded her.

Laura spoke up. "I don't see how you get everything done. The gardening, canning, and caring for the animals alone must be exhausting."

Emma nodded. "It is. Every night, after dinner, we check on the smokehouse and greenhouse, call in the goats and chickens, and start canning. I try to do at least two batches. While the jars process, I tell Gayla a bedtime story then send her off to bed. Then I read or…" Emma's eyes shifted, and she paused. "I check on the smokehouse one last time and go to bed. The next morning, we start all over."

Her guests were silent.

Emma inhaled, let out a gust of air, and lowered her eyes. "Mom and Dad used to talk about moving south where the weather was more forgiving and crops were easier to grow. But that would have meant leaving behind most of our livestock and supplies." She spread her palms and lifted her head. "And then, what would they find?" Her eyes lowered once more. "After Mom died, Dad never mentioned it again."

No one said a word. Emma's thumbs twirled, one over the other.

"I'm sorry for rambling. Dad used to say how tough this land was, and how nothing would give him more pleasure than taming it. I try. But to be honest, it's tough."

Laura walked over to Emma and reached out to hug her.

"Bless you. I hope we can give you some relief."

Emma tensed and tried returning the woman's embrace. Moving beyond years of seclusion would take time.

***

Jason was taking in the sight of Emma as she tried to accept her new neighbors when the children came running toward the house.

Gayla called out as she skipped. "Look, Emma. Look what me and my friends caught!"

Marcus held the massive string of fish in the air. "Gayla can sure catch fish. She had eight before we got there."

Jason introduced Gayla to the adults.

The women gushed all over her, and it was clear that Gayla loved every second of it.

"You are a beautiful young lady," Laura said.

"And from what Jason told us about you, you're pretty talented too," Iva told her.

"Jason swears you're better with a slingshot than anyone he's ever met," Leslie said.

Matthew laughed. "Alright, ladies. Let the girl breathe." He nodded toward his son. "Well, clean 'em up, Marcus. I'm darned near starved."

"I'll talk to you ladies later. Over here, Marcus." Gayla nodded toward the table by the hand pump. "This is where me and Emma clean fish. We save the guts and stuff for fertilizer."

"You can clean fish?" Marcus's forehead furled.

Gayla gave him a goofy stare. "Uh, yeah. Been doing it for years."

"Yuck." Shelley grimaced. "Fish guts are gross!"

Gayla twisted her lips. "I like gizzards." She smacked. "Nice and chewy."

Marcus gave Gayla a high-five. "I like 'em too. You scale, I'll clean."

"Okay. And I'll take the heads off."

"No. You just scale. I don't want you getting all nasty."

Jason chuckled at the spectacle, and Emma ran for the house.

"I'll be right back," he told the others.

Jason joined Emma as she sat on her bed. "What have I done? I cheated Gayla out of her childhood."

"Not from what I saw," Jason replied. "She seems to be fitting right in." He turned her chin toward him. "She'll be fine. Her only problem is that she knows far more than the typical eight-year-old." He kissed her cheek. "Like I said before, you did a fine job, Emma, a fine job."

***

42

Emma took everyone to the stream, and Jason pulled caged jars of butter, sour cream, and buttermilk from the water where she stored them during the warmer months.

"The stream is deeper here, so the water stays colder." She nodded her head toward the large burr oak. "Those branches help even more with all the shade."

Herbs mixed with buttermilk became dressing for their salad. Gayla's ground wheat and corn made the perfect pan of cornbread. Emma's canned beans became baked beans topped with thick slabs of bacon from the smokehouse. The potatoes roasting in the coals would soon be smothered with butter and sour cream.

The men had finished the evening chores and were cleaning up outside at the pump. The kids were exploring the property, and the women were busy putting dinner together.

Emma lamented, "Sorry, but I can't season with salt anymore. I save it for canning. Most of the time we eat flatbread because I'm low on baking soda and cream of tartar. Gayla loves pancakes, but I can't make them too often. Now I'm running out of sugar and molasses to make brown sugar." She sighed. "Dad stocked up on supplies before he died, but I haven't been able to meet the train to barter for more. In a few months, I'll have to rely on the beehives and use honey instead of sugar. When the salt runs out, I'll have no choice but to meet the train, or I won't be able to can my food."

"You have a beehive?" Iva asked.

Emma's brows lifted. "Doesn't everyone?"

"No." Leslie chuckled. "Trust me."

Jason walked in while Emma was talking about her shortages. His jaw tightened, and his eyes squinted. He stomped toward Emma. "Every time I visit, I ask if you need anything. You always say you don't. Now I find out you've been lying?"

"I wasn't lying!" she thundered. "I know how to make do, and I do not take charity!" Emma's face heated, and her arms flung in the air. "And talk about lying! Who was it that bought all the property around me and didn't tell me?" she spat.

Jason and Emma stood snarling at each other. Laura sat peeling potatoes for the morning hash browns. She put the knife on the table, stood, and walked toward Jason and Emma.

Jason was visibly shaking. He stuck a finger in Emma's face just as Laura got there. She took his pointer finger, slowly lowered it, and scowled at her young friend. After wiping her hands on her apron, she squeezed Emma's shoulder.

"Not to worry, Emma. We brought plenty of supplies. Shortages won't be a problem." She glanced back and forth at the two of them, then turned to Emma. "Jason was afraid to tell you about the land. He was terrified you wouldn't want him here, and all he wanted was to be close to you and Gayla. That was all he ever talked about." Then she turned to Jason. "And from what I've learned about Emma, she's a very proud and resourceful woman. But she would have told you she needed things before she ran out. There's no way she would let her pride hurt Gayla." Laura put her hands on her hips. "Now, I think the two of you need to calm down and apologize to each other."

Laura glared at Jason. He rolled his eyes and huffed. "I'm sorry Emma. I should have told you about buying the land. But if you weren't so…"

Laura shut him down. "Jason!" she snapped.

He took a deep breath. His head bobbed. "I apologize, Emma."

Laura smiled. "Good." She turned to Emma. "Your turn."

Emma was angry. But in all honesty, she was more furious at herself for letting her supplies run so low. Her only priority was to make sure Gayla did not go without. She crossed her arms over her chest and stared at the floor.

"I'm sorry. I should have told you I was running low on supplies."

Laura smiled. "Now, don't you both feel better?"

Jason didn't smile. He stared at the ceiling and nodded.

Emma huffed. "Yeah." Then, her pointer figure flew up, and she sneered. "But he started it!"

Laura threw her arms in the air. "Oh, for the love of…"

Iva and Leslie burst into laughter just as the other men walked in. They separated to allow Jason stomping room as he rushed from the cabin.

"What the heck is going on?" Matthew asked.

Emma turned her back to them and tried to calm herself.

Laura rolled her eyes and shook her head. "Let's just call it a lover's spat!"

Emma spun around, snatched off her apron, and tossed it on the counter before rushing to her room and slamming the door.

***

44

Jason was furious. He'd lost his appetite and walked feverishly toward the barn. Ole' Guss. That's what he needed. He'd saddle up his stallion and take a ride. A nice long ride.

When Jason walked into the barn, he heard the kids giggling and stepped to the side. They didn't need to see him so angry.

"So, you like Jason?" Shelley asked.

"Heck yeah!" Gayla said. "But I'm not sure if he's more like my brother or my dad."

"What do you mean?" Marcus asked.

"Well, if he marries Emma, that means he's sort of my brother. But Emma's not just my sister, she's been my mom too."

"Gayla," Marcus said, "Jason is a good guy. I don't think he'd mind being your dad."

"Really? Jason has a mom and dad. I'd love to have a grandma and grandpa!"

Jason had to cup his mouth.

"Me and Emma were so alone until Jason came. He changed our lives, you know. Do you think his mom and dad will like me?" Gayla released a few soft, mournful moans.

Jason's hands gripped his mouth tightly when he heard Gayla's choked sobs. He couldn't take any more. He rushed from the barn. Emma was hard-headed. He'd always known that. Their argument would not fester. He wouldn't allow it! If he had to grovel, so be it. He chuckled. Well, at least this time.

He picked up his speed and trotted toward Emma's cabin.

***

Laura knocked on Emma's door. "Emma. We need to finish dinner. I'm not sure what to do."

The door eased open. Emma peeked out and whispered. "Laura, I'm a little embarrassed to come out."

Laura thrust her hands into her hips. "Nonsense! You have no idea how many times we've tied up with our husbands!"

Emma opened the door wider and smiled. She was about to step out when Jason burst through the front door. She slammed it and put her back against the cold wood.

The screen door slammed as Jason shouted. "Emma! Get out here! This is ridiculous! We're acting like little kids!" He waited for a moment, but her bedroom door remained closed.

Emma looked in the mirror. She grabbed the cloth in the washbasin and held it to her face. The water was tepid, but it seemed to help. She checked her reflection one more time before opening the door and walking out.

She imitated Laura and shoved her hands into her hips. "Well, I'm glad you finally came to your senses! I'm starving."

Jason's grin grew. "Me too. I'll get the kids."

He stopped and turned as he was about to walk out the door. "Emma. I'm sorry." The screen door shut behind him.

"Me, too, Jason," Emma said softly. "Me, too."

***

As they put the food on the table, Laura reminded Emma that she didn't need to skimp on salt and sugar anymore.

Emma's eyes lit up. "I can bake cookies again and put brown sugar in my oats?"

"You can bake anything you want," Laura said. "With us working together, we can meet the trains and barter for whatever we need."

"What would you want for a pound of salt, five pounds of sugar, and a jar of molasses? Oh, and some soda and cream of tartar."

Laura squinted. "Nothing. You are welcome to anything you need."

Emma paled. "No. I can't do that."

"Are you serious?" Laura pointed to the bounty they were about to enjoy. "How much are you going to charge us?" Before Emma could answer, Iva rested her hand on Emma's shoulder. "If I came to you and asked for some butter and cream, what would you ask for in return?"

Emma balked. "Don't be silly. All you need do is ask."

The other women nodded their heads.

"I think I understand." Emma looked down. "Thank you." She grabbed her jar of precious salt from the counter and lifted it into the air. "This makes fish and potatoes so much better."

The adults gathered around the table, and the children took their plates to the front porch. Emma thanked them for the apparent new friendship between Gayla, Marcus, and Shelley. "I've never seen Gayla so happy."

Leslie shook her head. "The act like they've been friends for years."

***

As they cleaned up after dinner, Emma studied the cabin. They couldn't all sleep in the house. The living area, including the kitchen, was about twenty by twenty. The two bedrooms were small. Just big enough for a

46

double-sized bed and dresser. Her face warmed when she thought about the linens, quilts, and blankets in the cedar-lined wardrobe. They'd need to be aired out, and most had seen their better days.

She wondered what her new neighbor's homes were like back at Hudson Ranch. She'd never been ashamed of her tiny place before. Now an embarrassing heat consumed her face.

Were they appalled when they saw where they'd be cooking and eating? She kept her home clean, but it was old. As she wiped the wooden countertops her father had built, she felt a bit of guilt. He'd worked so hard to make the place "homey." Her mother had never complained. She said the cabin was "adorable." But now, Emma wondered. The rustic cabinets, also built by her dad, were nothing like the kitchen cabinets in the magazines. And she didn't have fancy curtains. They enjoyed the view, and her mom said drapes were dust collectors and one more thing to clean.

Laura handed Iva a freshly washed plate to dry. They were white plates several years ago. Now, they were scraped and scuffed. Emma bit her lip and looked at the china cabinet. She should have pulled out her mom's china so her new friends could have eaten off them. She and Gayla only used them for Christmas and Thanksgiving dinner.

What was she thinking? Elliot's house. It was much larger, and Emma's best linens and new sets of kitchenware were stored there. Most were unused. She bet the adults would like a peaceful night without the children. Gayla, on the other hand, would love their company.

"Canning is on hold until tomorrow night. We need to make sleeping arrangements before dark," Emma said.

"If you can make room for the women and children, the men and I will sleep in the barn," Jason said.

Emma placed her hands on her hips. "And let a perfectly good three-bedroom cabin go to waste?"

"What are you talking about?" Laura asked.

"The Elliot's cabin. I keep it clean and aired out. Plus, it has three bedrooms. It was our safe haven in case something happened to our house. Gayla and I often talked about moving there, but it's farther from the garden and stream." She placed her hands on her hips. "Geez, Jason, you checked the roof a few months ago."

Jason slapped the side of his head. "What was I thinking?"

"Other than firewood, it should be fine. I kept it well stocked with household items." Emma rubbed the back of her neck. "That's where my newer and nicer stuff is." Emma looked at the wooden slats of her floor. "It's a lot nicer and bigger than my tiny cabin. I'm sure you'd feel more at home there."

Leslie tilted her head. "What do you mean?"

Emma shrugged and lifted her eyes. "Well, I'm sure you're used to much finer things and bigger houses."

The room was quiet for a minute, then erupted in laughter.

Emma scanned the room, unsure of why everyone was laughing.

Laura chuckled, went to Emma, wrapped her arms around her, and squeezed before stepping back. "Emma, I think we need to explain some things. When we started building homes on the Hudson ranch, we used one simple floor plan. A twenty by twenty common area that included the kitchen, and two ten by ten bedrooms." Laura spread her arms. "Just as you have here."

Emma's head went back. "Uh, well, I just assumed…"

"Sit!" Laura pointed to the chair at the table. Emma sat. Laura went to the bookshelf, scanned the magazines, and pulled out a copy of "Modern Homes." She sat next to Emma, flipped through the pages, and landed on a beautiful, four-thousand square foot home. She turned the magazine toward Emma. "Is this how you think we live?"

"Uh. Yeah."

Again. The giggles. Emma twisted in her seat. The other women and men shook their heads. Jason had covered his eyes and was chuckling.

Laura took Emma's chin. "Sweetie, the only thing we have beyond what you have here is a small refrigerator, gas stove, and bathroom. And we didn't have those until a few years ago. Hudson Ranch can only produce so much energy. Some of us can afford to buy gas for hot water for bathing. Some can't."

Emma smiled and stood. "Well, you should feel right at home living at the Elliot's old place. The kids won't have bedrooms, but the adults will."

***

They called the children in and made arrangements for housing. "Jason, you can sleep in Gayla's room. The kids can have a slumber party in the living room."

"A slumber party?" Gayla's voice was almost a whisper. "You mean like we did when I was little?"

Emma grinned. "Yep. And we'll set up a sheet tent, too."

48

Marcus seemed sad. "Mom, can we bring some board games over so we can play tonight?"

Laura's lips trembled, and she glanced at her husband.

"I'll bring the wagon over," Matthew said. "We'll dig through it and pull out the games. And thank you, Emma, we brought everything we need to set up the house, but we sure didn't think we'd be using it so soon."

CHAPTER 8

The kids hovered under the makeshift tent on the living room floor. If it aggravated Marcus and Shelley to teach Gayla to play the board game, Emma didn't hear it. How could they be so patient? Emma smiled. The only game her parents had was Monopoly. If she never had to play it again, she wouldn't complain.

Emma took Jason's hand and led him to the porch. They sat in the rockers and stared at the night sky. "I have a feeling this may work out well," she told Jason.

"I wish you'd have let me help sooner."

She tucked her hands under her arms. "Don't start, Jason. This way, it feels like I'm bartering. Besides, you've been sneaking hay and corn here for years." Her lashes batted. "Thank you."

"I should have known you'd figured it out." Jason wore a sly grin. "But, there's more."

Emma raised her brow.

"In a day or so, we begin turning our ranches into replicas of my parent's place."

"How do you mean?"

"By now, the turbines and propane are on their way."

"Turbines? You mean those big fans that make electricity?" Emma's eyes widened.

"Yep." He leaned back and let out a long sigh.

Emma giggled. "Hate to tell you, but there's nothing here to power."

"Not yet."

Emma squinted. "Don't tease me. What's going on?"

"Oh, only a real gas stove, a refrigerator, a walk-in cooler and freezer, electric lights, an electric pump for the water well—and a gas water heater for the sink and tub." He snickered. "Yep. A real bathroom—with a flushing toilet." Jason rolled his eyes. "I'm getting carried away. We won't be using the gas water heater much to start with. Not until we have more power. We'll need propane to keep the generator going. We'll install a roof-top tank and heat it with wood chips for now. When the weather warms, the sun will heat the tanks and hoses to supply warm water. We'll only use the water heater if we have plenty of fuel."

"You're talking about doing this on your ranch, right?"

"Eventually, but we'll do it here first."

Emma jumped to her feet. "I can't allow that!"

Jason stood and towered over Emma. "Don't start with your charity crap! Do you know how long it'll take us to build houses? We need a place where we can feel at home and make our lives easier. With a real stove, we can prepare larger meals faster, and canning will be a heck of a lot easier."

Emma tried to lighten her expression when the children asked what was wrong. "Oh, nothing. We were just *practicing*." She was sure that fire was spitting from her eyes as she glared at Jason. "I have a feeling you should get used to it."

Jason chuckled and urged her to sit. "Listen, Emma, if anyone gets the raw end of this deal, it's you. People will be in and out of your house all the time. You won't have much privacy for a while."

She stared at her feet. "I've had enough privacy to last me a lifetime."

"We'll see. That may change after months of dozens of people swarming around."

"But there are only nine of you, plus the men bringing turbines."

"Guess I need to explain a little more."

Her head jerked, and she snapped. "Sounds like it."

"Emma, there's no way any of us could do what you did for six months, much less six years. I think you'll understand how impressive your accomplishments are once you have help and can breathe and sleep."

Emma clenched her teeth and began to pace. "I'm not sure about this, Jason. Maybe I don't want people taking over my house and chores." She spun and faced him. "Maybe you should do these things at the Elliot house."

"Hmm. Not a bad idea. That way, my friends can stay out of your way."

Emma's face burned. "No. That's not what I meant."

"No. No." Jason threw his hands in the air. "Perhaps you're right. They'd hate to feel like they were intruding."

Emma's scowled. "Okay, I give. You know darned well what I meant." She rested her fists on her hips. "You know how I am, Jason Alvise." She took a deep breath and asked Jason if he drank.

Jason drew back. "You mean alcohol?"

"Yes." Emma let out a loud huff. If she was going to accept all these grown-up responsibilities, well, maybe she wasn't too young to drink. She let out a chuckle at the thought. Heck, if that were the case, she could have started drinking at fourteen. Emma felt her grin grow. She looked at Jason and tapped her lips. "I've had my fill of tea tonight. Mom and Dad drank a glass of wine or whiskey every night. They said I couldn't drink until I turned twenty-one. That's about six months from now. I think they'll forgive me."

"Wait. I'm embarrassed to admit I never asked when your birthday was." His face turned red. "Great. I don't even know when Gayla's birthday is. I'm sorry."

"It's no big deal." She chuckled. "I never asked when yours was either. I was born in October. The year the lights went out. When were you born?"

"Wait a minute. What was the date?"

"October fifteenth."

"No way." Jason's head went back. "That's my birthday, too."

"You're kidding. We were born on the same day?"

"The same day. The same year! Is that crazy or what?"

"When is Gayla's birthday?"

"In a week. April 20th."

Jason grinned. "I feel a birthday party coming."

Emma's hands flew to her mouth. She'd love that!

Emma poked her head inside the door. "Jason and I are going for a walk. We'll be right back," Emma told the kids.

The kids peeked out of their tent. "Okay, but no kissing!" Gayla ordered. "You're already having twins!"

Shelley covered her mouth and giggled. Marcus squinted and scratched his head.

Once they reached the yard, Jason asked where they were going.

"To the cellar to get some booze," Emma smirked.

"I've been coming here all this time and had no idea you kept liquor in the cellar."

"Never crossed my mind until tonight." As Jason lifted the door, Emma glanced at her parent's resting place. "I hope you don't mind." In that instant, a strong wind snatched the half-opened door from her hand and exposed the stairs to the cellar.

"Okay," he muttered. "That was downright bizarre."

"Uh, yeah. You go first." She giggled and pushed Jason toward the opening.

As he made his way down the stairs, Emma made spooky sounds. He turned before reaching the bottom rung. "Cut it out, Emma, or you can go by yourself!"

She chuckled and shoved him forward. "Some knight in shining armor you turned out to be!"

He snarled. "Sometimes you can be a real pain!"

She bent and covered her mouth to smother her amusement.

He grabbed the lantern at the bottom of the stairs and lit the wick. "Good grief. You have twice the jars you had when I was here last time."

"I had a great crop. I try not to let anything go to waste."

He studied her, shaking his head. "Okay, where's the alcohol? All I see are hundreds of jars and boxes of vegetables."

She pointed to the far end of the cellar. "Back there. I would have never found it if Mom and Dad hadn't shown me." She stuck her finger in a knot in the wood panel and swung open the door.

The door led to an eight-by-eight room lined with bottles of wine and other spirits. Jason burst into laughter.

"Is that a lot?" Emma asked.

"Uh, yeah."

"When Dad started bartering with the folks at the train depot, he always came home with a case or two. Sure wish he would have bartered for more salt, sugar, and molasses. I was getting worried." She huffed. "That was awfully generous of your friends to offer me what I'm short on."

Jason let out a puff of air and shook his head. "You amaze me, Emma Harding. You can be so hard, and a moment later, so kindhearted. You expect nothing for what you give, yet feel you have to give to receive." He placed his hand on her shoulder. "Emma, my friends share because they care, not because they expect something in return." He took her in his arms and kissed her. She did not pull away.

"Great," she giggled as she slowly pulled away. "Triplets."

They chuckled as they searched the cellar for the right bottle.

"So, you've never had a drink?" Jason asked.

"Nope."

"What did your mom like best?"

"Red wines."

"Okay. Red wine it is." Jason grabbed a bottle, wiped the dust away, and shrugged. "Cool label. Let's try it."

"Okay."

When they returned to the cabin, Emma pulled out her mother's wine glasses and made them shine. Jason opened the bottle of Cabernet, and they sat on the porch and toasted their new adventure.

"Yuck." Emma quivered and stuck out her tongue. "No wonder Mom only drank one glass a night. It's disgusting." She sighed and leaned back in the rocker. "So, exactly how many people are you bringing in to set up your ranch?"

"Let's see: one electrician, five cowboys, six farmhands, and six carpenters. That would be eighteen men. They're all married, and several have children. There will be around fifty of us with the kids."

Emma gasped. "My goodness. That's an entire city."

He chuckled. "No, Emma. That's a community."

She grimaced as she took another sip, then held her chest. "How do I feed them all?"

Jason grabbed her hand and squeezed. "That's not your responsibility. We'll have plenty of food and feed, and the farmers will start planting as soon as they arrive. That's why we chose April to come." He rested back in the rocker. "The cowboys will be here in a few days with five-hundred head of cattle. Pigs, goats, and chickens won't be far behind. With all the livestock, we're not likely to starve." He chuckled. "And Gayla will surely keep us supplied with fish and rabbits."

Emma yawned and leaned back in her rocker. "Gayla can sure catch a fish. And don't let a small animal get within sight of her slingshot!"

***

Jason looked at Emma, brushed her hair back, and whispered, "Let the wine work its magic. If anyone deserves an early night, it's you."

They sat in silence for a while. Jason raised his glass to take another sip and snickered. After only one glass of wine, Emma was sound asleep. The children, engrossed in their board game, didn't notice as Jason slipped past them and carried Emma to bed before returning to the living room.

"Kids. Stay up as late as you want, but please try to be quiet. Emma's gone to bed, and I think I'll turn in as well."

"Emma's asleep?" Gayla sat up and looked worried. "Is she sick?"

"No, only worn out from the excitement."

Gayla glanced at the clock and back at Jason.

54

"Cross my heart, Gayla. Emma just needs some rest, and we're going to make sure she gets it, okay?"

"Okay. Goodnight, Jason."

After he crawled into bed, Jason felt Gayla's apprehensive eyes on him. The little girl tiptoeing past his door and into Emma's room filled his heart with warmth. He envisioned her small hand resting on Emma's forehead as she checked for a fever. What a great kid. Jason smiled and drifted off to sleep.

CHAPTER 9

Emma sidestepped the children on the floor to add logs to the fireplace. How odd. The fire was roaring. She glanced at the clock Jason had given her a few months earlier. A little past four. She scratched her head and stared at the wood-burning stove. What the heck? It was already going. Emma glanced around the room. Gayla and her friends must be playing a trick on her. Before she could let them know she was on to them, the front door opened.

"Good morning," Laura greeted her in a whisper. "Your hens are fine layers. Almost three dozen eggs this morning." She raised the basket and smiled. "The milk is about ready to bottle. Did you know one of your sows was pregnant?"

"What's going on?" Emma squinted and backed against the sink.

"We wanted to surprise you. We decided to do your morning chores. Best we can figure, if we start at four, we can finish in time for breakfast at six. How did you do it, Emma? And Jason says your cooking is right up there with Rusty and Tracey." Laura placed the basket of eggs on the counter and let out a gust of air. "We took a vote. Unless you disagree, we do the morning chores, and you make breakfast."

Emma wasn't smiling, and she fought the urge to stick her fingers in her ears. So much chatter first thing in the morning was irritating. Mornings were quiet until Gayla got up. "I'm confused. And who are Rusty and Tracey?" she asked a little too loud.

Jason walked in with a bucket of milk and smiled at the scowling Emma. Laura stared at him and bolted for the door. "Did I hear you ask who Rusty and Tracey were?" he whispered and sat down his heavy load.

Emma stomped toward him and snatched the bucket. "You can fill me in while I pour the milk into jars. They need to go to the stream. I don't like it out for too long," she snarled. "The oldest jars of milk and cream need to be brought in. Today is butter churning day, and I need to make cream cheese and yogurt. And the clabber is ready. The buttermilk needs to go in the stream as well."

"Whoa." Jason laughed. "You lost me."

Gayla moaned and rolled over.

"Shhh." Emma glared and stuck a finger in his face. "You're going to wake the kids up!" Emma stared at the sleeping children. "Since everyone insists on being so chatty first thing in the morning, we should move them to the bedroom so they can sleep."

Gayla stretched and yawned. "I heard that. We can go back to sleep?"

Emma grinned. "Yep."

Gayla sat up and stretched. "But it's dairy day."

"Not for you, Jellybean," Jason said. "We need to learn to do some of these things the way you and Emma do. Guess you're chore-free this morning."

"Wow!" Gayla woke up Marcus. "Hey. We get to go back to bed and not do chores this morning. Let's go to my room."

Marcus opened his eyes and blinked. "Am I dreaming?"

"Nope," Gayla said. She shook Shelley. "Wake up."

After the kids left, Emma turned and glared at Jason. He lowered his head in surrender and stepped back. "Okay. Okay," he said softly. "Let me help you fill the jars, and you show me what we need to do."

"I need to go to the outhouse first." Clenched fists shoved into her hips, and her nose curled. "Or is it occupied?"

"Don't think so." Jason raised his hands and almost ducked.

Emma's mouth thinned. "Since you're so determined to take over, I expect my cup of tea will be ready when I return!"

Jason watched Emma storm from the house and gave a slow whistle. Whew. They sure ruffled her feathers. Or maybe she's just a mean drunk. He chuckled, put the water on to boil, and tossed her tea leaves into a mug. He had the feeling all hell would break loose if he didn't do this right. He stared at the cup and wiped the sweat from his upper lip.

While the water heated, he went outside and tried to explain to the others what Emma wanted from the stream.

"Not happening." Laura waved her hands. "When she's ready, she can show us. No way I make a move without her permission."

"Well, I'll go to the smokehouse and grab a slab of bacon," Matthew said. "I'm starving."

The look everyone sent Matthew caused Jason to erupt in laughter. "Are you seriously that brave? I say we wait on Emma."

"Can we at least make some coffee," Iva asked. "I'm not used to starting my day without a cup."

"Sure. I'll make it. Water's on the stove. Did you bring the pour-over cones?"

Iva opened her pack and handed Jason the coffee brewing cone and coffee. "Make it quick. I'm having withdrawals."

While Jason's group sat on the front porch, he cautioned everyone to remain quiet as Emma ran to the barn where she housed the milk cows and chickens. Then they watched as she headed to the smokehouse and pigpen. Emma was checking behind them.

***

"Morning," Emma said as she approached the porch. "I see you're drinking tea."

"Actually, it's coffee," Leslie told her. "I hope you don't mind; I got a jar of cream from the stream. I think this is the best cup I ever tasted."

"Of course, I don't mind." Emma lightly scratched her temple. "You said you're drinking coffee? My mom and dad loved coffee." She sniffed the air. "Would you mind if I tried a cup?" Before there was a response, she laughed then grimaced. "But then again, my parents loved wine too."

Leslie stood. "I'll make a cup for you."

"Thank you. Thank you all." Emma stared at her feet. "I have a confession. I checked behind you. For the first time in my life, I don't have anything to do but cook breakfast." Emma wasn't sure how she felt about her routine changing in the blink of an eye. She didn't know whether to be grateful or resentful.

Jason burst into laughter. "Are you kidding? You barked out a ton of orders this morning. Drink your coffee or tea, then show us what we need to do."

"Whoa. Not before she shows us what meat we need to pull for breakfast," Matthew said. "The smell from the smokehouse is making me crazy."

"Which meat do you prefer," Emma asked.

"Bacon," the group shouted.

"Regular or honey smoked?"

"Honey smoked?" Matthew licked his lips.

"Honey smoked bacon it is." She was about to stand when Leslie walked out with a cup of coffee. She accepted the mug and took a sip. "Oh, my. This is wonderful."

"Don't stop drinking your herbal tea," Laura said. "It's full of antioxidants to keep you healthy."

Emma giggled. "For a moment, I was sure my mom was preaching again." She took another sip. "Mmm." She lowered the cup. "Mom was what you'd call a health food nut." She glanced toward her mother's grave. "Too bad it didn't protect her from dying when she gave birth to Gayla."

"Do you have any idea what happened?" Leslie asked her and took a seat on the porch.

"Dad and the Elliot's believed it was her blood pressure." She sucked in her lips and glanced at the crosses under the tree. "A heart attack? A stroke? It happened that fast." She snapped her fingers. "Mom was in labor for two days." She looked away. "They believed a cesarean would have saved her. That's all I know."

"I'm so sorry." Jason squeezed her shoulder. "I hope giving birth won't be so frightening in the future. We'll have a doctor and nurse here soon. Doc and his wife, Angie, volunteered to come for a while. Later, my cousins, Bella and Julien, will be joining us with their kids. Julien's parents are doctors. His dad's a surgeon, and his mom's an obstetrician. They've been teaching Bella and Julien for years." He shot a glance at the others. "Things won't be easy, but at least we'll have people around us with experience."

Emma looked away. Surely Jason wasn't speaking directly to her. Her face heated. Just because they had kissed a couple of times didn't mean… And even if they ended up growing closer, she'd seen too many of the farm animals giving birth. That wasn't for her.

Emma stood and swept her hair back. "Well, no one has to worry about that happening to me. Between how painful I imagine it is and losing my mother?" She huffed. "Not me! No way I will ever have a baby."

Jason's head went back, and he had a strange look on his face that Emma didn't recognize. It was a mixture of sadness and pain. Emma noticed the uncomfortable faces around her.

"I always dreamed of a big family," Jason said softly.

Emma felt the heat rise. "I'm sure you won't have a problem finding dozens of women happy to give you your dream."

Jason started to respond then paused. He nodded to the others. "You'll have to excuse me. I seem to have lost my appetite. I'm going to check on the cows."

Jason strolled to the barn. The other men stood.

59

"I think we should help him. We'll come back later for breakfast." Matthew gave his wife a sideways glance before he and the other men left.

Laura walked over to Emma and pointed her finger toward a chair. "Sit."

Emma sat and looked away.

"Listen to me, young lady. You just crushed Jason."

Emma turned to look at Laura. "What do you mean?"

Laura frowned. "You can't sit there and honestly say you don't know how much Jason cares for you." She threw her arms wide. "Look at the lengths he's gone to so he can be with you."

Emma stared at her feet and nodded.

"And I think we need to talk about giving birth." Laura tried to explain how, yes, it was painful, but the pain vanished immediately. "And there's not a more beautiful moment in the world than when you see your child for the first time."

Emma continued to stare at her feet. "I guess I did it again." She tried to laugh and looked at Laura. "I don't know how to fix this."

Laura smiled and patted her shoulder. "We'll work on it." She turned to Iva and Leslie. "Right, ladies?"

Both women smiled and nodded.

"I'm going to call Matthew and have the men come back so we can start breakfast. I'm starving," Laura said.

The men rode in a few minutes later.

Jason was smiling. "I'm glad Laura called us back. I'm starving now."

Emma looked at Laura. She had a feeling her new friend had said more than, "come back for breakfast."

Emma grinned. "Well, let's go pull some bacon."

Once she and the men reached the smokehouse, she warned them to stand back. Emma opened the door, and dense smoke curled as it made its exit.

Matthew inhaled the aroma pouring from the shed. "Oh, my Lord. That smells unbelievable."

Emma and the men walked inside, and she checked the thermometer. "Perfect. Sixty-two degrees. I generally cold smoke." She coughed, waved the smoke away, and walked toward a slab of bacon hanging from the rafter. "This is honey cured. Sounded like you never had it." She reached for it, but the men intercepted.

"Gee. Are you trying to be nice, or are you starving?" She snickered.

"A little of both." Jason chuckled.

"I made maple bacon until I ran out of syrup. I don't have the time or energy to tap the birch trees. Honey will have to do for now."

"Rusty would be impressed," Jason said.

"Who the heck is this Rusty you keep talking about?" She squinted.

"I'll tell you all about him at breakfast."

When they walked outside, Emma began giving orders. "We need to take the slab of bacon to the house, take the fresh milk to the stream, and bring back what we'll need to make butter and stuff." She reached for one of the small wagons next to the smokehouse.

"I've got it," Jason said.

"Uh, thanks."

Matthew was holding the bacon. "I'll meet you there after I take the bacon to the house.

The women joined them at the stream, and the men pulled the cages. Emma pointed to the ones with slips of green twine wrapped around the jars. "It's important to keep the jars in order. These are the oldest. The jars at the front of the next cage get the green bands and take their place. I think the oldest is best for cream cheese and yogurt. From the other batch, we can separate the cream, make sour cream, and add the clabber. Need to make some buttermilk. I use a lot to tenderize tough cuts of meat. We need the whole cage of cream so we can make plenty of butter." She put a hand on her hip. "We need to make more cheese, but that will be another day."

Wide eyes stared back at her. "Did I say something wrong?"

Iva shook her head. "Geesh. You really *are* Super Woman."

"I'm not sure what you mean."

"Of course, you don't, dear."

Laura had shredded potatoes the night before. Emma had put them in jars of water and placed them in the stream.

"It makes getting breakfast together a lot easier. Plus, Mom said the water helped remove the starch. They do seem to cook. I do it whenever I can."

Iva and Leslie shredded the onions, and Laura sliced the bacon. Emma added wood to the stove and pulled out the churn, jars, and other accessories. The men went to work churning butter and separating cream.

Emma handed Jason a large stainless-steel bowl, a piece of worn linen, and string. "Put the linen in the bowl, fill it with clabber, tie it up, and hang it from the hook over the bowl."

"What's that for?" he asked.

"Cream cheese," all four women said.

Laura winked. "Make Rusty proud."

"There you go again," Emma said. "Would someone please tell me who the heck Rusty is?"

"Rusty and his wife, Tracey, are chefs at Hudson Ranch," Jason explained. "They're more than fine cooks. Everyone adores them. President Walker used to threaten to steal Rusty. They say that next to my mom and dad, Rusty is the most well-known person in the country."

"Rusty is a fine man." Laura interrupted. "When Jason was about two years old, he got lost in a snowstorm. Rusty risked his life to find him."

"Yep. I'll never forget that day," Matthew added. "They found Rusty, unconscious, cradling Jason in his jacket. All he had on was a thin shirt and jeans. He saved Jason's life."

Emma looked at Jason and grinned. "I'm glad he found you. He sounds like a wonderful man."

"None better," Jason said.

Emma felt a little awkward. She was sure Laura had told her husband about their conversation, and he'd told Jason. If not, Jason wouldn't be in such a good mood. Sweat formed on her upper lip, and she wiped it away. She decided the best way to break the awkwardness was to keep talking.

"My mom and dad told me all about your parents. They said they saved the country from becoming a dictatorship a few years before the EMP, and then saved Riverton, Lander, and a lot of others." Emma bobbed her head and grinned. "I doubt I'd have a clue how to make all the dairy products, especially cheese, if it weren't for the women at Hudson Ranch."

"What do you mean?" Laura asked.

"They gave lessons to the people in Riverton and Lander. My parents passed the knowledge on to me."

Jason smiled. "Emma, my parents, and the folks at Hudson Ranch did what was necessary to save themselves and others."

Leslie chimed in. "You've done the same thing for years, all on your own. Gayla is one lucky little girl to have you for a sister."

Emma massaged the back of her neck, peeked inside the Dutch oven hanging in the fireplace, and changed the subject. "Geez. I didn't put the bread on soon enough" She stood and placed her hands on her hips. "Sorry. We can wait for it or eat it for lunch."

The aroma of grilling hash browns, sizzling bacon, and baking bread brought the kids to life.

Marcus came out. "Mmmm. For a minute, I thought I was at Hudson Ranch. I dreamed that Rusty was barking out orders and telling everyone to get out of his way."

Emma watched in amusement as the others giggled.

"Oh, I forgot to tell you," Jason said. "Rusty loves to pretend he's annoyed. There's not an angry bone in his body. It's part of his charm." He raised his eyebrows. "Sort of reminds me of someone."

He smiled at Emma. She huffed.

"I say we wait on the bread. Uh, is there any chance we can make some more coffee?"

"Four cups? You'll be jumping out of your skin." Leslie laughed and went to refill Emma's mug.

"But it's *so* good," Emma said as she reached to turn the Dutch oven.

"I'll get that," Jason insisted.

A tremor ran down her spine as he touched her shoulder. "Thank you."

Gayla walked out of her bedroom and snorted. "Will you two stop?"

"Stop what?" Emma asked.

"Acting all goofy when you look at each other."

Emma's face was on fire, and the other adults camouflaged their smirks behind their coffee cups.

Once the snickering winded down, Laura asked about her parents' old friends. "Emma, you never told us about the Elliot's. Why did they leave? Did you ever see them again? We found several things of theirs. Like a picture album. It surprised us that they left it."

Emma's face burned hotter, and her heart raced. She glanced at Jason then looked away. She had never talked about it. Not even to Jason. One day she would tell him. But today wasn't the day.

***

Emma was cleaning the pig pen while her dad and Gayla worked in the garden. The rattle of a wagon in the distance startled her. She grabbed her shotgun and ran toward her father.

"Someone's coming!"

He dropped the plow, grabbed three-year-old Gayla, and rushed toward his oldest daughter. He took the gun and handed Gayla to Emma. "In the house! Now!"

Emma cradled her little sister in her arms and ran. She put Gayla in the bedroom, shut the door, and snatched the 30-30 rifle that rested above the door frame.

She walked onto the porch. Her father stood, watching the dirt lane that fed off the old paved road. The rumbling sound of a wagon grew louder. He turned and glared.

"In the house! Now!"

Emma gritted her teeth and defiantly loaded a round into the chamber.

"Damnit, Emma!"

She walked down the porch steps and waited.

Her father spun and focused on the wagon entering the clearing. He raised his shotgun, and Emma inched closer.

"Harding!" yelled the driver as he slowed to a stop.

Emma watched as her father lowered his weapon. His shoulders shook for a moment before he raised his arm and waved them in.

Emma lowered her weapon and squinted. "Mr. Josh! Mrs. Lorna!" She ran back up the steps, placed the gun on the rack over the door, and grabbed the crying Gayla. The girls made it to them just as her father helped Mrs. Elliot from the wagon.

"God, Almighty! It's good to see you two!" Her father said. The four had a good cry as they wrapped each other in their arms.

Her father wiped his eyes and laughed. "You should have called. The place is a mess."

Mrs. Elliot chuckled. "We would have, but I lost my I-Phone several years ago."

The commotion got to little Gayla, and she began to cry again.

Mrs. Elliot reached out. "May I?" she asked Emma.

She took Gayla into her arms and cooed. "How beautiful you are, little one."

Gayla stopped crying and began wrapping one of Mrs. Elliot's long curls around her finger.

Emma offered to take their wagon and horses to the barn. "Dad. Take them inside so they can rest and get something to drink. I'll be there in a few minutes and make dinner."

Josh looked at the small cabin that Emma had nodded toward. "Why didn't you move to our old house? It's a lot bigger."

Her dad slapped him on the back. "I always hoped you'd come home."

***

"So why did you come back?" her father asked as they sat at the table.

Josh and Lorna lowered their mugs and looked at each other.

"One accident too many," Josh said. "Plus, there's no place like home."

Mrs. Elliot leaned back in her chair. "Food. Lord, how we miss the taste of real food."

"What do you mean, Mrs. Lorna?" Emma asked.

"We worked for the government. They did their best, but we were in New York City. That's a long way from cornfields or the livestock in Wyoming."

Josh nodded. "Yep. Sometimes we wondered what we were eating."

They both laughed, then Josh clenched his wife's hand. "We'd been talking about leaving for some time, but we didn't earn a salary. It was room and board. We lived in a twenty by twenty room. Thankfully, it had a working toilet, shower, and a wood-burning stove." He rubbed his forehead. "Once a month, we got a small amount of silver. We kept every piece. That's how we managed to make it here."

Her father let out a gust of air. Emma didn't miss the moisture in his eyes.

Josh lowered his head. "I'm almost afraid to tell you the rest." His eyes met her father's. "I don't want you to think of me as a coward."

Her father tossed his head back and laughed. "Not a chance in hell."

Josh hesitated. "Okay." His eyes darted toward his wife, then back to her father. "My job was bringing down buildings that hadn't completely collapsed. I set explosives. Lorna worked loading debris. The day before we left, a building came down on me and my men. It wasn't the first time, and I knew it wouldn't be the last." His mouth tightened. "I made sure my men were safe and found Lorna." He reached over and grabbed her hand. "She was covered in dust and had cuts on her arms from where she'd shielded her face." Josh's lips trembled, and he squeezed his wife's hand harder. "I couldn't do it anymore. I couldn't leave Lorna a widow, and she couldn't keep hauling and loading debris." He let out a gust of air. "That night, we packed our belongings and left."

Her father stood. "You're not a coward. And you're home now." He slung his head to the side. "Let's grab some meat from the smokehouse and have a real dinner."

Josh stood. "I thought you'd never ask. But there's one other thing." He smiled at Lorna. "We need to meet the train every month." Josh looked at his feet for a second, then back at Emma's father. "I hate to drag up old memories, but she's three months along. I'd feel better if the doctors on the train saw her each month."

Emma's father grabbed the back of the chair. A tear slid from his eye, and he looked at Lorna. "Every month, without fail!"

***

It had been a joy to have the Elliot's back for the past two months. Gayla was thrilled with the extra attention, and Emma loved having help and companionship. Her father? Well. Emma hadn't seen him so happy since before her mother died.

Lorna was feeling a tad queasy, and Emma insisted she go home and take a nap. Her father and Mr. Josh were feeding the animals in the barn. Emma was prepping vegetables to can and watching the loaf of bread baking in the Dutch oven. Emma jerked at the distant sound of a gunshot.

Oh, no. One of the cows had seemed sickly. Emma hoped they hadn't had to put her down. Emma grabbed a towel, wiped her hands, and walked toward the front window. Gayla chased a goat in the front yard. Emma giggled, then froze as her father and Josh raced from the barn. Josh had his rifle raised and was searching for something. Emma's father ran for Gayla, scooped her up, and rushed toward the house. Then he stopped, turned, and put Gayla down. She ran after the old goat. He was yelling at her.

"Run, Gayla! Run!"

Emma's mind became foggy. She opened the front door so she could hear better. That's when she saw them. Three men. The one farthest away laughed and staggered. He lifted a bottle to his lips and held a pistol in his other hand. Two others eased toward her father, Mr. Elliot, and Gayla.

An echoing shot rang out. Mr. Elliot fell to his knees, then crumpled to the ground. The man aiming his gun at Mr. Elliot spun sideways and clutched his shoulder. An instant later, the wounded man sent several rounds Mr. Elliot's way.

It happened so fast. Her father's scream. Him lifting his rifle and yelling, "Run, Gayla! Run!"

Emma wasn't sure how the 30-30 made it to her hands.

She watched as her father's head went back and he fell to the ground. Gayla was crying and didn't move. The man that shot her father set his site on Gayla. Emma lifted the rifle and fired. He went down. Two seconds later, the others had joined him on the ground.

Emma heard Gayla's wailing, but she was numb. She walked amongst the men. She had to make sure they couldn't hurt Gayla. Her dad was dead. Mr. Josh was dead. She was afraid to check on Mrs. Lorna. That had to be the first shot she heard. Tears rolled from both eyes.

As Emma approached the man who'd laughed and raised the bottle of booze, she heard him whimper.

"Help me."

She stared at him for a moment, then looked at her little sister as she squatted and sobbed next to their father. Emma snapped another round into the chamber. At the age of thirteen, she realized not everyone deserved a second chance, and she didn't even close her eyes.

Emma looked away from the man in front of her and stared at Gayla and her father. What was her sister saying? She slowly walked that way. How did she tell a three-year-old that her daddy was dead? As she neared them, she saw the rise and fall of her father's chest. The rifle slipped from her fingers.

Emma found Mrs. Elliot's body about fifty yards from their home. She buried her and her husband under a large oak where she remembered they loved to picnic years earlier. She thought about burying them with her mother but figured they'd probably like their own place.

Luckily, the man who tried to kill her dad wasn't a great shot. Emma had to dig a bullet from his side, but within a week, he was doing okay.

He discussed what happened with Emma and tried to make her understand how what she'd done had saved them and how proud he was. He let her cry and vent, and they never mentioned it again.

CHAPTER 10

Emma suggested the children take the day off to explore and get to know each other. Gayla's delighted expression brought Emma's hand to her chest. "You've earned it," she said quietly. "Many times over."

The adults sat around the table, making plans for the day. "You need to unpack and settle in," Emma told them. "I'll take care of the other chores."

"I have a better idea," Laura said. "The men unload the household stuff we didn't get to yesterday, then you show them around and let them handle the chores while we set up the Elliot House."

"Sounds good to me," one of the men said.

Emma rubbed her arms as if a chill had caught her. After a few deep breaths, she reluctantly accepted the offer.

"I can't believe we're going to have a house to live in," Leslie said. "We thought it would be months."

"The others will be arriving soon. We need to build the shelter as soon as possible," Jason said.

"They can't all stay here, or at Elliot House, that's for sure." Emma tapped her lips. She counted the soon to be population. "We can't let the women and children sleep outside or in the barn or shed."

"They're bringing tents and mattresses. They won't be on the ground," Jason said. "It won't take long to build the pavilion."

"How long?"

"Two or three weeks."

Emma shook her head. "That won't do. I say we tough it out and let the women and young children stay inside. I have tarps. We can enclose the front porches. If we make it tight, the fireplace should keep it warm. The men can set up tents in the barn."

The strange looks puzzled Emma. "I'm, I'm sorry. It was only a suggestion."

"Wow, Emma. You'd be willing to do that? I mean, they're total strangers. That's a lot of people to have around after being alone your whole life," Eric said.

She leaned in and rested her chin on her clasped fingers. "Hmm. If I came to you and had nowhere to sleep, would you turn me away?" She smiled and glanced at Iva. "You offered me molasses and sugar and wanted nothing in return. You didn't know me but made the offer anyway." She stood and suggested they get to work. "Sounds like we have a lot to do."

***

Emma had shown the men around. She'd told them to decide what they wanted to work on but warned them that the garden was hers. She leaned on the wooden handle of her hoe and watched Gayla, Marcus, and Shelley chase each other in the field. For the first time in her life, Gayla was getting to be a little kid. Emma had never seen her so happy.

Since moving to the farm, the only other people Emma had seen besides her parents and the Elliot's were census takers that showed up every few years. Gayla only knew Emma. She didn't remember their dad. Her only encounter with others was when she was four years old and more census takers showed up.

Almost sixteen. That was how old Emma was when they came. She had been terrified and threatened to shoot them. They had backed off and set up camp several yards from the house.

Three men occupied her front yard. "Ma'am, we are not here to harm you. We just want to know who you are. We need to know how many people are alive. We've lost so many, and we are trying to reunite families. Please, let us help you! We are not leaving until we know you are okay and what your names are."

Emma and Gayla listened to the message several times before nightfall. They didn't even make a trip to the outhouse. Emma refused to sleep and watched the men. They had to know that she and Gayla were alone. The next morning, Emma changed her normal routine. The animals would have to wait to be fed and watered. She quietly made her way to the chicken coop for eggs, pulled milk and butter from the stream, and grabbed bacon from the smokehouse.

Emma shook her head as she carried her stash inside. Pitiful! She'd wasted a night of rest on *them*? They could sleep through a stampede.

An hour later, Emma walked onto the porch and let out a few powerful whistles. The men roused.

"If you wished us harm, it would have been done by now." She slung her head toward the door. "Come in. Breakfast is ready."

The census workers took her information and encouraged her to follow them to a safer location. Emma declined.

The men spent about an hour playing chase with Gayla, and she hugged and kissed them all before they left.

"You made my little sister happy," Emma said as she offered them a bag of canned food she'd packed up from her cellar. "Thank you."

***

Emma went to work in the garden. The metal hoe hacked through the soil for several minutes before it hit a hard object and sent a jolt through her spine. Emma yelped, tried to straighten, and winced. She was stretching out her back when she heard Jason laughing.

"What? You don't get enough exercise?"

"Huh?"

"All that bending and stretching."

"Oh. No." Emma looked at the ground. "The hoe hit something hard, and it almost knocked my teeth loose."

"Are you okay?"

"Yeah." She winced and pointed to the shovel. "Would you bring it to me?"

Jason grabbed the splintered wooden handle of the shovel and turned it in his hands. He looked at Emma. "We need to make a new handle. This thing could darn near shove a spike through your hand!"

Emma rolled her eyes. "I know. I know. I'll take care of it in my spare time." She waved him over and snickered.

Emma reached for the shovel, and Jason pulled away. "Seriously? I'll dig it up. Probably a rock or stump." As Jason dug, his brows furrowed.

"What is it?"

He didn't answer and dug faster.

"What in the world?" Emma stared at what appeared to be a wooden trunk.

Jason scooped the dirt from around it and tried to lift the box, but it proved to be too heavy.

"Is your back okay?" he asked Emma.

"Yeah."

"See if you can help me lift this thing."

After much effort, they lifted the box and placed it next to Emma's garden wagon. Emma turned her water bottle up and chugged before offering it to Jason.

"Thanks." He turned it up and finished it off. He wiped his mouth. "Let's put it in the wagon and hope the tires hold."

Once the struggle to load the box was over, Jason broke the rusted lock, lifted the lid, and took a few steps back.

Emma gasped. "Is that what I think it is?"

"Whoa!" Jason grabbed his head and brushed his hair back before turning to Emma. "The whiskey cellar. No one knows about it, right?"

"No, not even Gayla."

"That's where we take it. Not a word to anyone, and I mean no one! This much gold might get you killed."

"So, it *is* gold?"

"Oh, yeah! And I'll bet the jewels are real." He exhaled and shook his head. "I'm serious, Emma, *no one* can know about this!"

***

Jason leaned against the whiskey cellar door, gasping for breath. Not so much from the hauling as from the pure adrenaline rush. "Let's bring out a few cases of whiskey and wine. We don't care for it, but some of the men and women will love it. We don't want the door exposed. We'll stack the booze in front of it."

After they set the whiskey in place, they headed back to the garden and tried to act normal.

Emma quizzed him on the walk. "Do you think it was from a stagecoach robbery back in the old days?"

"No way. The lock is too new. But those are ancient gold coins. Most likely, they came from a sunken ship. How the heck they got here, or how long ago, beats me. Once things are under control, I'm going after my dad. He'll help us figure it out." He smiled at Emma. "Looks like you may be a wealthy woman."

Jason froze. "Do you hear that?"

"Hear it? I can smell it!" Emma giggled. "I've never smelled so much cow in my life!" She laughed.

He'd never seen anything so beautiful. How was it possible for anyone to be so rough yet so generous and tender-hearted? He'd expected her to go wild when she realized the gold had made her wealthy, but instead, it was merely another day.

71

How could things get more exciting? Emma found hundreds of pounds of gold coins, and his cattle had arrived. He grabbed Emma and kissed her. She didn't pull back.

Jason let out a loud whoop. "Let's meet your new neighbors and cattle."

As they neared the wagon, Emma staggered and waved her hand. Jason knew she was nervous about meeting even more people. He held her hand. "You'll love them, Emma. Hudson Ranch has to cull sometimes. Some people get lazy. They don't want to contribute but demand their share. It's happened many times over the years. Dad gives them supplies and then sends them packing. What's left is the cream of the crop."

"I'm sure they're great people. I'm just a little nervous."

"I understand." How Emma remained composed with all that hit her at once was beyond him.

"I bet they'll be starving. I have a smoked ham we can have for dinner. I was going to can what Gayla and I couldn't eat. And mashed potatoes with gravy. I think spinach and chard salad; maybe pole beans and cornbread." She scratched her head. "Or would rolls be better?"

Jason stared for a moment, then burst into laughter.

***

The cowboys rushed to greet Jason. After a few slaps on the back, he reached for Emma's hand and introduced her.

"So, we finally meet the mysterious young lady that has everyone at Hudson Ranch captivated." The man took her hand and gave it a quick kiss. "My name's Mark, and if half of what Jason told us about you is as true as your beauty, you're one heck of a woman."

"Trust me," Matthew said as he greeted his old friends. "Jason's stories only scratch the surface."

Emma blushed as the rest of the men introduced themselves.

"Nice to meet you, gentlemen. I don't mean to be rude. I know you've got a lot to do. I'm going to take my wagon back home. I have quite a bit to do myself," she told them and hurried away.

Jason waited for Emma to be out of earshot. "We need to give her time to adjust. Remember, she's accustomed to being alone." Then he told them about her offer for sleeping arrangements.

"For someone accustomed to isolation, she sure seems to be adapting well," Mark said. "But there's been a change. The women and children will be staying behind for a while. The doctors agreed it was best to wait for a shelter. The men should be here at any time."

CHAPTER 11

"Gayla, Marcus, Shelley," Emma shouted. "Can you come here for a minute? I need a favor."

The three children came running. "What do you need?" Gayla asked.

"I hate to break a promise, but I need help. Jason's cowboys are here with the cattle. I need to pick the lettuce, baby spinach, and swiss chard leaves for dinner and gather what's ripe in the greenhouse. And I want to enclose the front porch, so we need the tarps, ladder, and hammer and nails from the shed."

"Why are you doing that?" Gayla asked.

"Because fifty people will be here soon, and they'll need somewhere to sleep. Some of the women and children can sleep on the porch."

Gayla jumped up and down and clapped her hands. "More children?"

"About a dozen, from what I hear."

Gayla threw her arms around Emma. "We're going to have a big family, just like in the books."

Emma found it difficult to swallow.

"Ms. Emma, I'll bring the stuff from the shed. Gayla and Shelley can pick the vegetables, and I'll help you," Marcus offered.

Emma's throat was so tight she could barely thank him. She sat on the porch and watched as the children ran off to do their chores. This might turn into a beautiful thing.

***

Marcus stood atop the ladder and nailed the tarp around Emma's porch. "Marcus, are you sure you're only ten? You use that hammer like a grown man."

"Thanks. You don't make it at Hudson Ranch if you're too lazy to learn." His chest puffed. "I learned to use a hammer before I could walk."

Emma giggled. "Lord, you sound like me."

"Phhh. Not. Everyone at Hudson Ranch knows about you. When Jason came back with stories after he visited, the grown-ups cried. Heck, some of the kids cried, too. Especially when they heard about Gayla."

73

Marcus descended the ladder. "I'm pretty sure me and Gayla will get married one day." He let out a heavy sigh. "I sure hope she can cook as good as you." He grabbed the end of another tarp and headed back up the ladder.

Emma chuckled. She thought back to the day she met Jason when they were seven, and how he had told her he was going to marry her one day. She smiled. Must be a Hudson Ranch thing.

"Would you mind helping put up the tarps at Elliot House?"

"No problem." He smiled down at her through a mouth full of nails.

Emma bragged on Gayla and Shelley as they wheeled in a wagon full of fresh vegetables. "We'll have a lovely salad for dinner, thanks to you."

"Do you need us to do anything else, Ms. Emma?" Shelley asked.

"Hmm. Let me think." She tapped her lips. "In fact, I do. Go play."

Gayla threw her arms in the air. "I love this." She grabbed Shelley's arm. "Let's play hide and seek again."

Gayla meeting others and making friends so easily far exceeded Emma's wildest dreams. It was so natural. As if they'd known each other for years.

Marcus jumped off the ladder. "All done. Should we tie the tarps up or secure the bottom?"

"Why don't we let them hang for now. We should take the rest to the Elliot House and put them up." She grinned at her young helper. "Or should I say *you* can put them up?"

Marcus extended an arm, curled his fist, and growled, "Ready when you are."

So much laughing. How Emma wished her parents were here to see this. She glanced at the crosses beneath the tree and caught her breath as a strong wind swept through the branches. Emma rubbed the raised hairs on her arms. "Thank you," she whispered.

"Marcus, rest a while. Get some water and a snack. I'll load and hook up the wagon."

"I just need to grab some water. I'll take care of the wagon. Don't you need to do something with those?" He pointed to the cart of vegetables.

"Wow. Give me some help, and I get lazy. Thank you, Marcus."

"Can I eat one of those tomatoes from the greenhouse?"

"Of course. Help yourself."

"Okay, and I love cucumbers."

"Eat anything you want." She placed her hands on her hips. "Don't ask again. You are more than welcome to anything grown here."

"Thank you." He picked up a tomato and examined it. "Is this a Brandywine?"

"Yes. Yes, it is." Emma shook her head. *He can identify a tomato?* "I'm going to pack this stuff up and put it in the cellar. I'll be back in a few minutes."

***

Emma carried the vegetables down the steps of the cellar. When she reached the bottom, she paused, stared at the cases of whiskey blocking the entrance to the secret room, and sat on the bottom rung. Why didn't finding the gold and gems thrill her? Instead, it triggered an unsettling feeling. Something was wrong. She felt a cold chill as a gust of wind whipped down the opening. She closed her eyes and prayed. "Mom, Dad. You're going to have to help me out on this one. Something about that box scares me." She left the cellar and bolted the door. The wind was still, yet the tree in the distance danced. Emma shuddered and went to meet Marcus.

"Hey," Marcus yelled. "Took your own sweet time. Let's roll."

"Okay, smarty-pants, I'm on my way."

***

Emma and Marcus had loaded into the wagon and headed for the Elliot House when she saw Jason riding toward them. Emma caught her breath. At six-foot-four, he seemed to dwarf the stallion. *My, my, my. Some people are put together* really *well. His unbuttoned shirt flapped in the wind, exposing his Herculean chest muscles. Her eyes grew wider as he approached. Dear Lord. Whew. Breathe, Emma, breathe.*

"Hey," Jason smiled when he stopped his stallion beside the wagon. "I figured you'd be up to your eyeballs making dinner plans and doing chores."

Look away, Emma. Do not stare. After she caught her breath, Emma told him what she and Marcus were up too. "Marcus is incredible. He enclosed my porch, and we're headed for Elliot House."

"You're a good man, Marcus."

Jason's stomach muscles rippled as he fought to control the prancing stallion, and Emma again averted her eyes.

"Once they're installed, the men can sleep easy. The women and children won't be coming until we build the shelter. The doctors convinced them it was a bad idea."

Emma glowered. "It would have been nice if you'd told me!"

75

"Like when?" Jason scowled. "I've been a little busy."

Emma's head jerked. "Doesn't matter. Now the men won't have to sleep in tents." She whipped the horse's reins and headed for Elliot House.

Marcus stared back at Jason as their wagon pulled away. "Whew, Jason looks a little ticked off."

"Misery loves company," Emma scoffed. Now she'd have to explain to Gayla that the children wouldn't be coming until later. She took a deep breath and told herself to stop being silly. What was a week or two after a lifetime of seclusion?

***

Emma and Marcus unloaded the wagon and told the women why they were there. "Jason said the women and children would be coming later. We, uh, Marcus, enclosed my porch. With yours, the men won't need to sleep in tents."

"We'll be happy to do whatever we can to help," Laura said.

Marcus was installing the first tarp when Jason arrived, stepped from his horse, and approached Emma.

"I'm sorry," they said in unison and laughed.

Emma stared at her feet. "It's just that I told Gayla about the new kids coming."

Jason embraced her and rubbed her back. "They'll be here, Emma. But the doctors were concerned about them living outdoors." He held her back. "I'll explain to Gayla."

"I think I'll take you up on that offer." Emma rubbed her forehead. "Jason, it seems so strange. I haven't done much of anything since everyone arrived, yet I'm exhausted. I don't understand."

"Seriously? Your entire world changed overnight. Go home. I'll help Marcus. Enjoy your afternoon for once. The women will come over later to help with dinner. Spend a few hours doing something you've always dreamed of."

She stepped back. "I will. By gosh, I will." She turned to head home.

"Hold on. I'll take you home in the wagon."

She threw her arms wide and spun. "Thank you, but I think I'd like to take a leisurely stroll home. I've read about the experience in books, but never actually done it." She grinned and lifted her shoulders in anticipation.

CHAPTER 12

Jason watched as Emma walked away. He hoped she would have many more leisurely walks. She surely deserved it. He wondered how many Emma's were out there. How many others had never known a day filled with joy? Thousands, perhaps millions. The EMP stole more than electricity, running water, the internet, television, and radio. For twenty years, the world's occupants struggled to survive. Even with the trains running now, fuel productions increasing, and goods brought in from other countries, most people still focused on their day-to-day survival. The majority of fuel supported the military. But even they had a tough time traversing the country. The roads had become inhospitable, and it would be many years before they were passable.

With only a tenth of the population before the EMP, it would be difficult to rebuild, even if they had access to the old "modern-day technology." The demolition of large cities to prevent the spread of disease caused smaller towns to spring up across the country, and there were no direct highways to join them. It would take years to rebuild cities like New York. The removal of debris alone might take a lifetime.

Jason shook his head. "What did you say, Marcus?"

"I asked if you wanted the tarps nailed down."

"I guess we nail them since the cowboys will be staying there tonight." He grinned at the young carpenter. "Thank you for your hard work."

Marcus jumped from the bottom rung of the ladder. "Just doing my part."

Jason reached for the hammer and apron full of nails. "I'll take care of it. You deserve a break. Why don't you go to Emma's and see if you can go fishing? Tell her I'd sure love to see some fish hanging in the smokehouse."

"You sure? She was kind of mad at you a while ago."

"I have a funny feeling she'll be thrilled." Jason nodded toward his stallion. "Why don't you take Guss? I'll take the wagon."

Marcus backed off. "Uh, thanks, but I'd rather take the wagon. My dad says Guss is a mean SOB. Not sure what SOB means, but *I* ain't riding him. Dad says no one can ride the beast but you."

Jason erupted in laughter. "Nonsense. Guss is just a little on the feisty side." He approached Guss and offered Marcus the reigns. "If I ever met a young man capable of handling Guss, it's you."

Marcus's hands shook as he reached for the reins.

"No." Jason gently pulled back and spoke softly. "Don't *ever* let an animal know you're afraid. They'll lose respect for you." He waved Marcus in. "Come on, son. Pet ole Guss."

Guss snorted, then stomped, and Jason calmed him. "Walk away, slowly. Take a deep breath. When you can control your fear, walk back. Be confident. Guss can sense your anxiety."

"But he scares me, Jason."

"Yeah. He knows—and he loves it. Once you can walk up to him without fear, he's a pussycat."

Marcus held his head high and took steady breaths as he approached Guss.

"Do *not* let an ounce of quiver come from you. Tell him it's time to go home and firmly take the reins."

Marcus shot him an uneasy eye and Jason grinned. "The worse that can happen is you land on your backside and he runs off. More than anyone else at Hudson Ranch can say."

Marcus took another deep breath, rubbed Guss's nose, mounted him, and spoke in a deep, confident voice. "Time to go home, Guss."

Jason beamed as Marcus rode Guss toward Emma's barn. "Sure hope Guss doesn't come back with an empty saddle." He chuckled.

***

Emma strolled toward Marcus and Guss as they neared her front porch, and she took the reins. "You did more than enough today, Marcus. Enjoy yourself. I'll put the horse away."

"But Ms. Emma, this is Guss. Jason's stallion."

"I know. Ornery as a mule, isn't he?" She patted Guss's haunches. "He tried to bite me the first time we met, and I had to give him a stern talking to." She rubbed his snout and kissed him. "Come on, old man. Let's go inside." Guss nuzzled Emma. "I love you too," she said and led him away.

Marcus allowed himself to absorb what he'd seen. This is crazy. He'd fought against sheer terror as he rode Guss. How in the world did he let

Jason goad him into riding the monster? Then he watched Emma rub and pet the revered giant while he nuzzled her and gave snorts of love. Marcus rubbed his sweaty forehead.

Gayla's and Shelley's giggling distracted him, and he ran toward them. "Jason wants us to go fishing. He wants to smoke some fish."

"I'll go ask Emma." Gayla rushed toward the barn.

"Wait!" Marcus yelled, but Gayla kept running. She's going to spook Guss. He covered his eyes, unable to watch. When he peeked through his fingers, Gayla was petting Guss while she spoke to Emma.

Marcus stared in disbelief as Gayla skipped toward him. "Emma said to catch all we want. Let's grab the poles."

He couldn't believe it. Jason must be right. Guss can sense fear. Emma and Gayla had the stallion acting like a puppy dog. One more story to pass around about the women at Emma's Place. Marcus chuckled. He couldn't wait to tell his dad. He won't even get close to Guss.

Marcus wobbled his shoulders from side to side. "Hey, Gayla. Guess what. I rode Guss home from Elliot House."

She smirked and hunched her shoulders. "And?"

Marcus kicked a clod of dirt. "Never mind."

***

Emma glanced at the clock and decide to start dinner. She closed her book and put it on the shelf. After gingerly wrapping her colored pencils, she placed them in the felt-lined box. Nothing but nubs. She rubbed the wooden container. New pencils, paint, and brushes would be a dream come true. She stole another moment and flipped through the art book on the coffee table then slapped it shut. In another life, Emma. In another life.

Emma pulled a small wagon into the smokehouse, lowered a twenty-pound ham, then went to the cellar for jars of green beans and potatoes. Bourbon and wine. Jason said they'd appreciate it. Sweet potato casserole. She grabbed four jars of yams and a can of her precious stash of pecans.

While the rolls were rising, she went to the stream, pulled out a jar of cream and buttermilk, and gathered herbs on the way home.

As she prepared dinner, the fresh breeze from the open front door wafted through the screen and filled the house. Emma couldn't remember being happier about making dinner.

"Hi Emma, we came to help with..." Laura paused. "Oh, my. I'm drooling."

The cinnamon apple pies resting in the windowsill were begging to be sliced. Baked ham, mashed potatoes, and green bean and sweet potato casseroles lined the counter. Emma was tossing a bowl of salad and had made a bottle of fresh dressing. Rolls were waiting to bake over the hot coals in the fireplace.

"Come on in, ladies. I was about to slice cheese in case anyone wanted to put it on top of the warm apple pie. I almost wish it were winter so I could make ice cream." She sighed. "Sorry, no ice in April."

"Uh, I think we need to call the men over. We figured it would be an hour or so."

"Oh, I started a little early. I knew you were busy, and I imagine the cowboys have a lot to do. It'll be dark in two hours." Emma bared down on the knife as it cut through the thick chunk of cheese. "I'll put the rolls in later. Dinner can wait. I just wanted it to be ready."

Laura's eyes drooped. "You should have told us. We would have helped."

"I know you would have." Emma smiled. "But you had things to do, and honestly, I enjoyed it."

"I'll let the men know to wind things up," Laura said quietly. "You guys see if there's anything you can do to help." She rushed away. The screen door slammed behind her.

"Oh, my." Iva stood over the ham.

Emma wiped her hands on the apron and stood beside Iva. "It *is* lovely, but I can still remember Mom's hams covered in pineapple rings, with a cherry in the middle. I wish I had them, but the glaze will have to do." She crinkled her lips. "Okay. Our biggest dilemma is how we seat everyone."

"We can fix a plate and eat wherever. That's okay with us," Leslie said.

"No! I'd feel horrible." Emma's brows raised. "The old doors. Dad stored several in the shed."

The women seemed confused, and Emma giggled. "We can use the sawhorses and lay the doors on them. The front porch will be fine. I'll tie back the tarps. The weather is perfect for an outdoor meal."

***

Jason gasped as he and the men pulled up in front of Emma's house. A long table covered in white linen graced the front porch. Stumps used for chopping blocks supported wood runners and served as extra seating.

The kids were dressing their fish for smoking, and Leslie and Iva were placing Emma's mother's china on the table. They paused and smiled at the approaching crew.

"Welcome home, boys," Laura said.

Jason walked inside. Emma hummed as she filled the dining room table with the evening meal. Captivated by her beauty and spirit, he hated to break the spell.

She saw him and scowled. "Well. It's about time. The food's getting cold."

Jason felt a twinge of Deja vu and spoke to himself. "Okay, Rusty."

"I thought we could make our plates in the dining room." Emma's expression contorted. "Or is that bad manners? Should we place the food on the tables outside?"

He needed to remember that Emma was struggling with how people outside of her solitude behaved. One day she'd be at ease with herself.

"We served ourselves, buffet style, back home." He saw the wine and whiskey set off to the side and smiled. "On special occasions, Dad set up the bar. Why don't we put the booze and glasses on the coffee table? That will make everyone feel at home."

Emma's expression caused his face and neck to warm. The gossipers were right. He was in love with Emma Harding. There was nothing he wouldn't do for her.

"May I have the honor of slicing this magnificent ham?"

Emma handed him a fork and knife. As their hands touched, she pulled back. "I'll slice the pies."

***

Jason watched with pleasure as his old friends laid praise on Emma.

"What a feast." Mark massaged his belly and took a sip of his bourbon. "You'd make Rusty proud."

Emma almost inhaled her cup of tea. "I swear, if I don't meet Rusty, I'm going to burst." She scrunched her brows.

"If we didn't know better, we'd swear you were his kid. You've got *so* much in common," Iva said.

Emma stood and began gathering dishes.

"Whoa. What are you doing?" Leslie asked.

"I'm going to wash the dishes."

"After this wonderful dinner? We're doing the dishes," Laura insisted.

Emma scowled and placed her fists on her hips. "You'd best remember this is my kitchen and stay out of my way."

The adults erupted in laughter.

"What's so funny?" she snapped.

"Rusty," Jason said. "He does that all the time."

Emma plopped in the chair and crossed her arms. Jason took her hand. "This is the deal. You cooked; we clean. Simple as that."

"Actually, *we* clean," Laura interrupted and nodded toward Iva and Leslie. "You men get yourselves set up at Elliot House. Kids. Use Emma's seasoning and hang the fish in the smokehouse. I'm sure Gayla can show you how."

"Yes, ma'am," Gayla said with pride.

Laura turned to Emma and Jason. "The two of you—take a hike, and stay out of our way," she said and walked inside.

Gayla glared at Jason and Emma. "I swear, if you two kiss again, you can forget me changing diapers." She called for Marcus and Shelley and headed for the fish.

The others stared at Jason, confused, as he and Emma giggled. "It's a long story. I'll tell you later," he said.

***

Jason held Emma's hand as they strolled to the stream. It felt right. It felt normal. He'd love to hold her tiny hand every day. They sat on the log by the water's edge and gazed at the star-filled sky. When he rubbed the calluses on her finger, Emma snatched away.

"Did I do something wrong?"

Emma glanced at her hands. "No. No. It's just, well, they embarrass me. They're so rough and ugly."

Jason reached out and lifted them. "Are you talking about these hands? They're beautiful and full of character."

A tear rested in the corner of an eye, and she told Jason about the day her father spoke the same words.

***

Her dad squatted. "Where are those horrible hands you keep complaining about?" He took her hands in his. "You're not talking about these, are you?" He lightly massaged her palms. "They're beautiful and full of character."

Emma rolled her eyes. She'd seen the women's hands in magazines, and her rawhide paws were far from beautiful.

Her father lifted one to his ear. His eyes widened, and he coaxed her in. "Listen. They have a story to tell."

"Dad, you're just being silly."

He turned her right palm up. "Do you see that?" He tapped the callus on her trigger finger. "That's from when you took down your first deer with a rifle. Remember him? And check out *those* beauties." He hooted and rubbed the thick tips of her pointer and middle finger. "These are from all the game you brought home with your bow. And the calluses on your palms are from hours of holding the fishing pole while you caught our dinner. That doesn't include the ones the hoe caused while you grew our food!" Her father stood. "Yep, those are some remarkable, fine-looking hands."

**

Emma chuckled and glanced at her palms. "Dad never was a good liar. They're just plain ugly."

Jason kissed her fingers. "Your father was right. Don't ever think you need to hide them from me." He grimaced and scratched the side of his right ear. "Now, if your feet are like that…"

Emma smirked and playfully punched his shoulder.

Jason snickered, wrapped his arm around Emma, and pulled her close. She rested her head on his shoulder, and they stared at the darkening sky. "Can you believe there was a time when people never saw them?"

"What do you mean?"

He pointed toward the evening sky. "The stars. Before we lost electricity, the big cities glowed with artificial light and drowned them out."

"That doesn't seem possible."

"I know. You and I have never known cites filled with lights. One day, maybe we will."

Emma stared at the brightly lit heavens. "I'm not sure that's a good thing. Gazing at the stars is so peaceful. It's like they have their own energy. They calm me."

They sat quietly for a while. Then Jason mentioned the wooden trunk. "As soon as I can, I'm going after my dad. He'll know what to do."

"Jason, something about the trunk scares me. I think we should put it back."

He laughed, then noticed the terror in her eyes. "You're serious?"

"Yes. I've had a bad feeling since we found it." She cupped her mouth and shuddered. "Every time I go to the cellar, I get this awful feeling."

"Tell you what. I'll move it somewhere else. Perhaps it won't bother you if you don't know where it is. I think knowing what's hidden in the cellar makes you paranoid."

"No, Jason. I want it reburied. At least for a while. There's something evil about it. Please, let's put it back."

He could sense fear emanating from her. "Okay, okay." He pulled her close. "I'll find a time when no one is around and return it. We can always dig it up later." She relaxed, and he rubbed her back. "I still want my dad's opinion. I'll keep a few coins to show him."

A loud rustling in the bushes caused them to leap to their feet. Jason grabbed Emma, pulled her back, and stood between her and whatever was rushing toward them. He released a gust of air as two Australian shepherds entered the clearing.

"Brute. Callie." Jason slapped his thighs, and the dogs came running. After a few seconds of talking and roughhousing with his old friends, he glanced at Emma. Her expression ripped through his soul.

"Dogs," she whispered. "Gayla's never seen a dog. I haven't seen one in years." She lowered to her knees. "Brute. Callie." The dogs were all over her, giving her kisses. She cuddled with them and allowed the dogs to lick her face as she giggled. "You're *so* soft."

Jason stood as Emma nuzzled and petted their fur. Then he saw it. He couldn't believe it. Tears slid down Emma's cheek. The dogs licked the moisture away, but he'd seen them. Emma was crying! No way! Not the big bad Emma! Jason took a step back and slowly lowered himself on the fallen tree.

A knot grew in his throat when he noticed Emma's shoulders twitch ever so slightly. He needed to give her privacy for a while. Not to mention that he might lose it if he kept watching.

"I need to go for a minute. I'll be behind that tree over there." He pointed, but she didn't look. She simply nodded.

He watched from behind the tree. When the giggling returned, so did Jason.

"Why don't we go to the house and introduce them to Gayla?"

Emma held tightly to his hand as they headed to the cabin. "I can't wait to see Gayla's face!" She stopped and looked into Jason's eyes. "Thank you. I don't think I've ever really said that. Mom always said everything happens for a reason and works out for the best." She looked down, rubbed Brute's neck, and looked back up. Then she took his other hand.

"I believe you're here for a reason. I don't exactly know what the reason is, but I'm glad you're here."

Jason thought back to his childhood. How many sleepless nights did he endure? Why had he survived when so many other children had died? The guilt had plagued him for years. And his mother, Sierra, told him the same thing.

Jason grinned and shook his head. "That's crazy. I've heard my mom say those same things so many times that I started rolling my eyes." He squeezed Emma's hands tighter. "Maybe our mothers were right. Maybe everything does happen for a reason."

CHAPTER 13

As Jason expected, it was love at first sight. Mark told Gayla some commands to give the dogs. She giggled when she squatted and held out her hand. "Brute. Shake." She did it repeatedly. She threw so many sticks for them to retrieve that Gayla complained about her shoulder hurting.

Emma laughed. "Gee. I can't imagine why. I'll get you some balm."

When the cowboys decided it was time to turn in, Mark called Brute and Callie to come. The dogs sat by Gayla and whined.

Mark placed his hands on his hips and laughed. "Gayla, it looks like you made some new friends." He squatted beside her and ruffled Brute's mane. "But they have a job to do. They help us herd. If I let them spend the night, it will be your responsibility to make sure they're at work in the morning."

"We'll be eating breakfast here for the time being," Jason told him. "Unless you think we need them with the herd tonight, it would be wonderful if they bonded with Gayla."

"Bond with her?" Mark stood and laughed. "This is the first time I've ever called them and they didn't come. I think the bonding is complete." He squeezed Gayla's shoulder and whispered, "You're the first to know. Callie is going to have puppies, and you get first pick."

Gayla sucked air. "How many times did they kiss?"

Mark scrunched his brows, Marcus rolled his eyes, and Jason and Emma burst into laughter.

"Seems Gayla believes you have a baby every time you kiss," Jason said. "Emma promised to talk to her." He smiled at Emma and raised his brow.

"Oh, I see," Mark chuckled. "In that case, they probably kissed five or six times—maybe more."

"Wow!" Gayla paused and appeared concerned. "Their babies don't wear diapers, do they?"

"Good grief," Marcus groaned.

***

Early the next morning, the sound of the door opening and closing woke Jason, and he went outside to investigate. "What the heck are you doing?"

Gayla hid something behind her back. "Nothing in particular."

He watched as the dogs devoured whatever it was she'd given them. Jason held out his hand. With her eyes on her feet, Gayla handed him the empty venison jar.

"They were hungry."

He could swear the dogs were smiling. "Jellybean." He lowered himself to a knee. "Let the grownups decide what they eat from now on. Okay? And Emma may not want them eating her jars of food."

"Okay." Her eyes pleaded. "Please, don't tell on me."

"Tell you what, I only woke up because I heard you. Let's slip back to bed till Emma wakes up."

Gayla threw her arms around him. "Thank you, Jason."

He watched the trio run back to Gayla's room, laid on the sofa, and glanced at the clock. Three a.m. He'd never get back to sleep. Then he remembered the empty jar he'd left on the counter and decided to hide it from Emma. Might as well get a jump on the day's work. He grabbed the jar and headed for the door.

"Did you get hungry?" Emma whispered and lifted her brows.

He looked at the glass in his hand and rubbed his belly. "Uh, yeah. Fine venison."

She walked across the room, took the jar, and put it in the sink. "So, how many jars did she feed them?"

"What are you talking about?"

Emma chuckled. "Don't be ridiculous. I must have a hundred jars. Some of it's getting old, and we can add it to their food. There'll be plenty more." She rolled her eyes. "I'll let you off the hook. She'll never know you ratted her out."

Jason smirked, "I didn't rat her out. I just can't get anything past you. Thanks for not spilling the beans to Gayla."

"You're welcome. The ladies left us coffee. I sure wish I had some cream."

"I can take a hint." He laughed as he reached for the flashlight and opened the door.

"Oh, and some buttermilk. I'd like biscuits this morning. A jar of cream cheese too. I like it with the jam. Jam's in the cellar."

Jason leaned against the door. "Should I grab a pencil and paper, or are you finished?"

Emma glanced around the kitchen. "Hmmm. Some ham and bacon would be nice."

His heart raced as he stared at her. "How could anyone tell you no?"

***

After Jason gathered the items Emma had requested, they sat on the front porch. "I've decided to install the turbines as soon as they arrive. We need a way to contact the outside world. Can't do it without power."

"I don't understand."

"We have a ham radio. We can talk to people from all around the world. But we need electricity to operate it."

"My dad used to talk about those. He said your parents gave one to Riverton. How exciting." Emma's eyes widened. "My mom spoke a little French. Maybe one day, I'll hear someone speak it."

"Peut-être mon cher."

Emma gasped and held her throat. "Was, was that French?"

"Yeah. My parents made sure we learned several languages." He chuckled. "I learned just enough to butcher them and get by."

"Your mom and dad sound like such wonderful people." She sighed and dropped her head. "I wish I could talk to mine in person instead of under the tree."

"At least you got to know yours. I couldn't love my parents more, but a part of me will always wonder what my birth parents would have been like."

Emma glanced up and crumpled her brow. "What on earth are you talking about?"

"I'm sorry. I assumed you knew. The people who gave me life died the week of the EMP. My father, Joseph, went down in an airplane. My mother, Renee, was wandering the woods a few days later as my parents, the Alvises, made their way to Wyoming. My birth mother was diabetic and dying. She said she'd prayed for a miracle, and there they were. She begged them to take me, laid me down, and disappeared into the woods. The Alvises raised me as their own."

He hesitated as Emma begged his forgiveness for rambling on about the loss of her parents when he'd never met his own. Jason held her hand. "You don't understand. The Alvises *are* my parents. I'm sure my birth parents loved me, but the Alvises didn't have to. They *chose* to. Destiny put

88

us together." He lightly squeezed her hand. "The same destiny that brought me to you."

He grasped her hands and went down on a knee. "Emma. My father said he lost seven years of being with my mom because he was afraid. He doesn't believe in wasting years that you could spend with the one you love." He squeezed her hand tighter. "I love you, Emma Harding. I've loved you since I was seven. I want to spend the rest of my life with you. I've carried this in my pocket for two years." He pulled out a case, opened it, and exposed a ring. "Will you marry me?"

Her lips trembled. "I love you too, Jason Alvise. Like your father says, love isn't something you waste." She threw her arms around his neck. And, without hesitation, Emma replied, "Yes. Yes. Yes!"

***

Jason could hardly keep his eyes off his fiancée. The old saying holds some truth: she positively glowed.

They wanted to tell Gayla first, and Jason hoped she would approve. If she didn't, he'd threaten to tell Emma about her feeding venison to the dogs. He laughed at himself. He never felt so happy and alive.

He had finished most of the work by the time the others arrived. Emma had coffee brewing, biscuits baking, the ham and bacon sizzled, and her famous hash browns grilled.

"Good grief," Laura barked. "Did you two stay up all night? It's five a.m., and there's nothing to do but eat this feast."

"Gayla woke me up at three. She was outside spoiling the dogs. Emma woke up too, so we decided to get a jump on the day."

"Lord Almighty," Mark bellowed. "It smells like I just walked into heaven."

"Help yourself to *your* coffee," Emma said.

"Ms. Emma, can I wake up Gayla?" Marcus asked.

"Sure."

***

They gathered on the front porch to eat breakfast. As they began clearing the plates, Gayla had a question for Jason. "So, are you going to start sleeping in Emma's room like Mommy and Daddy used to? Emma says that's what you do when you get married."

Her question caused him to choke on his coffee. He watched as Emma turned to the sink and held on for dear life, trying to suppress her chuckles. He was on his own.

89

"Uh, I'm confused, Gayla. What do you mean?" Jason asked.

Gayla rolled her eyes. "I was going to sneak out with Brute and Callie after you went back to sleep. I saw you ask Emma to marry you. Does that mean you'll sleep in her room? I sure hope so, and then we can have slumber parties in my room!"

Jason stared at Gayla. The room was quiet, but he sensed the many eyes on him. "I'd love to marry Emma, but only with your approval."

"Well, heck yeah. I was wondering what was taking you so long. It's been almost three darned years!"

Jason smiled, shook his head, and looked around. "I guess the surprise announcement is off."

The morning air erupted in cheers.

Laura, Iva, and Leslie folded Emma in their arms. "That was the best, most bizarre, wedding announcement I ever witnessed. Congratulations!" Laura cried.

CHAPTER 14

"People headed this way!" Marcus gasped for breath as he rushed into Emma's house. "Looks like lots of wagons."

Jason bolted for his rifle and binoculars while the other men grabbed their firearms and headed outside. The women armed themselves and stood by the front door.

Jason lowered the binoculars and smiled. "You can calm down. It's the others." More than a dozen men approached.

"Well, ladies," Emma said, "If the numbers Jason gave me are correct, I assume fourteen hungry men will be here soon. I never cooked breakfast twice. Guess there's a first time for everything."

Laura patted Emma's back. "No one could ever doubt why Jason adores you so much. I'll get the buttermilk, butter, milk, and cream."

"I'll start the coffee, get more potatoes and onions, and grate," Iva said.

"Guess I'll pull out the ham and bacon and start slicing," Leslie said.

Emma smiled, tossed more wood in the stove and fireplace, then took a deep breath. "I'll make sure everything's clean and ready to go."

Jason interrupted. "Thank you, ladies. But we'll gather everything for you. The men will be thrilled. Bet they ate beans for breakfast, lunch, and dinner the past few days." He turned before he left. "Let's wait until after breakfast to tell them about our engagement." He smiled and winked at Emma. "I'd like to surprise at least a few people."

Iva snickered. "It's Gayla you need to talk to, not us."

He pointed his finger and clicked the side of his tongue. "You're right. We're about to have a little chat."

***

Jason chuckled at the abrupt greeting he received from the men. They were more excited about meeting Emma and Gayla Harding.

"Wow! You heard about me?" Gayla asked.

"Yes, and you're lovelier than Jason described. And believe me, he described you and Emma repeatedly." Randy kissed her hand.

Jason stepped forward and introduced the men. "Don't listen to half of what they say, ladies. They're all full of bull."

"So, perhaps you *slightly* exaggerated?" Randy shot Jason a sidelong glance and nodded toward Emma. "You expect me to believe this slip of a woman could do *half* of what you bragged about?" He sent Jason a twisted smile with raised brows. "I think, maybe, there's more to the story."

Jason took note of Emma's narrowed eyes and inhaled a whistle. Randy's comments were sure to bring the wrath of Emma Harding.

Emma stepped forward and stretched out her hand. "I'm sorry, but I didn't catch your name."

Jason smirked at Randy's red face. "Sorry, ma'am. My name's Randy."

"Nice to meet you, Randy." Emma gave him a crooked smile. "We already had breakfast, but I assume you could use a hearty meal and some coffee or tea."

"Thank you, but we ate some beans and rice around two this morning. We'll be okay for a few hours."

"Nonsense. Gayla and Marcus will stable the horses. We're brewing coffee. You gentlemen can chat on the porch while we make you a proper breakfast."

She gave Jason a sugary look and went inside.

Randy was about to pay. Jason approached her and whispered. "Emma. Be nice. Randy is tired. He didn't mean to offend you."

She scoffed at his insinuation. "I can't believe you'd think I'd be vindictive."

"Oh, Lord," he murmured.

***

Jason chuckled as the new arrivals commented on the aroma coming from the house.

"Are you sure we're not back at Hudson Ranch?" one asked.

"I ate enough beans this morning to last me for hours, but that smell has my stomach growling," said another.

Randy smiled at Jason. "Why do I have this sick feeling Emma is about to show me a thing or two?"

"Because she is?" Jason smirked. "Not sure what her plan is, but I'd bet you a hundred to one she has one, and you'll be groveling to apologize soon. I haven't been able to slip one thing past her yet. Lord knows I tried, but she always seems to be one step ahead of me."

Randy wiped his face. "Oh, brother. Me and my big mouth."

***

The women came out with plates filled with eggs, bacon, ham, hash browns, and pancakes. Syrup, jellies, jams, cream cheese, and milk lined the center of the table.

Each received a hearty platter—everyone except Randy. Emma walked out with the last dish and laid it in front of him. "Sorry, Randy. I guess I didn't prepare well enough." She slid the bowl of rice and beans to him.

Randy stared at the plate and burst into laughter. He stood, bent over, and pointed to his rear. "Right there, Emma. Kick me right there as hard as you want. I deserve it."

Emma giggled. "Sit that nasty thing down. No telling how long it's been since you washed it."

Gayla came out with his *real* plate. "Ha. She got you, didn't she?" She leaned in. "When I asked why she was doing it, she said it was 'come-up-pants.' Sounds kind of weird to me. Do *not* ask her what it means. She'll make you look it up." Gayla nudged him and walked off.

Jason chuckled as Randy scratched his head at Gayla's comment. He slapped Randy on the back. "I think Gayla meant comeuppance, your payback, so to speak."

***

Jason enjoyed watching the men dig into their breakfast.

"Emma, the bacon and ham were amazing. The pancakes melted in my mouth. And the syrup and jams? Good Lord," Randy said. "Rusty would be impressed."

"I'm glad you enjoyed it. And I hope to meet the famous Rusty one day." She frowned and looked around. "I hear his name constantly."

"Meet him, you will," Randy said. "He and Tracey are coming to help us set up food storage."

Jason laughed. "Seriously? They'll be wasting their time. Emma can teach them a thing or two."

"Yikes!" Randy grimaced as Emma huffed off. "I think I just earned another strike. I need to learn to keep my mouth shut!"

Jason grinned and gripped Randy's shoulder. "She'll be fine. Emma's dealing with a lot right now." He watched as Emma stomped into the kitchen. "Whew," he whispered. "She's not too happy. I think we need to go a little slower." He shook his head. "Honestly, I'm not sure how we do that. There's too much to do." Jason turned to Randy. "So, what did you bring, and what do we need to do?"

"The first thing we do is wire Emma's house."

"Oh," Jason broke in. "I forgot to tell you about another house here. The Elliot House, as Emma calls it. Do we have enough wiring for both?"

"More than enough. I came prepared for the future." Randy rubbed his chin. "Two houses? What a blessing! Won't it be wonderful to have two homes equipped with electricity, gas stoves, and running water?" He nodded. "One day, we'll have enough power and fuel to run the water heaters twenty-four-seven."

Emma walked onto the front porch. She seemed frozen.

"Did I hear you right? You're going to do all that for both houses?"

"Yes, ma'am," Randy said.

Jason went to her and held her hands. "Your life is about to become easier, Emma. If anyone deserves it, you do."

Gayla's eyes grew wide. "Are we going to get water like they used to? You turn a handle, and it pours out? I won't have to pump the well?"

"Well, most of the time, Gayla," Randy said. "We'll have limited power for now. But one day…"

Gayla flung herself into his arms. "Thank you. I can't tell you how relieved I am. Washing baby diapers will be so much easier." She held Randy at arm's length. "Jason and Emma already kissed twice. There's no telling how many babies they'll have once they're married."

Randy and the new men turned toward Jason. He and Emma buried their faces in their hands, and the porch echoed with chuckles. Jason took Emma's hand.

"Thank you, Gayla." Jason rolled his eyes before addressing the men. "We hoped to surprise you with our wedding announcement. Guess Gayla figured we'd stalled long enough."

CHAPTER 15

Jason scanned the small living area and kitchen. Twenty by twenty. Just like the cabins at Hudson Ranch. Two windows over the front porch separated by an oak door. One window in the kitchen area on the right wall. There was a deep red handpump that, while picturesque, required a great deal of energy to pump even a gallon of water. The hand pump would stay, even when the new faucet and waterline became operational. Some things you just counted on.

Jason scratched his head and tried to picture the new appliances in the kitchen area. The pantry and table made the vision difficult.

He turned to Emma. "We need to figure out where to put them. Randy needs to run wiring and a gas line."

Emma caressed the still warm top of the pitted cast iron cooker. "I want to keep the wood burning stove."

"Of course. It will always be here." He patted the stove and thought of the handpump. "Some things you can just rely on, and we'll be using her often. Especially during winter. We can't count on always having propane and need to limit its use when we can."

"Can you bring the appliances inside? It's hard for me to imagine..."

"I'll be right back." Jason winked and rushed for the door.

Randy was outside preparing the wires and barely looked up. "Figure it out?"

Jason didn't respond and looked away. A moment later, when their eyes met, Randy's filled with compassion.

"No. Sometimes I forget that Emma doesn't remember things we take for granted." He shook his head. "It's sad, Randy. She only remembers stoves and refrigerators because of pictures in magazines. She can't decide where to put them until she sees them. Can you help me get them inside?"

Randy grabbed his shoulder and squeezed. "Yep. I'll get the wagon."

***

Emma tried to imagine the size of the appliances. She opened the kitchen makeovers magazine her mother often stared at and tapped her lips.

The men returned to a completely rearranged room that left a ten-foot span of wall space vacant.

Randy burst into laughter. "How in the world did you do that by yourself so fast?"

"I figured if I waited on the two of *you*, it would never get done."

"You're a puzzle, Emma Harding," Randy snickered.

"Is that enough room? I spend so much time over the stove, and I'd love for it to be under the window."

"Well, let's find out," Jason said.

As they rolled in the appliances and set them in place, Emma clapped her hands and jumped up and down.

The men chuckled as she inspected every inch of the new additions.

Randy rubbed his chin and sucked his back teeth.

"What's wrong?" Jason asked.

"They're too close. The stove and fridge need to be separated."

"That's okay," Emma said.

"Let me think." He paused for a minute. "Okay. You have that el-shaped counter. We could put the stove next to it where the pantry was. The carpenters can build another cabinet to go between the stove and fridge. You'd have about four more feet of counter space. But, unfortunately, the counter would be under the window. Not your stove."

Emma began clapping and jumping up and down again. "That's even better! More room to prep. And I spend more time doing that than cooking." Emma spun around with her arms out wide. "Am I in heaven, or what?" She giggled.

She threw herself at Randy and hugged him before kissing his cheek. Her face heated, and she stepped back. "I'm sorry. I got a little carried away."

Randy laughed. "That's okay. You can get carried away anytime you want. It's been years since a beautiful young woman threw herself at me!"

The three laughed, and Emma hugged Randy without a moment's hesitation. "I don't know how to thank you."

"Simple. Don't feed me beans for at least a month."

"I promise."

After they moved the appliances, Emma checked them out. "I can't believe how much room the refrigerator has. She opened the top of the refrigerator and pulled out four plastic containers. "These are ice trays, right?"

"Yep." Randy nodded

She ran to the sink, pumped water, filled the containers, and put them in the freezer. Emma stepped back and covered her mouth before looking at Jason and Randy. "So, when you get the refrigerator running, I'll have ice? Even during the summer?"

Jason and Randy nodded again.

Randy patted the refrigerator. "This one is a little different than what most people used to have."

"How?" she asked.

"Well, since we live so much of our lives without power, we buy up as many refrigerators that run off electricity and propane as we can."

"I don't understand."

"The fridge runs off propane if there's no electricity."

Emma knotted her brow. "That makes no sense. A refrigerator is cold. Gas makes fire."

Randy chuckled. "Trust me. Fire and ice, honey. Fire and ice."

Emma rolled her eyes and headed for the oven. She opened the door. "Wow!" She spun around. "I can cook a whole pig in there!"

Jason grinned. "Do you know how it works?"

"Not a clue," she said as she closed the door. "But I'll figure it out." She turned and faced the men. "But, you may have to get used to burnt food for a while."

For now, each house would have one central light fixture, a porch light, and an outlet in the kitchen and living area. While the others installed the electric pumps and plumbing, Randy ran the wiring and hooked up a propane generator at Emma's Place. Once the generator was humming, he handed her the plug to the refrigerator. "Would you like to do the honors?"

Her hands shook. "What if I get electrocuted?"

"It's okay, Emma. I'll plug it in for you." Randy reached for the cord.

"No. No. I can do it. It's kind of scary, though." She shoved the prongs into the outlet and jumped back.

Mark grinned. "Now the scariest part of all. You have to turn it on." He opened the door and pointed. "It's off right now. We need to set it to five for a while."

Emma turned the dial. The motor kicked on, and she shrieked.

Jason laughed and pulled her close. "Okay, tough girl. Now, we shut the door and wait."

"Emma. Come over here, and flip this switch," Randy said.

"What is it for?"

He pointed to the light fixture in the ceiling.

She raised the switch, and light filled the room.

"Now, flip the other one. It turns on the porch light."

She flipped them off and, on several times, then sat on the couch and rocked.

Randy excused himself. "I'm going to run the gas line for the stove. I'll need to turn everything off when I hook it to the propane tank."

"I'll be out in a minute," Jason said.

He sat beside Emma and held her.

Emma rocked back and forth. Her eyes darted from the refrigerator, to the oven, to the light, and back again. As she absorbed Jason's warmth, her head fell back, and she let out a deep sigh. She gently pushed him away. "Go help Randy. I'm fine. I'm just a little overwhelmed."

She couldn't hide it any longer. Emma needed some privacy.

Once Jason was gone, Emma jumped up, spread her arms, and spun. Watery streaks ran down her face and stained her cheeks. She couldn't remember these kinds of tears. She grew dizzy from spinning, but the tears continued. Emma ran to her room, threw herself on the bed, and thanked God for reuniting her with Jason.

***

"I say we build the bathroom now. Bathing in a tub in the shed isn't much fun," Matthew said.

John and Eric agreed.

"How long will it take?" Jason asked.

Matthew scratched his chin. "Only a few days if we keep it small."

"It only needs to be big enough for a sink, toilet, tub, and water heater."

"We're on it. Is there enough room to add a door to the house, or is it going to be a stand-alone?"

Jason laughed. "I'll ask Emma. I'm sure she'll figure it out. She likes to rearrange."

The men left to gather supplies, and Jason went inside to talk to Emma. Her head was in the refrigerator. "What are you doing?"

Emma jerked and banged her head. "Ouch. I was just checking. It's getting cold."

"Not if you leave the door open," he chuckled.

"I can't wait for Gayla to see this. I can make ice cream in the summer."

"She'll have more to see in a few days. The carpenters want to go ahead and build the bathroom."

"Really? Where will they build it?"

"Wherever you say. They'd like to attach it to the house if you can figure out where they can put in a door."

Her glowing, huge eyes gave him pleasure.

"So, if I can make room for a door, we won't need to go outside in bad weather?"

"That's the idea."

"How big will it be?"

"Not big. Maybe eight by eight."

"What if they build it on the porch? It's ten feet deep." She pointed to the left window. "Can they use the space where that window is for a door?"

"Sure. But are you really okay with giving up some of your deck?"

"For a real bathroom? Are you kidding?"

"I'll tell them. It won't take long if they don't have to start from nothing."

Randy walked in and asked Emma to turn off the fridge. "The gas line is ready to be hooked up."

She didn't hesitate to turn the knob.

"Not so scary now?"

She giggled. "Having a refrigerator and freezer is worth risking electrocution. And did you hear? John, Eric, and Matthew are building a real bathroom." She rushed toward the window. "They're going to put a door here and build it on the porch."

"Great idea. I'll run some wiring for a light and a gas line for the water heater."

"I'm going over to help load the materials. They'll be thrilled with your idea, Emma," Jason said.

"I need to go to the garden. It's about time for lunch, and I haven't done a thing all day."

"Good," Jason said. "Time you took a rest. As far as the garden goes, it's been taken care of. The kids are helping Laura, Leslie, and Iva prep the vegetables."

"Don't fret, Emma," Randy said. "You'll have plenty to do. In a few minutes, the stove will be waiting on your canning jars."

***

Emma spun around the room and laughed. Maybe she *was* in heaven. The canning jars lined the counter, ready to be sterilized. She thought of her aggravation with keeping the pressure canner at the correct temperature when she processed meat and vegetables. Her mom said it was much easier on a stove. She stared at the digital canner and decided to give it a shot. The sound of the weights bobbling on the weighted canner kept her alert, but she always wanted to try the digital. Her mom believed they were more reliable. As she reached in the cabinet, she changed her mind. An old memory surfaced of her mom saying it wasn't safe to use it now. Emma nodded. Now she remembered. Having the pressure gauge checked periodically was important. There was nowhere to do that nowadays.

"Oh, well." She reached for the weighted canner. "Guess it's just you and me, old friend."

Emma was pulling out jars of soup for lunch when Randy walked in laughing. "Couldn't wait, I see."

"No. I'm so anxious to try the stove. I vaguely remember seeing one, but I certainly never used one."

"You'll love it," Laura said as she and the other ladies walked in with baskets of prepped vegetables.

"Randy, you never cease to amaze me. I hear the hum of the fridge," Iva almost yelled.

"I'm about to light the stove and oven. Emma, I'd offer you the first lighting, but it can be tricky the first time."

Emma took several steps back. "Please, be my guest. Let's just hope we don't have charred Randy for lunch."

"Keep it up, and you'll have *me* scared. Stand back, ladies," he hooted.

He turned the knobs, and a quiet hissing sound came from the beast. Emma pictured a fire-breathing dragon and waited for the blaze to shoot out. Then he turned off the nobs and waited a moment.

"It doesn't work?"

"I'm clearing the lines of air," he said. "And they don't light by themselves. You use matches."

Emma backed away. "This is scarier than electricity."

Randy smiled. "Cross your fingers, ladies." He struck a match and held it to one burner. Whoosh. A ring of fire appeared. Then he lit the other three and let them burn while he lit the oven.

"Voila," he said as he turned the knobs off. "Come over here, Emma. I need to show you where the pilot light is so you can light the oven. You, too," he said to the other women.

Emma was less enthusiastic than the others. Laura wrapped her arm around her shoulder. "It's okay, Emma. We've been doing this for years. One or two times, and it won't bother you at all."

Her first lesson was lighting the burners, and her hands trembled. Randy coaxed her into doing it several times. Laura was right. It became more comfortable each time.

"Now for the oven." He pointed inside. "That's the pilot light." He struck a match, placed it near the pilot light, and a small fire lit. When he turned the oven knob, the burner flamed.

Emma's tremors returned, and again, Randy made her light it several times. She laughed at her silliness. "It's so simple."

"Yep," Randy said. "If you want to brown or crisp something, you put it in the lower drawer. That's called the broiler."

"Wow. So, I can put my baked beans in there, and it will get the bacon crispy?"

"You're a fast learner," Randy said. "But remember, for now, we use the gas stove as little as possible. Hudson Ranch has a large stockpile of propane, and they sent us a decent supply. We can buy more when the train comes through, but it's pricey. Very pricey!"

"Oh." Emma's finger went to her mouth, and she chewed the nail. "I wasn't thinking." She tried to disguise her momentary sadness as she massaged the tight ache in her throat. "I guess I need to keep using the woodburning stove."

Randy frowned. "I'm sorry, Emma. I didn't mean to alarm you. We have months of propane for the stove. Use the wood burning when it feels more comfortable, or you don't think the stove is necessary. I'll let you know if we start to run low on propane." He squeezed her shoulder. "Trust me. We'll find more." Randy crossed his arms over his chest and pointed to Emma's new kitchen gadget. "For now, young lady, I'd suggest you get busy and learn to use this thing!"

Emma threw her arms around him. "I'll never make you eat beans again."

Iva smiled. "Let's heat some soup and bread."

Emma grabbed the pot and baking pan.

***

Jason strolled in with the kids, and Emma smiled and stirred the soup over her new stove. The smell of bread heating in the oven hit him when he walked in the door.

Gayla stood in the doorway and froze as she stared at the new kitchen. Emma rushed to her side, picked her up, and swung her in the air. She put Gayla down, moaned, and grabbed her back. "I hope you enjoyed that. You're too big for me to do it again." She ushered in the shocked Gayla. "Look, Jellybean. She pointed to the two switches by the front door. "Lift that one."

Gayla's mouth opened, and she walked toward the light glowing from the ceiling. "There's one on the porch, too. Now, if you come dragging in after dark—well, it won't be dark." Emma giggled.

Gayla ran to Jason and wrapped her arms around him. "Thank you." She looked at the others in the room. "Thank you all." She ran to her bedroom and slammed the door.

"I think she likes it." Emma was delighted with Gayla's reaction. "She didn't even check out the stove and refrigerator."

"Speaking of which," Randy said. "I put a thermometer in the fridge. Let's see how cold it is."

He pulled it out. "If the dial is in the shaded blue area, it means it's reached a safe temperature. After lunch, I think we can fill her up." He pulled out the ice trays and smiled. Ice was already forming.

Emma covered her mouth. "I'm making tea. Iced tea."

***

Gayla came out of her room about an hour later.

"I'll heat some soup and bread for you," Emma smiled. "Grab some ice and pour a glass of tea."

Gayla seemed confused.

"The ice is in the top door of the fridge. The tea is in a pitcher in the door."

Gayla opened the top door, and frigid air spilled out. She took a step back, then pulled out the bowl filled with tiny cubes of ice. She put some in a glass, then opened the bottom door. Jars of dairy products lined the shelves. Gayla grabbed the pitcher of tea, filled her glass, and turned it in her hand.

"I'm having iced tea, and it's not even winter." She took in the new appliances and looked up at Emma. "So, this is what it was like?"

"Yes."

"Every day?"

"Yep."

"And this is the stove?"

"Yes."

Gayla was about to touch it.

"It's hot!" Emma warned. "It's heating up so I can cook a loaf of bread."

"But it's not hot in here. Not like the wood burning stove makes it."

"It's insulated." Emma opened the oven door, and heat rushed out.

Gayla stepped back. "Wow!"

"Let me heat some soup for you." Emma lit the burner under the pan, and Gayla shrieked.

"It's okay. I did the same thing the first time."

"Can I stir it?"

Emma handed her the spoon.

Gayla ate her lunch and stared at the new strangers. "We won't have to go to the stream every morning? We'll have milk right here in the house?"

"Isn't that wonderful?"

"Emma, can I make the light come on again?"

"Sure. But we need to remember that the electricity comes from the generator and propane gas. They said something about batteries storing the extra power, but I'm not sure how that works. All I know is, if we run out of propane, we don't have electricity until we get more. At least until they install the wind turbines."

"What are the wind turbines?" Gayla realized her mistake and kicked the rungs of her chair. "Darn it."

"Look it up," they said in unison.

Gayla reached for the dictionary.

"Look it up in the Encyclopedia," Emma suggested. "You may find it interesting."

Gayla read about the turbines and pointed to the picture. "Wow! We're going to have these?"

"Soon."

"When we get them, can I have a light in my bedroom?"

"We'll have to ask Randy. They're building a refrigerator and freezer so big you can walk in them. They get power first."

"Hold on a minute." Gayla pointed to the refrigerator. "They're going to make one of those things so big I can *walk* in it?"

"It won't look like the fridge. It will be more like a small house. Half for cooling, half for freezing."

"I'll do extra chores for a light. I'm reading a lot, and the lanterns make it hard."

Emma grabbed her chest. "Gayla, have you been sneaking oil lamps into your room?"

Gayla grimaced. "I'm sorry. I always put them back before I go to sleep."

Emma's heart raced out of control. Gayla could have burnt the house down. Worse yet, she could have gone up in flames with it. She forced herself to calm down.

"I would never want to discourage you from reading. You know how important I think it is. But the oil lamps are dangerous. You could fall asleep and knock one over." Emma shook her head and rubbed Gayla's shoulder. "Jellybean. Please. Don't do that anymore. Tell me you want to read, and I'll take care of it. Okay?"

Gayla stared at her feet. "Okay, Emma. I'm sorry."

Emma smiled. "I love that you enjoy reading, but things are about to change around here." Emma turned and looked at the new kitchen. I think I need to explain some things about our new oven."

Emma stressed the importance of never turning the knobs on the stove unless they were cooking. "Gas comes through a pipe to start the fire. If a knob gets turned on by accident, the house will fill with gas. The fumes could kill us or cause the house to explode." She saw Gayla's wide, terrified eyes. Great. She'd scared Gayla to death, and with all the kids that would be running around? Emma snatched the knobs off and placed them on the windowsill. "There. No need to worry now. Can't turn the knobs if they're not there."

She ruffled her little sister's hair. "There's more. Soon, the window over the porch will be a door leading to our bathroom. We'll have an indoor outhouse. They're going to build it on the front porch."

"Yuck!" Gayla took a step back and held her nose. "That's disgusting!"

Emma shook her head. "No, silly. I don't think you understand. We'll have a real bathtub and flushing toilet."

"On the porch? No thanks. I'll keep using the outhouse. I'm not gonna have my poop under the porch!"

Emma laughed and shook her head. "Never mind. I'll explain later. I've got chores to do. I'll be back when I finish." She turned and glared. "Do *not* touch the stove, and leave the refrigerator door shut."

***

Randy stood atop a ladder busy hooking up power at Elliot House when Emma approached. "I hate to bother you, but I have a problem." Randy climbed down and listened as Emma told him about Gayla sneaking lanterns into her room to read and her fear of the knobs on the stove being so accessible.

"Taking the knobs off the stove was smart. As far as Gayla and the lanterns? No way I'd discourage a kid from reading." He stared at Elliot House and laughed. "Sometimes, I don't think things through. Powering a light bulb isn't a big drain. I'll make sure all the bedrooms have a light." He scratched the side of his face. "Ah, What the hell. I'll install outlets too. I sleep better with a fan blowing on me. We have plenty of batteries for backup, and, as I said, Hudson Ranch has enough propane to keep us going for months."

"You're not upset?"

"Why would I be upset?"

"Because... that's a lot of extra work."

"Nonsense. I'm the power guy." He pounded his chest.

"But you have so much to do, and I'm asking for more."

"Whew." Randy hung his apron on the ladder. "I need a break. Care to join me?"

He clasped elbows with Emma and poured them both a glass of water.

"This is the deal, Emma. If you have a talent, you use it. If you don't have one, you do what you can. The other alternative is hitting the road. It just so happens my talent is supplying energy." He chugged his glass of water. "I want to tell you something. Jason's dad, Chris Alvise, is one of the gentlest souls I've ever known. It took him years to find the courage to tell freeloaders goodbye. But we count on each other and all profit from what others contribute. Hudson Ranch is different from any community I've ever heard of. Everyone has a home, but it belongs to the Ranch. You don't have a *right* to live there. It's a privilege. I consider it an honor to use my talent to help others."

"So, you like what you do? I mean, it makes you happy?"

"Absolutely. The smiles when someone flips a switch and a light comes on make me proud. It's my art."

"I guess I understand. I've always wondered if I could paint pictures that make people smile."

"You ever tried?"

She kicked a clump of dirt. "I've drawn some things with my pencils, but I don't have paint or brushes anymore, and my crayons disappeared years ago. I scan my artbook every day and dream. Sometimes I picture my paintings lining the walls of art galleries next to The Highwaymen." She giggled. "Of course, mine are *much* better."

"Emma, do you understand how talented you are, even without a paintbrush?" Randy stood and finished the last of his water. "Most of us thought Jason's bragging was because he was in love. But he was right. You are an amazing, gifted woman." He nodded. "Please excuse me. I need to get to work. I'll fix the lighting problem in the bedrooms when I finish here."

As Emma walked away, he yelled, and she turned. "Tell Gayla she'll have a light in her room tonight."

Emma broke into a huge grin.

***

Jason salivated as he approached the cabin. He stopped on the front porch and inhaled. The aroma of baking bread filled the air. He reached for the handle, looked through the screened door, and paused. Emma, Laura, Iva, and Leslie stood over the counter preparing dinner. To see Emma laughing so hard that she had to wipe tears away, well, the sight took his breath. After years of being alone, how in the world was she able to adjust so fast? His friends. That's how. They were so easy to be around that even someone unaccustomed to people would find their companionship hard to resist.

He opened the door and let out a loud hoot, "Ladies. You're killing me."

Emma ran to his side. "We're practicing baking bread in a real oven. We've made several kinds already. And we have two pies baking at the same time. Can you believe it?"

Jason didn't care who was looking. He grabbed Emma, kissed her, then laughed with vigor. "Sorry. I am not apologizing. I love this woman. "

Emma blushed, and the other ladies giggled.

Jason eyed a freshly baked loaf of bread.

106

"Go ahead," Laura said. "That's cinnamon bread. Cut us a slice while you're at it." She put the bowl of soft butter on the table.

They gathered at the table and sipped ice-cold milk with the warm bread smothered in butter and honey.

"Delicious," Jason said. "But I must say, it's no better than what you make in the Dutch oven, Emma."

"Same recipe, but I don't have to stay on guard to keep it from burning. The oven keeps it at the right temperature. Now I can do other things without worrying."

Emma took another mouthful of milk. "The only time Gayla and I have milk this cold is in the winter." She let out a gust of air. "Oh, it's so good!" Emma grinned and looked at the others. "You know what I want to do? I want to pull out the churn and have ice cream and pie this Sunday."

"Oh, yes!" Leslie said.

Iva grinned. "We have vanilla beans."

Emma's eyes widened. "You do?" She placed her hand on her chest. "Dad came home with a few from the train years ago. He said they cost him a fortune."

"They're still pretty expensive when they have them," Laura said. "I have several bottles of vanilla extract that I made with mine."

Emma's eyes squinted. "We used to have that. You said you made your own?"

"It's easy," Laura told her. "You split a few beans down the middle but keep them whole. Then you toss them in a jar and fill it with vodka. I'd shake the jar a couple of times a week, and in two months, I have vanilla extract. The longer it sits, the better it gets."

"That's it?" Emma asked.

"Yep." Laura raised her brows. "And you can use bourbon or other whiskeys to get a different flavor."

"Wow. I'd love to try that one day," Emma said.

Jason interrupted the lesson. "Before I forget, I need a list of items we're short of." He looked at Emma. "I guess vanilla beans go on the list. We realized today the train would be passing by next week. Eric and I will leave in a few days." He glanced at Leslie. "Sorry. That was rude. I should have let Eric tell you."

Leslie let out a puff of air. "Don't be silly. I just wish *I* could go."

"When the others arrive, you can. Just like we did at Hudson Ranch. In the meantime, if you ladies would make a list, it would be helpful. We'll

107

have to figure out how much gold and silver we each need to contribute once we have it." He stood to leave. Before he reached the door, he turned, "So you know, the list isn't just for necessities. If you have any personal items you'd like, write them down. We'll see what we can do."

Jason noticed the worried look on Emma's face. When her father died, almost everyone still bartered. Not many people had gold or silver to make purchases. Emma would approach him soon, concerned about how she'd pay for her and Gayla's part. Jason shook his head. Emma had more gold than anyone there, but he knew she wouldn't use it. A smile crossed his face. They were to be married. He would be paying her share, and he wouldn't hear her crap about charity!

"Sorry, What?" Jason asked.

Laura handed Jason the loaf of bread, tub of butter, and honey. "I said to take this to the others to tide them over till dinner."

"Thanks. By the way, where are the kids?"

"They're practicing with the net you gave them." Emma's smile seemed forced. "If we're lucky, they'll be busy for hours prepping fish for the smokehouse."

Jason needed to talk to her soon. He didn't want Emma to worry about paying her share.

CHAPTER 16

Jason brought in the fresh cow and goat milk and expected to see Emma over the stove, but Laura met him at the door.

"Jason, something's wrong. This isn't like Emma. It's the second day in a row she wasn't awake when we got here. Plus, she seemed sluggish yesterday. I'm afraid she's ill. You know she'd never tell us."

Jason would never forgive himself for not making the radio a priority if Emma was ill and needed a doctor. He went to Emma's room and sat by her side. "Emma." He kissed her forehead. "It's after six. Are you okay?"

Emma sat up and clutched her chest. "No. Not again. How embarrassing!"

"Embarrassing?" Jason asked. "Emma. You're sick! Lie down." He stood. "I'm going to get the radio working so we can get Doc here. If it doesn't work, I'm heading to Hudson Ranch to get him!"

"No. You don't understand. I have these dreams. They've started again. They keep me awake all night."

He sat back on the bed. "What kind of dreams?"

She stared into Jason's eyes. "You'll think I'm crazy, but before mom died, I had this recurring dream," Emma whimpered. "Mom had a little girl. She brushed the child's head, told her how much she loved her, and wished she could be there to watch her grow up." Emma's hands curled into fists and covered her eyes. She rocked back and forth. "Before dad died, I had dreams of him clutching his heart and staring toward heaven." Her hands lowered. "He said he was going to see Mom and told me I had to be strong." She looked at Jason. "You think I'm crazy, don't you?"

"No. Not at all."

"Maybe I am!" she shrieked. "I've been awake for two nights because trees decorated with sparkly things are chasing Gayla and me." She threw her arms around Jason. "I don't know what it means, Jason. But I swear, it's evil. Something bad is going to happen. I just know it."

Jason eased Emma down. "You're staying in bed today." He brushed her hair with his hand. "I believe in dreams. Maybe if you get some rest, you can figure it out."

"I don't want to sleep. I don't want to dream anymore. I'm afraid."

Jason stayed to comfort her. A few minutes later, she was sound asleep.

He walked out of Emma's room, dazed, and sat at the table. "Ladies, I don't know where to start."

After Jason retold his conversation with Emma, Leslie spoke up. "First, we cover her window so it's dark. It'll help her sleep. I had an aunt whose dreams came true. You can make fun of it if you want, but I saw it. The things my aunt dreamed happened all the time."

"Leslie, Emma's just tired," Jason said.

"Oh, so you think she's lying about having dreams about her mom and dad?"

"Uh, no."

"I say better safe than sorry. I believe Emma's having a premonition about something bad that will happen. We need to put our heads together and figure out what the sparkly trees mean in case she can't."

***

"Can someone set up the ham radio. We need to be able to contact my dad." Jason told the men about Emma's dreams. "She's terrified."

"Trees with sparkly things are chasing her? That's downright bizarre," Eric said. "Leslie had an aunt that used to freak everyone out with her dreams."

"She told me, and Emma swears she dreamed about her parents dying."

"I'll set up the radio," Matthew volunteered.

"Thanks. I hate to leave right now, but we can't afford to wait another month for the next train." Jason brushed his hair back. "We're short on supplies."

"I'm ready when you are," Eric said.

After they hitched the wagon, Jason and Eric went inside to tell the women goodbye. Emma and the others sat at the table drinking coffee. Emma's cheeks blushed, and she stared down at her cup.

Jason brushed her hair with his fingers. "Are you feeling better?"

"I'm fine. I'm probably overreacting. I'll make some herbal tea to help me sleep tonight."

"Matthew is going to set up the ham radio today. If anything happens while we're gone, he'll contact Hudson Ranch. They can get here in a few hours with the jeeps if it's an emergency. Do you ladies have the list ready?"

Laura slid it across the table. "We added a few luxury items."

"Humph. You wouldn't call deodorant a luxury item if you had to sleep next to John," Iva snorted.

John entered as Iva made the comment and laughed. "I wouldn't be talking if I were you." His lips twisted, and he chuckled at his wife's angst. "Jason, I was hoping to catch you before you left. We need more batteries. Mostly AA's, but we're low on all of them."

"Whew. I'll see. They're hard to find, and pricey, with only one plant supplying the whole country."

"Well, without the AA's, we don't have handheld radios. No C's means no flashlights."

"We're that low?"

"I just put the last AA's in a radio."

"Keep your fingers crossed. Are you all sure we didn't forget anything? A month will seem like an eternity if we run out of any essentials. And if there's any personal stuff you forgot, you need to speak up now."

Emma inhaled and was about to speak, then paused.

"You were about to say something?" Jason asked.

Her face turned bright red, and she stuttered. "Oh, uh, don't forget the coffee and sugar."

Jason smiled. "Never." His grin widened. "Darn. I almost forgot. I'm hoping we make it back in time for Gayla's birthday. Since we have refrigerators and ovens here and at Elliot's House, I was hoping you would make some ice cream and cake. If you could keep it a secret, we could give Gayla a surprise party when we got back. A real birthday party with cake, candles, and ice cream. If I can find birthday candles."

Emma sat. "That would be wonderful!"

His chat with Emma about paying her and Gayla's share had turned nasty until Jason used her parents as an example. "So, if your parents hadn't already been married, you don't believe your dad should have taken care of her needs? Let's reverse roles. Would you not help me?" Jason had towered over Emma and not backed down.

Jason kissed her goodbye and turned to leave. Finally, he'd won against the big, bad, Emma. Still, she asked for nothing for herself, only for Gayla.

CHAPTER 17

Jason couldn't shake Emma's dream from his thoughts. Sparkly trees. No. Trees with sparkly things on them. He closed his eyes and tried to picture things that sparkled. *Jewels.* He'd only heard Emma use the word evil one other time. It was when she'd referred to the chest of treasure. He'd done as she asked and reburied it. Jason sighed in relief. The treasure was what troubled Emma. He was sure she'd be able to relax once he told her. He shook from the sudden chilly wind.

"Where the heck did that rush of cold air come from?" Jason asked.

"What are you talking about? Please, don't tell me you're getting sick." Eric looked worried.

"No, no. I'm fine." Jason thought of the sudden gust of wind that snatched open the cellar door after Emma spoke to her deceased parents. Then he remembered his father's story about a rogue whirlwind crossing the plain and resting in the tree he sat beneath and how it sent down a shower of leaves. His father believed it was his dead parents showering him with love and forgiving him. Both strange. Both explainable. He broke the silence to erase the weird thoughts.

"You plan on getting Leslie and Shelley any special treats?"

"Of course. Shelley's getting toys, books, crayons. Whatever I can find and afford. And she needs some clothes and shoes."

"What about Leslie?"

"I don't have a clue," he sighed.

Jason laughed. "Some exotic fruits?"

Eric scowled. "Already on the list."

"Hmm. Perfume?"

"She still has a dozen bottles from before the EMP. She only uses them for special occasions."

"A fancy dress?"

"Yeah. It's been a long time since she bought a fancy dress. And her boots are looking bad. Maybe a pair of work shoes and some socks. What are you getting Emma and Gayla?"

"Gayla is getting books, writing tablets, colored pens, pencils, and crayons." He let out a loud gust of air. "If they have them." His smile grew. "Her birthday is next week. She's never had a birthday party, and I want it to be special. "Clothes, shoes, and hats. And she needs a new jacket. Heck. Maybe two! Maybe they'll have some toys, games, and dolls she'd like." Jason chuckled. "She's darned good at making slingshots, but I'm hoping they have some fancy ones." Jason sighed. "I always bought them gifts for Christmas, but I knew not to go overboard. Emma would have gone berserk!"

"I can imagine."

Jason grinned. "We'll be returning on or close to Gayla's birthday. The women are going to bake a cake and make ice cream." Jason's jaw tightened. "We'll give Gayla her first real birthday party."

"Oh. Wow!" Eric wiped his nose. "What about Emma?"

"Hopefully, she'll get her dream come true."

***

"We need parts for the ham radio and Jason's long gone." Matthew rubbed his chin. "I doubt he could find them anyway."

"We'll have to wait until he goes back to Hudson Ranch or puts in an order," Randy said.

"I should have rechecked it before we brought it. It's a mess," Matthew said. "If they don't have what we need at Hudson Ranch, it could be a year or more waiting on the order to get filled."

"Let's put it aside and finish the bathroom. I want a real bath so bad I can't stand it," John said.

"When you finish the plumbing, I'll hook up the gas water heater. We might be taking a warm shower tonight," Randy said. "As soon as we can, we need to install the water tank on the roof. It'll be a pain to crawl up there and heat it with coals in the winter if we don't have propane, but it should save us a lot of gas during the summer when the sun heats it."

"I'm going to run the greywater line down the slope," John said. "It may be a few days before we build the septic tank. Until then, we'll have to use the outhouse and not the toilet."

"Let's jump on it. A shower is calling. I'll bet the cowboys will try and beat us to it," Matthew said.

"Ha. I'd love to see them get in there before the women."

Randy was more solemn. "Men. As much as we'd all like to take a long, hot shower, I say Emma and Gayla go first."

"Yeah." Matthew nodded. "We can wait."

***

The sun was setting when the cowboys strolled in and took a seat on the porch. Emma mused at how chatty Matthew, John, and Randy were.

The children poured everyone a glass of iced tea. The cowboys drained their drinks, and the kids refilled them.

"Now?" Gayla asked.

Emma nodded.

The kids ran for the smokehouse. Iva and Leslie brought out a baking dish of baked beans and a bowl of salad. Laura carried a bowl of baked potatoes. Emma held a tray filled with cups of sauces and a wicker bowl filled with freshly baked rolls.

Randy let out a hearty laugh. "What did I do now, Emma? You promised me no more beans."

"These are my special baked beans. The kids will be back in a minute, as will we," Emma nodded and went inside.

Emma and the other ladies returned with glasses and goblets, a bucket of ice, and bottles of wine and whiskey. The children each carried a tray and placed them on the table.

"The kids have been dying to feed you their smoked fish. They harassed us all day," Emma told them.

"We made several different sauces to put on them," Laura said.

"I say we give grace and eat," Randy said. "Thank you, kids, and of course, you, ladies."

Emma was beginning to enjoy the taste of red wine. "This doesn't seem so bad now."

"A glass or two will help you sleep," Iva said.

The mention of sleep made Emma's heart race, and she took another sip. She didn't want to dream again.

"You're still not sleeping well?" one of the cowboys asked.

"No." Emma re-told the dream she'd had for the past two nights.

"Sparkly things in the tree?" he asked. "Do you mean like Christmas decorations or jewels?"

Emma's eyes widened, then she smiled. How silly. The dream was about the treasure. "Thank you," she said and squeezed the man's hand. "I think I know what it is now."

"Well," Leslie questioned. "What is it?"

114

Emma hated to lie, but she had no choice. No one could know about the treasure. She had to think fast. "My parents are buried under the burr oak on the hill. I think I was missing my mother. You know—big tree and Mom's diamond ring and earrings."

Leslie grabbed her hand. "I'm so relieved. I thought something bad was going to happen."

"I'm sorry I worried you." Emma held Leslie's hand and realized how natural it felt. There was no urge to pull away. Instead, she pressed tighter. The last time she'd lovingly held and squeezed a female's hand was her mother's after Gayla was born. Emma felt Leslie's grip tighten and saw the tiny drop of moisture in the corner of her eye before Leslie released her grip. Emma's jaw tightened. She understood now. This was what it was like to have friends. She looked away and focused on the kids. "Thank you for the wonderful dinner."

"Sure!" Marcus said. "By the way, we're cleaning up and putting the food away, too."

"Really?" his mother responded. "And what price do *we* pay?"

Marcus flashed his bright white smile. "We go fishing and don't have a curfew."

Everyone erupted in laughter. Emma gave a thumbs-up, and the others agreed to the deal.

While the children cleaned up after dinner, the adults caught up on the day's events.

"Did we forget to mention we have a working shower, tub, and hot water?" Randy asked.

Silence followed.

Randy winked. "Emma, you and Gayla go first."

She stood but felt uneasy. "I... I can take a real bath? In a real tub?"

"A bath, a shower, or both," Randy said. "We decided that tonight the bathroom would be for you and Gayla." He winked. "Use all the propane you want tonight." Randy sighed. "If it was me, I'd stay in there for an hour or two."

"I can't thank you enough. There are no words." She looked around. "I need to tell Gayla."

Matthew interrupted. "I'll tell her when they finish cleaning up. Bath salts, bubble bath, soap, shampoo, conditioner, and loofah pads are waiting for you."

"Bubble bath and loofah pads?"

"We'll show you," Laura said as the women escorted Emma to her new bathroom.

***

Emma's mind drifted as she soaked in the tub filled with silky bubbles. The slight knock on the door sobered her.

"Emma, can I come in?" Gayla asked.

"I don't know. *Can* you?"

"Geez. *May* I come in?"

Emma laughed at the vision of her sister rolling her eyes. "Yes, you may."

Gayla walked in and cupped her mouth.

"We're a little old for this, but would you like to join me?"

Gayla undressed and joined Emma in the tub of warm bubbly water. "This feels so good! And I can lay my whole body down in here."

"Doesn't it feel amazing?" Emma asked. "Do your hands like this in the water." Emma brushed her hands back and forth quickly, and bubbles formed.

Gayla giggled and helped make more.

They laid there in silence for several minutes before Gayla shivered. "I need to get out. I'm getting cold."

"Wait." Emma pulled the plug and allowed water to drain out, then re-plugged it. She pointed. "See that knob? Turn it to your left, but be careful. Hot water will come out."

Gayla's eyes widened as steaming water rushed from the spout. They soaked for an hour, reheating the tub several times before washing their hair under the spray of the shower.

"This stuff smells *so* good," Gayla said as she lathered her hair. "And it's like playing in the rain."

"Just remember to push the button on the sprayer so you don't use water until you need it."

"Geez. I got it, Emma." Gayla rolled her eyes.

Emma snickered. "Dad had planned to install an outdoor shower before he died. Now I wish I'd done it. This is wonderful!"

They dried off, put on fresh clothes, and ran to tell everyone how much they enjoyed their bath. Marcus sat alone in the living room reading. He smiled as they rushed out. "The others went home. They wanted to give you some privacy. Randy said to tell you he has a timer on the generator.

116

He set it to go off late for tonight. After ten, everything's running off the batteries."

Emma glanced at the clock. Almost ten. She felt guilty for using so much propane.

"Oh. And Randy said he didn't want to hear your crap about using the propane."

Emma couldn't help but chuckle.

"We had a deal. Gayla and I don't have a curfew tonight, and I want to go fishing. Shelley went home. If it gets too late, I'll clean the fish, and Gayla can go to bed."

Marcus's manliness struck Emma. Maybe he was too old for Gayla to be hanging out with all the time.

"Too late for me? I'll kick your butt just like I do every time." Gayla headed for the pantry and turned. "Hate to tell you, Marcus, but sometimes when you clean fish, you leave too much meat on the backbones. And you're not exactly the greatest fisherman in the world."

"Oh yeah? And who would that be?"

"Why, me, of course."

The two laughed as they grabbed snacks, a lantern, and raced for the stream.

Emma relaxed. "Have fun," she whispered. They'd earned it. Gayla wasn't your typical nine-year-old. She could handle it.

CHAPTER 18

"What a haul," Jason yelled as they loaded the wagon.

"You're not kidding! We're going to see some happy women and kids." Eric laughed. "Can you believe how much the prices came down on fruit?"

"A good growing season for them, a great buying season for us." Jason smiled. "We need to keep a close eye on the seafood and eat it as soon as we get home."

"I'm not so sure about the fishing net you got the kids. It's a lot different than the small one you gave Marcus. I'm afraid they'll get lazy and strip the streams."

"Nah. They love pole fishing. But once they learn to use the real net, they'll take care of us when we need a big batch."

"I guess you're right. What do we do about batteries?"

"What else can we do? We make do till next month and hope they can fill our order."

"From what you told me, Emma and Gayla are going to be so happy." Eric shook his head. "I still can't imagine what they went through all those years."

Jason put an arm on Eric's shoulder. "They deserve some happiness and rest. Did you know that neither of them asked for a thing? Not one lousy thing. Boy, are they in for a surprise. And we're actually going to make it home in time for Gayla's birthday. This feast my parents paid for should make her one happy kid."

A few hours after heading home, they stopped for the night, fed themselves and the horses, and reorganized their goods.

***

Emma and Laura finished prepping vegetables for the canner while the jars sterilized. Iva, Leslie, and the kids were planting and weeding. The men had finished the bathroom at Elliot House. The septic tanks were up and running. Now both houses had flushing toilets, but the outhouses remained an essential part of the community. The carpenters were busy

118

building the shelter for the new arrivals. The cattle and livestock grazed freely, allowing the cowboys time to help build.

Emma took a break, walked outside, and inhaled. She'd tasted the hint of a passing spring and the new coming fall before, but never had time to stop and appreciate it. Was this what life was like before? She eased into the seat of a rocker on the front porch and pushed her foot against the slats. The rocker swayed back and forth. The small creek each time it rolled forward made her smile. How was it she'd never noticed it before?

She looked around, and her eyes rested on the shed. "Home Depot and Lowes packed into a thirty by thirty building," her father used to say. Under the shed was Emma's lifeline. The cellar beneath protected her fruits and vegetables and kept her canned goods safe.

Her eyes shifted. A slight cloud rose from the smokehouse. How many months of food did that tiny shack provide her and her sister, year in and year out? The barn, where she housed the horses, milking cows, goats, and chickens took a lot of energy to keep it clean and stocked, but, without the effort, she doubted they would have survived. As she continued to scan the area, her eyes landed on the greenhouse. Emma heaved a huge sigh. Her parents had told her that few people could have summer crops in Wyoming without one. Emma enjoyed tomatoes, cucumbers, squash, and bell peppers, pretty much year-round.

Her grin threatened to snap her jaw. By God! She'd done good! Maybe Jason was right. She deserved a break. Then, memories of her nightmares returned and broke her happy mood. Emma stood and called out to Laura. "Do you mind if I go for a walk? I'd like to talk to my Mom and Dad."

Laura came to the door and wrapped her arm around Emma's shoulder. "Go." She nudged her. "Talk to them. I'm sure they've missed you."

Emma's walk to the tree was slow. How could she go from such joy to dread in an instant? Damn her dreams! One minute she was so full of joy, the next, she was terrified. She missed her parents and needed to talk to them about her dreams. They meant something. Her dreams always did.

Emma sat beneath the tree, talking to her parents when a loud rumbling echoed. She sprang to her feet, prepared to warn the others. When she squinted and scanned the horizon, she yelled in relief. "Jason!"

Moments later, her fiancé jumped from the wagon and swung her in the air before kissing her.

"Thank God! I was terrified something would happen to you."

"It's okay, Emma. I figured out your dream. You're worried about the treasure."

"I know that now, but it doesn't explain the trees chasing Gayla and me."

Jason glanced at the tree shadowing her parent's grave. He leaned in and whispered, "Perhaps they're trying to tell you to dig it up and become a wealthy young lady."

"No." She shoved him away. "You don't understand. The trees in my dreams are evil." Emma stared at her feet and stammered. "I'm sorry, Jason. That was a lousy greeting after so many days. I don't know what came over me." She hugged him. "I'm just glad you're home and safe."

"There goes that word again. Evil." Jason rubbed her shoulder "I'm here now. I won't let the trees get you."

Emma playfully slapped his arm and pulled back. "Don't make fun of me."

"Come on." He nodded toward the wagon. "Let's go home and unload."

Emma lifted the lid of a box. "No peaking, young lady."

She curled her nose and dropped it. "Fine."

As they approached Emma's house, Marcus came out of the barn, let out a whoop, and ran for the bell.

They were unloading the wagon when the others arrived.

"No one opens a box until I say so. Got it?" Jason and Eric laughed at the loud moans. "We got almost everything on the lists. Unfortunately, we couldn't find any batteries."

"That's bad news," Matthew said. "And you were already gone when I found out we needed parts for the ham radio. She won't work without them."

Jason let out a puff of air. "That *is* bad news. We'll have to make a run to Hudson Ranch and see if dad can help us. For now, we bought a lot of fantastic stuff. Emma, have you and Gayla ever had shrimp, oysters, or lobster?"

"No," they said.

"You will tonight." Eric removed the lid of a chest filled with melting ice and lifted the bags one by one. "Check it out."

Gayla stared at the strange items. "They look just like they do in the books."

"And they're delicious." Marcus licked his lips.

"We don't open boxes with names on them. We'll set those aside for later," Jason said. "Perishables first."

Boxes lined Emma's porch: mechanical, staples, personal, and perishables.

"What is this?" Gayla picked up a piece of fruit.

"That's a mango," Laura said.

Gayla clapped her hands then pointed to the fruits. "I've seen some of these in books. Bananas, grapefruits, oranges, lemons, and pineapples."

Jason grinned. "You nailed it, Gayla. When we build the walk-in cooler, we can buy a lot more if you like them."

"Which one is best?" she asked.

"Hard to say."

"Can I cut up a mango for them to try?" Marcus asked.

"Hmm." Jason rubbed his stubbly chin. "How about you take some of everything and make a platter?"

"Cool," he said and began picking out the ripe ones. "Look, Gayla. This is a tangerine. You eat it like this." He shoved his thumb into the center and peeled off the skin.

Gayla tossed a wedge into her mouth. Her eyes lit up, and she giggled. "Oh, Emma. You have to taste this." She offered her a piece, and it was Emma's turn to chuckle.

Once they stored the perishables, they went to work on the staples. Everything from sugar to coffee lined the walls of the living room.

"I have the secret room under my bed. We can store a lot of this there."

"A secret room?" Iva asked.

"Well, not exactly a room. More like a small storage area. My dad found it when he was working on the foundation after we moved in. I used to hide in there when I was little."

Once they stored the dry goods, Jason sat on the sofa. "Eric and I are worn out. Can we call it an early day and cook dinner? Then we open the other boxes."

Emma grinned. "Why don't you guys relax and take a bath?"

"I'm not up to it, Emma," Eric said. "I'm too tired to be lugging water. I'll take a sponge bath later, or better yet, go to the stream."

Leslie laughed. "No. You guys stink to high heaven." She pointed to the bathroom door.

"It works?" Jason asked. "Eric, you go first. I may not come out for an hour or two. We need to set up a lottery and take turns until we build more."

Randy chimed in. "We have two. There's a bathroom at Elliot House also. The septic tanks went in days before expected. We officially have two fully functional bathrooms!"

***

Emma immersed herself in learning to prep the seafood while the men waited for their turns to shower.

She learned to head and devein the shrimp they would fry and grill. The ones they'd steam were left intact. Lobsters were split, sprinkled with salt and garlic, and smothered in butter. They'd eat oysters fried, raw, and made into an oyster "stew." Emma had a tough time grasping a "stew" consisting of sautéed oysters, onions, garlic, salt, pepper, butter, and cream. It made no sense.

Her homemade ketchup with lemon and grated horseradish root from the buying trip would complete the cocktail sauce. Emma's eyes watered from grating the horseradish root.

"Whew. It burns, but it smells wonderful. Does horseradish grow like a ginger root?"

"Sure does," Laura said.

Her mother planted a single ginger root when they first arrived at the ranch. Now Emma had pots filled with them. She loved ginger tea. Every year she dried, ground, and pickled them.

Emma delighted in her cooking lesson, but when the women tried to coerce her into eating a raw oyster, she back away. "No! It's disgusting."

Laura laughed and picked out a small one. "Come on. Try it."

"No. I can't." Emma grimaced and turned her head away from the offensive thing.

"So, the big bad Emma's afraid of a little oyster? I don't believe it." Jason walked over, grabbed one, dipped it, and tossed it into his mouth. "Mmmm. Perfect cocktail sauce, ladies."

Emma grimaced, grabbed an oyster, dipped it in the sauce, and tossed it in her mouth.

"Oh, my. I don't know what's better. The salty oyster or the horseradish." She pulled out her handkerchief and blew her drippy nose. "Sorry. First, it made my eyes run, and now it's making my nose run."

Everyone chuckled.

She broke off a piece of root. "I'm planting this."

Jason grinned and kissed her forehead. "It's my turn to shower. Is there time before dinner?"

Emma looked to the other women for guidance.

"We won't start until the potatoes finish roasting. Go ahead," Laura said.

***

Laura and Emma finished frying the shrimp and oysters and broiling the lobsters while Leslie and Iva set up the table. The men separated supplies while the kids brought in the chickens and goats and fed the animals.

Emma caught her breath when Jason strolled out of the bathroom. His handsome, shaved face and ruffled wavy hair made her knees weak. "Dinner is almost ready." She tried not to stutter. "Can you bring some wine and bourbon from the cellar? This is a special occasion."

He walked toward her and held her from behind. The scent of his freshly washed body and hair was intoxicating. "Wow. You need to bathe more often. You smell…" She let out a long sigh.

"I'd bathe every night if we didn't have to draw numbers. I'd hate for you to think of me as your smelly fiancé."

He playfully smacked her rear, and her face burned. "Don't be silly." She waved the tongs. "Go to the cellar."

"Get a room, you two," Laura said.

Emma looked puzzled.

Laura grinned. "Never mind."

***

Jason lifted the door to the cellar, paused, then turned to the large burr oak and the two crosses that stood beneath. "Mr. and Mrs. Harding, I hate to bother you. But is there something you want to tell me?" He sat on the top rung of the stairs and stared at the graves. "You see, Emma's having bad dreams. She thinks trouble is coming. If anything happened to her or Gayla…" Jason sat for a second before laughing at himself and headed down the stairway. His lantern illuminated the floor of the cellar. Oak leaves, covered with dew, glistened. *That's not possible.* He ran to the top of the stairs and yelled at the tree. "What are you trying to tell me?" He waited, then hesitated before heading back down into the cellar. He lifted the lantern and laughed. "I thought I'd lost my mind." The light reflecting off the cellar floor did indeed resemble leaves covered in dew. Jason grabbed

123

a bottle of wine and bourbon. "I'm not telling anyone. They'll think I'd already had a few."

***

Jason was delighted with the reaction to dinner. His parent's generous gift of gold coins to buy seafood and other extravagances had made the entire group happy. The others had tasted the treats before. But this was Emma's and Gayla's first experience with what the rest of the world had to offer.

"I can't breathe." Gayla moaned and held her tummy. "That was the weirdest stew I ever tasted. But if I could eat more, I would. What did you say it was called?"

"Oyster stew," Jason said.

"It was so good!"

"Do you have enough oomph left to open your box?" Jason asked.

Gayla bolted up. "I got a box?" She looked at Emma, then Jason. "But I didn't ask for anything," she said quietly.

"I know." Jason nodded and shot a glance at Emma. "We don't meet the train without bringing something back for everyone. Never. You make our trip much more difficult when you don't tell us what you want or need, even if you can't pay for it. We work that out later."

Emma's head dipped, and she stared at her feet.

Jason slapped his hands. "Let's clean up, then see what everyone got."

***

Jason slid the box next to Gayla. "Open it."

Gayla fidgeted with her hands. "Let the others open theirs. I can wait."

"I thought you'd say that, and I kind of like the idea." Jason pinched his nose and mouth. "Since you and Emma were the only ones without a wish list, I think you should go last. It would be neat to see if we fulfilled your *secret* desires."

Jason stood and addressed everyone. "You should know, most everything we brought back was used. People bartered them. Not a whole lot of factories making stuff yet."

Knowing what they'd received wasn't brand new didn't concern anyone. They were all thankful to those who'd passed things on to them. The adults were thrilled with their new clothes, hats, gloves, jackets, and boots. Shelley loved her package, but it was clear what she loved most as she cuddled her doll. Marcus's new clothes and shoes didn't excite him, but he was appreciative. Then he opened the box with the fishing gear and marveled at his rod and reel. He focused on the last item and pulled up the corner. "Is this what I think it is?"

"It's a *real* fishing net," Jason said. "But once you learn to use it, it's only for hard times."

"Yes, sir!"

Jason and the men put several boxes in front of Emma.

"Open up," Jason said.

"Me?" Emma asked. "I, I don't understand. I have all I need."

"Consider it a Christmas gift," Jason said.

Emma swallowed hard and nodded. Emma's hands shook as she lifted one of the lids. "Oh, my," she gasped. Dresses, pants, shirts, hats, gloves, socks, shoes, boots, and a coat. The second box had every item a woman could want: perfumes, lotions, soaps, makeup, and manicure items.

"I don't know how to thank you," Emma said softly.

"Hmm." Jason scratched his chin. "Eric, did we miss something?"

Eric smiled and nodded. He pulled the final box across the porch and placed it in front of Emma. "Don't know how we missed this one."

Emma's hand went to her heart. "Another box? It's huge."

Randy beamed. "Open it."

Emma lifted the lid, clasped her chest, and stared at Jason. "How did you know?" Her eyes darted toward Randy.

He smiled. "I expect to see your art hanging in galleries next to The Highwaymen. Of course, yours will be better."

Emma laughed. "You *do* know I was kidding, right?"

"We don't care if you scribble," Jason said. "You wanted to paint, and now you have no excuse. The brushes and paint look to be in decent shape. I put in an order for more, but it could be a while. A wish list goes out at every stop, so people know what others want to barter."

Emma stared at the box and the variety of paints, brushes, trays, and canvases. Every tool an artist could want lay at her feet. She lifted the books. "They teach you to paint."

As Emma thumbed through the collection, Matthew and John went to the barn and returned with a stool and a wooden structure.

"We built these after Randy told us you wanted to be a painter," Matthew said.

John smiled. "Yep. Every artist needs an easel and stool."

Emma rubbed her face. "I don't know what to say."

"Go through your box. We'll be back in a few minutes," Laura said as she, Iva, and Leslie excused themselves. Laura turned before she entered Emma's cabin. "Gayla can't open her boxes until we return."

Marcus and Shelley followed them inside, returned with a white sheet, and covered one of the outside tables. Then, they ran inside and came out with Emma's mother's china side plates and bowls and placed them on the table. Beside each plate and bowl, they laid down a fork and spoon.

Jason picked up a small box. "Excuse me for a minute," he said before he walked through the front door.

Marcus and Shelley went inside. A few minutes later, everyone in Emma's house walked out wearing a party hat. They carried balloons and blew rollout whistles as they handed the others party favors to celebrate Gayla's birthday.

"Happy birthday, Gayla!" everyone shouted.

Gayla's eyes grew wide, and a tear slid down her cheek. "How did you know?" she asked as her chin trembled. "Only me and Emma knew." She shot a glance at her sister.

Emma grinned. "I told them, but I had no idea what they were planning." A tear dripped from Emma's eye. "Happy birthday, Jellybean."

Jason slid Gayla's boxes closer to her. "You didn't know it, but that was your birthday dinner we just ate." He grabbed her face and kissed her cheek. After you open your gifts, we have another surprise."

Gayla's hands shook as she cautiously opened her first box. "Books. All kinds of books, Emma." She pulled out the other items. "Puzzles and paper. Lots of paper. Crayons and colored pencils. Board games." She tore open the other box filled with clothes, shoes, socks, gloves, coats, and hats. "Emma, I got new clothes and shoes." She looked at Jason. "I never had so many new clothes." Then she reached the bottom and gingerly lifted the doll. Gayla stroked her. "She's beautiful."

Marcus walked toward Gayla with a new rod and reel. "This is from the rest of us."

Gayla took the reel in her hand and looked around. A tear clung to her cheek. "I always wondered what it was like to have friends and a real birthday party." Her damp eyelashes batted several times, and her mouth trembled. "Thank you."

Laura, Iva, and Leslie disappeared into the house again. A minute later, they walked out carrying a cake with nine brightly burning candles and a

126

huge bowl of ice cream. Everyone at Emma's place began to sing happy birthday to Gayla.

She went to Jason, wrapped her arms around his neck, and squeezed. She didn't cry out loud, but her twitchy shoulders made it difficult for him to breathe. "I'm glad you're happy." He led her to the table. "Make a wish and blow out your candles."

Gayla shook her head. "I don't have anything else to wish for," she whispered.

Marcus walked over and whispered in her ear. Gayla chuckled. "That's a good one, Marcus."

He nodded. "But you can't tell anyone, or it won't come true."

After Gayla made her wish and blew out the candles, they all sat at and ate cake and ice cream. Once they'd finished, Gayla stood. "I just wanted to thank you all again. Me and Emma were lonely. We waited our whole life to meet you. I'm so glad you finally showed up."

"Thank you. Thank you all." Emma stood. "If you'll excuse me." She ran to her room.

Marcus cuddled his whimpering mother. "I'd say the party was a home run. Hey, Gayla and Shelley. I say we try out the new fishing gear." He looked at his parents. "That's okay, isn't it?"

"Scoot," Matthew said.

***

The next day, Emma sat on a stool with her easel facing the burr oak and her parent's graves. The others insisted that she spend time every day learning to paint. How different her life was since they'd arrived. She still struggled with the idea of free time but had to admit she enjoyed every second of it.

Emma opened the tattered folder and stared at the pictures she'd drawn years before. The childlike drawings with crayons, pencils, and watercolor paint made her chuckle. The pencil drawings she'd made over the past few years were better, but certainly not gallery-worthy. She unfolded an ink drawing she'd found after they moved in and stared back at the house. Once again, she tried to picture the child who'd drawn it. Emma had used crayons to color it in and remembered wondering if all those trees were there before. She placed it back in the folder, took a deep breath, and began to paint the tree.

A couple of hours later, Emma stepped back from the canvas and covered her mouth. After a few minutes, she gathered everything and headed home.

The painting rested on the windowsill. Emma wasn't sure if she wanted anyone to see it. She sliced potatoes and kept staring. "I really did that?"

The ladies were full of chatter when they came in to help prepare dinner.

"What a beautiful day," Laura said.

"I wish it were like this every day," Iva added.

"So, did you practice painting?" Leslie asked Emma.

Emma exhaled. "I tried." She nodded toward the window where her first painting dried.

"Oh, Emma! That's spectacular," Leslie said.

"Really?"

All three ladies took a seat and stared at Emma's first painting.

"How could you have possibly painted something like that on your first try?" Leslie asked.

"I, I just dipped into the paint and..." She looked at them. "You think it's okay?"

Laura sniffled. "Emma. If this is any sign of what a wonderful artist you are, we *will* see your art hanging in a gallery one day. It's stunning."

The women's eyes were damp when the men walked in. "Is something wrong?" Jason rushed over.

Laura pointed. "Emma's first painting."

Jason turned, stared, and chuckled. "Ha. Good one, ladies." He walked toward the painting, stuck a finger to the canvas, and stared at the wet goo on his fingertip. He spun around. "Is this a joke?"

"No," Iva said.

Jason lowered himself into a chair and stared at Emma. "Wow!"

Randy smiled and gave Emma a bear hug. "I knew you had it, Emma. I knew it."

The kids came in to show off their catch before they cleaned them. Marcus seemed worried about the adult's behavior.

Emma wrapped her arm around him. "Nothing's wrong. They're just acting silly because I did my first painting." She pointed to the picture in the window.

Marcus glanced at the painting, then back at Emma. "You painted that?"

CHAPTER 19

Marcus was cleaning the stables while Emma and Gayla gathered vegetables. An engine. He ran toward the garden. "Emma. There's a vehicle headed our way."

Emma ran from the garden and ushered Gayla inside. Marcus stood in the front yard. "Marcus, get in the house!" She grabbed her rifle and headed for the handheld radio.

"Wait, Emma. It's okay. It's the military."

"They scared me to death!" Emma lowered her rifle, placed it inside the door, and turned to Gayla. "It's okay. Probably census takers."

The jeep paused a few feet from the entrance sign to Emma's Place, then made a slow approach.

Gayla ran outside, waved, and jumped up and down as three men stepped out. "More people. Do you think they're thirsty? Can I make them some iced tea?"

"Sure."

Gayla rushed inside.

Emma and Marcus went to meet their visitors, and she offered her hand. "Census takers, I gather?"

The three men glanced at one another and smiled.

"Yes. Yes, we are. I'm Colonel Dean." The man took her hand and kissed it. "These are my men, Privates Sole and Lyndsey."

"It's so nice to meet you. My sister is pouring you a glass of tea. Please, come in."

Marcus's head swirled. Something was wrong. The man who called himself Colonel wore the insignia of Major. The men he introduced as Privates wore badges of Corporals.

Marcus tried to remain calm and stretched out his hand. "I'm sorry, sir. It's not every day we're lucky enough to see members of the Marines. I'm a little nervous about meeting you and didn't catch your name." Perhaps he heard wrong, or the man was tired and misspoke.

"A young man with manners. Impressive." He took Marcus's hand and gave him a firm handshake. "I'm Colonel Dean."

Marcus forced himself to return the handshake. Do not snatch away. Act normal. Learning to identify military uniforms and insignias was mandatory at Hudson Ranch. The men were imposters. Their uniforms were Army, not Marine. A strong wind blew, briefly exposing the forehead of one of the men. Marcus didn't breathe. A cross! The warning sign Mr. Alvise started a few years after the EMP. Anyone caught stealing or butchering livestock had their forehead branded so others would know. The ritual quickly spread throughout the country.

"It was a pleasure to meet you." Marcus turned to Emma. "I finished cleaning the barn, ma'am. May I leave now?"

"Of, of course, Marcus. And thank you."

"Do you mind if I take Gypsy for a ride?"

"Uh, sure."

Marcus turned to the men. "I hate to be rude, but I never get to ride, what with all the chores and all."

"No problem," Colonel Dean said. "It was a pleasure to meet you, young man."

Marcus forced himself to take his time getting to the stables. They could not suspect he knew they were frauds. He hated leaving Emma and Gayla but saw no alternative. Jason and the others had to be warned.

Marcus considered going inside and getting Emma's rifle. But, if he managed to get it, she could end up dead in the crossfire. He'd chosen his words carefully and hoped his request to leave and go for a ride would alert Emma, and that the men wouldn't realize there were others at the ranch. He never called Emma ma'am, and he hoped it would send a message.

His pace slowed as he neared the barn. The radio. I could call on the radio for help. He stepped inside the barn and thought for a moment. Gayla's inside. If I go back, I can tell her to run and call for help. His heart raced. I can't. If they realize she's gone, the men will know something's up. No, I need to get help. I can't do this alone.

He was frantic as he saddled Gypsy. Emma's horse was a sweet creature and easy to handle. He eyed Ole' Guss and shivered. The massive, bad-tempered creature was as fast as they came. He walked toward him, reigned in his fear, and had a talk with the beast.

"Listen, Guss. I'm not putting up with your crap. Emma and Gayla may be in danger. You're going to behave and go as fast as you can to Jason. Understand?"

Marcus struggled to saddle Guss. It took all the strength he could muster to toss the saddle over his back. He slid the bit in his mouth and thanked the stallion for staying calm. Marcus stretched his leg, about to mount the monster when the sound of the jeep alerted him. He ran from the stable and saw one of the men enter the vehicle before it sped off. He sighed in relief and apologized to the stallion. "Sorry. I guess I got a little carried away. I'll be back in a minute to unsaddle you." He ran for the house to tell Emma about their close call.

***

Emma's heart pounded. Why were they acting so strangely? Something was wrong. It was like they were canvassing her home. They seemed angry that she had electricity. Even the ice cubes in the tea seemed to anger them.

The Colonel pushed past Emma and went to her bedroom. She followed.

"What are you doing? Get out of my house!"

The man's eyes scanned the floor. He tossed the bed over, snatched up the rug, and exposed the door to the hidden room. He opened it and crawled inside.

"Where is it? Where's the damned map?" he seethed.

"What map? What are you doing?"

One of the men grabbed Gayla and put his hand over her mouth. Emma wanted to scream but had no voice.

"So help me, lady, the kid dies unless you tell me where the map is," the Colonel yelled.

"Please, please. I don't know what you're talking about. Please don't hurt her."

"Maybe you just need a little time to think."

She saw the pistol about to throttle her temple and tried to duck. The room erupted in a burst of light.

***

Marcus flung the door open, called out, and met silence. He ran to Emma's bedroom. Her mattress rested against the wall, and the cover to the secret room was open. He ran for the door and froze. Deep red drops puddled on the kitchen floor. Blood. That's blood. The radio. He grabbed

131

it and began calling. What's wrong with this thing? He slapped it in his hand. Dead batteries. He flung it aside and rushed to the stable.

What do I do? Track the jeep or go for Jason? The jeep. We need to know which way they went. "Alright, Guss." He reached for the reigns of the ornery stallion. "No crap. Understand?"

He and the beast rode with fury for several minutes. The jeep's trail was visible until they reached an old paved road. Marcus jumped from Guss and checked out the marks. He couldn't make it out. He saw no sign of which direction they headed. There were tracks on the overgrown road headed east and west and in both directions. He held his arms wide and screamed. "No!"

Guss stomped his hoofs, snorted, and turned to the east. Marcus crawled on his back. "Okay, boy. If you think they headed east, I trust you." He laid on the stallions back, stroking his neck. "But if we find them, what would I do? We need to tell Jason." It was as if Guss understood. He reared, whinnied, and headed for the ranch. Marcus held on, never so much as touching the reigns. Guss knew where he was going.

***

"What the hell?" Matthew yelled. "Marcus is headed our way, and he's riding Guss!"

Jason smiled, proud of Marcus's courage, then paused. What the heck would cause him to saddle and ride the beast? Something was wrong. He ran toward them and grabbed Guss's reigns when he stopped.

"What's wrong?"

Marcus leaped from the saddle and grappled with speaking. "Fake military. Radio's dead. Took Emma and Gayla. Blood on the floor." Marcus took deep breaths and tried to slow down. "Me and Guss went after them so we'd know which way they went. We hit a paved road, and Guss wanted to go east." Marcus's knees buckled, and Jason grabbed him.

"I'm sorry. I couldn't save them by myself, so I came back. I let them down." Marcus sobbed as the men armed themselves and mounted their horses.

"Laura," Matthew called out. "Marcus has to go with us. Get his gun."

She ran out with a rifle. "You'll find them, son. I love you."

"You ride with me." Jason pulled the boy onto the stallion's back. "Stay inside and arm yourselves," he warned the women. "They may come back."

When they reached the paved road, the men examined the tracks.

"Look at the bend of the weeds," Jason said. "Bent in both directions." He rubbed the side of his face. "I'll ride east. Matthew, you go west."

About fifty yards in, Jason shouted, "They went east!" He rushed Guss back to the others.

Matthew agreed. "It looks like they came in from the west and passed the road to the cabin a few times. But when they left, they were definitely headed east."

"Marcus, you need to stay here. Hide. If they come back, call us." Jason tossed Marcus a radio and spoke to the men. "Mark, can you go back and get Brute? We can't bring Callie. She's too far along."

"I'm on it." Mark kicked his horse into a run.

Jason bent over and placed a hand on Marcus's shoulder. "You're a remarkable young man." Guss reared and headed east.

The men scanned the sides of the road, searching for signs of tire tracks leading off into the woods. Jason reigned in Guss and raised his hand for the others to stop. "They could be miles from here by now." He lifted his radio. "Mark. When you get Brute, would you bring Marcus a horse?"

"Got it, Jason."

"Thanks. We're going to keep moving."

CHAPTER 20

Twenty-one years. Twenty-one *long* damned years. Jordan Dean had waited for this day—the day he'd begin the journey to reunite with his fortune. Thousands of pounds of gold awaited him, not to mention the cases of rare coins and jewels he'd stashed away over the years.

His bitter laugh garnered a stare from the man accompanying him. Let him stare, the stupid, useful tool. He needed him and his friends—for now. He'd kept them all these years out of necessity. How was he supposed to grow food, raise animals, and hunt? He examined his smooth, soft hands. Hands not meant for hard labor. He glanced at the small farmhouse he'd called home for almost twenty years. Better than the jail cell he'd sat in for more than a year, but still, a pathetic place for a man like *him*.

His thick black hair and beard had grayed since the day the judge ordered him jailed. He turned the rear-view mirror and gazed at himself. Still handsome, if he did say so himself. Elizabeth would miss him, but he was glad to be rid of her. She was beautiful once, but she'd grown old. She must be forty-five by now. He deserved better.

Jordan wondered how long she'd last. Elizabeth didn't have a clue about growing vegetables or taking care of the animals. She'd lived a pampered life. Her problem, not his. She should have learned. Instead, she waited for the day they'd retrieve the gold. He leaned out the window and waved toward the farmhouse. "Goodbye, my dear. And good luck." He threw his head back and laughed.

Elizabeth, the last of his original crew, knew he'd buried *some* gold in Wyoming. She went with him and the men on the last trip. He fed her whiskey on the ride to and from the location. There was no way she'd ever find it, and she was only privy to the one load. Elizabeth was lucky. Her loyalty and beauty spared her the fate of the others who'd helped him hide his stash.

He hoped the judge who sentenced them to jail until they disclosed the location of the gold, rotted in hell. The investors knew the risk. They had *no* proof he'd found the ship, only the word of one disgruntled man. And he wouldn't be talking.

He remembered the haul that led to his capture. The "rat" said there was a vast discrepancy in what Jordan reported to the investors and what they had recovered. Jordan was sure he'd convinced the young man it was an error, but he couldn't risk it. Instead, there'd be a horrible "accident." Unfortunately, the incident occurred *after* the new crew member contacted authorities.

Jordan thought about his last visit to Wyoming. His men had dug a trench for the boxes filled with gold and lowered them inside. He coaxed them to stand in front of the ditch so Elizabeth could take a group photo. She stood beside the truck and pretended to struggle with the camera, and Jordan offered his help. When he reached the truck, he pulled out a machine gun and mowed them down.

"Whew," Elizabeth sighed. "Thank God you had them dig their graves. Can you imagine having to bury them all? That would take hours."

Jordon used his foot to push them into the trench. One man moaned and grabbed his leg. Jordan tore loose, shoved him into the hole, and buried him alive.

***

Jordan had been skimming treasures from investors for years. He had two old shacks restored to make it suitable for him to live in when he was there—one for him, the other to house his men—temporarily. A secret crawl space under the bed in the cabin hid his map.

His crew had gone along with his plans believing they'd split the treasure and become millionaires. Jordan had offered up just enough to keep the investors coming. Then, one small-minded recruit with his heart set on finding the lost ships, not with what lay inside, brought Jordan's hunting to an end. *Idiot.*

He and Elizabeth had spent a year in jail when the EMP hit. The sheriff had no choice but to release the two non-violent offenders.

While in jail, Jordan began recruiting men. They'd eventually meet the same fate of his crew, but he had no idea he'd have to wait more than twenty years. The three men he'd chosen believed there were a thousand pounds. What some men would do for such a small amount of gold amazed him. Half would be his. After all, he was the treasure hunter who found it. The three men would split the rest.

They took over the small farm after the EMP. Jordan never asked what happened to the family. He didn't care. He needed it to survive.

He was the greatest treasure hunter of all time. If the government didn't take his bounties, the damned investors did. The gold was his. No one would stand in his way.

After the EMP, Jordan struggled with the urge to go after his treasure but knew he had to wait for the right time. Until recently, there was no easy way to sell it. And how would he survive if he went to Wyoming? With the price of gold on a steady incline, the desire to go after his haul had grown stronger.

He'd made sure Elizabeth would never find the place again. He damned sure didn't want her knowing where it was so she could conspire with the men. If he had to kill them, who would grow food and raise livestock? Jordan wasn't willing to starve or work.

He could have taken the train to Wyoming, but he didn't have enough to barter for the things he'd need. Things like plenty of food and a way to dig up and transport the gold. An evil smile crossed his lips. After more than twenty years, the government and military graciously supplied him with what he required.

The three jeeps loaded with food, weapons, survival gear, and fuel were a godsend. The men told Jordan they were headed south to deliver the items to a small outpost that housed census workers. Jordan had wooed them, fed them well, and provided the men with a well-deserved night of rest. It was their last. A few days later, Jordan and his men made their clandestine escape for Wyoming.

They took all three jeeps. Once they reached a safe spot, they would unload, keep what they needed, and ditch one of the vehicles. They'd need as much fuel as possible to reach their destination.

Jordan felt a pang of regret. Not because he'd left Elizabeth behind, but because she might find some way to pay him back. He should have had the men kill her. He shook his head and smiled. No. She only knew of the one stash and had no idea where it was. Besides, she'd starve to death within a few weeks.

Jordan had one concern. He couldn't be caught with the map. When he'd hidden it in the cabin, he thought he'd be back in a few weeks. The house and the map could have gone up in flames. It didn't worry him much. He knew exactly where the largest stash was hidden. Once they dug it up, he'd buy a metal detector. He'd find it—every ounce.

"Jordan," Elizabeth called out and clutched her throbbing head. There was no response. Where was everyone? Silence surrounded her. Her stomach rumbled. "Ugh. Sorry bastards." She walked to the pantry and opened the doors. Empty. She rubbed her temples and tried to clear her mind of the alcohol-induced fog. She rushed to the bedroom and opened his drawers. Empty. She swung open the closet door. His clothes were gone. Elizabeth grabbed a lantern, ran to the cellar, and stumbled down the stairs. Her stomach ached with dread. Elizabeth screamed and stomped her feet. She knew she'd find an empty basement. She rushed up the stairs and shouted to no one. "You bastard! You think you outsmarted me?"

Elizabeth ran back to the bedroom, pulled out the top drawer, flipped it over, and removed the pieces of paper she'd secretly copied twenty some-odd-years earlier. Did Jordan honestly think she was so naive? Her hand slid under the pillow and pulled out a revolver. Sleeping with one eye open for twenty years was over. Why didn't she take care of Jordan when they got the jeeps and supplies? She gripped her hair and stomped. "Damn it!"

Elizabeth calmed, pulled a trunk from under the bed and tapped her lips. "Hmm. What do I want for breakfast?"

While she ate a jar of stew, Elizabeth plotted. The easiest thing would be to alert the authorities and have Jordan arrested. But that was a twenty-year-old strategy. They may not care now. Traveling from Florida to Wyoming sent chills down her spine. Even with her hidden stash of food, weapons, and ammo, it would be a daunting task. And he had a lead and three jeeps filled with supplies. There was no telling when he'd left. Now she understood why he pulled out the whiskey and encouraged her to drink. Hell, he could have gone a day or two ago.

"You're on your own," Elizabeth told the chickens as she opened the door to their pen. At the last minute, she reconsidered. Eggs. Food. The chickens were essential. She stared at the ornery milk goat, cows, and pigs. "I'm taking some of you with me. The train should be passing through in a week or so. You'll help me barter my way to Wyoming." She scanned the small farm and screamed again. "You won't get away with this, Jordon. Do you hear me? You'll pay!"

Elizabeth spent several days improvising cages for the chickens and figuring out how to attach the cart to one of the horses. She loaded the chickens, two goats, and two small pigs. She'd tie a milk cow behind the cart.

Elizabeth got on her horse and whipped her. "Move it." The mare balked at the load, and she whipped her again. "Move, you lousy piece of flesh." After several minutes of abuse, Elizabeth began her journey of vengeance.

A smile crept across Elizabeth's face. The former President's ranch was in Wyoming but out of the way. It didn't matter. She'd go there and play the role of a twenty-year hostage of a notorious treasure hunter gone rogue. Plus, she'd always wanted to meet Chris Alvise. What a fine specimen.

She'd have to come up with a new name. It wasn't likely anyone would recall her or Jordan, but better safe than sorry. Her new name needed to be simple, something she could easily remember. Jane. Her name was Jane.

In the military jeeps, it would take Jordan at least a week, perhaps two, to make it to Wyoming. Maybe longer from what she'd heard about the condition of the roads. Hell, she'd probably beat them there.

***

What an idiot. Assuming she was drunk and passed out, Jordan had left a map and a drawing on the table after they'd killed the men. The picture was familiar. It looked like the cabin they were staying in. But what was with all the trees? There were only a couple of trees close to the house. Then, Elizabeth realized one row of trees stood for the spot where they'd buried the men and the treasure. She smiled at the many trees and shrubs scattered in the child-like drawing. It was a map. Some of the trees stood alone. Some were in clusters. The trees represented buried treasure. She'd made a quick sketch and wrote directions to the cabin.

Jordan's constant insistence that he'd distributed the gold in many locations always amused her. It was *all* there. She was sure of it. Years of cheating investors, and the riches lay buried on a single piece of property. She hadn't wasted twenty years on that SOB for nothing. Hopefully, he'd be arrested, or better yet, killed. Jordan would die before disclosing the location of the gold. Once he was in jail, or dead, the gold was hers.

She'd been willing to share the bounty, but now? He could rot in hell.

CHAPTER 21

Emma struggled to focus. The violent throbbing in her head and Gayla's crying confused her.

"I thought you were dead," Gayla choked and cried harder.

"What happened?" Emma winced and clutched the side of her head. A sticky wetness coated her fingers. She lowered her hand and stared at the dark red goo.

"They wanted a map. You said you didn't know what they were talking about, and one of them hit you with a gun. Are you okay?"

"I think so. Did they hurt you?"

"No, but they're mean, Emma. They threatened to kill me."

The memories came rushing back. Emma forced herself upright and grabbed her little sister as they bounced around in the back of the jeep. They had to jump. Her stomach churned. Perhaps from the injury, or maybe from the motion sickness she'd read about. She eased to the back of the jeep and peeked out. The shadows rushing by on the paved road made her dizzy, and she quickly shut the flap. Her stomach churned. She tossed back the flap and threw up.

"Emma! Emma!" Gayla cried.

Emma waved her hand behind her as she fought to catch her breath. "I'm okay. The motion is making me sick." She wiped her mouth and crawled back to her little sister. Emma found it difficult to breathe. "Listen to me," she gasped. "We have to jump!"

Gayla's eyes grew with fright.

"We don't have a choice. They're not going to let us go." She squeezed Gayla's shoulders and began to throw up again.

Gayla brushed Emma's hair back and cried louder.

Emma took several deep breaths and held her abdomen. "Dad said that if you find yourself in hell..."

"I know," Gayla choked, "you have to fight your way out, or that's where you'll stay."

Emma nodded and laid down on the floor of the jeep bed for a few minutes. Then, she sat up and rubbed her forehead. "I feel better now."

Thank God they didn't leave a man to guard them. Emma pulled up her pants leg, stared at the knife, and let out a gust of air.

"We wait for a pause. A turn, maybe. If we jump out at this speed..." Emma clutched Gayla and eased her toward the back of the jeep.

"We'll die," Gayla sobbed.

"I'm not leaving you behind. When I jump, you're coming too!"

Emma made her way to the back of the jeep, lifted the flap, and stared out. She felt the waves of nausea and fought to hold it back. Dizziness. She tried to focus on the scenery. There was a long shadow behind the vehicle. Remember everything, Emma. Remember. She couldn't look anymore and closed the flap.

Gayla threw her arms around her sister. "I'm scared, Emma. I'm scared."

"I know you are. But you need to be strong." She tightened her grasp. "Now is the time to fight our way out of hell, just like Dad taught us."

"Yeah." Gayla gasped for breath. "I guess this is when I need to cowgirl-up."

Emma nodded. "Yep, Jellybean. Time to cowgirl-up."

They squeezed hands and waited. It seemed like an eternity before the jeep slowed and slung them to the left.

"Now!" Emma yelled. She jumped and pulled Gayla with her. They tumbled to the ground, and the jeep continued. Her head swarmed as she staggered toward Gayla, who was lying crumpled on the ground. "Gayla!" Emma screamed.

***

Emma's eyes flickered. Dazed, she tried focusing on a fire burning nearby. Gayla was breaking limbs. Emma reached up and felt a damp cloth covering her forehead.

"Gayla," she whispered.

"Emma! Emma!" Gayla rushed to her side. "Try to sit up and drink some water."

"My head hurts." Emma tried to sit, but the pain forced her down. "We need to get as far away from the road as we can."

"Emma, we walked at least two hours after we jumped from the jeep. Don't you remember?"

"No. No. I remember jumping from the jeep and seeing you lying on the ground." She rubbed her temples. "That was two hours ago?"

"No, Emma. We walked for two hours, then you laid down. I made a fire and started building a shelter. We jumped at least four hours ago."

Emma stared at the fire. "How did you start it? Did you have matches?" She tensed. "You know you're not..."

"No, silly. I used the sun, just like you taught me. There's a stream down there." She pointed. "I found some old bottles." She lifted the one filled with water. "I broke the bottoms off the ones that were broken or cracked and found a sunny spot. One of them worked like a magnifying glass." She ran for the glass and showed it to Emma. "This is a keeper."

Gayla reached for the bottle of water. "Here, drink." Emma took the bottle and drank.

Gayla sighed. "We may be here for a while. I'll break more limbs for a shelter." She pushed her hair back. "You rest. I need to fill the other bottles with water. I'll try to find something to cook. I'm hungry." She bent and kissed Emma's cheek. "I'll be back soon. Rest."

Emma beamed with pride. Gayla and her slingshot. Now she's *my* caregiver. She wanted to help but didn't have the strength and drifted off to sleep.

***

Emma sat and squeezed her head. Gayla rushed toward her with a bottle of water. "Here. Drink some more water."

Gayla pointed to the fire. "I'm roasting firewood roots on that flat stone in the coals." She smiled. "Got a rabbit and two squirrels with my slingshot. I'm glad the bad men didn't see it and take it."

Emma blinked and tried to focus. Sure enough, a rabbit and two squirrels roasted over the coals.

"It's getting late. I need to finish our shelter. I'll wake you up when dinner's ready."

Emma watched as Gayla built a makeshift shelter. Good job, little sister, good job.

She thought she'd only dozed for a moment, but Gayla's plea told her otherwise.

"Wake up, Emma. Please wake up."

Her eyes flickered, then came to life as she took in her surroundings.

"Dinner's ready." Gayla helped Emma sit and returned with an old, battered aluminum pie tin filled with rabbit, squirrel, and roasted firewood roots. "I found the tin at the stream. It looks nasty, but I washed it good. We'll have to share. I only found one."

And Jason thought she couldn't make it on her own. "Thank you, Gayla."

After dinner, Emma felt renewed energy. She walked around the camp and praised Gayla. "You did all of this in a few hours?"

"Phhh. It's not nearly what you could have done."

"Gayla, you have no idea." Emma got on her knees and hugged her little sister. "You saved me, started a fire, got meat for dinner, found wild vegetables and water, and built a shelter. And Jason's friends call me Super Woman?" Emma repeatedly kissed Gayla's forehead. "I'm so proud of you."

Gayla giggled, pushed away, and wiped her brow. "Yuck! You just drooled all over me!" Then she lowered her head. "Emma, you taught me to do stuff like this." Gayla choked, and her jaw quivered. "But what if they find us? What if we don't find our way home?" She threw herself into her sister's arms.

"We'll be okay, Jellybean. I promise."

***

After dinner, Emma questioned Gayla. "Do you remember leaving the ranch? Do you recall the shift in the jeep when we hit the old paved road?"

"No. I was too scared."

"It's okay." She rubbed Gayla's shoulder. "What did I say when we jumped? Did I lead us in a particular direction?"

"Yeah," Gayla sniffled. "You said we had to head north and get as far from the road as we could."

Emma wiped her forehead. "Then we need to head south and find the spot where we escaped."

"No! They might see us."

"Listen to me, Gayla. The tracks will lead us home. Without them, I have no idea what direction to travel. We have to find the tracks before they're gone." Emma leaned back. "I'm so tired. I'm sorry. I need to rest for a few minutes." Emma curled up under the shelter and squeezed Gayla's hand.

Gayla stared at the sky. "I've got a little while before it gets dark, Emma. I'll try to find some food and get more water for tomorrow. I'll take care of you." She rubbed Emma's shoulder. "Just like you've always done for me."

Emma closed her eyes and drifted off.

***

Emma tossed and turned, tormented by nightmares. Marcus asked to leave after he'd cleaned the barn. She didn't question him but was curious why he'd promised to help her all day. That wasn't like Marcus. Then he asked to take a horse instead of walking and said he seldom rode. That made no sense. A man covered Gayla's mouth and threatened to kill her. She tried to dodge the pistol as it swung for her head and woke up in the bed of the jostling jeep. The swaying motion made her ill. The jeep made a sharp turn. She held Gayla tight, and they jumped.

Emma bolted upright. Marcus was a smart young man. Either he recognized something she missed or had a bad feeling about the men. He'd never skimp on his chores to take the horse for a ride, and he'd called her ma'am. He never did any of those things. She shook her head and wondered how she could have missed the tell-tale signs. Marcus wanted to take the horse so he could move fast and alert the others. They're looking for us. We need to stay put for a while. She stared at the fire. Please, don't let the men see our smoke. Their only defense was her knife and Gayla's slingshot. Emma lifted her pants leg. That wouldn't do.

When Gayla awoke, the rest of the game she'd taken the day before warmed near the fire. Emma doodled in the sand with a stick.

"Good morning, sleepyhead."

"Morning," Gayla yawned. "How do you feel?"

"I'm fine, and you'll be happy to know we aren't going back to the road."

"Whew," Gayla sighed.

"I remembered some things last night. Are you positive I led us north?"

"Well, you said the sun rose in the east, and we had to go north. Then you led us this way. Why?"

Emma drew a line in the sand. "This is the road." She gripped Gayla's hand. "Think hard. Did we cross the paved road and go in the opposite direction of the jeep?"

"Yeah. Would have been kind of dumb to go the way they went."

Emma grinned. "If you're right, we're here." She carved an X into the ground. "There was a shadow behind the jeep, and it made a hard-right turn before we jumped."

143

Gayla closed her eyes and aimed her face toward the sky. Then she squinted and looked at Emma. "Wait a minute. I remember getting thrown on my left side."

"Physics."

"What's that?" Gayla asked.

Emma grinned and lifted her brows.

Gayla stomped her. "Darn it. You got me again. I'll look it up when we get home."

"We were headed east. That's why there was a shadow behind the jeep." Emma tossed the stick. "Our way home is to the west. But we stay put for a while. I think Marcus knew something was wrong. I believe he left to warn Jason and the others. Moving will make it more difficult for them to find us. Plus, we have the stream here. We don't want to find ourselves without water." Emma nodded toward the shelter Gayla had built. "Not to mention our wonderful living quarters. We'll give them a few days. If they don't find us by then, we move."

Gayla stood, tossed her shoulders back, and brushed her clothes. "Marcus is pretty smart. He'll find us. I'm going to the stream to rinse off. Maybe I can find some more things we can use. I can't believe all the stuff people used to throw away."

As Gayla skipped toward the stream, Emma noticed the large piece missing from the back of her shirt and glanced at the cloth that had cooled her head. Emma thought about how Gayla had truly cowgirled-up as she fiddled with the bracelet her mom made for her years earlier. The conversation about the gift flooded her memories.

"This is called a paracord bracelet, Emma. If you're ever in an emergency situation, it might save your life."

Her dad had knelt beside her and pulled out a short piece of paracord and separated it. "Check this out. A sturdy cord to a fishing line all wrapped together. You could even use the thinnest piece to sew up a wound."

Pages from survival books took the place of her memories. "Gayla!" Emma shouted. "If you find any cans, or lids from cans, bring them. Make a pile with anything you find. I'll explain later."

Emma kissed her bracelet, thanked her mother, and began to unravel the braided rope.

***

"Emma, Emma. I found lots of stuff."

Gayla was shirtless, and her top carried a stash of usable items. Emma's eyes widened. Oh, my lord. When did that happen? We laid together in the tub not all that long ago, and they weren't there. She ran for Gayla. "Good job. Now, put on your shirt."

"But it's all sandy."

"I don't care. Shake it out and put it on."

"Geez. Okay, okay."

"I'm sorry, Gayla. I just never realized how you'd matured."

Gayla squinted her eyes in confusion.

Emma giggled. "Never mind. Let's eat breakfast, and then we'll see what you scavenged."

After breakfast, Gayla laid out her find. "I left more at the stream."

Emma smiled at the beer and soda cans. The pull tabs would become hooks for catching fish.

"Look at this." Gayla lifted a large, white, plastic container. "This thing will hold a lot of water."

"Wonderful. I say we fill it up and heat the water in the cans before we drink it. We've been lucky so far, but I'd prefer to know we killed the cooties."

"Okay. I'll fill a lot of bottles and bring back the other stuff. You need to rest."

***

Whether for food or protection, Emma needed a bow. The paracord supplied the bowstring, and she scanned the forest for the other materials. What she wouldn't give to find a burr oak, but that was doubtful. She'd walked about a hundred yards when she spotted a Rocky Mountain Juniper and embraced it. "I knew I'd find you."

At home, she had a spinner her dad made to check for flaws in the arrows. Out here, she was on her own. She'd have to eyeball them for accuracy. She chopped several limbs for bows and dozens of smaller ones for arrows. On her way back to camp, Emma scoured the forest floor for feathers to make fletchings. Finding none was discouraging. She'd figure something out. Maybe plastic from the bottle.

Time slipped by as Emma worked on her bow and arrows. She glanced toward the stream. Gayla had been gone for a long time. Emma's heart raced, and she ran toward the creek. Emma braced herself against a tree before sitting on a fallen log. Her little sister was pulling a net from the

145

water and tossing fish on the bank. When she threw the fourth ashore, she saw Emma.

"Look, Emma. I found this old net. It's full of holes, but it still caught dinner, and then some."

"Wow." Emma forced herself to stand and went to help Gayla gather the fish and supplies.

"Gayla, we only need to keep a few. Let the others go. You can catch them tomorrow."

"I know. Can you help me? There's so many."

As they released the fish, Emma quizzed Gayla. "I can't believe you found the net and all this stuff just hanging around."

"Well, I had to walk a long way." Gayla pointed. "There's a lot more stuff that way."

"Gayla. Dear God. You were headed for the road."

"I, I was?"

"Yes." Emma exhaled. Her voice was husky. "Never go that way again."

"I won't. I'm sorry," Gayla said.

"It's not just that. You have to stay close. What if you wandered off and something happened to you, or you got lost?" Emma yelled.

"I'm sorry. I'm sorry." Tears filled Gayla's eyes, and her nose began to drip.

Emma embraced her. "Forgive me. I allowed myself to forget we weren't at home. You need to stay close." She stepped back and spread her arms. "Look at this. Look what you did. All these useful items *and* dinner. You are amazing, Jellybean."

Gayla's sobs continued. Emma seldom yelled at her.

"I'm sorry. I was just scared. I don't know what I would do if something happened to you. Let's take your find back to camp."

***

Gayla separated the items she'd found as the fish roasted over the fire.

Emma stretched her bow and smiled. "Perfect." She chuckled. "Well, sort of."

Gayla clapped her hands and licked her lips. "I smell venison."

"Yeah. Let's see if I can make some arrows first." Emma raised the bow. "I could toss this thing at a deer all day, and we'd go to bed hungry."

"I'm going to try and find some more greens and roots," Gayla said.

"Okay, but don't wander too far."

Gayla rolled her eyes. "You already told me once."

146

Emma went to work on her arrows. She was trying one out when Gayla ran toward camp.

"Lambs quarters, Emma. Lots of it. I only picked enough for dinner."

"Good job, Gayla."

"Hey, you got an arrow ready?"

"Yep. Let's eat some fish and greens. Then we'll see how she flies."

They pulled out the old pie tin and scarfed down their meal.

"Drink plenty of water," Emma said.

"I know, I know. Stay hydrated."

Emma strolled away from the fire, closed her eyes, and lifted her head. She'd been standing like that for a minute or so when Gayla's arm wrapped around hers. "I do that too. You're listening for them, aren't you?"

Emma exhaled. "I'm listening for the bad men, but also for Jason and Marcus." She patted her sister's hand. "Let's wash our plate and gather more firewood. Then I test the bow and arrows."

"Deal." Gayla raised her hand for a slap then giggled. "But I caught dinner, so I'll clean the plate while *you* gather wood."

She followed Gayla back to the fire. Gayla lifted the tin plate and was about to toss the scraps onto the fire.

"Wait!"

Gayla jerked back. "What's wrong?"

Emma's finger rubbed across the tops of her bottom teeth. Then she chewed a nail for a second. "Don't toss that on the fire. Throw it in the stream and wash the pan there."

Gayla shrugged. "Okay."

***

After she'd gathered firewood, Emma completed her work on the arrows. It was time to try out her new weapon.

"I found this feather when I was gathering wood, but I want to save it. I'm trying plastic from the busted jug first, but I don't want to risk the plastic whacking my thumb off." Emma slid her hand into the makeshift glove she'd made with a squirrel skin and paracord. She pointed to the arrowhead. "This one is wrapped in metal from a can. I want to make some with blades later. Let's see how she does." She drew back, aimed, and let go.

Gayla danced as the arrow hit almost dead center of the target.

Emma threw her head back, rocked her shoulders, and flipped her hair. "Guess we don't play around with perfection."

Gayla rolled her eyes and chuckled. "Oh, brother." She pulled out her slingshot, aimed, and hit the target inches closer than Emma's arrow.

"Smarty-pants." Emma ruffled her little sister's hair.

Emma put down her bow and examined Gayla's fishing net. "I can't believe you found this." She tugged on the monofilament net. "There's no way this has been here for twenty years."

"How do you know?"

"It's too strong. After twenty years in the woods, I imagine it would be falling apart. This stuff is strong. That's good. I need to cut some. We need the line."

"No! We need it to catch fish."

"Don't worry, Gayla. I'm only cutting some of it loose. I want a piece long enough to go around our camp."

Gayla's lips twisted. "Why?"

Emma pointed to the stack of tin cans. "We're going to tie a few of them together and run the line around the camp. If any animals come close and touch the line, the cans will rattle and warn us."

Gayla's mouth sagged, and her eyes filled with fear. Emma took a deep breath and tried to play it off. "I figured if a rabbit hit it, you could get it with your slingshot."

"Oh. I thought you meant wild animals like bears." Gayla relaxed.

"Phhh. Any old bear that runs into it will run off when the cans start making noise." That was most likely a lie, but Emma hoped not.

Emma began cutting the fishing net. "And another thing. Starting tomorrow, we cook at the stream, not at our camp."

"Why?"

Emma lowered the net. She didn't want to frighten Gayla, but at the same time, her little sister needed to understand that things were different here.

"Free food attracts lazy hunters. The smell of cooking meat and fish can travel for miles. I'd prefer any animals too lazy to hunt find their meals away from our camp."

"Okay," Gayla said quietly.

She knew Gayla was worried. But there was nothing Emma could do about it. Things were different now. Still, she didn't want Gayla to be afraid or to panic.

Emma turned and lifted a long shaft of wood into the air. She handed it to Gayla. "I made you something."

148

Gayla took the gift and look confused.

"A spear," Emma said.

"I know what it is," Gayla said. "We used to make them and toss them at targets."

"Well, don't toss this one. Always keep it with you for protection. I heated the tip to harden it. If anything or anyone tries to harm you, shove that sucker in them as hard and fast as you can."

Gayla's eyes grew wide with fear.

"I'm sorry, Gayla. But I told you. We aren't at home. We need to be prepared."

Gayla's face paled. Her eyes closed and she nodded. "Okay."

Emma was proud of Gayla and all she could do; all she could withstand. But she was only a child, after all. A couple of things about Gayla stood out if you knew her well. If she felt someone considered her just a little kid, or if she thought you didn't believe she wasn't brave enough, Gayla would push herself to prove you wrong.

Emma pulled the fishnet close and forced a chuckle. "Whew. This is going to be tough, Gayla. I wish I could promise you an easy trip home, but I can't." She rested her elbows on her knees. "It's probably gonna get harder every day." Emma tightened her lips and pretended to examine the net. "Dad used to tell Mom that the only easy day was yesterday."

Emma continued cutting line from the fishing net and waited for Gayla to relax.

"By the way, are you still a good tree climber?" Emma cocked her head and looked down her nose.

Gayla smirked, and her hands flew to her hips. "Probably one of the best in the country!"

Emma couldn't suppress her smile. "Good." She lifted what remained of her paracord bracelet. "We have about ten feet of this. We need to find a tree you can climb and tie our food to a branch."

Gayla's eyes scrunched, and her lips puckered.

Emma chuckled. "Gayla, what do you think Brute and Callie would do if you left out... say, some venison, and went to bed? Do you think they'd go after it when you went to sleep?"

Gayla paled. "Jason said he wouldn't tell!"

Emma laughed. "He didn't. He tried to pretend he'd eaten it, but I'm not that naive."

Gayla looked at her feet.

"That doesn't matter, Gayla. It never did. I'm trying to make you understand that animals could smell our food and look for it. If we cook away from camp and tie our extra food up high, they probably won't mess with us."

"Okay. I understand." Gayla's fists went together and covered her mouth.

Emma had no idea what she was supposed to say and blurted the first thing that came to mind.

"Cowgirl-up! You've been living with wild animals your whole life! Just because you don't have a cabin and a gun doesn't mean you're not smarter than them!" Emma reached her hand out for Gayla's.

Gayla snatched away and wiped her eye. "I'm not a baby, and I'm not letting some wild animal outsmart me. You just tell me what I need to do."

CHAPTER 22

"What the hell do you mean they're gone?" Jordan stomped to the back of the jeep and flung open the flaps.

"We need to go back and find them," one of his men said.

Jordan seethed and considered the request before he snapped the flaps closed. "No. No way they survived a jump as fast as we were going. If they managed to live, they'll be dead soon. We must be eighty miles from their place."

"Let me at least ride back to the road," one man offered. "Maybe they jumped when we made the turn."

Jordan scoffed. "We're not wasting fuel to search for two dead girls. Like I said, if they jumped on the road, they're dead. If they jumped when we turned on the dirt road, they'll never make it home alive."

"But one of them may know where the map is."

"If they knew, they would have used it to save themselves. More than likely, it was gone before they moved in."

One of the men got in Jordan's face. "So, you're telling us someone may have already dug up the gold, and we've wasted twenty years?"

"Back off." Jordan shoved him back. "If anyone found the map, they'd have no idea what it was. It looked like a kid's drawing. I didn't mark a damned X where I buried it. The gold's still there." Jordan exhaled. "I need to think. Start a fire. We need to eat. I'll be back in a minute."

Jordan walked away and headed for one of the jeeps. One of the girls had found the map. He was sure of it. He'd brought them along to refresh their memory. Most likely, they had no idea what it was. He'd hoped to question and prod them until they remembered. The youngest girl was Jordan's leverage. Now he'd lost any chance of recovering the map.

Jordan's breathing was erratic. He needed to calm down. If he could do away with the men now, he would, but he needed them. There was no telling how many people were living in the cabins. No, he'd have to wait. He crawled into the back of the jeep and opened his chest filled with whiskey. He pulled out a bottle. Two of the men knew the location of the treasure now. He didn't feel like having his throat slit that night.

Jordan walked toward the fire and raised the bottle. "I've been saving this for a special occasion."

As his men drank, Jordan contemplated his next move. He should have taken the boy. If there were others, he would have warned them by now. Jordan smiled. If so, they'd probably be looking for the girls. How many miles could they travel on horseback each day? He guessed thirty or less if they were searching for signs. They had three or four days before the men would find their tracks.

Tomorrow they would go back to the paved road, cover their tracks, and head closer in. Once the men looking for the girls passed, they'd head for the cabin. When they returned, Jordan and his men would wipe them out.

Pleased with himself, Jordan poured a drink and told the men his plan.

***

Elizabeth had nothing left to barter when she and her horse left the train. She'd been taken advantage of, but all she cared about was making it to Hudson Ranch and wooing the unsuspecting ex-president. It was only twenty-five miles, but she had to appear worn out, frightened, and angry. It shouldn't be hard. She *was* angry and worn out. As she neared the ranch, a jeep rushed toward her. She laid down on her saddle and pretended to struggle to stay atop the horse. Look feeble, Elizabeth. Gain sympathy.

"Halt!" The soldier ordered. "What business do you have here?"

Crap. Time to go a little overboard. She rolled her eyes and forced herself to tumble from the horse.

Several soldiers surrounded her. "Ma'am. Are you okay?"

"Water," she mumbled.

"Get her some water."

She took a few sips and began choking, imitating the old westerns she'd seen on television.

"Get her in the jeep. We need to take her to the ranch. She needs a doctor. What's your name, ma'am?"

"Jane. My name is Jane." Elizabeth fought her smile as they rushed her to the infirmary.

Chris Alvise and his wife, Sierra, hurried to her side.

"The doctors are on their way," Chris told her.

"I, I just need water." Elizabeth didn't want damned doctors butting in.

Sierra offered water, and she drank.

Elizabeth shook her head. "Thank you. I'm fine. I think I was dehydrated."

***

Chris's brows furrowed. Sierra continued to fawn over the woman as they waited on the doctors. He'd never seen anyone recover from dehydration so fast.

Doc showed up first and checked on the new patient. "She's fine. She may have been a little dehydrated, but most likely, the trip itself caused her turmoil."

Jane was the main topic at dinner.

"Did you hear? She was a hostage of a pirate released from prison after the EMP. He held her captive for twenty years!"

"Yeah. Jane escaped with directions to his old hideout. She heard him talking to some men about going after the treasure before they abandoned her."

"She rode alone from Florida. I can't imagine!"

Chris listened to the chatter. Something didn't feel right.

Ryan, his adoptive nephew, approached him after dinner. "Uncle Chris, may I speak with you in private?"

They went to the pool room and had a drink.

"Uncle Chris," Ryan whispered, "I'm positive I saw Jane get off the train at Shoshoni Depot. I remember because, well, frankly, she's attractive and was struggling with her horse. I was about to offer help when she rode off. No way she was suffering from dehydration or exhaustion." He shook his head. "Something isn't right."

Chris tossed his drink back and wiped his mouth. "Thank you, Ryan. You're right. Something's wrong with this picture. Keep this conversation between us."

Chris returned to the dining hall and interrupted Jane's adoring fans. "Ma'am. You said you had a map. I need it if we're to catch the man who held you hostage."

Of course. Elizabeth pulled the folded paper from her bra and held Chris's hand a moment too long. "I made a copy of where he said they'd hideout." She batted her lashes. "He said the treasure was buried about twenty miles from there."

"What was this notorious pirate's name?" Sierra asked.

"Jordan..." Elizabeth's eyes darted. "James... James Jordan."

153

Chris grinned. Sierra's question had caught "Jane" off guard. Either his first or last name was Jordan. James was a lie. And he doubted that Jane was her real name. "My men are on it. Don't worry. We'll find him."

Elizabeth grasped his hand and placed it on her chest. "Thank you, President Alvise, or may I call you Chris?"

He fought the urge to snarl and leisurely pulled away. "Mr. Alvise is fine, I am no longer the president."

Chris handed the paper to one of his men and saw the fireworks shooting from Sierra's eyes. He took his wife's arm and went back to the pool room. His old friend, Frank, racked a set of balls.

Chris looked at Barbara, Frank's wife. "Grandma and Grandpa would be proud of that rack." Chris chuckled. "They turned your husband into a pool shark before they passed."

"Yeah." Barbara shook her head and rolled her eyes. "Why don't you see if you can humble him. He's getting a big head."

Chris always thought twice before taking on Frank. He'd become known as the Hustler.

***

Chris found it difficult to concentrate. Frank beat him handily three games in a row. Sierra sat in the corner, nursing a drink, seething, and whispering to Barbara.

"Another round?" Frank smirked.

"Maybe later." Chris leaned his cue against the bar and slammed his mug on the counter. "I need to have a talk with my wife!" He walked toward her, and Sierra lowered her drink. "Spill it, Sierra. What's your problem?"

"Jane." She sat tall. "You didn't seem to mind her advances."

"How dare you question my loyalty," Chris said a bit too loud. "What have I ever done to make you question me?"

Sierra stared at her drink. "Nothing. Absolutely nothing." She choked for a moment. "I'm sorry. I don't know where that came from. But that woman had the nerve to caress your hands then put them on her chest with me standing right there. I almost screamed. I apologize for lashing out at you, but I refuse to apologize for having a bad feeling about her. Something's not right."

Chris smirked. "You're jealous!"

154

"Phhh. Of what? A gorgeous younger woman making advances on my husband and placing his hands on her breasts? Why in the world would that make me jealous?"

Chris burst into laughter. "Sierra, there's not a woman on the planet who could tempt me. You're my soul-mate." He kissed her hand. "You're the only woman I've ever loved. A tryst with a gorgeous younger woman isn't worth the risk of losing you."

The daggers that came his way caused Chris to laugh harder. "For some reason, I don't think I gave the right response."

Sierra's frown slowly curled into a grin as Frank and Barbara burst into laughter.

"Laugh if you will," Sierra blurted. "But something's wrong with Jane's story. I don't trust her."

"You have every right to distrust her." Chris turned to Frank and Barbara. "Your son saw her getting off the train at the Shoshoni Depot. She hadn't ridden alone from Florida. Her trip was only twenty-five miles."

"What?" Frank jumped from his barstool.

"Yeah. For now, we keep it quiet. I don't want "Jane," or whoever she is, running off."

"Jordan... Jordan," Sierra tapped her lips. "Treasure hunter. Why does that sound so familiar?" Sierra asked. Then she gasped. "Jordan Dean. I did a story on him. He cheated investors out of tons of gold. He and his girlfriend were captured and jailed until they told the whereabouts of the treasure. It was about a year before the EMP." Sierra snarled. "Jane, or whoever she is, is probably his girlfriend. I can't remember her name."

"Oh, my gosh," Barbara whispered. "I remember that story. And the men and women here are gushing all over her."

"As I said, we keep this quiet," Chris said.

One of Chris's detail rushed in. "Sir, I need to speak with you."

"I'll be right back." Chris kissed Sierra's forehead.

***

Chris entered the room with his security detail. "Sir, we have a problem." He asked Chris to look at the map.

Chris rubbed his temples. "Wait. Am I reading this right? Is that Emma's ranch?"

"Afraid so, Sir."

Chris lowered himself into a chair. "Dear God. Have we heard from them?"

155

"No, Sir."

Chris stood and set his jaw. "Load the jeeps. We move within the hour."

"Yes, Sir."

Chris ran back to the pool hall and told Sierra, Frank, and Barbara.

"I'll be ready in a few minutes," Frank yelled as he and Barbara went to pack his bag.

Chris stopped them. "Frank. I appreciate the offer, but we have buyers coming in a few days. You need to stay and oversee things."

"Guess you're right." Frank slumped and sat on a stool.

"Well, I'm going," Sierra said.

"No," Chris barked. "Jim, Lena, and Barbie need you here."

"Jason is my son." She stood defiantly. "I'm going."

Chris towered over Sierra. "I don't like being in this position, but this time, it's *my* decision. You will not be going. You have other children to think of. I'll send for you when I know it's safe."

CHAPTER 23

Mark, Marcus, and Brute caught up with Jason and the other men two hours later.

Jason scanned the anxious faces surrounding him. "I know you're all eager to find them, but at least two of you need to stay behind to help the women in case they come back. Any volunteers?"

Randy and Eric looked at each other before Randy spoke. "We discussed this. I need to stay behind in case of an electrical or gas problem, and Eric is an excellent shot. We'll stay at Elliot House and take care of the women."

Mark snickered. "Hell, Randy. Tell the truth. The women can outshoot you any day of the week."

Randy tossed a hand. "Yeah. Yeah. Whatever."

Jason allowed himself a grin. "Okay. Let's head out."

"I'm going, too," Marcus said.

Jason hesitated, glanced at Marcus's father, Matthew, for approval, then nodded. "Of course you're going."

Marcus's jaw set. "We'll find them, Jason. We'll find them."

Jason slapped the boy's shoulder. He wanted to agree, but hundreds of miles could separate them. He closed his eyes briefly. The image of Emma and Gayla dead in the woods would not haunt him.

Jason mounted his stallion. "Let's roll."

Jason and his team headed out. About an hour later, Jason raised his hand, and his men stopped. Jason rubbed his forehead. "Something just struck me. Emma and Gayla are smart." He let out a small chuckle. "And neither one of them seems to be cowardly. If the men put them in the back of the jeep, they may have jumped. We could have already passed them. I think we should let Brute walk for a while. Maybe he'll pick up their scent."

Matthew lowered his passenger, Brute, to the ground, and Marcus stuck one of Gayla's shirts under his nose, then one of Emma's. "Find Gayla and Emma, Brute."

At the mention of Gayla, Brute's ears lifted and he began to whine and sniff the ground.

"That's right, boy. Find Gayla!"

Brute let out a loud howl and bolted east down the old paved road.

Jason smiled. "Looks like they didn't jump. At least, not yet."

Jason stroked his horse's mane. "You were right, Ole Guss. You knew the whole time." Ole Guss let out a loud snort and fought the reigns to follow Brute.

"Follow that dog!" Jason yelled, let out a hoot, and gave Guss free reign.

***

Matthew talked to Jason while they let the dog and horses rest. "We need to stop and set up camp, Jason. The animals need to rest."

Jason tossed Matthew's hand from his shoulder. "No. We still have at least an hour of daylight left."

"Damn it, Jason. Killing Brute and the horses won't help the girls!"

Jason didn't answer.

"Jason," Matthew spoke calmly. "You need to remember who we're dealing with. Emma and Gayla Harding. If there's any chance of making it, those two figured it out." He squeezed Jason's shoulder again. "They're alive, Jason. I know it."

"Phhh," Marcus walked up behind them. "Heck, Gayla probably took them all out with her slingshot."

Jason didn't feel like smiling, but Marcus had conjured up a vision he couldn't shake. "Ok. We set up camp." His eyes narrowed, and his jaws clenched. "But tomorrow, we find those bastards and kill them." Jason walked toward the woods and eagerly broke limbs to start a fire.

Jason returned a few minutes later. "I apologize for trying to push the animals. Let's take care of the horses. Then we'll eat some of Emma's fine canned stew." He ruffled Brute's head. "Yeah, buddy. You can eat a whole jar." He gave a sad smile. "Gayla would like that." Jason had to walk away.

***

It had to be past midnight. Jason's eyes drooped. He was so tired. He shook his head. No way he'd go to sleep with Emma and Gayla out there. He'd lifted the cup of coffee to his lips when he heard it. Engines. Sounded like jeeps.

"Wake up! Wake up!" Jason shouted.

The men stirred and listened to the sound of approaching engines.

"Sounds like a lot more than one," Matthew said.

"Yeah," Jason checked his rifle and pistol. "We don't know how many they had or how many men." He shoved the gun in its holster. But if it's them…" He paused.

"We've got your back, Jason," Matthew said. "If it's them, it'll be their last ride."

"We have to be careful. I don't want Emma or Gayla hurt." Jason walked to the middle of the blacktop, pulled out his holstered pistol, turned on his flashlight, and aimed both at the oncoming vehicles. The other men surrounded both sides of the road.

Jason yelled out to them. "If they don't stop, take out the tires."

The men leveled their rifles.

Four jeeps rolled to a stop about fifty yards away.

"Jason," someone yelled through a loudspeaker.

Jason lowered his gun and fell to his knees. He'd recognize his father's voice anywhere. The other men began cheering as Chris ran for his son and embraced him.

***

Chris had never seen his son cry. Not since he was six and a stallion tossed him on his backside. The tears rolling down his son's cheeks shredded his heart.

"They took Emma and Gayla, Dad. Marcus found blood on the cabin floor."

"Let it go, son. Let it go." Chris tightened his embrace. They rocked back and forth as Jason wailed and pounded his father's back.

"I can't lose her dad. I can't lose her." Jason released his hold and wiped his eyes. "And Gayla." His shoulders shook.

Chris held Jason again for a moment, then kissed his forehead and placed his hands firmly on his son's shoulders. "We *will* find them. We won't leave until Emma and Gayla are home."

Chris didn't know how else to say it. From what he knew, he feared Emma and Gayla might be dead. But he wasn't lying to his son. Emma and Gayla would return home—one way or the other.

Once Jason gained control, he asked why his father and men had come.

"I don't understand how you showed up when we needed you. Did someone get the radio working?"

"It's a long story, son. Let's go to your camp, have some food and coffee, and I'll fill you in."

***

159

Jason stood by the fire with his back to the men while his father told them about the mysterious woman who showed up at Hudson Ranch. His stomach twisted. Why hadn't he listened to Emma? She was right. The chest she found *was* evil. He should have gone straight to Hudson Ranch and asked for his father's advice. If he had, Emma and Gayla would be safe. Now?

When his father finished, Jason turned to them. "I could have prevented this if I'd listened to Emma."

"How's that, Jason?" Matthew asked.

He wiped the sweat from his brow. "Do you remember Emma's dream? Trees with sparkly things chasing her and Gayla?"

Jason's father and his men scrunched their brows. The men who knew about Emma's dream nodded.

Jason hung his head. "I'm embarrassed to tell you this, but Emma found a box filled with gold coins and jewels a while back."

"What?" several men blurted.

Chris Alvise stood. His eyes narrowed.

"Yeah. It has to be worth millions." He sheepishly raised his eyes. "I told her she couldn't tell anyone." He wiped his mouth. "My... what can I call it? Distrust? Greed?" He shook his head in shame. "Telling her that may have cost Emma and Gayla their lives."

Everyone was silent.

"Emma made me re-bury the box. She said it was evil and wanted no part of it." No one said a word. "Please. Don't think I distrust you. It all happened that fast." Jason snapped his fingers.

After Matthew thought about what Jason said, he started laughing. "Dear Lord. That reminds me of before the EMP. I used to tell Laura if we won the lottery, she'd better keep her mouth shut, or one of our relatives would slit our throats." Matthew slapped his knee several times, and the other men chuckled.

Relief flooded Jason.

His father scanned the camp. "You're some fine men. We have about three hours until daylight. I say we get some sleep. No way a lazy pirate will be running about this late."

CHAPTER 24

"Gayla. Wake up."

Gayla's eyes rolled, and she responded groggily. "Aww. I was having a good dream."

"I'm sorry, Jellybean, but I made a bad mistake." Emma was talking way too fast.

Gayla's eyes popped open, and her eyes widened. "What's wrong?"

Emma pointed to the sky. Black clouds surrounded them, and there wasn't a hint of sunlight. "A storm's coming. A really bad one!" At that moment, the eastern sky erupted in streaks of lightning.

Gayla gasped, bolted upright, and stared at the thick dark horizon.

"We need food, Gayla. Lots of it. I should have let you catch all the fish you wanted. We could have been smoking it." Emma squeezed Gayla's shoulders. "Take your net to the stream and bring back enough to last a few days."

"I'll try."

Emma grabbed the lone fish resting on the stone by the fire and handed it to Gayla. "So you don't get hungry."

Gayla pushed the fish away. "No. You eat it."

"I already ate," Emma lied.

"Oh. Okay." Gayla took the fish and headed for the stream. "How many, Emma?"

"Like I said. All you can catch. I'm going to work on our sleeping quarters." She glanced back at the sky. "I have no idea how we stay dry or keep the fire going if that storm's as bad as it looks." The fear in her little sister's eyes caused Emma to catch her breath and calm the panic. "Hey, don't worry about it. Catch us a ton of fish, then help me add on to your wonderful shelter."

Emma yelled as Gayla strolled toward the stream. "Gayla. Run! Don't walk! We don't have much time!"

Gayla's eyes widened again, and she rushed to the stream.

The fear of wild animals drawn to the cooking fish worried Emma, and she shuddered. Just the small amount they'd been cooking could have brought in numerous preditors.

Emma stared at the sky and shook her head. They could be in for days of non-stop rain. They needed a fire inside the structure. She envisioned a tee-pee so the smoke could escape, but had never made one. She remembered something about a wikiup. Emma closed her eyes and hoped she could build it in time.

The fire caught her attention, and she added more limbs to feed the fading flames. Without the sun, they'd never get one started if it died.

Gayla's structure was between two trees and on flat ground. The time spent teaching Gayla to build a forest shelter hadn't been a waste of time. With a little tweaking, Gayla's fortress could become a cover for extra firewood. Emma's envisioned teepee would have a small fire where they could smoke fish and stay warm and dry.

Emma rushed to collect every broken branch and limb she could find. With only her knife, it was a challenge to cut branches of green fronds from the Juniper trees. But they needed them. The green branches wouldn't go up in flames easily and would better protect them and their precious fire. Plus, they'd provide a decent bed for her and Gayla.

Three hours later, Emma's makeshift shelter was almost complete. No rocks or stones were left behind. Every one went toward building the firepit. A fireplace if you wanted to get technical. A large flat rock lay on the top of the stone structure and covered all but the backside. Emma hoped the smoke would escape through the small opening at the top of the shelter, and the heated rocks would give them extra warmth. She sighed, partially from exhaustion and a lack of food, partly from fear that she wasn't making the right choices.

She pulled out her knife and was about to head back for more Juniper branches when she heard Gayla whimpering.

"I'm sorry, Emma. This is all I caught." She held up three small fish. Her head bent and rested on her chest.

"I'm impressed." Emma inspected Gayla's fish. "With the weather headed our way, I didn't think you'd catch a thing. I'm so proud of you." Emma wasn't exactly being truthful and assumed her little sister knew. They usually caught more fish before a storm.

Gayla wiped her eyes. "What are we gonna eat?"

162

"Hmmm." Emma rubbed her mouth. "Fill some cans with water and find more of those wild greens. When you pick them, put the stems in the water so they don't wilt."

"Okay. There were lots of them."

"Pick all you can. I'll put the fish over the fire."

Emma watched Gayla rush toward her patch of greens, then quickly scaled and skewered the fish. Nothing would go to waste, not the head, a piece of skin, or even an eyeball. What they didn't eat would be turned into soup with the greens.

Emma glanced at the darkening sky and trembled.

***

After five days of hunting, the darkening sky chilled Jason. He took a deep breath and turned to his father and the other men. "It's about to get nasty. You all need to get back to Emma's Place. The jeeps are running low on fuel." He gave a halfhearted laugh. "Don't think there's a gas station nearby."

His father was sitting beside the campfire and stood. "Jason is right. The jeeps need to return to Emma's, but leave the extra cans of gas with us. Anyone wanting to go on horseback can come back. Make sure you bring what you'll need and some more food. Some of you need to stay and care for the ranch."

"I'll come back," echoed.

Jason had a difficult time saying, thank you. "Dad's right. We may be out here for a while. The animals need to be taken care of."

"I guess we draw straws," Chris said. "At least four of you should stay at the ranch."

Chris's military team would return, along with the others. The farmers and ranchers drew straws. Matthew refused. If his son was staying, so was he.

Jason agreed. "I say we keep moving. So far, there's no sign that they've turned and headed back to Emma's Place."

"Oh, they'll be heading back there eventually, son. You can count on it. And I doubt they'd risk going too far and running out of fuel."

Jason gritted his teeth. "I'm going a few miles farther before it gets dark."

"I'm going with Jason," Marcus said.

"Guess that means I'll be going too," Matthew told the others.

"Sir," one of Chris's men interrupted. "Don't you think we need to keep one of the jeeps? If we find the girls, we may need to get them home in a hurry." He glanced at Jason then quickly averted his eyes.

"Thank you," Chris said. "You're right." He looked at his son. "And if the weather gets really nasty, we'll have some shelter."

Jason's jaw tightened. "Not me. No way I sleep protected by the jeep while Emma and Gayla may be sleeping on the ground!"

Chris glared at his son. "Really? So, proving what a badass you are is more important than staying healthy and safe so you can find the girls?"

Jason's head flew back, and he sucked air. His eyes lowered. "No, sir."

"Good! Glad you came to your senses!" Chris turned and started to walk away. Then, he turned back to face Jason. "Son. I learned something in Iraq. A dead man can help no other."

The men readied to leave so they could be home before dark and prepare for heading out early the next morning.

"Jason." His father gripped his shoulder. "Son, Brute needs to go home." He examined the horizon. "If we were expecting a light rain, Brute could track. But it doesn't appear Mother Nature is going to cooperate."

Jason's head bobbed. "I know."

Jason knelt, stroked Brute, and thanked the loyal canine for his help before addressing the men.

"Keep your eyes out on the way to Emma's. If you see anything, a fire, tracks—anything—call us. If Brute acts weird, you should trust him. He loved…" Jason realized what he'd said and cupped Brute's face. "Brute loves Gayla. Don't cha, boy?" he whispered and ruffled the dog's mane.

Brute whined and pawed the ground a few times.

As they escorted Brute to the jeep, his tail went between his legs. He broke loose and ran for Jason. He whined and pawed at Jason's leg. Marcus squatted beside him, and Brute licked his tears away. Then, the Aussie turned, ran, and pounced into the back of the jeep. As they pulled away, the dog barked and walked in circles.

"What is it with animals? That damned dog knows. I swear, Brute knows," Jason said.

***

The men had been gone for about an hour when they radioed back. Jason's father answered. "What do you see?"

"Smoke from a fire, Sir. We stopped about a hundred yards this side of it in case someone's watching the road. Should we investigate?"

"No. Hold your ground. Marcus is the only one who can ID them. We're on our way. Don't let Brute take off."

They left one man behind to tend the horses, and the others loaded into the jeep.

Chris glanced at the sky. "All hell is about to break loose, son. Not sure if that's good or bad."

"I don't care about the storm. I just want to find Emma and Gayla."

His pleading eyes broke Chris's heart, and he squeezed his son's hand. Why did he promise to bring the girls home—no matter what? If the camp his men spotted was Jordan Dean and his men, it didn't mean the girls were still alive. They could be anywhere. He should have never made such a promise.

"We'll do all we can, Jason. We'll do all we can."

They'd been on the road for about ten minutes when someone shouted over the radio. "Shot fired, Sir."

Chris grabbed the handheld. "At you? How many?"

"Not at us. In the woods. Only one shot. May just be someone shooting dinner."

"We'll be there as fast as we can. Let's pray it's Jordan Dean, and the girls are with him and safe."

CHAPTER 25

Jordan Dean had been pleased when one of his men rushed back to camp. He'd decided to move closer to the ranch and wait a few days. It had been a rough ride. Jordan had his men drive through the woods instead of getting back on the old paved road. They had to make dozens of stops to chop trees and clear the way, but Jordan and his men agreed it was a smart move. They'd done their best to camouflage where they'd made the turn off the main road. With the storm coming, it was unlikely their tracks would be found.

Not knowing how many he was up against made Jordan uncomfortable. When the lookout told him several men on horseback had just passed, Jordan's plans changed again. There was no telling how many stayed behind. But Jordan bet almost every man was out looking for the girls. Best he got rid of the ones looking first. They'd wait for them to return and wipe them out. There was no need to go to "Emma's Place" until they were gone. Jordan's nose curled at the remembrance of the sign. It wasn't Emma's Place. It was his!

Not long after his gloating ended, Jordan threw a tantrum. Several jeeps loaded with men and military passed. He had no way of knowing if they were merely passing through or if they were searching for the missing girls. He couldn't take the chance. They had to wait it out. What were a few more days after twenty years?

***

Jordan sat up and stretched after his afternoon nap. Almost time to waste more of his precious whiskey on his antsy men. They were becoming more agitated by the day. He was about to get out of the jeep when he noticed the sky. Great. The storm is about to hit. The smell of smoke sent him into a rage, and he slung open the door. "What the hell's wrong with you? Put that damned fire out."

"We need to cook before the storm hits," one man growled.

"I told you. No damned fires until after dark. You want someone spotting the smoke?" His lips gnarled. "Put it out."

"Go to hell!" another spat. "We're hungry."

Jordan pulled out his pistol. They'd gotten a little too cocky. He needed to make it clear who was in control. He aimed and pulled the trigger. The man who told him to go to hell collapsed.

"Your guns," he barked at the other two. "Toss them on the ground and back away."

Jordan bent to pick up the pistols. "You won't be needing these until the riders come back." One man took a step toward him. "Don't think I won't kill you both," he snarled. "And without me, you'll never find the treasure. Put out the damned fire and drag his body away from camp."

***

Jordan could kick himself. He was down a man. Worse yet, he doubted the other two would let him see daylight. He'd made the mistake of letting them know where the cabin was. Unless they were complete idiots, they'd know the treasure was there. No. They couldn't see daybreak. What a pain it would be to dig up the chests by himself.

He approached them, apologized for shooting the other man, and lifted a bottle of bourbon. "With him gone, your shares just got a lot bigger."

They smiled. Jordan filled their glasses, and the idiots drank. A few minutes later, they lay dead.

Jordan turned up the bottle and took a swig just as a loud rumble broke the silence, and the sky filled with light. Thick black clouds were rolling in from the east. He flinched as the sky again lit in flames. "Damn it!" he shouted. He was slipping. The old Jordan would have tricked them into walking far from camp before he shot them. Now he had to drag their sorry asses away before the storm hit.

***

"More shots fired, sir."

"Hold your ground. Like you said, it could be someone hunting dinner." Maneuvering the old overgrown roads was a challenge at times. He pushed the mic. "We're moving as fast as we can."

Chris looked at his son's paling face and squeezed his hand. "Keep the faith, son. At this point, it's all we can do."

Jason clenched a handful of hair then brushed it back. "What if it was Emma and Gayla? What if the shots were at them?"

"Stop it. Stop it now!" Chris barked. "We don't even know if it's Jordan. Pull yourself together!"

A few minutes later, they met up with the others.

"We go on foot," Chris said.

The sky darkened as they inched through the forest, and the constant rumble of thunder and flashes of lightning was closing in. When they neared the camp, Chris handed the binoculars to Marcus. "Are these the men we're looking for?"

Marcus raised the binoculars. "I only see one man." He inhaled. "Wait! He's dragging someone into the woods! That's him! The man who was in charge! I don't see Emma or Gayla."

Chris motioned for his men to encircle from the rear and search the campsite for signs of the girls. He glanced at Jason and whispered, "Let's move in closer, but we let my men do their job."

The sky was black, and the rain was beginning to fall. Chris watched as Jordan laughed and chugged whiskey. He froze when soldiers stormed the camp. "Who the hell are you?"

"On the ground!"

"Go to hell," Jordan spat.

The men inched closer, and one spoke. "We found a few of what we assume were your friends, dead in the woods. Mr. Alvise would like a word with you. Oh. You might want to consider disarming."

The leveled military rifles seemed to humble Jordan. He dropped a pistol from his waistband, waved his hands, and laughed. "This must be some horrible misunderstanding. I'm alone and found the jeeps and clothes. I meant no harm."

"Shut up!" Chris stepped out of the shadows.

Before he could react, Jason bolted past him and grabbed Jordan around the neck. "Where are they? Where are Emma and Gayla?"

Jordan's legs swung in mid-air, and he tugged at the arm cutting off his oxygen. "Don't know," he choked out.

Chris struggled to free Jordan from Jason's grip. "Let him go. If you kill him, we may never find the girls!"

Jason released his grip, and Jordan fell to the ground, gasping for air.

"My son asked you a question. Where are they?"

"I have no idea what you're talking about." Jordan rubbed his throat.

Marcus stepped forward and yelled. "You're a liar. You came to the farm and took Emma and Gayla. There was blood on the kitchen floor."

Jordan's lips turned into a snarl. "The kid doesn't know what he's talking about. I've never seen him before."

Jason lunged for Jordan. Chris allowed him to pummel the man for several seconds before intervening. "Not so tough without your gun, are you Jordan Dean?"

Jordan's head shot up. His mouth slack and eyes wide.

"That's right. We know who you are. We had a visitor at our ranch. She said you'd held her captive for twenty years."

"Elizabeth's a liar! She was with me willingly!"

Chris smiled. "Elizabeth? So that's her real name? She told us her name was Jane." He smirked. "Thank you for confirming that, and also that you are indeed Jordan Dean."

Jordan spat next to Chris's boots. Chris smiled. "So, do you want to tell us where the girls are? Or would you prefer I allow my son to beat the answer out of you?"

Jason took a step toward him, and Jordan cowered. "Alright, alright."

CHAPTER 26

"Sierra," Chris's voice cracked over the radio. "We caught Jordan Dean."

"Thank God." She clutched her chest, but a long silence forced her to sit. "Emma? Gayla?" A tear rolled down her cheek as the quiet continued.

"Sierra, Jason's a mess."

She could sense her husband's fear. Sierra didn't want to hear his answer, not really, but asked anyway, "Please. Please tell me you found them. Tell me Emma and Gayla are at least alive." Sierra's throat constricted. It hurt to speak.

"I wish I could. Jordan told us they jumped out of the back of the jeep somewhere. We don't know where or even if he's telling the truth. He'd killed the men who were with him."

Again, the silence.

"Jason is still looking for them. He's going to need you here." He gripped the mic a moment too long, and Sierra heard his sobs before he went quiet. After a pause, he spoke again. This time, there was no attempt to hide his sorrow. "I promised him, Sierra. I promised Jason we'd bring the girls home. I don't know what came over me. How could I have promised such a thing?"

Sierra lost control, and Frank took the mic. "Frank here, Chris. I'll get things together and have Sierra there as soon as I can."

"Thank you, Frank. Keep this quiet. And make sure someone keeps an eye on his girlfriend until she's arrested."

"So, she *is* his girlfriend?"

"Yeah. And her name is Elizabeth, not Jane. The only bright spot in this whole mess was watching Jordan Dean's reaction when I told him about our visitor. That, and how President Cully was sending a chopper to take him in."

"Are you going back out to look for Emma and Gayla?"

"Yeah. The chopper did a few flyovers but didn't see any sign of them. Me, Jason, Mathew, and Marcus are about to head back out. We're going to scour every inch until we find them and bring them home—just like I promised. We're going by horseback, so we'll only have the handheld radios. Oh, and Frank, bring batteries. A lot of them. It could take a while."

Sierra took the mic. "I love you, Chris." She shoved the mic into Frank's hand and rushed from the room.

***

Frank's wife, Barbara, wanted to come along. Frank convinced her it was best if she stayed and watched Jordan's girlfriend.

"We can't tell anyone what's going on. If word spreads about that woman's true identity, it could be a big problem. There's most likely a lot of gold buried somewhere near Emma's. We can't risk anyone getting any funny ideas."

"Okay. So, no one can know about Jordan?"

"That's right."

"What do I tell everyone when they arrest her?"

"Only that she was a wanted woman."

Sierra walked back into the room and ran for the door. She snatched it open, looked outside, and let out a gust of air.

"What in the world?" Barbara asked.

"Sorry. I thought someone was at the window," Sierra said. "Guess I'm getting paranoid."

***

Elizabeth ran to her room. She wanted to curse the fact that Jordan was alive, but part of her was glad. Outsmarting him? Picturing his anger as she claimed the riches he'd stolen as her own? Ahh. What pleasure that would bring.

The habit of watching the radio room and listening in had paid off. They knew who she was, and Elizabeth needed to get out of there. Frank and Sierra would be leaving soon. She wouldn't be far behind.

She scanned the small room. What few clothes Elizabeth owned would have to stay. No way she wanted Barbara to know she was gone and alert anyone. Her smile grew. It was all there—every ounce of gold and the gems.

Washing day was a blessing. She snatched a pillowcase from the clothesline, a few pieces of clothing, and stuffed them inside the pillowcase. Food. Rusty and Tracey didn't like her. Perhaps, if she told them she wanted to be alone and would rather eat in her room for a few

171

days, they would give her a few jars of food. She couldn't pretend to be ill and risk a trip to the infirmary.

Elizabeth was right. Tracey happily handed her several jars of canned food, some fresh fruit and vegetables, and a loaf of bread. She added her food to the stash and hid it in the woods behind the stable. She'd need more food. Elizabeth decided to volunteer at the greenhouse but had to hurry. If Frank and Sierra got too far ahead, she might lose her way. Elizabeth smirked as she offered her services.

After gathering a few cucumbers and tomatoes, Elizabeth slipped out the door and headed for the stable. It was easy to convince the young man to saddle a horse. Elizabeth's over exaggerated admiration of his bulging muscles and sprouting facial hair garnered her one of the finest horses at Hudson Ranch. She wouldn't be taking her worthless piece of flesh. Her mare would stay. One less chance for Barbara to realize she was gone.

Sierra and Frank had taken a wagon. It would take them several days to make the trip. Elizabeth wasn't willing to sleep in the open air, and she needed something to start a fire.

"Sweetie," she cooed and massaged the stable boy's shoulder. "Any chance you can get me a small tent, a sleeping bag, and some matches?" She batted her lashes. "I need to spend the night out there." She spread her hand toward the outdoors. "I miss it terribly. But, of course, it would have to be our secret. I wouldn't want anyone worrying about me."

"Okay. And I can get that stuff for you." He smiled and rushed away.

Weapons. Chris Alvise insisted she turn hers over when she arrived at Hudson Ranch. He said they were forbidden until the community felt a newcomer was safe.

"Wait," she yelled for the young man. "Do you think I should take a weapon?" She widened her eyes and put a finger to her lips.

He looked at his boots, and she took notice of the slight pink his face took on. "I could come with you if you want. I'm a great shot."

She cocked her head sideways. "I'm sure you are, and it's sweet of you to offer. Maybe next week. Right now, I need some alone time. Do you mind?"

"Of course not, Ms. Jane." The young man tossed his shoulders back. "You wait right here. I'll be back in a few minutes." He stopped and turned. "Oh, you'll need some water and food. And something to cook with. I'll take care of it for you."

Elizabeth batted her lashes again. "Thank you, sweetheart."

The boy grinned and gave a thumbs up.

Extra food, tent, matches, water, and firearms. What else did she need? Elizabeth held her laughter until he was out of sight.

There were probably a dozen people she'd have to get rid of. She thought of the map, pulled out her copy, and smiled. One small box would give her enough money to hire men to help her. There was no way she could do it all on her own.

Sierra and Frank had a three-hour head start. Once the eager young man loaded her horse, Elizabeth headed out. She paid close attention, so she didn't miss the spot where the wagon veered off the road. About an hour later, she saw the tracks and sneered. "I'm right behind you, Sierra. I'm right behind you." She kicked her horse into a run to close the gap.

**

Four terrifying, miserable nights outdoors with only a small fire for comfort had taken its toll. The thought of suffering another night, possibly more, made her anxious. Elizabeth watched from the forest as Frank and Sierra met with the others at the girl's ranch. Damn. There were a lot more people than she'd imagined.

Elizabeth pulled out her map and searched for what she assumed would be stashes of treasure. Even the smallest should be more than enough to buy help. Her problem would be finding the right time to dig it up. Dig it up? Dig it up? Her head spun, and she clenched her temples. She didn't bring a shovel. Idiot. The night sounds were scary, but fear wouldn't stop her now.

Elizabeth couldn't risk the luxury of a fire. Dinner was cold stew and a cucumber. Then, she waited. Once everything went dark, Elizabeth rushed toward the barn. She slid the door open, closed it, and pulled out the pack of matches. Her fingers shook, partly from fear, partly from excitement. She snapped the thin stick against the box. Light. Not much. Elizabeth cupped the small flame and turned to take in her surroundings. She grinned when she saw the oil lamp.

Shovels. Several leaned against the barn wall. The milk cow let out a moo, and Elizabeth licked her lips. She wasn't sleeping outside tonight. Tonight, fresh milk and hay would keep her full and warm and help her sleep.

Elizabeth ran for her horse and bags. She wasn't sure what to do with the horse. It couldn't stay. She slapped it's flanks and yelled. The mare bolted. Good. Elizabeth dragged her bags to the barn and searched for a hiding spot. She drank her fill of fresh milk and fell asleep.

The next morning, the barn exploded with activity. Elizabeth woke, barely breathed, and hoped she was invisible. When the commotion ended, she made her way to the barn door and peeked out. Sierra hugged Frank before he mounted a horse and rode off. Elizabeth smiled. She bet Frank was going to meet up with Chris. Good. Good. Now it was just her and Sierra.

***

Sierra scanned the cabin, then closed her eyes and tried to imagine Emma and Gayla sitting at the kitchen table as they planned their day. How could she face her son in his hour of such pain? How could she possibly console him? Her mind reached for old memories. She should have known he loved Emma, even when he was a young boy. How many times had Jason questioned her and Chris about Emma? How many times over the years had he wondered if she was okay? Some may think it silly, but Sierra knew that Jason had fallen in love with the little girl the day they met.

Sierra's head rested on the table, her hand lightly rubbing the worn wood. Was she supposed to break down when she saw Jason? Or was she supposed to get it out now and be strong for him when he returned? A salty pool of water dampened her cheek and the tabletop. Sierra raised her head and wiped the mess away with a dishtowel that someone had tossed on the table. A grin crossed her lips. She imagined Emma would have none of that. She looked around again. Organized. Not a thing out of place.

Sierra found herself drawn to the rows of books lining the upper half of one wall. She ran her fingers across them and grinned. The genre first, then author, and alphabetically. That had to be John Harding. Chris said he was an avid reader and had a vast library. The lowest shelf on the left held the 2019 version of The World Book Encyclopedia, a worn, leather-bound dictionary, and a family bible. The shelf next to it held only magazines. Sierra found herself chuckling. Chris told her that Harding had every magazine ever published. Her husband had considered it ridiculous.

Sierra took a few, sat on the sofa, and flipped through the pages. No, Chris. You were wrong. Not ridiculous. Without the old magazines, Emma and Gayla would have no idea how the world used to be or how it could be again one day.

When Sierra stood to return the magazines to the shelf, her eyes fell on the single hardback on the coffee table. She sat and caught her breath. *The*

174

Highwaymen. For Emma to keep the book on the coffee table meant it held special meaning to her. Sierra grasped the book, held it to her chest, and rocked. "I have dozens of their paintings. You can have them." She placed the book on the coffee table and whispered, "But you have to come home to get them." Sierra stood and scanned the room again. Her eyes rested on one of the Highwaymen's paintings hanging between the two front windows. She approached to see who'd painted it and gasped. The signature was Emma Harding. Sierra stared for several seconds before sitting on the sofa. The little girl she'd met years earlier had grown into a gifted woman.

Sierra refused to cry. Like Jason, Marcus, and Randy, she believed Emma and Gayla were alive. There was only one reason for Jordan to take the girls instead of killing them then and there. He needed them. Sierra inhaled and brushed her cheek. Jordan could have taken them hundreds of miles from home. If they did indeed jump, they could have died. If they didn't, how would they ever find their way home?

Sierra shook her head. No! Emma was smart enough to figure out how to survive alone all these years! No way they were dead. They were alive, and Emma would make damned sure they found their way home.

***

The morning chores seemed to last forever. Then the barn door closed, and it was quiet. Elizabeth could finally breathe. She took some of her stash for later and hid the rest. The forest gave her cover as she paced and kept an eye on the cabin.

Several women visited Sierra around sunrise with what appeared to be dishes of food. A sliver of drool eased from the corner of Elizabeth's mouth. She licked it away and rubbed her rumbling belly. Most likely they'd be bringing Sierra lunch and dinner. Elizabeth would watch today and figure out their routine. Tomorrow? Tomorrow she'd show Sierra a thing or two before she dug up some of the treasure.

Elizabeth opened a jar of stew, spooned the cold concoction onto a plate, then ripped off a chunk of bread. The loaf was stale but dipped in the juices tasted like heaven. She smiled and stirred the plate. No more jars of cold stew after tomorrow. She glanced at the cabin. Tomorrow, the bitch would pay, and Elizabeth would finally be on her way to the life she deserved.

***

The sun had barely been up an hour. Breakfast was on hold. Perhaps they'd find something soon.

"Emma, I'm tired and hungry."

Emma stopped, lifted the spear, and slid the blade beneath the wire handle of the fire can. She placed the smoldering tin of embers on the ground and lowered the sled that carried their collection. "I was holding out until you complained. I'm hungry, too. Let's eat the rest of the squirrel and have some water."

They sat beneath a large burr oak and ate in silence. Emma felt a pang of guilt as Gayla licked her fingers clean. The little bit of squirrel wasn't nearly enough to stop their grumbling stomachs. "Maybe you should rest. I'll hunt for a while. We should stop in an hour or two and make a shelter. I'm running out of energy."

"No," Gayla said. "I'll help hunt. I'd rather have food than shelter tonight."

"Alright. Let's dig a hole for the fire can and feed it so it doesn't go out. We'll build a fire if we get something to cook."

"You know, I would have just left it sitting on the ground before you showed me that."

Emma grinned. "Just made sense to me. With all our other problems, we sure don't need to start a forest fire, and we darned sure don't want it to go out."

They each grabbed a tin can and began to dig.

"That should be deep enough." Emma dumped the contents of the fire can and slowly added tinder. "We have to keep the coals going." She wagged her finger at Gayla. "If there's one thing you need to pay attention to, it's the embers! If something happens to me, you keep them going!"

Gayla shuddered. "Don't say that!"

"Stop it!" Emma snarled, stood, and brushed the dirt from her hands. "This is life, Gayla!" She thrust her hands into her hips and frowned. "I have no intention of going anywhere other than home! But we never know what lies around the corner."

'Well, don't talk like you might be gone."

Emma shook her head. "I don't plan on it. But Gayla, you know anything can happen."

Emma wrapped her arm around her little sister and nodded. "Let's head that way." She rubbed Gayla's arm. "Let's see what you and your slingshot can get us for dinner."

About five minutes into their hunting trip, Emma gasped.

"What is it?" Gayla's eyes widened.

Emma raised her hand and pointed her finger toward the partial blacktop that stood out beneath the overgrown grass.

Gayla stepped back. "It's the road. The bad guys might see us."

Emma placed her hand on Gayla's shoulder. "It's been about two weeks, Jellybean. I doubt they're looking for us, but maybe Jason and Marcus haven't given up. I say we get our sled and walk on the road. We'll hunt as we go. Plus, the road is bound to take us to people."

"Okay, but I'm so hungry. We've only had a couple of squirrels since the storm. We should have stayed at the stream. At least there was fish and water."

She couldn't look at Gayla. The decision to head out so soon was a bad one, but the fishing net was worthless after Emma used it to secure their structure. After the storm, it was no more than dangling threads. She should have salvaged it and tried to stock up on food before they headed out.

She couldn't let Gayla know how anxious she was. Emma had barely slept since their ordeal began. She always needed to be on alert. For Gayla's sake, she had to appear in control. But Emma was no fool. She knew the many dangers the darkness of Wyoming held.

Their dad had invested heavily in ammunition. Gayla would be terrified to go outside if she knew how much went toward fending off wolves and bears that threatened their livestock. Her parents said very few predators used to live in their area, but the animal population had exploded after the EMP.

Now, here they were, alone in the woods. Emma glanced at her makeshift spear. Her knife was strapped to a long sturdy branch when she wasn't using it to chop. The wooden spear with the blade attached, and the bow, were all that stood between them and Mother Nature's predators. Emma chuckled. She couldn't forget Gayla's slingshot and spear.

Gayla grabbed Emma's arm, placed a finger to her lips, and pulled her down. She nodded toward a doe eating grass a few yards away.

Emma had never taken a doe. She'd never had the need.

Emma's stomach rumbled, and she glanced at Gayla. There was nothing she wouldn't do for her.

The doe was there for a reason. Gayla needed food, and so did she. If she brought her down, she'd thank the sweet lady for saving them. Emma slowly lifted her bow and zeroed in. "I'm sorry little lady," Emma whispered just before releasing her arrow.

The doe ran a few feet, then fell to the ground. Emma rushed toward her as she unstrapped her knife from the spear.

"I'm sorry sweet lady." Emma knelt and used her knife to end the doe's misery. "Thank you."

Emma searched the area for a low-lying branch then tossed the rest of her paracord to Gayla. "Can you shimmy up there and tie it? We need to hang the deer so I can clean her."

Gayla crawled up the tree, and together they lifted the deer.

"Gather wood. We need to build a fire and camp," Emma said as she began processing the deer.

"Okay." Gayla scouted for firewood and anything they could use to build a shelter. She brought her first stack of wood to where Emma was cleaning the deer.

"Wait!" Emma said before Gayla could drop the timbers. "We need to find a place away from here. I don't want animals smelling the scent and harassing us tonight." Emma looked around. "Put the wood down, and let's find a good spot."

A few minutes later, Emma stopped. "Perfect!" She couldn't believe their luck. A boulder at least ten feet long and surrounded by juniper trees would be the perfect camp. "Look at this!" Emma threw her arms wide and spun. "We can start a fire by the rock. We'll have plenty of heat and food tonight! We'll cook the venison over there." Emma pointed.

Emma and Gayla embraced, then rushed back to the deer.

As Emma skinned, Gayla built a fire and set up poles for cooking and smoking the meat.

"Let's get her skin dried as much as we can." Emma briskly rubbed Gayla's shoulders and hugged her. "Can you imagine? It'll be like we have a warm blanket tonight!"

Gayla jumped up and down and clapped her hands.

Emma threw her head back and laughed. "That's not all. Tonight, we eat ribs. We'll strip the other bones of meat and dry it today. The bones will make some great broth later."

***

After they had the last of the meat hanging over the fire, Emma sat on the ground. "We'll be eating ribs soon."

"I can't wait! I am so hungry." Gayla grabbed her stomach.

Emma turned her stained hands. "I hate to waste our water, but I have to get this off. No way I want to smell like a blood-soaked doe."

She grabbed a can and began digging.

"What are you doing?" Gayla asked.

"I'm going to wash the blood off with dirt first, then you can pour a tiny bit of water in my hands." After she cleaned her knife, she handed it to Gayla and nodded toward a juniper tree. "Can you cut some branches? I'll rub them all over myself to cover the scent." She glanced at the deer on the cooking rack. "Cut as many branches as you can. When the meat's done, I'll wrap it in juniper before we hang it from a tree. It may help keep the critters away."

**

Frank met up with Chris, Jason, Matthew, and Marcus. He hugged Jason and promised to do all he could to help find the girls. "We decided Brute should come. Actually, Brute decided that for himself."

He went to Marcus. "Young man." Frank held out his hand for a shake. "I hear you're quite the hero."

"No, sir. A hero would have saved them."

"Nonsense. And risk your life knowing you were the only one who could warn the others. A true hero would have done exactly what you did."

Everyone's attention turned to the Australian Sheppard. He was frantically sniffing and walking one way then the other. "What is it, boy?" Jason asked. Brute began to bark before breaking into a trot.

"Jason, Marcus. Be prepared." Chris's jaw tightened. "That's all I'm saying."

Jason looked away. His father's expression said it all. "I know, Dad. I know. But I have to find them—one way or the other." Jason kicked Gus into a run and followed Brute's lead.

A few minutes later, Brute was rummaging through a makeshift teepee. Jason eased himself from his horse. His legs grew weak and barely supported him. As he tried to force his way toward the campsite, his father grabbed his arm. "I'll go in, son."

He bit his lip and nodded. Just then, Brute came running toward him with something in his mouth. Jason's hand shook, and he took the cloth the dog offered. His throat ached as he stared at the piece of Gayla's shirt.

179

He turned toward his father. "I brought Gayla a shirt with this same design. I know it's hers."

Chris looked inside the shelter. Empty. Then he, Frank, Matthew, and Marcus searched nearby. Jason sat inside the small fortress and touched and smelled every item.

After several minutes, he walked outside. Relief flooded him when he was greeted with smiles.

"Son, if that's Gayla's shirt, I have a feeling the girls are alive."

Marcus lunged at Jason. "I told you. I told you. I knew they weren't dead."

"Jason, look at all the items here. Cans, bottles, and if I'm not mistaken," Chris pointed to the covering, "that's a piece of fishing net holding the branches in place." He grinned and shook his head. "There's a stream down there. I bet the girls used the net right up till the day we had that bad storm. Emma was smart to use it to keep the cover from blowing away."

Jason laughed for the first time in two weeks. "That's my Emma. Let's find them and take them home."

They mounted their horses, and Jason gave Brute the go-ahead. "Alright, boy. Find Gayla."

Brute backed up a few steps, barked, then headed off.

***

They'd been walking for about four hours and had finished off the last of the deer earlier. Their best efforts hadn't thwarted an animal from stealing most of the deer two nights before. Emma prayed they'd find more food soon. And water. She was deep in thought when Gayla whipped out her slingshot, and a squirrel hit the ground. Gayla smiled and winked. "Looks like we eat tonight."

Emma grabbed her and tried to swing her in the air. "Never mind. You're too heavy," she giggled before plopping Gayla on the ground. "I guess this means we set up camp. I'm so hungry I could almost eat it raw."

As dinner roasted over the coals, the girls talked about how lucky they were. "I wonder how many people died when the lights went out because they didn't know the stuff we do?"

Emma was silent for a while before she let out a heavy sigh. "Mom and Dad said millions died."

"How sad." Gayla shook her head. "I can't even imagine millions of people. When I was little, and you read me stories about the big cities, I thought you were making it up. When I learned to read, I was jealous of them."

"You were jealous? Why? They died."

"Because I never got to see all the things I read about. When I read, I try to picture what it would have been like to see those movies where people acted out the story. And the pictures of houses and cars and stuff they had? Well, I wished I could have had them."

Emma never told Gayla how she got to watch movies before they moved to the farm. Every Saturday night, the entire town of Riverton would pack into the school gym. Emma shook her head. One more thing to thank Jason's parents for. It was their idea to have movie night at Hudson Ranch. As the mayor of Riverton, her dad had simply copied them.

Emma squeezed Gayla's hand. "You'll have them one day, Jellybean. I promise."

That evening, Emma sat by the fire and watched Gayla as she slept. Her mind drifted back to the chest of treasure. It had to be the reason the men became so angry about not finding a map. Emma was glad it all happened so fast. If she'd shown them where the treasure was buried, they would have surely killed them both. Gayla didn't know about the chest, and Emma wasn't mentioning it now. Perhaps the bad men went back to find the chest, and her friends had stopped them. She prayed no one at the farm was injured or killed because of it.

Until Gayla confessed her jealousy, Emma wanted nothing to do with the gold and jewels. Now she was rethinking things. Gayla deserved better. A lot of people did. Emma had no idea what the chest was worth, but Jason said she was a rich woman. When they made it home, she'd use the gold and jewels to help as many people as possible, especially little kids. She found herself praying it was still there.

Emma drifted off to sleep, and for the first time in a while, she dreamed of the trees with sparkly things. But they weren't chasing her. They seemed happy as their branches swayed slowly in the breeze.

The smell of roasting squirrel woke Emma. "Thanks, Gayla."

"I decided we needed a full belly today."

Gayla stepped away from the fire, and Emma's mouth slackened. A rabbit hung over the coals next to what was left of the squirrel. "I don't believe it. You, little sister, are remarkable."

Gayla grinned. "Yeah. I had a good teacher."

181

CHAPTER 27

Emma lowered the sled and wiped her parched mouth. She picked up the almost empty jug of water and shivered. They drank sparingly, but the bottle was running dry. They couldn't make it much longer without water, and they'd seen no sign of it since leaving their first camp. They'd used leaves to collect as much as they could, but the small amount only added a few sips a day.

The few prickly pear cactus loaded with fruit they'd found had been a Godsend. Without the fluid and fruit it provided, Emma doubted they'd have made it. Emma had skewered them and roasted them over a fire to burn off the needles. They lasted a few days, but they hadn't found any since.

She handed the water bottle to Gayla. "Take a sip. But only a sip."

Gayla stepped back and shook her head. "No. I'm okay."

Emma shoved the bottle closer. "Drink!"

Gayla took a small sip, then a larger one, and handed the container back to Emma. She turned the bottle up, filled her mouth, and let it sit for a moment before swallowing.

"We have to find water soon. Dad said there were streams everywhere. It's only a matter of time before we find one. And he told me that, just like roads, all rivers lead to men." Emma raised her head and stared at the sky before letting out a gust of air. "At least, that's how it used to be."

"But we've been walking for days, Emma. What if we don't find any?"

"We will. Keep an eye out for large leaves so we can collect more dew, and look for cactus."

"Mmm." Gayla licked her lips. "I'd love to find some more cactus. Some of those pieces tasted so sweet."

"Yeah. I don't think they grow too good with all of the shade. If we come upon a wide-open space, I say we give it a good search." Emma exhaled.

They'd walked for several hours when Emma stopped. She sniffed the air. "Gayla, do you smell that?"

"Gayla curled her nose and inhaled. "Smell what?"

"Mint."

"You mean like those herbs you grow and say we have to keep in pots, or they'll take over the world?"

"Yes."

Gayla sniffed again. "I don't smell it."

"Well, let's hope my nose isn't playing tricks on me. If that's field mint, it means water is nearby."

Emma followed the scent, and it grew stronger.

"I smell it, Emma! I smell it!" Gayla yelled.

Their pace increased.

About thirty minutes later, Emma froze. The sound of trickling water caused her heart to skip a beat. Gayla grabbed her around the waist and held her tight. "You did it, Emma. You found water."

Emma's voice was husky. "I got lucky, Gayla. We got lucky." She kissed the top of her little sister's head. "I say we fill the jugs, have a bath, and make a shelter. Then we go hunting."

They ran for the stream, ready to take their fill of the fresh water before filling the jugs. Emma placed her hand on Gayla's chest. "Wait."

Gayla looked down at the flowing water. "Oh, Emma."

Emma pulled out her arrows and loaded her bow. Gayla readied her spear. Five large fish would soon roast over the coals.

Gayla gathered firewood while Emma prepared the fish. As dinner roasted, Emma and Gayla soaked in the cool spring.

"This feels so good, Emma."

"Yeah. But we need to make a shelter and hang our clothes next to the fire to dry. It won't seem so warm in a couple of hours."

When they made their way back to camp, Gayla began to strip. Emma paused. "Gayla. Our shirts will dry fast. Maybe we should just hang our jeans up to dry."

Gayla looked confused. "I'm already getting chilly." She slid off her shirt and hung it on a stick next to the fire.

Emma looked away. Gayla had no idea how much she'd matured. She took off her jeans and hung them next to Gayla's clothes. "I'm going to look for branches for our shelter. So help me, if you let our clothes go up in flames…"

Gayla giggled. "I'll watch them. No way I want to go home naked!"

Emma had wandered about a hundred yards from where they'd set up camp when a distant sound caught her attention. She wasn't sure what it was until it passed overhead. She yelled through the woods, "Gayla, wave your arms. Wave your arms. It's a helicopter. Find a clearing. They might see us. Wave your arms." Emma's heart sank as the chopper disappeared, and she fell to her knees. After a moment, she let it go and got back to work. It was doubtful they would be able to help anyway.

Perfect. Emma spied a juniper tree with dozens of low-lying limbs and began chopping. She stacked the last one on top and took a deep breath before she had to drag them back to camp. As she bent and reached for the bottom limb, another sound caught her attention. She rubbed her ears. Perhaps she was hearing things. It was faint, but she was sure she heard cows.

Emma raised her hands, palms facing away from her as if to silence the forest. There it was again. Her heart raced. She had to stay calm. It could be home, but it might be a wild heard. She decided to keep it from Gayla. She raced back to camp, pulling the limbs for their shelter, and trying not to shred her bare legs in the process.

Gayla had been tending the fish and drying their clothes, but still managed to find several sturdy limbs to support their shelter.

"I heard the noise. I heard you yell. That was a helicopter, wasn't it?" The naked Gayla ran toward her sister.

Emma looked away and slipped on her still damp jeans. "Yes. But they wouldn't have known what to do if they saw us. Put your clothes on, and let's build a shelter. I want to see if I can get a few more fish before it gets too late. Then, we get a good night's rest."

"Okay."

"In the morning, we head back to the road."

***

The next morning, Emma and Gayla headed out with a full jug of water and several roasted fish. She wanted to tell Gayla about hearing the cows but didn't want to get her hopes up.

The road didn't look like the ones in magazines, but it was easy enough to see even with years of growth springing up through the asphalt. She thought of the road close to home. Every year, before winter, her father and Mr. Elliott left for a few days to clear the path of sprouting trees.

"We have to keep the road as passable as we can, Emma. It's our way to the train station."

After her father died, Emma had taken over the job. But she only went as far as she could in a day.

Emma saw the bent and flattened weeds. They went in both directions for as far as she could see. There were no vehicles at her farm. The tracks had to be from the bad men. Emma shuddered.

They had been walking for about two hours when Emma suggested they stop for some water and rest.

Gayla didn't respond. She gazed off in the distance, and a tear dripped from her chin.

Emma dropped the sled and held her sister. "We'll be okay, Jellybean. I promise."

Gayla's hand raised, and she pointed. "Emma, that's my tree. The one with the fat limb a few feet off the ground."

Emma squinted and followed the direction of Gayla's finger. "What are you talking about?"

"Don't get mad. I know I wasn't supposed to go to the road. But until the others came, I used to sneak away and sit on that big limb. I'd pretend people were driving by, and I'd wave at them." Gayla burst into tears. "But no one ever came."

Emma hugged Gayla again. "It's okay. It's okay." Then she held her and wiped Gayla's cheek. "Jellybean, a lot of things look the same..."

"No." Gayla's mouth trembled. "I'm telling you, that's *my* tree. There's a road beside it, and our house will be at the end of it."

"Okay. Okay." Emma handed Gayla a jug of water. "Drink."

Gayla smiled, chugged the water, then wiped her lips. "We're almost home. I can drink all I want."

She handed the jug back to Emma, and she took a few sips. What would Gayla do when they reached the tree and realized she was wrong? Emma's throat constricted. She'd find out in a few minutes.

Emma's legs felt like heavy metal as she made her way toward the tree. Soon, it was painful. Gayla whistled and skipped. Emma's throat grew tighter.

As they neared, Gayla's arms flapped like an Osprey taking flight. "Hurry, Emma. Hurry."

Emma was at least a hundred feet behind. She watched as Gayla climbed on the lower branch of the tree. "Home's that-a-way." Gayla pointed, giggled, and wrapped her arms around the oak.

Trapped in a fog, one foot barely stepped in front of the other. Emma's breathing deepened. A dirt road did indeed run next to the tree. The sled slipped from her grasp, and she scanned the area. Tracks. Tracks everywhere. Horses, wagons, dogs, vehicles. People! Emma fell to her knees. Gayla jumped from the tree and embraced her sister.

"We're home, Emma. We're home."

CHAPTER 28

Hopefully, it would be Elizabeth's last miserable night in the barn. After everyone finished their morning ritual, she rushed toward the house and crawled beneath it. She wanted to hear what the women talked about this morning. The day before, they worked in the garden. It was too close to the house for Elizabeth to get rid of Sierra and search for the gold. She hoped they'd move on to something else today. Maybe Sierra would go with them. Elizabeth could take care of Sierra another day. It was more important to dig up some treasure and get out of there.

When the women brought food for Sierra, the aroma of bacon, fresh bread, and coffee wafted beneath the house. Elizabeth grabbed her growling belly and silently cursed them. After a few minutes, the women sat together on the porch. She inched her way closer.

"So, what are you doing today, Sierra?"

"I thought I'd help in the garden."

Elizabeth cringed. Not the garden.

"If you're sure. But we're only working it until lunchtime. We harvested so much yesterday, and it's going to take forever to get it prepped and canned. I still don't see how Emma did all of this."

"I can help with that, too."

"Only if you want or need the company," another woman said.

Elizabeth rolled her eyes as Sierra spoke again. The boo-hooing made her ill as she talked about her son's girlfriend. How many times did she hear the name, Emma, while listening in on radio conversations? Emma this. Emma that. And she had a bratty kid sister named Gayla. When she heard Jordan had taken them, she knew the girls were dead. If she ever got to confront Sierra, she'd twist the knife deeper and explain just how wicked he was. Perhaps she would embellish and describe how she assumed they'd died.

"I wish I'd have met them," Sierra said softly. "I've tried to imagine what they look like. We could pass each other and never know."

"Sierra, if you need to be alone, it's okay. We have more than enough help. If you want to come over and eat lunch or watch us prep and can, fine. If not, take it easy."

"You know what. I think I'll stay here and get this house sparkling clean. Emma and Gayla may be home any day now. I have a feeling Emma would be furious if she came back to a dusty, dirty house."

Elizabeth could barely make out the soft-spoken agreements. The clop, clop, clop of boots hitting the wooden deck above was a delightful sound. Just get the hell out of here already. She was starving. Elizabeth rushed for the woods where she would wait until the women left the garden.

After she wolfed down her cold stew and last piece of crusty bread, Elizabeth pulled out her pistol and made sure it was ready. Unfortunately, the gun was a last resort. Firing it would mean facing a small army in no time. She pulled out a rope and practiced.

***

It was past noon, and the women were leaving the field. Sierra had washed sheets and towels, and they snapped on the clothesline every time a good breeze came. Elizabeth dashed to the barn and saddled one of the horses so it would be ready once she dug up the gold. After carefully studying her map, she decided the bush Jordan had drawn on the back side of the house was a small chest. It was her best choice. And she'd be well hidden in case anyone decided to show up.

But she wouldn't leave without giving that bitch, Sierra, a little lesson!

Elizabeth rechecked her pistol, then grabbed her rope and bolted for the cabin. Her heart raced as she eased onto the front porch and peeked through a window. Sierra had her back to her as she scrubbed the stovetop. This was too easy. Elizabeth pulled out the gun and slowly turned the doorknob.

The door creaked as it opened. Sierra turned, and her smile faded. "You!"

"Surprise, surprise." Elizabeth laughed and waved Sierra toward the kitchen table. "Have a seat." She walked over and put the gun to Sierra's temple and forced her to sit.

"If you shoot me, you'll never make it out of here alive. They'll be all over you," Sierra snarled.

"That's a risk I'm willing to take. I've been dying to tell you a little story." Elizabeth savored every second as she watched Sierra's pained expression as she told how she and Jordan took care of problems. "So, you

188

see, my dear, your son's girlfriend and her sister are most likely rotting in the woods. Unless the wolves gobbled up the evidence," Elizabeth taunted Sierra, threw her head back in laughter, and pulled the rope from her shoulder.

It was a fraction of a second. Sierra dove at Elizabeth, and the two women wrestled for control of the gun.

***

Emma pulled Gayla aside when they saw the house in the clearing. "I know you want to go running. So do I. But we need to be careful. The bad guys were looking for something. They may have come back." She squeezed Gayla's shoulders. "They could be there."

"Okay, Emma. What do we do?"

"I'll sneak toward the cabin and peek inside. If it's safe, I'll call you." She let out a gust of air. "If not, I'll come back, and we make a plan."

The sound of screaming and the crashing of glass sent Emma bolting for the cabin. She turned and stuck a finger in her sister's direction. "Stay there."

Emma ran as fast as she could, eased herself onto the side of the porch, and looked through the window. Two women fought for control of a revolver. Emma pulled out her bow, placed the arrow, and kicked the partially open door wide. "Drop the gun," she shouted.

The brunette screamed. "Thank God! Shoot her! She's trying to kill me!"

The other woman's eyes pleaded. "Run. Run now!"

Emma had taken the lives of dozens of animals for food and thanked them for their sacrifice. But this was different. Memories of the day the Elliot's were murdered came back to haunt her. This was a human life. She wasn't sure she could do it again. She had no idea who the women were, but the woman telling her to shoot reminded her of a Bible story. She had to be the bad one. Emma had to make a decision, and she had to do it quickly. Her chin quivered, and she was about to warn the brunette to drop the gun when the dark-haired woman screamed, let go of the pistol, and both hands flew to her left temple. Emma's eyes furrowed as the woman collapsed.

The other woman slowly went to her knees and shoved the gun away. She looked past Emma, took a few short breaths, and spoke quietly. "I take it you're Gayla."

"Yes, Ma'am."

Emma spun. Gayla stuck her slingshot in her back pocket. The hint of proudness didn't escape Emma.

"Thank you, young lady. My name is Sierra Alvise. I'm Jason's mother."

It was Emma's turn to fall to her knees and thank God. Her moment of indecision could have cost Jason's mother her life.

Sierra went to Emma and embraced her. "You must be the famous Emma. I knew it the minute you walked in. When I saw the hesitation in your eyes, I knew Jason was right. You're a strong, compassionate woman. I am glad you didn't release your arrow and have to live with that decision for the rest of your life."

Emma threw her arms around Sierra and shook uncontrollably. She wanted to tell her the truth. How she wasn't sure she could do it again, but she couldn't. "I hesitated. I could have gotten you killed."

Sierra eased back and lifted Emma's chin. "Listen to me, young lady. After all the stories I've heard about the amazing Emma? I have no doubt you'd have done whatever was necessary to protect me had you known who I was."

Emma thought back to when she'd taken the lives of those men. What Jason's mother said. It echoed what her father had told her. She'd done it to protect her sister. She had no choice.

"But, but Gayla didn't hesitate," Emma sniffled.

"Geesh, Emma. When I heard her tell you to shoot, I knew she was the bad person. And I was just hittin' her upside the head with a little rock. Didn't figure I'd kill her. I knew if you shot her with the bow, we'd have a nasty mess to clean up."

The two women stared at Gayla, who stood, scowling with her hands on her hips.

Sierra laughed so hard she had to hold her side. "Gayla, Jason was right. You are something else. I love you already."

Gayla's smirk turned to a mixture of joy and sadness. Sierra rushed over, got on her knees, and embraced her. She rocked back and forth. "You heard that right. I love you. The truth is, I loved you long before today."

Gayla's arms flung around Sierra's neck, and she whispered. Her words were hard to make out. Emma covered her mouth and pinched her nose.

"Can you be my grandma, Mrs. Sierra?" Gayla asked. "I've never had one of those."

Sierra hugged Gayla with one arm and covered her mouth with the other. Her eyes swelled, and the whites turned deep red. "I'd be honored, Gayla. I'd be honored."

CHAPTER 29

Sierra and Emma used Elizabeth's rope to restrain her.

"I want her out of here as soon as possible!" Sierra spat. She turned to Gayla. "Would you mind letting everyone know what's going on?"

"Sure will. I can't wait to see Marcus's reaction when he finds out I'm not dead."

Sierra knelt in front of Gayla. "He's not here, Sweetie. He and his father are with Jason and his dad, and our friend Frank." She rested her hand on Gayla's shoulder. "Marcus never gave up hope."

Gayla's lips trembled, then she lifted her head and placed her hands on her hips. "Figures," Gayla scoffed. "Probably just trying to get out of chores." Gayla brushed a finger under her right eye and pointed to the unconscious woman on the kitchen floor. "I'd watch her if I were you."

"I will," Sierra promised.

***

Gayla's heart pounded as she ran for Elliot House. Marcus was still looking. He hadn't given up on her. Tears streamed down her cheeks, and she sat beneath a tree and allowed them to flow. There were only two times Gayla could remember being so overcome with emotion; the day Emma left to find the milk cow, and when Emma lay lifeless in the back of the jeep. She never told Emma, but both times, Gayla feared her sister would die.

Unable to control her cries, Gayla clutched her stomach with one hand and massaged her aching throat with the other. She hated the feeling. It was painful. Was it because Marcus was still looking for her? Was it because of what she and Emma went through? Or was it because she was so thankful to be home? After several minutes, a peace fell over her when she realized it was all of those. She stood, spread her arms, and spun as she shouted, "We made it, Emma! We made it!"

The women were hanging laundry when Gayla reached Elliot House. "Mrs. Laura!" she wailed and ran for Marcus's mother.

"Gayla." Laura clutched her chest and grabbed the clothesline for support before falling to her knees. "Dear God. It's Gayla."

Leslie and Iva seemed paralyzed as she ran toward them.

"We're back, Mrs. Laura," Gayla said as she reached for her hand.

Laura sluggishly rose, then gripped Gayla in her arms. "Thank you. Thank you," she wailed.

Leslie and Iva inched toward them, swallowed Gayla in their arms, and gave thanks for her return.

"Okay," Gayla said as she eased out of their grip. "We've got this bad lady tied up in the kitchen. She tried to kill my grandma. We need to get the men so they can get her out of the house." The women looked confused.

Gayla rocked her head from side to side. "Okay. Okay. I know Mrs. Sierra isn't really my Grandma." Gayla rolled her eyes. "But she said she would be." Gayla shrugged. "I didn't want to hurt her feelings."

The response was a mixture of laughter and sobbing. Laura kissed Gayla's forehead and looked at the other women. "Go to Emma's house. I'll get the men and meet you there in a few minutes."

***

Within the hour, Emma's house echoed with a mixture of tears and laughter. Randy sat on the couch, and Emma went to his side. His nose ran, and he wiped it away. He shook his head and stared at his boots. "I'm so ashamed. I gave up on you."

Emma held him close. "Randy. It's okay. I understand. After what Mrs. Sierra told me about Jordan Dean and Elizabeth, I'm surprised we survived." She rubbed his back. "Pure luck, or we'd have been coyote food." She tried to make light of the situation.

Randy rubbed his eyes and huffed. "Pure luck? Are you kidding?" His pointer finger tapped the side of Emma's head. "No, my dear. Knowledge." He wiped his eye with the back of his hand. "We survived the lights going out, but I'm not sure we could have made it without guns, matches, or water."

He looked around the room and spoke loudly. "Hey! Be honest. How many of us could have survived with only a knife while we spent several weeks trying to find our way home?" Heads shook, "not me."

Randy looked back at Emma. "Honey, we've had a village of support from day one. You only had yourself, a knife, and what your parents taught

193

you." He gripped her hand. "You're a legend, Emma Harding. One day, they'll write books about you."

"Hey," Gayla quipped. "Don't forget me."

The room erupted in giggles, and Emma hugged Gayla. "Don't you worry, little sister. Everyone will know we would have starved to death without you and your slingshot."

Randy wiped his runny nose one more time. "Sorry, Gayla. Didn't mean to slight you. Your heroics were next." He winked, stood, and slapped his thighs. "Okay. Let's see if we can make some men happy. I say we try getting in touch with the boys on the handhelds. Keep your fingers crossed that they're close enough." Randy took a deep breath, grabbed the radio, stepped outside, and called out. "Jason. Are you there? Can you hear me?"

***

Frank heard the call several times and whipped his horse to catch up to Jason. "Hey," he said as he held Jason's reigns. "Randy's been trying to call you. Can't you hear him?"

Jason looked at his radio. "Thanks, Uncle Frank. Guess the batteries are dead."

Frank handed his radio to Jason and reached into his backpack for fresh batteries.

"I need some too," Chris said.

"Me too." Marcus tapped his handheld.

Emma's voice echoed through the forest. "So, I'm gone for a few lousy weeks, and everything's gone to hell? I expect you to be home soon and get things back on track. Gayla and I are tired and dirty. We're gonna get a bath, eat, and go to bed."

Jason stared at the radio and slid from Guss's back. He went to his knees, and his hand covered his heart. After he pulled himself together, he offered a simple, choked reply. "Don't use all the soap and hot water—I kind of stink." He paused. "I love you, Emma and Gayla."

Then Gayla's voice came from the radio. "This is for Marcus. If you think you can get out of chores, you're crazy. I looked. Not one lousy fish in the smokehouse."

Marcus wiped his eyes and took the radio from Jason. "I'll get on it as soon as we get back, Gayla. I promise."

Sierra took the radio and told them how Gayla saved her and swore that Elizabeth was no longer a threat. The men had her under lock and key.

Chris laughed. "Sounds like the Gayla I heard tales of. Give Elizabeth a message for me. Tell her she'll reunite with her boyfriend in a day or two."

A few moments later, the men gathered and high-fived each other as they gave thanks.

Matthew, Frank, and Chris gathered wood and built a fire. Chris was about to tell Jason and Marcus that dinner was ready when he realized they were sound asleep. He offered the extra plates to Frank and Matthew.

Frank grabbed a dish. "What the hell. I'm starving."

CHAPTER 30

Later that evening, Emma eyed Elizabeth as she sat tied to the pillars on the front porch. Gayla approached her and squatted. "Hey, lady. It must be miserable being tied to that pole. Can I get you something?"

"Some water and food would be nice. And I need to use the outhouse." Elizabeth sent Gayla her sweetest smile.

Gayla doubled over in laughter. "Ha. Got you. They say a chopper will be here soon." Gayla rubbed her chin. "Hmmm. Wonder what prison food tastes like?" She stood and placed her hands on her hips. "You're an evil woman, Elizabeth. I hope you and that Jordan fellow spend the rest of your lives locked up. I just heard about what you two did." Gayla squatted again. "I have to ask. Was it worth it? I mean, killing all those people so you could be rich. Was it really worth it?" She placed her hand on Elizabeth's shoulder. "Don't worry. We'll use the treasure to make a lot of people happy."

As Gayla skipped away, Elizabeth screamed and screamed and screamed.

Emma laughed harder than she'd ever laughed before.

***

Sierra offered to stay at Elliot House so Emma and Gayla could get a good night's rest.

"Grandma." Gayla looked at her feet. "I don't want you to think I'm a scaredy-cat." She looked up at Sierra and let out a puff of air. "But I sure wish you'd stay here and sleep with me." She looked back down at her shoes. "Grandparents do that in some of the books I've read."

Sierra brushed back Gayla's hair. "It would be my privilege."

Gayla fell asleep within minutes of going to bed.

Sierra slipped out of Gayla's room and watched Emma as she sat at the table, her face in her palms. Sierra placed her hand on Emma's shoulder. "Can I get you something? Maybe some herbal tea to help you sleep?"

Emma's hand instinctively went to Sierra's and rubbed it. "Thanks, Mom. But I'm okay."

Both women gasped at the remark. Emma stood. "Um. I think I just need to go to bed."

A tear slid down Sierra's check, and she smiled. "Get some rest. Jason should be here tomorrow."

Emma nodded and turned to go to her room.

"Emma," Sierra called out.

Emma turned.

"Thank you. Thank you for saving my son." Her hands cupped her mouth. "Jason spent years wondering why he was spared while so many others perished. I told him it happened for a reason." Her lips clenched. "I believe that reason was you and your sister."

Emma didn't know what to make of her comment. She nodded. "Sleep well. I'll see you in the morning."

***

But as tired as she was, Emma fought for rest. Old dreams kept her shuffling in her bed. She just wanted to sleep. Please, let her sleep. Finally, Emma drifted away and dreamed.

Twelve-year-old Emma held her ear next to the bedroom door. Mr. and Mrs. Elliot were talking to her father. "She's not well. We need a doctor. I'm afraid she won't survive the delivery," Mrs. Elliot whispered.

"I'll take her to the depot when the train comes through next week. They always have a doctor," her father said.

Then Emma heard a door creak open, followed by her mother's voice. "Stop it! Stop pretending. I'm no fool. I know something's wrong." She cried softly and said what a wonderful life she'd had and how her biggest regret would be not being there to see her children grow up."

Emma woke and realized she didn't have a vision about her mom dying. She'd overheard the conversation when she was a child. Then, she recalled her father's dizzy spells before his heart attack and how they had worried her. Once again, she hadn't envisioned his death in a dream—she'd feared it would happen. Emma rolled on her side and allowed her tears to fill the pillow. She missed her parents so much.

When Emma drifted back to sleep, the nightmares began. Jordan was screaming at her and demanding to know where the map was. The trees with sparkly things returned. Emma pictured her younger self finding the child's drawing years earlier. She sat at the table and colored in all the trees. Proud of how pretty they looked, she had folded the picture and placed it in her art book.

Emma awoke and bolted upright. It couldn't be. Jordan had searched the hidden space while demanding to know where the map was. That's where Emma found the drawing. She threw back the covers, raced to the bookcase, and pulled out her folder of art.

Emma spread the picture out on the table. Her fingers caressed the old paper. "This is what he was looking for. It's a map," she whispered. As her fingers brushed over a small bush, Emma gasped. She grabbed her measuring stick. The bush was about six inches from the side of the house.

Emma held a tight grip on the flashlight as she went outside. She counted her paces from the side of the house to the spot where she'd found the chest. About sixty paces. Her heart raced. The trees, the bushes. If she was right, they marked the spot of buried treasure. Emma ran to the barn, grabbed a shovel, then went back inside to check the map.

The drawing of another small shrub was less than an inch behind the cabin. She went to the spot and started digging. After a few minutes, the shovel struck a solid surface. Emma clutched her chest, took a deep breath, and exposed the top of a wooden box. She quickly recovered it, remembering Jason's warning. Best she kept it quiet.

A little later, the others began doing chores at the barn, Emma called them over.

"Fresh coffee and rolls."

***

Gayla was still asleep, so they had coffee and rolls on the porch.

"I'm sorry, but I'm not up to cooking this morning," Emma said.

Everyone lowered their mug and stared.

"Are you serious?" Sierra asked.

Emma's face heated. "I, I just feel tired."

Laura stood. "For goodness sake, Emma! We don't expect you to cook." She shook her head. "I'll be back in a while with breakfast for you and Gayla."

Everyone stood to leave. "Go back to bed!" Laura ordered as she and the others left.

Emma asked Sierra to stay when the others left, and she gladly accepted the offer. "I'd love to spend time with my future daughter." Her grin grew. "And my new granddaughter."

After another cup of coffee and some small talk, Emma pulled out the map. "I need to tell you some things." Emma explained how she always believed she was clairvoyant. She now realized that her visions were from conversations she'd overheard or things she'd observed. "And then there's this." She handed the drawing to Sierra.

Sierra smiled. "I take it you drew this when you were a child."

"No. I found it after we moved in. I colored it, that's all."

Sierra seemed confused.

Emma told her about finding the chest, believing it was evil, and having Jason rebury it. She pointed to a small bush. "That's where it is." Then she pointed to the little shrub behind the house. "I dug up this one early this morning."

Sierra paled. "Are you telling me you believe all the trees and bushes represent buried treasure?"

"Yep."

"Oh, my." Sierra put a hand on her chest.

Emma laughed. "Jason will sure be busy when he gets home."

Sierra chuckled. "Somehow, I don't think he'll mind." She became serious. "I need to ask. If you're right, what are you planning on doing with all the money?"

"I want to use every dime to rebuild Riverton and restore as much power as possible. My father loved that town. My mother eventually realized that she did too. I wanted nothing to do with the treasure until Gayla told me how sad she was that she never got to see the things in the magazines and books." Emma's jaw tightened. "I promised her she would one day. Her and a lot of children."

"That, my dear, is the most unselfish gesture I've ever heard." Sierra embraced Emma. "Jason was right about you. You are an amazing woman, Emma Harding."

Gayla strolled out of her room and rubbed her eyes. "Good morning, Grandma," she shouted and ran for Sierra.

CHAPTER 31

Rusty was busy barking orders as he loaded one of the wagons. "For Pete's sake. What's taking so long?" He could feel the heat as his face blistered. "Hurry it up!"

Barbara squeezed his arm. "Rusty, calm down. We just found out the girls were safe two hours ago."

Rusty's wife giggled. "Tell the truth, Rusty. You've been dying to meet your female clone for years."

Rusty scowled. "Don't be ridiculous. I'm just anxious to meet Jason's fiancee' and her sister, and I'm glad they're safe." He shook his head and pounded on the side of the wagon. "And I need to apologize to Sierra. I should have kept a better eye on that woman." His lips tightened in anger.

"Whoa!" Barbara said. "She tricked us, Rusty. And I was the one who was supposed to watch her. Not you!"

"Yeah? I was the one at the pavilion every day. I should have noticed!"

Rusty's wife interrupted. "Well. Then I guess I'm as much to blame as you!"

"Stop it!" Barbara barked. "If the stable boy had been honest, we'd have known she was gone long before now. Instead, he waited to tell us after the horse came home!"

Jason's younger brother, Jim, tossed a bag in one of the wagons, hopped in, and took the reigns. "Blaming each other is doing none of us any good. Stop this blame game, and let's go meet the other half of our family."

"Rusty," someone yelled, "hold up."

A man came running with a large bag over his shoulder and tossed it in the wagon. "Letters," he huffed, "from the kids at Hudson Ranch praying for Emma and Gayla to be safe and find their way home. We thought they should have them."

Rusty's lips tightened, and he nodded. "Thank you," he said as he nudged his team forward.

***

"Hi, honey. I wanted to let you know that Rusty, Tracey, Barbara, and the kids will be here in a few days," Sierra told Jason as he made his way home.

Jason turned his horse away from the others. "Mom, I realize this conversation can't be exactly private, but I'd like to speak to Emma alone if you don't mind."

"Of course, dear."

"Jason?" Emma's voice made his heart race.

"Emma. God. I can't wait to see you." He paused. "I need to ask you something. The most important people in my life will be at your ranch in a few days." He paused again. "I'm not sure how you'll feel about this." He paused longer. "Do we need a long drawn out fancy wedding?" His heart raced. "Would, uh, can't we just have a simple wedding when they get there?"

There was silence.

Jason stopped Guss and stepped from his steed after several seconds of quiet. "I, I'm sorry. That was selfish of me. It's just that I can't wait for us to be married."

Nothing.

Jason cleared his throat. "Emma, we can wait and have your dream wedding."

Gayla responded. "Hey, Jason. Grandma Sierra said I should tell you that they're checking out wedding ideas in the magazines." She sighed. "You do *not* want to talk to them now. It's kind of embarrassing. Your Mom is crying, and Emma is talking about having babies. Just so you know, I am *not* changing any diapers! Will you be home by tomorrow?"

Jason laughed, "We should be."

"Good!" she snapped. "Marcus has a ton of stuff he needs to take care of. I checked again. I was right. Not one fish in the smokehouse."

Jason eyed Marcus, and his smile caused a chuckle. Jason tossed the radio to his young friend. Marcus inhaled and attempted to act cocky. "Gee, Gayla," Marcus said. "I've been a little busy."

"Boo-hoo. You sound like a little kid making excuses."

"Fine," Marcus smirked. "See if I waste my time looking for you again!"

There was a moment of silence. "I've missed you, Marcus." Gayla's nasal response caused the men's eyes to tear. "Get your butt home."

***

The red bell the men had hung began to toll. Emma smiled, stared out the window, and wiped her hands on her apron cuff. Gayla heard them coming. The smile on her little sister's face as she vigorously tugged the rope overwhelmed her. Somehow, the many years of solitude hadn't damaged Gayla. Emma's heart was bursting.

Emma knew her little sister adored Marcus. How could she possibly chide Gayla about having feelings for a boy at such a young age? After all, she had fallen in love with Jason when she was only a child and had dreamed of him for years. If Marcus became half the man Jason had become…

Emma glanced in the mirror and straightened her hair. Her rough, bristly fingers snagged a few strands. She frowned, then extended her hands and examined them. A smile crossed her lips. Jason and her dad were right. Those were some fine hands, and they had a story to tell.

Emma rushed for the cabin door and stood on the front porch as Jason and the others returned. Five men approached on horseback. Yes. She counted Marcus as a man.

Emma let out a small whistle. Granted, she hadn't seen many men, but she had old magazines. The men riding toward her put those men to shame. Matthew, Marcus, and Jason rode in with two men she didn't know. The man between Jason and Marcus was handsome and had a kind and gentle look about him. She looked at the man to Jason's left. Was that his father? Was that the former President Alvise? Never had she imagined anyone as chiseled and magnificent as Jason—but there he was.

Emma tried to remain calm as the men dismounted. But as Jason ran toward her, her knees buckled, and Emma collapsed.

***

It finally hit her. All she and Gayla went through. The weeks of being lost. Wondering if they'd find their way home. The hunger. The fear.

Emma bolted upright in the bed. She glanced at the familiar surroundings and took deep breaths. It was okay. She was at home. She and Gayla were safe. Sweat dripped from her brow, and she pulled the covers tighter. Sleep. That's what she needed. But what if she was dreaming? Maybe she wasn't really home. Perhaps she and Gayla were still lost. Emma tossed the covers aside and shrieked. "Gayla!"

She sat, gasping for breath and clutching her blanket.

Gayla rushed to her side, curled up in the bed with Emma, and wrapped her arms around her. "Emma, it's okay. We're home. We're safe."

Jason sat on the edge of the bed and took Emma's hand. "We're here, Emma. You and Gayla are safe. Get some rest."

"No. No." Emma thrashed about. "He's gonna kill us. My head hurts. Which way do we go? Which way?" She could feel the heaviness of her eyelids. She needed sleep. "Great shelter, Gayla." Emma whimpered and gave a small laugh. "You and your slingshot." Emma sighed and rolled on her side.

***

Sierra and Chris had been standing by the door and rushed in as Gayla began to sob. Chris picked up Gayla and brushed her hair. "Shh. Shh. Emma will be fine, Gayla. She's just exhausted."

Sierra placed a hand on Jason's shoulder. "Son. Let's go. She needs rest."

"I can't leave her." Jason shook his head. "Didn't you see the terror in her eyes?"

"Yes. But hovering over her won't help. She needs time to process what's happened." Sierra tightened her grip on her son's shoulder and turned his face toward hers. "And you have no idea what else weighs on Emma's mind."

Jason's brows raised.

"Son. Come to the living room," Chris said. "We need to talk."

Chris placed Gayla on the couch and had Jason sit beside her. Then, he told them all that he knew.

"It appears Jordan and the other men didn't come here for one small chest of treasure," Chris smirked.

"What do you mean?" Gayla asked.

"We should have told you," Jason told Gayla, "But Emma and I wanted to protect you. We found a chest full of gold and jewels. Emma made me re-bury it." He looked at his father. "I was going to tell you about the trunk once things were running smoothly here. Then Emma and Gayla were taken."

"I found out about the man who took us when me and Emma got home. Grandma said he was a pirate. How much is the chest worth? Are we rich?" Gayla grinned and clapped her hands.

Sierra grinned. "It may have been a lot more than one chest, Gayla." Jason stood. "What?"

"There are possibly tons buried here," Chris said.

"Wow," Gayla said and clapped harder.

Jason looked between his parents. "I don't understand."

"Jason," Sierra said, "Emma found something."

She handed him the drawing, and he unfolded it. He shook his head. "I'm not sure I understand. What does a kid's drawing have to do with any of this?"

"It's not a kid's drawing," Sierra said. "It seems to be a map. Emma realized it when she got home. She's already found another chest right here." She pointed to the small shrub drawn behind the house. "It appears the trees and shrubs represent where Jordan buried his haul. Emma believes the larger the plant, the larger the stash."

Gayla jumped from the couch. "That man kept screaming at us! He wanted to know where the map was!"

"Had Emma known what he was talking about, you might not be here today," Chris said.

"So, what do we do now?" Jason asked as he lowered himself to the sofa. "Emma wants no part of it. She said it was evil. Looks like she was right."

Sierra smiled. "She's changed her mind, son. Your dad made some calls. This place will be swarming with the military in a few days."

***

The next morning Emma woke, rested and at peace. She apologized for what she could remember. "I've never been so out of it. I was sure I was awake, but it felt like I was dreaming. I must have looked like a complete idiot."

"Not at all," Sierra assured her. "The stress finally caught up with you."

"Yeah, Mom's right," Jason said. "If I know you, there was no way that you ever let Gayla know you were scared. Everyone has a breaking point."

She felt her face heat up and looked at her feet. "Thank you." A twisted grin crossed her lips. "The man who came into my room, that was your father?"

"Yes."

Emma let out a slow whistle. "My, my, my. Some people are certainly put together well."

Sierra and Jason busted into laughter.

"Don't get any ideas, young lady," Sierra chuckled. "He's taken."

"Okay…" Emma shrugged, looked at Jason, and sighed. "Guess I'll make do with you."

Sierra laughed harder, and Jason rolled his eyes. "What makes you think I still want you after that comment?"

Emma smiled, "Because you love me."

Jason grinned, "You got me there."

While they rocked on the front porch, Emma told Jason about her plans to rebuild Riverton.

"What a wonderful gesture, Emma. Now, let's hope you're right about the map. It's going to take some serious cash to do what you're proposing."

"Speaking of proposing," Sierra interrupted, "We need to finish the wedding plans. Rusty, Tracey, Barbara, and the kids will be here soon. Are you up to it?" she asked Emma.

"Absolutely." She reached over and took Jason's hand.

"I thought they'd be here by now. What's taking so long?" Jason asked.

Sierra grinned. "They'd forgotten some things. Jim and Lena went back to Hudson Ranch, and the others waited for them to return."

"Well, I say we get things going. Tell me what I need to do," Jason said.

"Would you mind if we got married under the burr oak?" Emma glanced at the tree. "I'd like Mom and Dad to be there."

Jason squeezed her hand. "Sounds perfect."

Their heads turned toward the stream. The sound of Gayla's and Marcus's laughter echoed. The two kids, walking toward the cabin, hand in hand, filled Emma's heart with warmth.

"Emma!" Gayla shouted, ran for her sister, and threw her arms around her. "You're awake. Are you okay?"

"I'm fine. Thanks for taking such good care of me."

Marcus held his hand out for a shake. "I'm so happy you're both home." A tear slid down his cheek, and he brushed it away.

Emma grabbed him and cradled him in her arms. "Thank you, Marcus." She could feel his body tremble. "Thank you for all you did and for not giving up on us."

Emma relaxed her hold, but Marcus tightened his. "I love you, Emma. I wish I could have stopped them."

Emma huffed. "Ha. I wish I'd paid attention to what you were trying to tell me. And I love you, too."

The sound of approaching wagons caught their attention. "They're here, Emma. You're about to meet some of my family." Jason let out a loud hoot.

CHAPTER 32

Jason ran to greet the wagons as his father and Uncle Frank escorted them to Emma's cabin. Marcus and Gayla followed.

Emma's breathing increased. "I'm nervous, Mrs. Sierra."

"No need. Trust me. And I'm Mom, not Mrs."

Emma nodded.

"Oh, one thing. I can practically guarantee Rusty will try to ruffle your feathers. Don't fall for his act. Rusty loves everyone, and everyone loves him. If you outwit him and his smart-aleck comments, he'll just love you more and try harder to outdo you."

"Trust me, I've heard all about Rusty."

The wagons stopped just off the front porch. Chris and the other man she now knew as Uncle Frank dismounted and rushed to greet her.

"Finally," Frank hugged her. "I've been waiting for years to meet you."

"It's good to meet you, Uncle Frank."

Frank grinned and gave a thumbs up.

Chris hugged Emma. "I was hoping to do that yesterday. You had us a little concerned."

"I'm sorry. I'm fine. I was just exhausted."

"I can imagine," he said. "Tomorrow will be better. Each day will get easier."

Jason, Jim, and Marcus helped the ladies off the wagon.

Rusty scowled. "Hey, a little help here? My rear is practically molded to the seat, and my back is killing me."

Emma rushed for his wagon. "I'll help you, Uncle Rusty. It must be awful getting old and arthritic." She reached for his hand.

Rusty's lip curled and twitched. Emma couldn't miss the amusement in his eyes as he reached for her offered hand. "Ha. At least someone around here has manners." When he got out of the wagon, he put his arm around her. "Mind if I lean on you till we make it to the porch? I'm having a hard time standing up."

"Sure, Uncle Rusty." Emma leaned in and gave a fake whisper. "But you stink. I think you should get first dibs on the shower."

Everyone chuckled. Rusty stopped and put his fists on his hips. "You sure are a real smart-aleck for such a cute little thing."

Emma's eyes widened. "Really? Huh. Everyone says I remind them of you."

Rusty struggled to conceal his smile, then leaned in and whispered. "It's an art, honey. You'll never out-do the master." He gave her a big hug and kissed her forehead. "Jason," he said, "I think she's a keeper."

Gayla walked up and stuck her hand out. "I'm Gayla. We heard a lot about you, Uncle Rusty. I'm not sure what Jason meant, but he said it would be fun to see you and Emma go head-to-head."

Rusty took a step back and seemed shocked. Then his smile broadened, and his eyes watered. "We'll find out, I'm sure." He cocked his head sideways. "Wait a minute. This can't be. You're the Gayla who can bring down a deer with a slingshot?"

Gayla laughed. "Now, that's just plain silly. Rabbits, squirrels, stuff like that. *No way* I could take a deer with my slingshot."

Rusty rubbed his scruffy beard. "I don't know. You hit him just right..." His hands slapped together. "Bam. Dinner."

Gayla rolled her eyes. "I'm too little to shoot a rock *that* big."

As the others from Hudson Ranch each greeted Emma and Gayla, another wagon headed their way. Laura, Leslie, and Iva waved and yelled in excitement. "We brought food," Laura shouted.

***

"Can we go fishing after we eat?" Marcus asked. "We're getting a little tired of all this grown-up talk."

Emma looked at the others and sighed. "I say they go. After all, they're responsible for keeping us supplied with fish."

Marcus grinned, gave two thumbs up, then told the girls, "Told ya. They're pushovers."

The adults chuckled.

"Don't push your luck, son," Matthew said.

After they finished eating, the kids left, and the discussion of housing came up. "Me, Jason, Gayla, and Marcus can sleep in the living room," Emma offered. "But that still only leaves two beds."

Jim, Jason's younger brother, spoke for himself and his two sisters. "I can sleep in the barn. There should be more than enough room for Lena and Barbie in the living room."

"I say the women bunk together at Elliot house. The men can rough it like we've been doing," Randy said. "Heck, with our mattresses and sleeping bags, the closed-in porches have been just fine."

Chris nodded. "Sounds fine to me."

Emma paled. There was nothing she could do about housing so many, but she felt it was her fault they were all here and had nowhere to sleep.

Sierra sighed. "Everyone at Hudson Ranch wanted to come when I told them Jason and Emma were getting married, but they knew it wasn't possible."

Barbara nodded. "It darned near broke Lilly's heart when I told her she couldn't come because of her baby. And with Ryan working on the train, he won't be home for at least a month."

Tracey and Rusty both sighed. "Yeah, same with our kids."

Emma stood. "Excuse me. I need to check on the kids and the smokehouse. Jason, can you come with me?"

"Sure," he said. He looked at his family. "You guys figure out the sleeping arrangements. Whatever you decide will be fine with us." He turned before he walked out the door. "I'm just glad you're all here. And I'm thankful you finally got to meet Emma and Gayla."

***

"Emma, what's going on?" Jason asked. "The kids haven't been gone for an hour, and we checked the smokehouse before we ate."

She clutched his hand. "I wanted you to be with me." Her hands flew to her face, and she let out her distress.

"Emma." Jason wrapped his arms around her. "What's wrong?"

Emma pushed him back and shook her head. She couldn't speak. Her throat ached. She took Jason's hand and led him to the burr oak. When they got there, she stared at the two crosses for a moment and knelt. "I need to tell them how sorry I am."

Jason knelt beside her and stroked her shoulder. "I don't understand."

"We can't get married."

She watched as Jason's face turned white.

"Why? Why, Emma?"

She grabbed his hands. "I don't mean *never*, Jason. I mean, just not now. You have a huge family that wants to be with us when we marry." Her arm spread out and waved across the farm. "We can't do it here. It has to be at Hudson Ranch. We've been waiting since we were seven. A few more months won't kill us."

Jason inhaled a deep breath of air, let out a small laugh, then rested his hand on her mother's cross. "Is that okay with you, Mrs. Harding?"

"Of course."

Emma and Jason gasped. Then Emma felt a hand on her shoulder and looked behind her. Gayla smiled. "I bet that's just what Mommy and Daddy would want."

***

"Great," Rusty huffed. "I spend several God-awful days to get here, then have to turn around and go back to plan a wedding?"

Emma squinted. "No. I can come over a couple of days before and take care of it."

Rusty smirked. "I don't think so. The cake alone will take days."

"Muffins will be fine," Emma grinned.

Rusty stared for a moment, then burst into laughter. "No muffins for you and Jason, my dear. It would be my honor to cater the biggest wedding Hudson Ranch has ever seen." He grabbed Emma and spun her around before dropping her and clutching his back.

Chris chuckled. "Gets harder every year, old man."

Rusty winced and hobbled to a chair. "You got that right."

"Emma, you and Jason don't have to do this," Sierra said. "This place will be a madhouse after the soldiers arrive."

Chris agreed. "And once the treasure is unearthed, it has to be taken to NORAD. We could be talking a couple of months. Maybe more."

"We can wait," Jason said. "Emma wants the whole family there when we get married."

"That's right. I don't have any family, other than Gayla. If I did, I'd want them there too," Emma said.

Sierra looked a little sad. "Emma, I lost my family. At least I know how and where. Do you have any idea about your family? All we ever knew was your mom and dad."

"I don't know a whole lot," Emma said. "My dad was an only child. He lost his parents before I was born. His father was a police officer and got killed by a drug addict." Emma shook her head and exhaled. "Grandma Harding was really special." She stared at her coffee mug. "At least that's what Dad said." She swirled her cup and blinked her eyes. "There must have been some terrible people back then. Dad said she was coming home from grocery shopping, and some guy killed her for her purse."

Sierra gripped Emma's hand. "Yes. There were some horrible people then. There still are, but not as many."

Emma let out a gust of air. "I kind of think my mom's story is sadder. She grew up in Aspen, Colorado. Her parents were wealthy and chose their kid's future. They didn't like my dad and constantly harassed mom to leave him and make her mark in a big city," Emma sighed. "It worked. Mom ran away before I was born. Then the EMP happened. I didn't meet Dad until I was around three-years-old. Mom said her parents decided my Uncle David would be an attorney. When he chose culinary school instead, they disowned him. He left and never came back. Mom tried to find him for years. She assumed they all died after the EMP."

Emma squinted and looked at Rusty. Something was wrong. Why had no one noticed? "What's wrong with Rusty?" she yelled.

Rusty clutched his chest and waved everyone off. "Go away. Go away. I need to talk to Emma."

Emma rushed to his side. Rusty gripped her hand, and a tear ran down his face.

"Emma, what was your mom's name?"

"Mona. Are you okay, Uncle Rusty?"

Rusty closed his eyes. "Mona? Are you sure?"

"That's what everyone called her. Her real name was Monika. Monika Baker."

"Noooo!" Rusty wailed. He buried his mouth. "No. No. No." He rocked back and forth and cried.

Tracey held him. After a moment of silence, she spoke for her husband. "There are things no one knows about Rusty. He didn't confide in me until we'd been married for years." Tracey struggled to speak. "Emma, Rusty knew your mom."

"What?" The comments made by everyone rushed through her head. "You act just like Rusty." "You sound like Rusty." "If I didn't know better, I'd think Rusty was your father."

Emma took a step back. "No." She shook her head. "No. My father is under the Big oak. I don't want to hear more." Emma placed her hands over her ears.

Jason rushed to her side. "Stop!" he yelled at Tracey.

"Emma." Rusty's lips quivered. "I'm not your father." He rested his head on his wife's shoulder.

Jason's eyes widened. "Wait...wait a minute."

Emma followed Jason's gaze. Everyone sat with their mouths dropped open or covered their mouths as if they were smothering a cry.

"Dear God," Sierra breathed.

"What's going on?" No one responded. Emma spoke louder and stomped her feet. "What the hell is going on?"

Rusty eased from Tracey's hold. "I'm okay." He patted her hand. "I'm okay." He looked at Emma for a second, then looked away. "Where do I start?" He wiped his nose, then looked her in the eyes.

"Years ago, I dyed my hair red. It earned me the nickname, Rusty. I legally changed my name to Rusty Rivers when I decided I'd be a famous chef one day." He gave a halfhearted laugh. "I couldn't keep my last name. No way I wanted to be called Rusty Baker." He exhaled. "Emma, my birth name was David, David Baker."

Emma blinked a few times, then her lips slowly turned into a snarl. "You're, you're my uncle? My mother's brother?" Her lips tightened, and her nose flared. "How could you?" she screamed. "How could you? My mother adored you. She searched for you for years." Emma had never known hate for someone, but at that moment, she hated Rusty. How could he have been so selfish and caused her mother so much misery?

Tracey jumped to her husband's defense. "Rusty loved your mother. He missed her so much that we named our first daughter, Monica, after your mom. And he tried. He repeatedly went to his parent's house. He was never allowed inside. He begged to speak to your mom. They said she didn't want to see him. Rusty knew it was a lie, and he tried over and over. He didn't stop trying until after the murder of his wife and children. Then he gave up on everything!"

Rusty gripped his wife's arm. She sat beside him and took sobering breaths.

"Emma," Rusty struggled for control. "The loss of my sister haunted me, just like the murder of my wife and children tormented me for years. I knew my wife and family were gone, but I had no idea what happened to my little sister. You have to believe me. I tried to find her."

Emma's eyes widened, and she bit her knuckle. "Your family was murdered?" Emma asked.

Rusty nodded and looked at the floor. His forehead wrinkled as he looked up. "Yeah. A long time ago. Years before you were born." He wrapped his arm around his wife. "Hudson Ranch and Tracey saved me from myself."

"I, I'm sorry." Emma glanced at her feet. "I have photos of Mom and letters she wrote you but didn't know where to send." Emma's jaw tightened. "I'll have to admit; I hated you for abandoning her and making her cry." Her mouth trembled, and her eyes filled with tears. "She loved you so much. She talked about you all the time."

"Rusty's eyes filled with tears again. I'd love to see the photos and read the letters. That is, if you don't mind."

"I don't mind." Emma stared at her feet. "I'd like to give them to you, but I don't know if I can. They mean too much to me."

Chris approached Emma and placed a hand on her shoulder. "I can help with that. We can make copies at Hudson Ranch."

Emma's eyes grew wide. "You can?"

Sierra walked up beside them. "Emma. Almost everyone who survived the EMP lost track of their families." Her head bobbed. "Most had died. But the census reconnected thousands of family members. Stories like your's and Rusty's? I'm sure it happens, but I've never heard of one quite like it. The government is copying and keeping an archive of the reunions. The hope is that one day those beautiful occasions will fill a museum."

Emma reached out. "Come with me, Uncle David, or Uncle Rusty. Whoever you are now, I don't think Mom will care. Let's go visit your sister."

Rusty stood and took her hand.

CHAPTER 33

The next morning, Emma crept off the couch and tried to start breakfast quietly. Marcus and Jason slept peacefully on the living room floor. Gayla slept with her new grandparents in her room, and Rusty and Tracey slept in Emma's room. The others all chose to bunk at Elliot House.

Emma slipped on her jacket and opened the front door. Maple bacon waited in the smokehouse. Her eyes fluttered. The front porch light was on. She reached for the knob. It was unlocked. She shook her head and scolded herself. Way too much confusion the night before.

As she was about to turn the knob, the door opened. Rusty stood in the doorway with a slab of bacon.

"Good morning," he whispered and raised the bacon. "Hope you don't mind. I don't know that I've ever seen a more spectacular smokehouse." He used a free hand to pull Emma close and kissed her forehead. "I'll deny it if you tell anyone I said that."

Emma grinned.

"Too late, old man," Jason yawned.

"Yeah," Marcus said. "You guys make too much noise."

Emma rolled her eyes. "Go back to sleep. It's not even four yet."

Jason tossed his cover aside. "Not a chance we'll be able to sleep once the two of you start arguing in the kitchen."

"Speak for yourself." Marcus pulled the blanket over his head and rolled on his side.

"Emma," Rusty said, "Why don't we have a cup of coffee with a slice of your fabulous bread and jam, then you go enjoy a nice warm shower. I'll get breakfast started." He glanced at Jason. "I'm sure your fiance' would enjoy helping me."

Emma was about to respond when Jason waved his arms. "Whoa. No way I get in your way in the kitchen, Uncle Rusty. I kind of like my head attached to my shoulders."

Rusty's brows lifted. "I have no idea why you'd say that. You make me sound like some kind of kitchen monster. I'd appreciate your help."

Jason approached and placed his hand on Rusty's forehead. "Hmm. He doesn't seem to have a fever."

Rusty swatted his hand away. "You are going to scare my niece. She'll think I'm some kind of a brute."

Emma tried to stifle her laughter. "Uncle Rusty, I've been warned about you for months."

Rusty placed his hands on his hips and glared at Jason.

"Hey." Jason raised his hands and backed away. "Wasn't just me."

Emma shook her head. "Let's make coffee before you two wake up the whole house." She rubbed Rusty's shoulder. "Thank you for the offer to shower, but I know where everything is. Plus, I'd love to watch a master chef in action."

Rusty threw his shoulders back and grinned. "From what I've heard and seen, I doubt there's much I can teach you."

"From what I've heard and seen, I think Emma can teach you a few things," Sierra said as she and Chris entered the living room.

Tracey walked out of Emma's bedroom and stretched. "Yeah. This should be interesting."

Marcus peeked from beneath his cover. "Emma, can I go to your room while you guys do whatever it is you're going to do?"

"Sure."

Marcus placed his hand on Emma's shoulder as he passed. "Good luck. I sure hope to see you in one piece at breakfast."

The room filled with snickers.

***

Emma and Rusty went about preparing breakfast. Rusty showed Emma how he prepared large batches of bacon. "If you put the slices on a baking sheet and bake it in the oven, it takes a fraction of the time. Plus, the equal heat surrounding it keeps the slices from curling."

"You mean they stay flat? Are you serious?"

"Yep. Perfect, flat, crispy bacon every time."

"Wow."

Rusty wagged his head at Sierra. "Told ya I could teach her a thing or two."

Sierra rolled her eyes. "Oh, brother."

Rusty was about to form the biscuits. "You didn't add enough lard."

"What? My biscuits are always moist, fluffy, and delicious."

Emma shrugged. "Whatever."

Rusty backed away and bowed. "They're all yours."

Emma huffed. "Sure, now that you over kneaded them."

"Duel," Rusty declared. "I'll make a batch, and you'll make a batch."

The two slapped hands and flour covered the floor. Both looked at the mess for a moment, then stared at each other before laughing.

Chris shook his head. "I'm not sure I believe this. Emma's survived thirty minutes in the kitchen with you, and you're laughing at flour all over the place?"

Rusty smirked. "I don't understand your confusion." He looked at Emma and waved his hands. "Pay them no attention, Emma."

"Sure, Uncle Rusty."

The smell of bacon and biscuits baking in the oven brought out Gayla and Marcus.

"It smells so good in here," Marcus said.

"Yeah," Gayla eyed the pan of biscuits on the table. "Hey, Marcus, why don't we make a biscuit sandwich and go fishing?"

Marcus looked at Emma. She stroked her chin. "Hmm. I think you should milk the cows in exchange. I'll cook eggs to go on the sandwiches."

Marcus and Gayla smiled.

"Done." Marcus raised his thumb, and they headed for the barn.

Emma noticed Rusty's pained expression. The kids weren't there when he'd revealed his true identity.

"We'll tell her later. Trust me, Gayla will be thrilled," she told Rusty.

"I hope so." Rusty hesitated as he reached into his back pocket. He pulled out a worn leather billfold and rubbed it before handing it to Emma. "The men who killed my family stole my wallet. I had this one in a drawer at home. It, and the pictures inside, are the only things I took before I went insane and left everything behind."

Emma's hands trembled. She was sure she was about to meet her aunt and her cousins. They were gone, and she wasn't sure how she'd react.

Rusty reached out and gripped Emma's hands. "Open it."

***

Everyone decided the biscuit duel was a toss-up. Rusty and Emma had certainly met their match. After breakfast, they went to the stream.

"Caught anything?" Rusty asked.

Marcus lifted a stringer full of fish and proudly wobbled his head.

215

"Good job."

"Can you guys stop for a minute? We'd like to tell you something," Emma said.

The kids pulled in their lines and sat on the fallen log while Rusty and Emma told them the story.

"This is so cool," Marcus said.

Gayla sat unemotionally.

Marcus nudged Gayla. "Isn't that cool, Gayla?"

A single tear ran down Gayla's cheek, and she looked at Rusty. "So, you never got to see your sister again because of me? Because I was born?"

Rusty took a step back. "Gayla, don't ever say that again! Never think that. Your mother would never want you to feel that way. And she'd be so proud of you!"

Gayla's lips trembled. "I don't know what it's like to have parents and lose them, but I know I couldn't take losing my sister or never seeing her again."

Rusty reached into his pocket and pulled out his wallet. "Trust me. I understand." He handed the billfold to Gayla. "Look inside."

Gayla flipped through the photos, and then looked at Rusty. "I don't understand. Why do you have pictures of me?" She flipped back and forth and looked at Emma. "I don't understand."

Emma's jaw hurt. She struggled to answer. "That's not you, Jellybean. That's Uncle Rusty's little girl."

Gayla looked at the pictures again. She seemed confused. "Are you sure?"

"I'm sure," Rusty said. "You can't imagine how it fills my heart to meet the spitting image of my daughter. Your personality. Your hair. Your eyes. It's like seeing Rebbeca again."

Marcus stood beside Gayla and placed his hand on her shoulder. "So Uncle Rusty lost his sister and then his wife and kids. I think your mom had a plan. Somehow, she knew her brother would never get to see his little girl again, so she made sure he did." He nodded his head. "I'd say that's pretty cool!"

Gayla glanced up, breathing short gasps, and long exhales. Once she calmed, she stared for a moment. "Is that true, Uncle Rusty? Do you think what Marcus said is true?"

Rusty nodded. A tear slid down his cheek. He spread his arms, and Gayla ran to fill them.

CHAPTER 34

Sierra and Chris would stay until the treasure was unearthed and transported to NORAD. Rusty and the others would be returning to Hudson Ranch the next day.

"I'll make sure you have the most spectacular wedding ever," Rusty promised Emma.

"Don't go crazy." She squeezed his hand. "Having a family is more than I ever dreamed of."

"Emma," Gayla said, "Marcus sure misses his old friends."

Emma frowned for a second. She had a sense of where this was going and let out a gust of air. "Why do I have the feeling I may not see you for a while?"

"Please, Emma. We haven't asked their parents yet, but Marcus and Shelley would like to see their friends." She looked down. "And I'd kind of like to meet some more kids."

Rusty and Tracey grinned. "We have plenty of room. They could stay with us," Tracey offered. "And, Gayla will get the chance to meet all the others and the ones that will be moving here later."

Emma tossed her head. "You'd better hurry and sweet-talk them. You'll have to pack, you know."

Gayla threw her arms around Emma, and she held her heart as she watched her little sister run toward Elliot House.

Tracey stroked her arm. "Are you sure, Emma?"

Emma huffed. "Am I sure? You're the one who offered to take her in." She attempted to laugh. "Hope you know what you're getting in to." Her gaze drifted toward her little sister. "It's time, Aunt Tracey. It's past time."

Sierra put an arm around Emma. "She'll have a great time, trust me. But, now that it's just the four of us, we need to talk."

"About what?"

"Your wedding gown."

"Oh. I hadn't thought about it."

"Come inside." Sierra took Emma's arm.

While Tracey made tea, Sierra asked Emma what she knew about Jason's birth-parents.

"Only that you rescued him on your way to Wyoming. He said his mom's name was Renee, and she was dying. His father's name was Joseph and died in a plane crash when the EMP hit."

Sierra smiled. "May I tell you a story?"

Emma nodded.

"Shortly after you and your parents left, Major Hall came to take a census. After a few minutes of chatting, the major shifted his focus to the children in the field where Jason was playing quarterback."

***

"Oh, my God!" the major spurted. "Déjà vu."

"Hey, the receiver screwed up," Chris laughed. "My son can darn sure handle a football, can't he?"

"That's your son?" the major asked as he pointed to Jason.

"Yep." Chris beamed. "Seven years old and a born athlete."

"Lord, looking at him brings back memories. Your son looks just like my best friend at his age. We were inseparable from second grade till . . ."

Chris patted his shoulder. "Sorry, Major. We know your pain. We all lost a lot of friends."

Major Hall said he tried to find his friend's family. He made it to their house about a week after the EMP, but they were gone. "I was hoping to save his wife and son. I doubt they lasted long." His eyebrows gathered, and he frowned. "Renee' had diabetes, and their son was only a few months old," the Major said. "I'd talked to Joe that night," he sighed and stared at the sky. "There was a problem with their plane. Instead of getting home at ten, it would be close to three in the morning. Damn it!" Major Hall wiped his eyes. "Joe went down in the damned plane. He was an incredible athlete. He'd just been recruited by the Atlanta Falcons when it hit." He shook his head slowly. "God only knows what happened to his family. Renee and Jason were such sweethearts. So damned sad."

Chris had grabbed Sierra's chair to steady himself. The rest of the group stared in disbelief.

"Your friend's name was Joe? His wife was Renee'?" Chris had managed to ask.

Major Hall smiled. "Joseph. Hell of a guy."

"Dear God," Sierra gasped.

Major Hall squinted. "Did I say something wrong?"

Chris told Major Hall how he and Sierra had become Jason's parents. The Major's knees weakened, and Chris offered him a seat.

"Would you write a letter to Jason? Tell him about his parents?" Chris watched his son. "It would be wonderful for him to know who they were."

"I can do better than that." Major Hall collected himself. "I took all I could when I went to their house." He glanced at the women. "I even grabbed Renee's wedding dress. I thought she might like it, you know, in case I found her. I'll make sure Jason gets it all."

***

Sierra wiped the tears from her eyes. "A few years later, when we felt Jason was old enough, we gave him the trunk. He asked if his sisters could get married in his birth-mother's gown."

Tracey walked out of the bedroom, holding the white gown laden with tiny pearls.

Emma gasped and cupped her mouth.

Sierra held her hand. "We've protected it all these years. I'm not sure Jason even remembers."

"How beautiful," Emma breathed.

"The dress is the reason they took so long to get here. When Jason said he wanted to get married right away, Jim and Lena went back for it."

"I don't know what to say," Emma whispered.

"Just don't tell Jason. I'm sure he'll remember when he sees you walking down the aisle. Since the wedding will take place later at our ranch, the seamstress can make it a perfect fit."

Tracey poured them a cup of tea and put the pot down. "I think we should let Emma try on the gown. I'm dying to see her in it."

Sierra nodded. "Lets' do that."

A few minutes later, Emma walked out in the gown. Sierra caught her breath and gripped the arm of a chair before sitting. "Oh, Emma!"

Tracey hugged herself. "How perfect is that?"

The light through the windows hitting the pearl laden gown resulted in an aurora. A tear slid down Sierra's cheek as she scanned the walls of the small cabin and watched the tiny lights dance off the wooden walls. She wiped the dampness away and laughed. "That dress was meant for you!" Her hands covered her mouth. "I have never seen anything or anyone more beautiful in my life!"

***

The next morning, goodbyes were said, and those heading back to Hudson Ranch loaded into the wagons. Emma tried to hide her heartache when Gayla gave her a quick hug and jumped in next to Marcus and Shelley.

Rusty went to Emma. "Don't be offended, Emma. She loves you, but she's excited about going on a journey and meeting a lot of kids."

"I know," she whimpered. "I just thought she might have a twinge of sorrow over not seeing me for a while."

Rusty cradled her. "We had a chat. She wanted to know what would happen if she missed you and wanted to come home."

Emma glanced up. "She did?"

"Yes. I said I'd bring her back any time she wanted."

"That makes me feel better. I thought all she could think about was leaving."

"Not a chance. And to be honest, since Shelley's parents said she could go, it will be a lot easier on all of you. From what I understand, you're going to be pretty busy for a month or so."

"Thank you, Uncle Rusty. Take good care of Gayla for me."

"Phhh. Piece of cake. You did a fine job raising that little girl."

Rusty gave her a final hug then loaded up. "Let's roll," he yelled.

Gayla, Marcus, and Shelley yelled from the back of the wagon until they were out of sight. "Bye, Emma. Bye."

She smiled. This was her Deja' Vu.

CHAPTER 35

It had been three days since they left. Emma still found it strange for Chris and Sierra to walk out of Gayla's bedroom. At the same time, her heart warmed, and she got a funny feeling in her throat. She understood why her dad had loved them. They were wonderful. Kind, generous, helpful. She couldn't come up with all the flattering ways to describe the Alvise family. She had trouble calling them Mom and Dad but was sure that those words would easily spill off her tongue one day.

Emma and Jason sat at the table sipping coffee when Chris and Sierra joined them.

Emma pushed her chair back. "Good morning. Have a seat. I'll pour some coffee."

Chris placed his hand on her shoulder. "We have it. But thanks."

Sierra was about to sit and inhaled. "Actually, he has it." She rushed for the bathroom and slammed the door.

"Whew! I'm sure glad they got the septic tank installed!" Chris chuckled as he filled his mug. "She's moaned and groaned all night." He shook his head and put the pot down. "I told her to slack off on your canned jalapenos last night. She was putting them on everything!" He smirked and took a sip. "She wouldn't listen. Said they were the best she'd ever had."

"Whoa!" Emma fanned her face. "I love those things. I add a little piece of cinnamon. But I learned my lesson." She laughed. "Actually, it took about a dozen times before I learned."

"Bet she'll listen to me next time." Chris chuckled and joined them at the table. "The military should be here in a day or so. I want the shelter finished today. Those fine young men are doing us a favor, and I don't want them sleeping outdoors in tents. I want a roof over their heads."

"We'll get it done, Dad. The septic tank is ready, and the pipes went in yesterday. We have six bathrooms ready to be hooked up. Randy said they'd have it done in no time."

Chris nodded. "That's good. After breakfast and chores, I say that's where we concentrate."

"We're going to need more propane. There's gonna be a lot of cooking and heating water," Jason said. "We won't have nearly enough with all the extra people."

"Oh," Emma's hands flew to her mouth. "I can use the wood stove for cooking. They'll need the showers."

Chris reached across the table and patted her hand. "Don't you worry about it. I took care of it. The men are bringing propane tanks. They're also clearing the road."

"What?" Emma and Jason asked.

"The President had a chopper do a fly-over to determine their best path." Chris grinned. "In light of your generosity, he decided you at least deserved a road to the train depot."

"That's wonderful," Emma said.

Sierra came out of the bathroom. "Chris Alvise. If you ever let me eat jalapenos again…" She grimaced and shook her head. "I'm going back to bed!"

As she stormed past Jason, he chuckled. Sierra stopped just long enough to swat his shoulder.

Emma giggled when the bedroom door slammed. "I feel her pain." She stood. "You two plan out what we'll do today. I'll run to the smokehouse and grab some ham for breakfast." She let out a loud puff. "With all the men coming, we'll need more pork." She shook her head and stared at the floor. "What will we do about beef? We don't have the walk-in cooler ready. I hung the beef in the barn during winter to age it. Then Gayla and I ate what we could and canned the rest." Emma's mouth twitched. "This reminds me of winter when I thin the herd. I know I have to, but I hate it."

Chris and Jason rose. "Emma," Jason said, "I'll get someone to help me take care of the livestock."

Emma bobbed her head. "Thank you," she said and rushed for the door. As her hand reached the knob, she paused and turned around. "Jason, Dad. I have dozens of chickens. Much more than we need." She stared at her boots. "I'll tag the non-layers." Emma opened the door and ran.

***

The screen door slammed behind her. Jason went to the door and watched Emma as she ran for the chicken coop. He turned and stared at his dad. "How did she do it, Dad?" He thrust his hand in the direction

222

Emma ran. "You just saw her. You saw how much it pained her to think of killing the animals for food. How did she do it?"

Chris approached Jason and gazed at the fleeing Emma. He squeezed Jason's shoulder. "She did what she had to, son. Didn't mean she enjoyed it." Chris rubbed his mouth. "One thing Emma said struck me. We don't have a walk-in cooler."

"There was no time," Jason said. "The last thing I thought about was the cooler when Emma and Gayla were taken."

"I understand," Chris said. "But they're safe now. As soon as we finish the shelter, we start on the cooler and freezer."

Jason sat at the table and ran his fingers through his hair. "Dad. There's so much to do. I'm overwhelmed. I'm not sure where to start."

"We play it by ear. If Emma is right about the map, you're going to be a busy man. For years."

Gayla's bedroom door swung open, and Sierra ran for the bathroom. Chris and Jason chuckled.

"Like I said, I tried to warn her," Chris laughed then raised his coffee mug. "Good luck, son. Emma's even more hardheaded than your mother."

Jason raised his mug and tapped his father's. "And you've adored every minute of it."

Chris grinned and nodded. "I have. Yes. I have." His eyes darted toward the bathroom door, and his face knotted. "I couldn't imagine life without your mother. I pray that you and Emma have the same connection."

"We do, Father. We've had it since we were seven-years-old."

***

Emma and Sierra were prepping vegetables when Chris rushed in and flashed a huge grin.

"Ladies. The carpenters have finally given the ok. I'm going to freshen up a bit, and then we get to check out the new pavilion. It's unbelievable!"

Sierra hunched her shoulders and grinned. "Emma, let's stash the vegetables in the fridge. I can't wait to see the new building."

"Shouldn't we wait on Dad?"

"Nope!" Sierra giggled.

"I can't believe they wouldn't even let us take a peek," Sierra said as she loaded the fridge.

"Yeah. It's been driving me crazy," Emma said.

Sierra put her hands on her hips as she loaded the final batch. "Okay. Let's go!"

They held hands as they trotted toward the massive new structure. As they neared, Emma stopped. "Mrs., uh, Mom. I still can't believe how huge it is!"

"Pretty darned big." Sierra grinned. "But I guarantee it will get bigger."

Emma squinted. "What?" She scratched her head. "Why? Are more people coming?"

Sierra grinned. "Eventually. You and Jason own a heck of lot more land than you think."

Emma clutched her chest. "What?"

Sierra grimaced. "Don't you dare tell a soul! Not even Jason! Chris will have my hide for letting that slip!" Sierra's head wobbled. "Okay." She pointed to a tree. "Let's have a seat under the shade while I explain some things."

They sat under the tree, and Sierra told Emma the whole story.

"Emma. Chris and I have been buying and homesteading as much land as we could for years." Her head went back, and she exhaled. "Some people say we own Wyoming." She looked at Emma. "To some extent, they're correct."

Emma stared at her soon to be mother-in-law and frowned. "So, it's not just a rumor?"

Sierra chuckled. "No. But you can't believe everything you hear or read." She clutched Emma's hand. "We had the means, and we used our money and position."

Emma's hand pulled away. Suddenly, the Alvise family didn't seem so wonderful.

Sierra nodded her understanding of Emma's reaction. "I think I need to explain."

Emma crossed her arms across her chest. "Yeah. Maybe you should."

Sierra grinned. "Emma. We're not greedy landowners. What we did was for the good of our country."

Emma's head shot back. "Really? So buying up all the land helped our citizens?" she snapped.

"Yep." Sierra reached for Emma's hand, but she pulled away. Sierra huffed. "Let me try again." She stared at the sky and shook her head. "When Chris became president, he had the census workers and military keep notes about small towns and homesteads." Her lips pursed. "The notes we got back were devastating." She shook her head. "Once proud, productive people were starving. We felt we had to do something. We

224

chose to use our resources to buy and establish as many farms and ranches as we could." Sierra leaned back against the tree and smiled. "The more land we owned, the more people we could feed and help get back on their feet. Our costs, sharecroppers, and hired hands get paid first. We donate most of the crops and livestock. Any profit we make goes into starting new farms."

Emma's eyes widened. "Are you serious?"

Sierra reached for Emma's hand, and she didn't pull away. "The Alvise family is a long way from being destitute. But much of what we have, we spend on saving our countrymen."

"I think you're telling me that the pavilion will expand because we'll be taking on new people."

Sierra nodded. "A handful of Hudson residents will call this place home. But soon, you'll be needing more help. Lord knows thousands are looking for a home."

Emma stood and brushed her pants. "So, is this what Jason and I will be doing?" Her head tilted. "You and Mr. Alvise, Dad, want us to continue your tradition?"

Sierra shrugged. "That will be your decision."

Emma grinned and offered her other hand to her soon to be mother-in-law.

When Sierra stood, Emma cocked her head side-ways. "So. Exactly how much land does Jason own?"

Sierra brushed the dirt from the seat of her pants and seemed confused. "My dear. I have no idea what you're talking about." A smirk crossed her face as she linked arms with Emma. "Let's have a look at your new pavilion."

***

Emma and Sierra walked inside the new building.

"This is what we started with at Hudson Ranch. Later, we added a pool room, bar, and an enclosed porch," Sierra said.

"A pool room? You had a swimming pool inside?"

Sierra shook her head and laughed. "No. We have pool tables and a bar. It's the one place on Hudson Ranch that no children are allowed. It's only for adults." Sierra's lips twisted. "No pool tables in your magazines, I take it?"

Emma shook her head. Then her eyes lit up. "Wait! Yes! I read about them! They're in dark smokey rooms that smell musky." Her nose curled. "Why in the world would we want one of those?"

Sierra burst into laughter. "Like I said earlier, you can't believe everything you read." She wrapped her arm in Emma's. "Let's go inside."

Emma was in awe. She spun around and tried to take it all in. Her hands glided down the sides of the wooden walls. "This is beautiful!"

"It is, isn't it." Sierra wrapped her arm around Emma's waist. "Eventually, it will resemble the pavilion at Hudson Ranch."

"What do you mean?"

Sierra spread her arms. "This will be the main dining hall." She pointed toward the stacks of stones and bricks at each end of the room. "Soon, those rocks will surround the brick fireplaces. They'll keep it warm during the winter, and they'll be large enough to cook a whole cow."

"You're kidding."

"Nope. Chris said they're going to start on the fireplaces in a day or so, but he wanted the cooler finished first."

"Jason told me that he wanted to hold off on the beef and chickens until we needed them, or the cooler was running."

Sierra nodded toward the wall near a set of double doors. "That's where the buffet tables will go." She slung her head. "Let's check out the room behind the doors."

Emma's hands flew to her cheeks when she entered the second room. "What in the world?"

Sierra giggled. "My goodness. The men have been busy. I wasn't expecting to see the kitchen this far along."

Emma's mouth opened wide, and her eyes searched the large room. "This is a kitchen?"

"Yep."

"And there's another huge fireplace over there." Emma pointed.

"Actually, that's a brick oven. But, trust me, it will help add warmth."

Emma strolled along a wall lined with all sorts of things that were unfamiliar. "What is this?"

"It's called a flat grill. Imagine cooking dozens of pancakes at one time."

Emma slid her fingers over the metal slats on the next grill. "I guess they haven't finished this one. Pancakes would fall right through those holes."

Sierra laughed and rubbed Emma's shoulder. "No, dear." She chuckled. "That's a grill for cooking meat. Steaks, chops, burgers."

"Hmm." Emma tapped her lips and nodded. "I get it. It's sort of like my cast iron pan that has ridges. Very clever. In my opinion, it's the only way to cook a steak."

"Agreed." Sierra grinned. "But unlike your pan, you can grill thirty or forty at a time."

Sierra patted the next item. "These are burners, like on your stove. They run off propane, and we use them sparingly." She raised her eyebrows. "You won't believe how much time you'll save when you're canning with so many burners."

Emma pointed. "What's behind those two big doors?"

"One will be a small walk-in cooler, the other a freezer."

"But, they're already building a cooler and freezer."

"Yes. But you'll also need them in the kitchen."

Sierra took her arm. "Let's check out the bedrooms and bathrooms."

Sierra opened the door to the first bedroom. "There are ten of these along this side of the pavilion. Small. Just enough room for a double bed, nightstand, and closet."

"It's not that much different from my bedroom."

"Yeah. Mostly for sleeping," Sierra said. "Let's look at the bathrooms. We have one for men and one for women."

Emma scratched her head when they walked into the first one. Walls separated the showers and toilets. "No tubs? That's sad. They sure can soak your pains away."

Sierra smirked. "This is the men's room. A room with four tubs is next. It's reserved for bathing children. And soaking pains away is much better in the hot tub."

Emma squinted. "A hot tub?"

"Yep. A hot tub is gigantic. Several people can relax in it at once. And you can make it shoot streams of water out and..."

Emma's squint deepened. "Uh, several people at once?"

"Yeah. It's for soaking, not bathing. You didn't see them in your magazines?"

Emma shook her head.

Sierra laughed and patted her arm. "Never mind. You'll see soon enough."

227

Chris walked in and took his wife's arm. "Couldn't wait for me, I see. Well! What do you think, ladies?" He reached for a knob in a shower. "Randy wanted me to see if the water was hot." After a few seconds, hot water poured out. He gave a thumbs up. "Yep."

"Mr., uh, Dad, I've never seen anything like this place," Emma said. "At least, not that I can remember."

"Emma, your future will be filled with discoveries." His grin grew. "Do you realize what your generosity will do for thousands of people. Imagine all the Gayla's out there who've never turned a faucet and had cold or hot water, or flipped a switch and turned on a light. Emma Harding. I couldn't be more proud or love you more if you were my own daughter!" Chris grabbed her in a bear hug and spun her around.

CHAPTER 36

Emma was cleaning the barn when she heard them. Engines. Probably the military, but she wasn't taking any chances. She grabbed the rifle leaning next to the door. The toll of the red bell brought almost everyone to her cabin.

The six-truck convoy pulled up just as Jason rode in. Emma lowered her rifle and wiped her brow.

Jason dismounted Guss and took Emma's hand. They were about to greet the men when Chris and his mount rushed in, followed by several others. He stopped between the men and his family and aimed his rifle.

"Identify yourselves!" Chris shouted.

Jason raised his gun. Emma was confused. She glanced around and realized the others had weapons drawn on the group of men.

"Whoa, President Alvise." One man exited a jeep, raised his hands, and stepped in front of his truck. "Major Hall, Sir. We're here to help."

Chris sighed and signaled for everyone to lower their weapons.

"Sorry, Major."

Major Hall raised his brows. "Scared me for a second there, sir."

He was about to give a salute.

"No! No salutes," Chris said. "Thank you for your respect, but I want no salutes. If anyone deserves them, it's you and your men." He nodded his head toward the house. "Have your men sit on the porch. We'll get them snacks and drinks."

Chris spoke to Major Hall on the way to the house. "No more salutes. To be on the safe side, I'd prefer no one knows who was who."

"Sir?"

Emma felt dazed. Almost queasy. Why had everyone reacted that way? What did Mr. Alvise mean about staying on the safe side? She turned to go inside, but Sierra stopped her. "Jason, Emma. Your Dad was obviously expecting trouble." She looked at her husband. "Something's wrong. Find out what it is. I'll take care of the men."

"Mom?" Jason yelled.

Emma didn't miss the flash of panic in Sierra's eyes. "I told you! Talk to your dad while I take care of the men." She let out a gust of air and squeezed Jason's shoulder. "Someone better damned well let me know what's going on pretty soon!"

***

As Jason and Emma walked toward Chris, he pulled Major Hall to the side. "Why don't we check out the pavilion?" He spoke a little too loud and then leaned in. "We need to talk," he whispered. Chris smiled and ushered Jason, Emma, and Major Hall away. Once they made it out of sight of the others, Chris stopped. "We have a problem." His brows heightened. "Jordan Dean escaped. I found out just as you and your men were arriving, Major."

Emma gasped.

"Sorry, Emma, but it gets worse," Chris said. "It seems he talked a lot of men into joining him."

Major Hall's eyes narrowed. "What are you saying, Chris? Are you accusing my men and me of being bought off by Jordan Dean?"

Chris gripped Major Hall's shoulder. "No. Not you. But how well do you know your men?"

"Very well."

"Are you sure?" Chris asked.

"Absolutely."

"I hope you're right, but this is the reality. Twenty-two men escaped from the prison at NORAD, and dozens of military personnel are unaccounted for. Jordan may well have a small army."

Emma held her chest and took a step back. "Dear God." She couldn't believe what she was hearing. Her encounter with Jordan Dean came rushing back, and the world began to spin. Jason wrapped his arms around her for support.

Major Hall's eyes widened. "How the hell is this possible?"

"Greed is a powerful thing." Chris shrugged. "If any of your men are involved..." Chris let out a gust of air. "No doubt Jordan knows we've been informed. He won't just storm in. Could be he was tipped off about your mission and will be waiting when we move the treasure to NORAD. Choppers are looking for them, but I'm sure he'd prepared for that. It's my understanding that your men have no idea why they're here. Correct?"

"Correct."

230

"Okay, once they settle in, we'll have dinner and fill them in. We'll need to pay close attention to them after that."

"Alright, but I don't believe any of the men I brought are involved. I've known them for years, and they all have the highest clearance."

"I hope you're right," Chris said. "Get them set up at the pavilion. We have bathrooms up and running. I'm sure they'd appreciate a shower."

Jason stuck his hand out. "Major Hall, I'm glad you're here, and it's good to see you again."

"Good to see you, too. I swear you look more like Joe every time I see you." Major Hall turned to Emma. "Jason is a lucky man. The stories about you have spread across the country. It's an honor to meet you, Ms. Emma."

"That's embarrassing." She looked at Jason. "But I'm the lucky one, Major."

He smiled. "You both are. I can't wait to meet your little sister. Every kid in the country talks about Gayla. She's their hero. Slingshots are number one on kid's wish lists nowadays. They even have one named "The Gayla."

Emma chuckled. "That will tickle Gayla. But she's at Hudson Ranch. She wanted to meet more kids."

"That's probably a good thing, considering... But, honestly, it seems everyone knows your story." He gripped her shoulder. "You and Gayla should be proud. You've given hope to thousands."

***

After dinner, Major Hall told his men about their mission and Jordan Dean's escape. Chris enlightened them to Emma's plan for the treasure.

One of the soldiers cocked his head. "You're really going to do that, Ma'am? You're going to use the money to rebuild Riverton?"

"Yes," she said. "We have no idea what we'll find. For all we know, there may not be enough to buy more than a few generators. But I promise every dime will go toward rebuilding my parent's hometown."

The young man bolted from his chair. "Harding. Oh, my God. You're John Harding's daughter?"

Emma felt awkward. "Uh, yes."

"Ma'am, I grew up in Riverton. I knew your father." Tears filled his eyes, and he brushed them away. "Pardon me. I never realized the connection. My family was close friends with your dad." The young man stood. "Ms. Emma, my father's brother and wife moved here with your parents."

Emma stood on shaky legs. "The Elliot's?" she asked.

He extended a hand. "Joshua, Joshua Elliot, at your service, ma'am." He stood at attention and gave a salute. "I promise to protect you with my very life."

Emma found it hard to speak. "You're Josh Elliot's namesake?"

"Yes, Ma'am. Uncle Josh died several years ago. He was helping bring down an old building when it collapsed." Joshua shook his head. "Aunt Lorna disappeared. No one knows where she went."

Emma rubbed her neck. He deserved to know the truth. But how could she tell him when she still struggled with telling Jason.

"I still have family in Riverton. The younger ones can't imagine electricity beyond the little they get from generators and solar." Joshua's head bent. "God bless you, ma'am," he whispered.

Emma went to the young man and hugged him. "I'm sorry. Let's pray I'm right, and Jordan buried enough here to make those children's dreams come true."

It took a few minutes for everyone to collect themselves. Then one of the soldiers broke the silence. "Major, are we expecting back-up?" one man asked. "If he buried that much treasure here…" The man let out a puff of air.

The Major looked at Chris.

Chris shook his head. "Probably a bad idea. We don't know who we can trust at this point," he said.

"Dad," Emma said. "I'm afraid they plan on attacking us. Unless someone told him, like you suggested, Jordan has no idea we know about all the treasure on the property." She sighed. "I'm sure he thinks he has enough manpower to get rid of us."

He put a hand on her shoulder. "We'll be ready, Emma."

"Will we?" she asked. "Jordan may be evil, but I don't believe he's stupid. He's clever."

"And?" Chris asked.

"Well." Emma felt her face warm, and her hands shook as she stared at the expressions surrounding her. "If I were him, I'd have made sure a rumor got around before I escaped." Her eyes darted, and she felt slightly foolish. "I would have had the men tell stories of how I'd only buried a small amount here. The rest? I'd have them say it was hundreds of miles away. Perhaps in several locations. You know, so they wouldn't be sure where to search."

Chris blinked his eyes, and Jason laughed. "You should listen to her. Emma's quite clever. Not much gets past her."

Chris cocked his head. "I'll find out if any rumors like that were heard."

"Oh, one other thing," Emma said. "He knows this is the first place they'd come looking for him. He won't come for a couple of weeks, maybe longer. He's already waited twenty years. If I were him, I'd want to make sure I'd thrown them off my trail before I made my move. But if they were tipped off, Jordan and his men will be here any time now, waiting for the moment to attack. He wouldn't risk the gold being dug up and slipping through his fingers."

Chris turned toward Major Hall. "Station lookouts. Every man at the ranch will help." Chris walked down the porch steps and paused. "I'm going to find out if NORAD heard any gossip."

***

Chris had the main radio set up in the pavilion. He put the mic down and leaned back in his chair. His fingers ran through his thick salt and pepper hair. "Son of a gun."

Major Hall walked in. "Hey. Jason, Emma, and your men know the property better than me. They're deciding where to station the men." He paused. "Is something wrong?

Chris let out a half-hearted chuckle. "Seems Emma was correct. Everyone at NORAD is being interrogated." He smirked and stared at the Major. "There was, indeed, a rumor about the treasure." He chuckled. "Damn near identical to Emma's theory. It appears to have started the day before they escaped."

"Go on," the Major said.

"The gossip was, Jordan buried a couple of small chests here, at Emma's, early on, then decided he needed to find a more remote area for the big stashes." Chris raised his brows and smirked. "Two-hundred miles from here."

The Major's jaw twisted. "Emma should have been special ops."

Chris rubbed his brow. "Yeah. Or the FBI."

"What do we do?"

Chris stood. "Clothes."

Major Hall squinted.

"We need to put your men in civilian clothes," Chris said. "I doubt they've made it here yet, but Jordan's recruits may be watching us shortly. We don't need anyone walking around in uniform."

"Gotcha."

"We need to think this out. Even with military binoculars, they won't be able to see us unless they're close. Too many trees. We need to have men stationed several hundred feet into the forest."

"Sounds good."

"Joshua Elliot," Chris said.

"Sir?" Major Hall asked.

"I'd appreciate it if he could be Emma's guardian."

"Consider it done, sir."

CHAPTER 37

It had been a week since Jordan's escape. The decision to begin excavating was agreed on. The next morning would prove Emma correct or destroy her plans to rebuild Riverton.

"I'll get that for you, Ms. Emma." Joshua Elliot rested his rifle against the porch.

Emma lowered the basket of wet clothes and put her hands on her hips. "Listen, Joshua, if you keep trying to do my chores, how the heck will you protect me if Jordan and his men show up?"

He grabbed his gun. "Sorry, ma'am. You're right. I just hate to see you carrying all that heavy stuff." He looked at his boots. "You work too hard."

Emma dropped her basket and nodded toward the cabin. "I need something to drink."

When they got inside, she filled their glasses with ice and tea. "Sit." Emma pointed to the couch, handed Joshua his drink, and sat beside him.

"Listen, Joshua. I appreciate you worrying about me, but if you think how I'm living now is hard, well, you're wrong. This is a breeze."

"I know, Ms. Emma. I lost a lot of my family, ya know." He looked up, and his lips tightened. "A lot of them. I always believed Mom and Dad worked themselves to death. Even in Riverton and Lander, where everyone worked together, it was hard. They worked all day trying to make sure we were fed and warm." Joshua bent over and planted his face in his hands. "They tried so hard. My little sister got sick. She didn't make it to six," he cried. "Why did this have to happen? Why?"

Emma wrapped her arms around Joshua and rubbed his back. "I don't know. I don't know."

Jason opened the door. Emma put a finger to her lips and shook her head as she comforted Joshua.

Jason backed out, waited a minute, then yelled, "Emma," before he came in. Joshua wiped his eyes and jumped to his feet.

"Emma. Joshua. They got Jordan and his men!"

"What?" Emma gasped. "Are you sure."

"I'm sure!" He grabbed Emma, swung her around, and then gave her a big kiss.

"A chopper spotted them yesterday," Jason said. "They were traveling at a high rate of speed. The pilot attempted to warn them that the bridge ahead had collapsed, but they kept going." Jason shook his head. "They said there's no way anyone survived. Three trucks plunged into the Platte River. One on top of the other. Three managed to stop. They captured everyone about an hour ago. Jordan Dean wasn't one of the survivors."

Emma sat on the couch. "I feel horrible for being relieved that people died."

"I understand. But remember, it was them, or us."

"I know."

"So, we go ahead with digging up the treasure?" Joshua asked.

"Yep," Jason said. "Tomorrow, hopefully, Emma will be a wealthy woman."

Emma smiled. "Only briefly, Jason."

***

That evening, everyone gathered at Emma's and celebrated.

"Major Hall," Chris said, "It appears I owe you and your men an apology."

Major Hall raised his eyebrows. "How's that?"

"For questioning your men's loyalty."

The Major raised his glass and smirked. "Apology accepted."

"So, how does the treasure search work?" Emma asked.

"I'd like to search for some of the smaller ones first," Chris said. "But it's your call, Emma."

"I kind of like that idea," she said. "And I've changed my mind about it all going to rebuilding Riverton."

Questioning eyes caused her to laugh. "Don't worry. I'm not getting greedy. Everybody here was willing to put their lives at risk to recover it. I'd like to give everyone a share."

Chris, Sierra, and Jason grinned. The others waved their hands and talked at once, saying they expected nothing.

"I know you expected nothing, but that's the deal," Emma said. "I guess how much depends on what we find."

"That's very generous of you, Emma," Chris said. "No offense," he eyed everyone, "but no one will have access to the map or metal detector other than me, Jason, and Emma. Not even you, my dear." He nodded toward his wife. "It's for everyone's protection."

Once the others left, Emma voiced her concern. "We can't just stack the treasure in the barn. What do we do with it?"

"Dad and I talked about that," Jason said. "We'll hide it in the secret room in the cellar and the little room under your bed."

Emma nodded and rubbed her forehead.

"I know that look. What's wrong, Emma?" Jason asked.

"Jordan Dean." She looked at them. "What if he didn't die?"

"He's gone, Emma. There's no way anyone could have survived," Chris said. "Even if he managed to live, he'd be horribly injured. You don't have to worry about him anymore."

"I'm sure you're right." Emma wasn't convinced.

***

Jordan grabbed his head and moaned. What a wicked hangover. A shivering cold engulfed him, and he reached for his cover. Unable to find it, he forced his eyes open. For a brief moment, he thought he'd gone blind. Surrounded by total darkness, the sight of a few faint embers of coals gave him relief.

Sorry bastards let the fire die out and left him passed out on the damp ground. He rolled over and got on his knees. The earth beneath him seemed to move, and he had to steady himself before he stood. He was about to wake them with a cursing rant when he realized he was alone. He spun and almost fell before taking a knee.

"What the hell?"

He made a slow turn around the campsite. No men. No trucks. He closed his eyes and tried to remember. They'd been celebrating the end of their week-long wait. Only about one hundred miles separated them from the treasure. By now, no one was looking for them. At least nowhere near where they were headed. He'd made sure anyone searching would be hundreds of miles away. One of the men had handed him a drink. That was the last he remembered. No. Several men stood over him. They were laughing and going through his pockets.

Jordan's breathing increased as he frantically searched the pockets of his jacket. His map. Jordan thrust his arms into the air, gritted his teeth, and shrieked. He took deep breaths and calmed. Okay. So they knew where the cabin was. They knew he'd buried some of the treasure there. It didn't matter. That's all they knew. He'd practically memorized the map. He

237

didn't need it. If they got lucky enough to find the gold and dig it up, they'd save him the trouble. Yeah. Let them take care of whoever was living there. He'd get there later and make them pay!

Jordan snickered and put tinder on the hot coals. Minutes later, he had a warm fire. As it burned, he walked toward the forest and retrieved his hidden stash. He should have been a Boy Scout. "Always prepared," he snickered and rubbed his bristly chin. Who was it that said, "Trust no one?" He searched through the packs he hid each night. Weapons, ammo, food, and survival gear. He pulled out the sleeping bag and unrolled it before tossing it next to the fire. "I was hoping I wouldn't need you."

He needed to get organized and recuperate from whatever it was they'd put in his drink. The next morning he would head out. Most likely, his idiot *friends* would stick to the old map. Bad idea. He'd made the trek a few weeks earlier. The roads were nothing like they were when he'd mapped it out twenty years ago.

Jordan raised a bottle of whiskey, threw his head back, and downed a shot. He swallowed, and his nose curled before he spit on the fire. "Fools! The whole damned lot of you!"

CHAPTER 38

"Emma. I miss you so much."

Emma fought to compose herself before she pressed the button on the mic. "I miss you, too, Gayla. Are you having fun?"

"Oh, yes. I have lots of Grandmas and Grandpas and dozens of Aunts and Uncles. Don't ask me to count how many cousins I have."

Emma wiped her eye. "I'm so happy for you, Jellybean."

"I'm giving slingshot lessons. You won't believe this, but they say people know about me. My cousin, Ryan, brought some slingshots they were selling on the train." Gayla giggled. "They're called The Gayla's. Is that awesome or what?"

Emma's grin threatened to crack her face. "That's very awesome, Jellybean."

"So, when are you coming? When are you and Jason getting married?"

"Soon, I hope. We still have a lot to take care of."

"Okay, Uncle Frank says I need to let you get back to work. I love you, Emma. I'll see you soon."

"I love you, too."

A moment later, Frank called out. "I hope I handled that okay, Emma. It sounded like you were overwhelmed."

"Thanks, Uncle Frank. Yes. It was kind of hard, but I'm glad she's so happy."

Frank chuckled. "Gayla is having a blast, but Rusty and Tracey say she cries almost every night because she misses you."

"She does?" Emma bolted up from the chair.

"Yep. When they offer to take her home, she refuses. She says you were right, and she needs to make friends like you always wanted."

Frank's attempt to sound jovial didn't fool Emma. She sensed a fake cheerfulness.

Frank paused, and his words were choppy. "Oh, and she's helping plan your wedding."

Emma eased back into the chair. Uncle Frank was crying. She knew it wasn't because he was afraid or sad. Uncle Frank was crying because he was happy for her little sister. It took Emma a few seconds to respond. "Thank you. Thank you all. Gayla and I have been truly blessed."

Emma laid the mic down, and Chris picked it up and clutched Emma's quivering shoulder. "Frank, we start exploring in the morning. Say some prayers. Hopefully, Emma and Gayla can reunite soon."

***

The next morning, Emma's theory about the trees and bushes in the drawing proved to be correct. Every bush contained a crate.

"We'll open the first one," Chris told everyone. "We want to be sure we're digging up treasure, but if we find others, they'll remain sealed."

Everyone gasped when Jason broke the lock on the first trunk. Gems, coins, and precious metals filled the container.

By noon they had retrieved four trunks, and Chris asked Major Hall to take his men to the pavilion so they could clean up before lunch. "Keep an eye on them, Major."

"Will do."

Sierra, Emma, and the other women made lunch while Jason and Chris placed the chests in the secret cellar. Emma stared out the kitchen window. About fifty yards away was the largest collection of trees in the drawing. If that group of trees represented treasure, there was no telling what lay beneath the surface. Emma's heart pounded.

She watched as Jason and Chris headed to the spot with a metal detector. A few minutes later, Chris wiped his mouth and said something to Jason. Jason rubbed his throat and nodded.

Emma's head fell to her chest as Chris and Jason made their way to her cabin. She'd hoped they would find much more treasure. What they'd found would change many lives, but there was no way it would make the impact she'd hoped for.

Chris and Jason sat down to eat, and Emma slid a plate to them. She'd told Sierra about what she'd seen, and Sierra wrapped an arm around Emma.

"Okay, Chris," Sierra blurted. "Get it over with."

Chris pushed his plate back. "We have a problem."

"I saw you on the hill with the metal detector." Emma fought her trembling chin. "I take it there's nothing there."

Chris's head went back, his eyes widened, and he let out a puff of air.

"Emma," Jason said, "Whatever is buried there is massive."

The thought of danger didn't slow her grin. "I don't understand. You said we had a problem."

"That *is* the problem," Jason said. "We can't trust anyone. Major Hall's men may be trustworthy, but like I told you before, that much gold can get you killed."

"Then, what do we do?"

Chris spoke up. "We send the men on a wild goose chase. They won't find more treasure. Tomorrow, I go with them to escort what we have to NORAD."

"But what about the rest?" Emma asked.

"I'll speak with the president. We'll need a much larger escort. And if possible, a chopper escort as well."

Emma huffed. "This is a lot more complicated than I imagined."

Jason laughed. "Emma, if you think it's complicated now, wait until all that money lands in your lap and you have to figure out how to spend it."

"I already know how to spend it. You two need to eat. The others will be back soon, and you need to plan your wild goose chase." Emma giggled.

*****

Four hours later, Chris leaned on his shovel. "I think it's time to call it quits men. Jason and I searched everywhere with the metal detector." He shook his head. "All we're digging up are old cans and hog wire. Looks like there wasn't as much gold buried here as we'd hoped."

Joshua Elliott walked over to Emma. "I'm sorry, Ms. Emma. I know you wanted to rebuild Riverton, but what we found should help a lot."

The other men echoed Joshua's comments.

"Maybe there's enough to buy all the kids and old folks some nice things for Christmas this year," one private said.

"That's a great idea," a few others chimed in.

"I promised you all a percentage and…"

"No, ma'am." Every man shook his head.

"Ms. Emma, we're as disappointed as you. We talked all night about how we hoped to be a part of rebuilding Riverton." Joshua looked at his comrades. "I like the Christmas idea. Maybe we could be there and help distribute stuff next Christmas."

Emma glanced at Jason and Chris, then stared at the men's sad eyes. "You'll have to excuse me," she said before rushing home.

*****

241

Jason followed his distraught fiancee'. "What's wrong, Emma?" he asked as he rushed through the door.

"What's wrong?" Emma spun around. "What's wrong? Didn't you see the men? We stood there and lied to them, and all they wanted to do was help!"

Jason went to her and massaged her shoulder. "And help, they will. Every one of them will return with Dad and more backup."

"They'll know we lied to them, Jason."

"Yes. And they'll understand why."

Emma backed away, snatched her bandana from her back pocket, and blew her nose. "I hope you're right."

"He *is* right, Emma," Sierra said as she walked in.

Emma took note of the expression Sierra wore. Tension. Anxiety. She'd never seen Jason's mother so concerned, not even when Gayla saved her from Elizabeth.

Sierra rubbed her hands and paced for a moment before stopping and taking a deep breath. "We're in a very unsafe situation. The trucks the men brought can't carry what's still buried. And one leak about what's on this small transport could cost the men their lives. It's worth millions. Imagine the danger once it's all unearthed."

"I guess you're right. I just hate lying."

Sierra took a deep breath and gripped her soon to be daughter-in-law. "Sometimes, it's necessary." She held her at arm's length. "This would be one of those times. I don't want to lose my husband over gold and jewels. The more men he has around him, the better I'll feel."

"Mrs. Sierra. I mean, Mom. I, I don't know what I was thinking. I don't want Dad risking his life on my behalf." She threw her shoulders back. "Jason, I'm going on the transport. I won't have your father…"

"Not a chance in hell," Sierra barked. "You are staying right here." She thrust a finger toward the ground.

"But…"

"There is no but!" Sierra snarled and shoved a finger in Emma's face. After a brief pause, she cupped her mouth. "I apologize," she spoke softly and looked at the floor. "My goodness. I don't know what came over me. I feel horrible." She took Emma's hands and gazed into her eyes. "Thank you for the offer. But that simply isn't going to happen. Chris has to meet with the president. They have to lay out a plan. I'm sorry for, well, for exposing my nervousness." She faked a laugh and looked at her son.

242

"You'd think after being married to your father all these years I'd have learned to deal with it."

Jason hugged his mother. Emma's heart filled with a throbbing ache. How she wished she could hold her mother or father right now.

Sierra righted herself and shook her head. "Whew. That wasn't why I came here. Sorry." She dried her eyes. "The ladies want to eat at the new pavilion tonight. There's plenty of room, and they've been preparing a huge feast since they heard the men were leaving in the morning."

"Of course. We'll need to set up some tables," Emma said.

Jason gave Emma a quick kiss. "I'll take care of that."

"What's on the menu?" Emma asked.

"Oh, let's see. Sweet potato and green bean casseroles, bread, salad, stuffing, and cranberry sauce."

Emma's forehead bunched. "Okay. I guess I should get a ham from the smokehouse."

"Oh," Sierra said. "Did I forget to mention turkey?"

"Turkey?" Emma and Jason asked.

"Turkey. A big old Tom," Sierra smirked.

"That's the shot we heard late yesterday? Someone got a turkey?" Jason asked. "Randy told Dad it was one of the cows being put down."

"He lied," Sierra chuckled. "Randy had that gobbler dressed and hanging in the walk-in cooler this morning."

Jason laughed. "You're telling us that Randy shot a turkey? Randy? The worst shot on the ranch?"

Emma's mouth dropped open. "Jason. She's also telling us the walk-in-cooler is working."

Jason sent out a "Whoo-hoo." Then he grabbed Emma and spun around before putting her down. He gripped her shoulders. "Can you imagine, Emma? Think of all the things we can keep in there."

Sierra laughed. "Save a little celebratory energy. The freezer seems to be working, too. The barrels of water froze today."

***

That evening, everyone enjoyed Thanksgiving a few months early. Randy was ribbed about being the worst shot but the only one to bring home a turkey.

"Yeah, well, I try to hold back. Don't want to embarrass the rest of you," he said.

Emma stood. She felt awkward and nervous. "I want to thank Randy for more than this wonderful turkey dinner." Her eyelashes batted. "Not just Randy. All of you. Without you, I'd still be running outside in a rain or snowstorm to get water or…" Her face heated. "Or, well, you know." Emma lowered her eyes. "Now I don't have to go to the stream every morning and hope my dairy products are still good. And I don't have to can food for several hours a night. I can put it in the fridge, freezer, or smokehouse." Emma lifted her tea glass in a salute. "To you all, Thank you!"

As Emma lifted her glass, there was a loud explosion. She instinctively threw her arms up to protect her face, and tea soaked her hair.

Chris bolted from his seat and pointed to the women. "Stay here." The men ran toward the noise.

"Put it out. Put it out." That was all Emma could hear. Her feet shuffled as she headed toward the door. Sierra tried to stop her, but Emma tossed her arm away. She walked outside and fell to her knees. The walk-in-cooler and freezer swirled with thick heavy smog. All the work. All the dreams. Gone. Just gone. Maybe it wasn't meant to be.

Emma crouched on her knees. The other women joined her.

"It's okay, Emma," Laura said. "We'll rebuild."

"Yeah," Iva agreed. "Things just happen."

"No," Emma whispered. "Payback. It's payback for lying."

Jason ran toward the women. "Everything is okay. No damage to the cooler or freezer. It was a bad generator. Randy has it under control."

Emma wiped her wet hair back in relief. Why did she always have to assume the worst?

***

Everyone met for breakfast the next morning at Emma's Place. Chris, Major Hall, and his men would leave at sunrise. Years earlier, it would have been about a six or seven-hour drive. Now, it would take twelve, maybe fourteen hours if they were lucky.

"We'll try to stay in touch," Chris told his wife. He glanced at Emma and Jason. "Don't worry if you don't hear from us for several hours. Give us at least twenty-four. There's no telling what conditions we may encounter. Some of the bridges aren't holding up so well."

"I understand, Dad," Jason said.

Sierra held her husband. "Please. Stay alert. Don't trust anyone."

"I'll be fine, honey." Chris nodded toward the Major's men as they told everyone goodbye. "Hell. Look at them."

"Mom," Emma said, "Dad's right. They're upset about us not finding more treasure. Not because they wanted to steal it, but because of what it would have meant to Riverton."

Sierra brushed her hair back. "I'm sure you're right." Her lips tightened and curled into a frown. "Chris, I couldn't bear to lose you."

Chris kissed her forehead. "I'll be back."

Joshua walked toward Emma. His eyes focused on the ground. When he reached her, he held out his hand, and she took it. "Ms. Emma, I've never been more honored to meet someone. I'm due to re-enlist." He shook his head. "I've decided against it. I'm going back to Riverton. Somehow, I'm going to help make your dream come true, even without all the money." His lips thinned. "I'm not sure how, but something inside me tells me I can make a difference."

Emma grinned. "I have no doubt. Make sure you stop by here on your way." She hugged her young friend then stepped back.

"Yes, ma'am."

Emma grinned and chuckled. "Will you please stop calling me Ms. Emma and ma'am?"

"I'll try." Joshua stood at attention and saluted her. One by one, the other men joined him.

Emma stood tall and saluted them back. Once they went to the trucks, she turned to her future mother-in-law. "They'll keep Dad safe."

Sierra rested her head on her husband's chest. "Emma's right. You'll be fine, Chris. You'll be fine."

CHAPTER 39

Jason made sure the radio was monitored continuously. There had been no contact with his father since noon, and the sun would be setting soon. "Mom. Emma. I'm going back to the pavilion. I won't be able to sleep until I hear from Dad."

"I'm going with you," Sierra said.

Emma stood. "Me too."

Jason shook his head. "No. Please." He let out a gust of air. "I'm sure Dad's fine. Mom, take a long hot bath and try to relax. Emma. Read or draw. Something. I'll let you know if I hear from him."

"I need to be there," Sierra insisted.

"Why? What good will it do for the two of you to be there?" He thrust his finger toward the bathroom door. "Mom, go relax like I told you!"

Sierra grinned, then snorted and chuckled. "God. You sound just like your father." She lifted her hand, and Jason helped her up. "You're right. There's nothing I can do." Sierra clasped a hand to her mouth. "But he's escorting treasure worth millions of dollars."

Emma wrapped her arms around Sierra. "Mom, I swear he'll be okay. I just know it." She glanced at Jason. "Heat the water. I'll get some things together so your mom can take a nice long bath, then I'll make her some Chamomile tea. Would you like a thermos of coffee?"

"Yes. Thanks, Emma. But I'll make the tea and coffee," Jason said.

"I'm sorry to be such a pain," Sierra said. "After all these years, you'd think I'd be used to my husband's dangerous escapades." She shook her head. "Maybe it's because we're older. He's not as quick as he was a few years ago." Sierra coughed as she choked on her words. "Dear Lord." She laughed and waved her hands. "Don't ever tell your father I said that!"

Emma and Jason chuckled. "Don't worry, Mom. That'll be our secret," Jason said. "But, if I don't hear from him soon, I'll be heading out." His dad had left about thirteen-hours ago and said to give him twenty-four. "I'm only concerned because he promised to check in every few hours, and we haven't heard from him since noon." He squeezed his mother's shoulder. "We have to remember that things aren't like they were years ago. A fallen tree alone could cost them hours. And communication can be spotty."

Sierra took a deep breath and hugged her son. "Your father is fine." She walked past him and went to her room. "Heat the water, please. I think I'd like that hot bath now. See you in the morning."

***

He'd been calling out for more than four hours, and Jason was losing hope. His head rested in the crook of his arm. "Two more hours," he whispered. "If I don't hear from you by then…"

"I hear you, son." Chris's reply was choppy. "Tried contacting you all day. Mountain interference. Bridge out. Had to detour. Go to bed. We'll be at NORAD within the hour. I'll call in the morning."

Jason jumped up and thrust his fists in the air.

"Thank God!" Randy said. He looked at the other men and wiped his eyes. "I say we get some sleep. We have about five hours before it's time to go to work."

"Time well spent," Matthew said.

"Thank you. Thank you all," Jason said. "I'll see you in the morning."

Once they'd left, Jason laid his head on the desk. He was okay. His dad was safe. He stood, rubbed his face, and headed back to Emma's.

The porch light was on, but the house was dark. Jason smiled. He pictured Emma and his mother sound asleep. They must be exhausted. So much had happened so fast. He toyed with the idea of waking them to let them know his dad was safe. No. He'd wait until morning. They needed the rest.

Jason glanced at the clearing behind the house and stared at the slight slope. He walked toward it. When he reached the spot where he and his father had used the metal detector, Jason crouched and grabbed a handful of earth. "What are you hiding?" After a few moments, Jason stood and brushed his hands. He hoped the small hill concealed enough treasure to make Emma's dreams come true. They'd know in a few days.

As he rounded the cabin and headed for the steps of the front porch, Jason saw his mother and Emma in the rocking chairs. He paused and eased out of sight.

"Jason saved me and Gayla." Emma shook her head, lifted a wine glass to her lips, and took a sip. "I don't know how I could go on without him." Emma looked at Sierra. "I could never forgive myself if something happened to your husband on my account." Her lips quivered, and she stared off into the distance.

Jason knew she was staring at the crosses under the burr oak, and his eyes blurred.

"I've always thought Dad held on till he figured I was old enough to care for Gayla. He missed Mom so much. I think he wanted to be with her."

"Stop it, Emma," Sierra snapped. "As much as I love Chris, I would never want to leave this world because he was gone. I have children, and hopefully, one day, grandchildren to love. Chris would never want me to follow him. And I knew your father. He would have never given up. He was ill. That's all there was to it. It wasn't his choice." She took a sip of wine. "Besides. Chris will be fine. He always is."

Jason waited a moment before he walked out of the shadows. He could ease his mother's mind. But, Emma? It was harder to deal with her old haunts. At least, for now, she didn't have to deal with harm befalling his father.

He took several steps back and jogged toward the cabin. "Hey." He pretended to catch his breath. "Glad you're still up. We heard from Dad. He should be at NORAD any minute now. A bridge was out, and they had to make a detour."

Sierra and Emma stood. Jason noticed the tears in his mother's eyes. "Did you guys save me a glass of wine?" he asked.

***

The next morning, a light rap roused Jason from his sleep. He slipped off the couch and opened the door. "Randy?" Jason yawned and glanced at the clock. "It's not even four yet," he whispered.

"Sorry, Jason. I got up early and went to the pavilion for a shower." Randy nodded toward the stove. "I could sure use some coffee."

"Sure." Jason scratched his head. "Give me a minute to make it and freshen up."

"Okay. I'll wait on the porch. I'd rather not wake your mom or Emma."

When the brew was ready, Jason joined Randy and handed him a cup. He sat in a rocker and took a sip. "So, what's up? What brought you over so early?"

"Someone was calling us on the radio. What I heard couldn't wait." Randy sniffed his armpit and winced. "As you can probably tell, I never got my shower."

Jason's eyes blinked, and he leaned forward. "Are you telling me Dad never made it to NORAD?"

Randy shook his head. "No. No. He's fine. But he had someone calling us all night."

"About what?"

"Jordan Dean wasn't with the men who went under on the bridge. One of the men finally broke. It seems they'd drugged Jordan and left him for dead about a hundred miles north of here."

Jason stood. "Damn!"

"Yeah. They took his map. He didn't have any gear. Most likely, he's dead or will be soon."

"We can't risk it. That bastard must have nine-lives." Jason wiped his forehead.

"I agree," Randy said. "As hell-bent as Jordan is, if he's alive, he could have walked twenty or thirty miles a day." Randy exhaled. "That SOB could be here already."

Jason released a long sigh. "Let's wait until after breakfast to tell Mom and Emma. We have to set up security again."

"Major Hall and his men are on their way back. They're bringing an extra dozen men with them," Randy said. "Your dad can't return until they work out a plan for excavating and transporting the treasure. They'll fly him in."

"So, Major Hall's men know we lied about there not being more treasure?"

Randy chuckled. "Not sure about that, but they gave themselves a nickname. *Riverton's Riders.*"

Jason's lips pinched. "Sounds like they know."

Emma stepped onto the porch and raised a coffee pot. "More coffee, gentlemen?"

Jason rolled his eyes and smirked. "Emma. Only the pot? You know I take cream and sugar with my coffee."

Sierra stepped out with a bowl of sugar and a pitcher of cream. She placed it on the table in front of her son. Her fists rested on her hips. "The smell of coffee woke us. I heard something about Jordan Dean. What the hell is going on now?"

***

Randy took it on himself to get the day started early by waking everyone. Once they'd fed the animals and milked the cows, everyone met at Emma's for breakfast.

Jason told them about the possibility of Jordan Dean paying a visit. "We can't count on him being dead."

Emma put her mug on the table. "He'll be here. I can feel it."

Daylight was breaking, and the sound of an approaching wagon rumbled in the distance. Everyone shot to their feet. Matthew snatched his binoculars from his pack and let out a hoot. "I think it's Rusty and the kids." He lifted the lenses again. "Yep. It's them!"

Emma clasped her chest. "Gayla."

Jason grasped her arm. "Emma, keep it together. Let Gayla know how proud you are that she was courageous enough to leave home and make friends."

"You're right." But as Gayla jumped from the wagon, Emma lost it. Shelley and Marcus rushed toward their parents. Gayla cocked her head and laughed as Emma sprinted toward her. She cuddled her older sister. "Geesh, Emma. It's not like I've been gone for months."

Emma pushed back and pulled herself together. "Well, excuse me for being so happy to see you."

A tear dripped from Gayla's eye, and she quickly wiped it away. "I missed you too. And I was worried about you. I harassed Uncle Rusty and Aunt Tracey for a few days about coming home. They couldn't contact you on the radio." She wobbled her head in victory. "Uncle Rusty finally threw his hands in the air and gave up." Gayla leaned forward and giggled. "I have them figured out. If you whine, they can't take it. Keep it up, and they'll do whatever you want."

Emma stepped back and put her hands on her hips. Her lips narrowed, and her eyes flickered. "Gayla. I don't think I like this new behavior."

Jason interrupted. "Emma. That's what kids do."

She glared at him. "What? They whine until they get their way?"

"Uh, yeah." Jason wrinkled his brows. "Are you saying Gayla didn't get away with it here?"

Emma glared at Gayla. Memories returned. A few moments later, she rolled her eyes and huffed. "Well. Guess I've been a sucker."

CHAPTER 40

Jordan Dean reached the Platte River. The damned idiots probably never saw the warning sign. He'd seen it weeks earlier when he and his men walked the bridge. It appeared safe to pass on foot, but there was no way a vehicle could cross. The detour had cost him days. Jordan imagined it cost the men from NORAD their lives. He hefted his pack onto his back and began to make his way across.

About halfway, the entire right side of the bridge had collapsed. Jordan stared down into the calm waters and smirked. Damned fools. He could see at least two trucks piled on top of the other. They got what they deserved. Jordan gave a mock salute, readjusted his pack, and continued.

A few steps in, his right foot broke loose a part of the road beneath him. Jordan lunged for the railing. "Son of a…" He took deep breaths and stared at the water below. As he wiped his brow, a creeping pain ran up the length of his leg. He was afraid to look. When he managed to lift his leg, agony and fear took hold.

Jordan's shin bone was scraped clean. The only thing that remained of his inside calf were feathery strips of meat. His head swirled. Perhaps from the pain. Or was it because he'd seen no need to pack medical supplies. All he needed was food, a weapon, and ammo.

He glanced at his mangled leg and shook his head. No first-aid kit would be helping that!

He could have been unconscious for hours. Possibly days. How would he know? Jordan glanced at his leg then quickly looked away. Raw meat and bone stared back at him. He rolled on his side and vomited.

**

The smell of a fire and roasting meat greeted Jordan. He blinked a few times. Someone held his head and offered water.

"Drink," the voice said. "Drink."

Jordan remembered and reached for his leg.

251

"No. Let it alone." Someone grabbed his hands. "I only have salt. No antibiotics. I've been treating your wound for three days now. It's looking better." The man offered water again, and Jordan drank.

Jordan let his head relax on the soft down pillow. "I'm cold," he whispered.

The stranger covered him. "We have antelope. Try to eat."

Jorda ate a few bites, but it took all of his energy to chew. It tasted so good. He wanted one more taste, but the heaviness of his eyes won.

"Sleep, friend. It's probably best. Thank God you were unconscious when I had to cauterize your wounds."

As Jordan drifted away, his mind replayed the past few days. He'd made it across the bridge and collapsed. At some point, he dragged himself to the river's edge and rinsed his wounds. "Charles!" someone had yelled. A woman stood over him, and a man was behind her. The man was tearing cloth into strips and ordering the children. "Get these in the pot of hot water. Damned if I want to see another man die."

Jordan woke, and for the first time in his life, he took in the beautiful darkness. The stars in the sky were mesmerizing, and he stared for several minutes. Then, he glanced to his right. The bed of embers next to him snapped and popped, begging to be fed. It was beautiful. Why had he never noticed before?

The small fire seemed to come to life, and a child's voice asked if he was thirsty.

"Yes."

After a few sips, Jordan asked the young boy to help him stand.

"I'll get my parents," he said.

"No." Jordan threw his hand up, then rubbed his stubbly chin and whispered. "I don't want to trouble them. I've been enough of a burden. I just need to see if I can walk."

The boy glanced at the wagon where his parents and sister slept. "I don't know, Mister. They'll be mad. Maybe we should wait till morning."

Jordan clutched his lower belly. "Kid, I gotta go. I can't wait till morning."

The boy glanced at the wagon, grimaced, then stood. "Okay, but when you're done, you have to lay back down."

"Deal."

The pain was excruciating. Jordan imagined it was more from lack of movement than a lack of healing. The skin around his wound needed to stretch. Warm liquid trickled down his calf, but he refused to cry out. He wouldn't even acknowledge it. The less the boy knew, the better. He'd be leaving later and taking one of their horses and some supplies. He was getting soft. He wouldn't kill them. Well, unless they tried to stop him.

"Thanks, son." Jordan ruffled the boy's hair. "Get some sleep. I'll watch the fire. It's the least I can do after all your family did for me."

"Are you sure, Mister?"

"Absolutely. I feel great," Jordan lied.

The young boy curled up on his mat next to the fire. Jordan couldn't believe the sadness that overcame him. How could he steal from the only people in his life who'd freely given him support? If not for them, he'd surely be dead.

Before the boy drifted off to sleep, Jordan questioned him. "What are your parent's names, and where are you headed?"

Jordan made a mental note about the family who'd rescued him. Once he'd recovered his treasure, he'd find and compensate them. The decision lessened his guilt. What the hell was he thinking? Why did he care what happened to them? While Jordan waited for the boy to fall asleep, he pulled some paper from his pack and wrote a note to himself. *Charles and Jean Crawford. One son. One daughter. Riverton, Wyoming. They sacrificed much to save my worthless ass. For the first time in my life, I feel I owe someone.* Jordan's fingers ran through his oily, matted hair, and he stared at what he'd written. He was about to crumple the reminder and toss it on the fire. Instead, he took a breath, folded it, and placed it in the front pocket of his pack. He glanced at the sleeping boy and made his get-away his plans.

CHAPTER 41

Emma ran behind the wagon as Gayla and the others returned to Hudson Ranch. "Bye, Gayla. Bye."

Jason caught up to her and swung her around. "Déjà vu, Emma," he laughed.

Emma smiled at the memory. "That was us years ago." Her face warmed. "I must look like a fool."

Jason wrapped his arm around her and waved at the departing wagon. "Wave, Emma. And smile. Gayla needs to know it's okay."

It hit her. How could she be so selfish? She wanted the best for her little sister, but her love was smothering Gayla.

Once the wagon was out of sight, Emma threw herself into Jason's arms. "It's so hard, Jason. It's so hard."

She knew he understood.

He held her back. "It's time to let go."

Emma's lips formed a sad frown, and she nodded. "I know. I know."

"Besides, Major Hall and his men will be here in a few days. Dad's coming right behind them. As soon as he gets here, we start digging." Jason winked.

Emma glanced toward the field where the large cluster of trees filled the drawing. "I'm almost afraid of what we'll find."

**

Three days after Gayla left, Major Hall and his men arrived. A few minutes later, a whooping sound filled the air and grew louder before it cleared the tops of the trees. Emma couldn't take her eyes off the chopper as it landed in the field near her house. It was the most amazing thing she'd ever seen.

Chris jumped out, rushed toward her, and took her hand. He nodded. "Come on. The pilot wants to meet you."

After he introduced Emma to the pilot, he slapped the empty seat. "Climb aboard, Ms. Emma. I'd be honored to take you for a ride."

Emma remembered how sick the motion from the jeep made her and took several steps back. "No, thank you. I'll keep both feet on the ground."

The pilot laughed, gave a thumbs-up, and wished them well. Chris led Emma away as the blades began to turn.

Emma waved as the helicopter flew away. "Part of me wishes I'd taken him up on his offer."

"You'll have plenty of chances soon, trust me," Chris said.

Chris asked Major Hall to join them at Emma's while his men cleaned up at the pavilion.

"I hate that we had to lie to you and your men," Chris said.

The major waved off his apology. "Nonsense. They understood."

Emma felt her face warming. "So, they knew we were lying?"

"Not until they found out we were returning with even more men." He chuckled. "Our supplies list ended any doubts they had. Two dozen shovels, metal crates, and locks? And it's not often six sharpshooters are sent on a mission."

"Still, I apologize," Emma said.

"Like I said, nonsense. So, where do we start?"

Chris looked at Emma. "It's your call."

"I say we dig up the other small shrubs first." She let out a deep breath. "And the huge cluster of trees?" She tapped the map spread out on the kitchen table. "We save it for last."

After breakfast, the shovels came out. Jason handed one to Emma. "You get the honor of breaking ground."

Emma chose to dig up the chest she and Jason found. When her shovel hit the hard surface, the men took over and placed the box in a wagon.

"I promised everyone a percentage. That promise still stands."

Jason grinned. "The rest goes to restoring power in Riverton. We'll have to figure out a percentage once we know what we're dealing with. Hopefully, you'll get a hefty nest egg."

Most of the men declined the offer.

"Listen, we're not talking millions. Just enough to make your lives a little easier when you leave the military. Or perhaps you can help your families." Jason looked at his father and patted the box. "Should we let them see what's in here?"

Chris nodded, and Jason lifted the lid. Whistles and gasps filled the air.

"How many of these are here?" someone asked.

"We have no idea," Jason said.

"I think there may be a few dozen this size or smaller," Emma said. "But, there may be several much larger."

"Show us where to start digging," one man yelled.

***

After a day spent separating and storing the unearthed treasure, Emma's living room was lined with dozens of metal chests filled with riches.

"We've barely touched the surface, Emma." Sierra sat on the sofa and wiped her brow.

Emma sat beside her and nodded. Many of the larger bushes on the map contained two or more trunks, and they were all loaded with precious metals, coins, and gems.

"Do you think there's enough?" She asked Sierra. "I mean, enough to build a power station for Riverton?"

"Honestly, I don't know. I have no idea what it will cost or what the treasure is worth." Sierra squeezed Emma's hand. "Chris said the first load he took to NORAD was worth millions." She scanned the cabin. "What he took was a fraction of what's filling your living room tonight."

Jason walked in, followed by several men with six more cases. "Thanks, guys." He slapped them on the back. "Go to the pavilion and get a shower before dinner. Oh, and Dad said we're watching a movie tonight."

The men threw their fists in the air. "Yes."

Only Jason and Joshua Elliot remained.

Jason poured himself a glass of wine then glanced at Joshua. He poured another. "You're not military anymore." Jason handed the goblet to his new friend.

Joshua stared at the offering. "Thank you, sir, but I don't drink."

Sierra stood. "I'll get some iced tea."

"Thank you, ma'am."

"I'm sorry, Joshua," Jason said. "We hated being dishonest. Especially with you."

"Hey, not a problem." He accepted the glass of tea from Sierra.

Jason pointed to the chair at the far end of the couch. "Sit. You've worked your rear off all day."

Joshua rolled his eyes. "Whatever," he said as he took a seat.

Jason sat next to Emma. "This is the last batch for tonight. The ladies cooked a feast. You and Mom go to dinner. Joshua and I will stay here and watch over things."

Emma went to Joshua. He stood as she approached. "Joshua, I hope there's enough treasure to rebuild Riverton." She held him and squeezed his shoulders. "Regardless, something tells me you'll play a big role in what happens."

"I don't know how that's possible, ma'am. But I'll do whatever I can."

Sierra and Emma headed for the pavilion.

Jason finished his glass of wine. "Okay, so do you take a shower first, or do I?"

Joshua laughed. "I'll start the generator then check out the area. Have another glass of wine while the water heats." His nose wrinkled. "And you go first. You stink."

Jason threw his head back and roared.

***

Dusk was taking over. Jordan looked through his binoculars and squinted. Damn it. He wished he could see better. He refocused. Son-of-a... It was her! The older female he'd taken weeks ago. How could that be? There was no way she could have survived, but there she was. Jordan felt something peculiar. Respect. What else could it be? He smiled at the sight of his adversary and chuckled. Damn. She'd outwitted him. Was the younger girl her daughter, her sister, or merely an acquaintance? Was she alive? Or had she died? Jordan lowered his binoculars and found it odd that he hoped the young girl had survived.

He scanned the area. What appeared to be dozens of armed military stood outside a new building, warming themselves next to a fire. He knew why they were there. He knew what they would find. There was no way he'd be leaving with his treasure. His best bet was a lifetime in prison. Most likely, he'd face the firing squad.

Jordan sat on a fallen tree, opened the front pocket of his pack, and read the note tucked inside. He returned it, zipped the pocket, and thought. He could run. He shook his head. No. He'd fought through the pain, but gave in the day before and looked at his leg. He'd almost gagged at the sight; bloody, swollen, dark red streaks, and covered in green and yellow puss. He huffed and shook his head. What a way to go. Karma. Yeah, that's what it was. Bad Karma had finally bitten him on the ass.

After a moment of reflection, Jordan made his choice. His years of evil would surely give him a seat in hell. Maybe it was too late, but they say there are no atheists in foxholes.

He stepped out of the clearing as Emma and Sierra passed. "I'd advise you to stand still and not make a ruckus." The women froze, and Jordan limped toward them. He shoved a pistol into Emma's ear.

"Call them. Tell them Jordan Dean is here."

Emma reached for Sierra's hand and squeezed. "I'll do no such thing," she whispered. "You'll not harm my loved ones."

Jordan burst into laughter. "How can I harm them? I'm only one man with a single bullet." He twisted the barrel of his pistol into her temple. "I could use it on you, but..." He put the barrel next to his ear.

"Stop!" Joshua shouted. "Drop your gun. There's no need."

Jordan spun and faced the soldier. "Young man, only once in my life can I remember an act of kindness thrown my way. Only once can I recall others giving to me without expecting something in return." He nodded toward his backpack. "Their names are in the front pocket." He took a deep breath and looked at Emma. "Is the little girl okay?"

Emma nodded.

Jordan smiled. "I'm glad." Jordan chuckled. "So, you found the map?"

Emma didn't respond.

"Well. I hope you put the money to good use. Do you mind telling me what your plan is?"

Emma hesitated, then told him how the proceeds would go toward rebuilding Riverton and, hopefully, Lander.

Jordan nodded. "Everything happens for a reason. I would have probably wasted it on women and whiskey." His free hand rubbed his mouth. "In that case, there's something I need to tell you. The most valuable stash isn't on the map."

Emma's eyes grew wide. Sierra took her hand and squeezed.

"Many years ago, I had a room added to the cellar. There's a knot in one of the panels just big enough for the tip of a finger. When you find the secret room, dig up the floor."

Jordan turned back to the man with the leveled gun. "Son, I'm not one to live on death row, and there's no need for you to live with taking a man's life." He closed his eyes. "I learned how that could change your life when I was thirteen." Jordan's lips thinned as he pressed the gun harder against his skull. "My Dad beat my Mom and me one time too many. The last time, she died in my arms, and I made sure he'd *never* hurt anyone else!" His mouth twitched, and his eyes teared. "They said it was self-defense. I moved from foster home to foster home. The last family I lived with owned a boat and went treasure hunting on the weekends. I watched and learned." Jordan chuckled. "That family was my first investor. They bought my boat, paid my crew, and covered all of my expenses for more than a year." Jordan rubbed his mouth. "They were good people, but hatred consumed me. I felt nothing for anyone! I never gave them a dime, even though I'd recovered millions in coins and jewels."

Jordan grabbed his bad leg and screamed in agony as he lowered himself to the other knee. He looked once more at Emma. "Please forgive me," he whispered. "There should be plenty to rebuild Riverton." He rocked back and forth in obvious pain. "My mom." Jordan tightened his lips. "She was an art teacher. She tried to protect me, but he was too evil." His head lowered to his chest. "She loved children. I'd appreciate it if you could find a way to honor her." A tear slid down his cheek. "Her name was Hazel. Hazel Dean."

A shot rang out. The gun slipped from Jordan's hand as he crumpled to the ground.

***

The men decided to bury Jordan several miles from Emma's Place.

"No!" Emma stood and addressed everyone. "He gets buried here. Like it or not, he's a part of this." Emma took note of the stares and lifted brows. "Everything is not as it seems." She shook her head. "Jordan Dean was evil, but there was a reason behind it." Emma took a deep breath. "He confessed his sins and asked for forgiveness. When he found out my plans for the money, he was pleased and told me where to find more. He said it's not on the map and was his most valuable stash."

"What?" Jason stood. "Where?"

Emma grinned. "In a place that only you and I know of."

Jason seemed confused for a moment. Then he nodded and sat down.

"Jordan gets a proper burial." She walked to the bottom step of the porch and searched the surroundings. "Over there." She pointed. "Along the tree line yet out of sight." Her eyes lifted. "Everything happens for a reason. Jordan's bad deeds may bring amazing things to life!"

***

After Jordan's burial, Jason wrapped his arm around Emma. "You have the final say. What do we do about the family that saved Jordan?"

She shrugged. "They didn't know who they were helping. But something tells me it wouldn't have mattered. I believe they should be compensated for their compassion to show others that being good samaritans still means something."

Emma stood by as Chris contacted the new mayor of Riverton. "Richard, we have info that a family named Crawford is planning on joining your community. Marshall and Jean Crawford. They have a son and a daughter. I'd be much obliged if you found them a nice home and a job. I'll compensate the owner or town."

Chris explained the situation without revealing Emma's plan.

"Sounds like the Crawfords are the kind of people we want here in Riverton," the mayor said. "I'll make sure it happens."

***

The next morning, Jason and Emma stood atop the slopping hill represented in the drawing.

"All the trees in the drawing. This should be huge. But Jordan said the one in the cellar was bigger. That's hard to believe," Emma said.

"We'll find out soon. Are you ready?"

Emma let out of huff. Her jaws clenched, and she nodded. "I'm ready." Jason gave the go-ahead.

Chris had a backhoe sent to Emma's from Hudson Ranch. "We can dig the area up in minutes."

After a few scoops, the backhoe dug deeper and dropped its load.

Emma weaved back and forth and fell to her knees as a skull rolled toward her.

Jason flung his arms and yelled. "Stop! Stop!"

Sierra rushed toward them. "Dear God!" She looked at Jason. "I'm taking Emma inside."

A few minutes later, the digging continued. Amongst the half dozen bodies, There were several dozen cases of treasure.

Jason exhaled. "Dad," he asked Chris, "What do you think this is worth?"

Chris rubbed his mouth and wiped an eye. "An untold number of lives, son." Chris tapped his fist to his lips. "To be honest, Jordan's evil may end up saving thousands. But, it wouldn't be happening without someone like Emma finding it."

CHAPTER 42

Emma was seven-years-old when she'd visited Hudson Ranch. Her first encounter as an adult was overwhelming. Many, working together, had created a beautiful community. She doubted it was possible. She should have known better. The men and women who'd come to her small parcel had taught her better.

Emma stared at the reflection in the mirror. Not one alteration. It turned out that Jason's mother's wedding dress was a perfect fit. She ran her hands down the length of the gown and felt the urge to talk to his mother. "Mrs. Renee', I love your son. I promise to do all I can to make him happy."

Gayla ran in, stopped, and cupped her face. "Oh, Emma."

Emma's eyes turned to slivers. "You'll keep the dress a secret?"

Gayla huffed. "Heck yeah," she snorted. "I can't wait to see Jason start boo-hooing when he sees you wearing Grandma Sierra's wedding dress."

Emma approached Gayla. "Jellybean, I don't think you understand. This dress didn't belong to Grandma Sierra." Again, Emma's hand slowly ran down the length of the gown before she looked back at Gayla. "This gown belonged to Jason's birth mother."

Gayla nodded. "Yeah. I know. It was Grandma Sierra's wedding dress."

Emma squeezed Gayla's hand. "I'm sorry. I thought you knew." Emma explained things to Gayla.

Gayla's eyes filled with tears, and she hugged Emma. "I'm sorry. I'm sorry. I didn't know. That's so sad."

Emma ran her fingers through Gayla's hair. "Sometimes, sad stories have happy endings."

***

What a blessing. Rusty wiped the fog from his eyes as the spitting image of his departed daughter held a bouquet of wildflowers, ready to walk down the aisle. Rusty approached her, got on a knee, and clutched her free hand. "Promise me. When you get married, you'll let me walk you down the aisle just like I'm doing for Emma."

Gayla kissed her Uncle's cheek. "No one but you, Uncle Rusty."

Rusty stood and nodded. "Let's get this show on the road."

***

Jason stood at the altar and stared at the door. It would begin any second. Soon, he and Emma would be married. The pavilion at Hudson Ranch overflowed with well-wishers, not only from the community, but also from the surrounding towns and homesteads. Many more stood outside, hoping to witness the wedding of Jason Alvise and Emma Harding. Rusty, his wife, and helpers had prepared a feast to serve hundreds. They would turn no one away.

When the door opened, and Emma entered, Jason gasped. Visions from nine years earlier flashed through his memory. As she walked toward him, Jason's mind whirled.

***

"Jason, are you ill? You barely ate dinner and haven't said a word."

"I'm okay, Dad." Jason looked at his feet as he tapped his toes together. "I just feel sorry for the other kids," he sniffed.

"The children at NORAD?" Sierra asked. "Trust me, they're fine."

"No, Mom." He slumped, and his chin dipped to his chest. "The *other* kids. The ones that live outside." He looked at his surroundings. "I don't feel right about things."

Chris fought the urge to join in his son's anguish. "Sierra, I think it's time."

She took a deep breath and left the room.

"Jason," Chris sat beside his son and held his hand, "We've told you the story of how you came to be our son many times."

"Phhh. I know, Dad. I was the luckiest boy on earth." His reply was filled with sarcasm.

Chris nodded. "That you were. And you know your mom's saying? Everything happens for a reason and works out for the best."

"Yeah." Jason rolled his eyes. "I'm sorry, Dad. I don't see how losing power and millions of people dying could have a good purpose."

"I can't answer that, son." Chris shrugged his shoulders. "I don't understand why good people like your birth parents had to die. Maybe it was to put you here, at this moment." Chris spread his arms wide. "Maybe this was where you were supposed to be."

Sierra rolled in the boxes and placed them at Jason's feet. Her face was damp, her eyes red and veiny. "We wanted to be sure you were man

262

enough to handle this." She caressed the boxes. "We received them from Major Hall a while back."

Chris placed his hand on Jason's shoulder. "Jason, Major Hall was your first father's best friend. He says you're his spitting image."

Jason stared at the boxes. "Are you saying these belonged to my birth parents?" he asked quietly.

"Yes. I believe you'll find a lot of yourself inside."

"May I open them in my room?"

"Of course."

Jason sat on his bed and stared at the boxes. Part of him wanted to rip them open and expose the contents. The other half feared what he'd find. Chris and Sierra Alvise were his parents—his mom and dad. He wondered if his feelings toward them would change once he met his real parents. He focused on his door, imagining his parents, Chris and Sierra, in the living room. He guessed they were crying and hugging each other, anxious over his reaction to the contents of the boxes. Jason smiled. He loved them. Nothing in the cases could change that! No! His love for them would *never* change. But unlike millions of others, he had the opportunity to meet the ones who had given him life. He carefully opened the time capsules. In one box lay an envelope from Major Hall. He took a deep breath and sat on his bed.

Major Hall wrote about how fortunate it was that Chris and Sierra rescued him. He believed their union was divine intervention. God had a purpose for bringing them together. Jason reread the letter before placing it to the side and lifting the dress from the box. He spread it out on his bed. His mother's wedding gown, covered with tiny pearls, shimmered in the light. He lay down beside it and clutched it to his chest, deeply inhaling as he imagined her scent.

Jason thought for sure he'd cry out in pain when he opened the cases; instead, he couldn't stop smiling. Every turn of the page showed genuine love and dedication. The only tears he shed were of happiness. His birth parents had lived beautiful, rich lives, filled with precious memories. He instinctively knew they would want no sorrow.

Jason closed the last photo album, gently folded his mother's wedding gown, and picked up his father's high school football.

When he entered the living room, it was much as he'd imagined. His mother's eyes were red from crying, his father was nursing a drink as he held her, and his three siblings were struggling with a puzzle.

"Hey, Mom." Jason broke the silence as he handed her Renee's wedding gown. "Do you think we can pass this down?" He smiled. "I thought it would be cool if all the ladies in our family wore it."

Sierra choked. "That would be wonderful."

Jason took a step to the side and faced Chris. His eyes thinned as he tightly gripped the football and pounded it into his left hand. "Well, old man?" He raised his eyebrows. "You up for it?"

"Huh?" Chris squinted. His jaw was tight, his eyes red.

"Well, from what I just saw, I'd say you have three, four years max before I kick your butt," Jason smirked and continued to taunt his father by slapping the ball in his hand.

Jason watched as his mother fought back more tears, and his dad stood and tried to act tough.

"Huh. Is that so?" Chris grunted as he wiped the back of his hand across his nose. "We'll just see about that!"

Chris kissed Sierra. "We'll be back after I teach this smart-aleck kid a lesson."

Jason turned before he left the room. "I love you, Mom." He grinned, and his mother burst into tears. Jason winked. "Dad doesn't know it, but I'm about to kick his rear-end." He chuckled as he walked out the door.

"I'm going long, old man. Run!" Jason hurled the ball down the corridor.

***

Emma was only steps away. Jason felt his knees give, and his father grabbed his arm to support him. Jason lifted his eyes and stared at the woman walking toward him in his birth mother's gown.

He knew now. He finally understood. Years of questioning why his life was spared while so many other children died began to fade. It was just like his mom always said. Everything happens for a reason. Everything works out for the best. Jason was supposed to be there for Emma and Gayla, and they, in turn, would be there for thousands of others.

Jason bowed his head and quietly spoke to his birth mom. "Thank you. Thank you for saving me."

CHAPTER 43

True to her word, every dime of Emma's treasure went to rebuild the town of Riverton. News of The Harding-Alvise Power Plant had people flocking to Riverton.

As people poured in, the problem with housing had to be addressed. As they figured out how to barter for shelter, the city council met for hours each day, and the arguments escalated.

One councilman slammed his fist on the table. "This is ridiculous! We have tents set up all over the city! These people need to be in houses! Some of them have young children! For God's sake! We can't leave them in tents with all the vacant homes we have!"

"So, you think we should just give everyone a house?" Another councilman shook his head. "No! We don't want freeloaders! We want people who are willing to contribute."

Joshua Elliot was the newest member of the council, and the youngest ever elected. Besides his duties as a councilman, he oversaw the installation of the powerlines and rewiring of homes. He'd sat through this argument every night for over a week. He'd had enough.

"Ladies. Gentlemen," he said. "I think we've heard these repeated arguments long enough."

One of the elders sneered. "What do you know? You're only here because of Emma and Jason."

Joshua smiled, slid his chair back, and stood. "Well, I guess that's one more reason you should thank them."

"Little smart ass," someone muttered.

Joshua chuckled. "I have a proposal if you think you can stop arguing long enough to hear it."

The mayor rolled his head and flipped his hand. "Go ahead."

"As it was pointed out earlier, we have hundreds of vacant homes that are owned by the city, and we can't keep them up."

"Yeah, yeah. We know. We've talked about it all week," someone said.

265

"Well, I propose, in exchange for housing, the occupants agree to work for the city or the Harding-Alvise Power Plant. I'm sure Mrs. Emma would agree. They would be supplied with food, shelter, clothing, daycare, and medical care. Everyone of age would be expected to contribute. Whatever skill they have would be used to pay back to the community." He glanced around the room. "Later, once we have currency, they start paying rent."

The mayor rubbed his forehead. "I can't believe I'm saying this, but go ahead, Joshua."

"Those with carpenter skills renovate the homes. Electricians, help with the power situation. We need teachers, babysitters, people to help with the gardens and livestock. The roads are a mess. Houses need to be painted."

Joshua received blank stares. "Listen. It would be like it is at Hudson Ranch. Everyone checks in, they do their chores, then clock out. If they don't pull their weight? Well, sadly, they have to leave."

Nothing. No response. Joshua was getting irritated but refused to show it. "Oh, and homes large enough to accommodate more than one family? Well, shared housing may be mandatory."

The mayor rubbed his jaw. Finally, he stood and began to clap. The rest of the council followed him.

"Looks like our streets may soon be tent free," the mayor said. "Hell, and the town may look like it used too."

***

With the installation of the power plant, the community's rapid economic and population growth brought a new train line and depot. With the new train line, stores, large and small, sprang up from Riverton to Lander, and eventually, the two towns merged. Several manufacturing plants opened and supplied the country with everything from batteries to shoes.

Money had been reintroduced, and slowly, people began replacing bartering for cash. Bartering would continue for years, but in the beginning, most store owners set up exchanges with other shops to supplement employee's cash pay with their merchandise.

Walking into a market and leaving with meat for dinner, strolling down the street to buy or trade for fresh fruits, vegetables, or bread? That was something many never experienced.

As cash became more popular, job openings exploded, and salaries were on a steady incline. Every day saw new residents clamoring to rent or buy a home.

While admiring the art in the newly opened museum, Emma grabbed her belly and bent. "Oh!"

"Hey," Jason scolded his unborn child, "don't kick your mother around."

Emma pointed and winced. "Jason." She nodded toward their daughter and massaged her soon-to-be little one.

Jason lifted their three-year-old in the air and spun her around. "Hey, you. Hands off the paintings." Lila giggled as her daddy nuzzled her.

Marcus and Gayla brought Emma's five-year-old son over. "We're returning him." Gayla let out a puff of air.

Marcus chuckled. "If our child is as wild as Daniel, I'm sending it back."

Gayla grabbed her swollen tummy, rubbed, and shook her head. "Uh, I don't think so." She smirked. "If you hadn't kissed me, we wouldn't be in this situation. And for the record. At my first birthday party, you said I should wish to never have to change poopy diapers. You also said if I didn't tell anyone, my wish would come true." She rolled her eye. "Ha! That was a lie! And now I'll *really* have to change them." Gayla let out a gust of air and shook her head. "Guess I have to cowgirl-up."

Everyone erupted in laughter.

Rusty, Chris, and Sierra joined them. "I'm so proud of you, Emma. Everyone is talking about the gallery," Rusty said.

Randy strolled up and kissed Emma's forehead. "Your art gallery seems to be a success. Everyone starts crying when they get to the wall of connection." He shook his head. "Whew! Reading those letters that reconnected families and friends tore me up!"

Emma smiled. "Well. I have to say. The wall dedicated to honoring Jordan's mother, Hazel, filled my heart. Hundreds of pictures drawn by children." She lifted her shoulders. "How could that not fill you with joy?"

Randy nodded. And your dream has come true." He pointed to Emma's art hanging next to one of The Highwaymen paintings that Sierra had donated. "Of course, yours are much better." He winked.

Emma clasped hands with her husband and looked into Jason's eyes. "Thank you, Randy, but my dream came true when I was seventeen."

I hope you enjoyed *Out of Darkness*.

If you have time, please leave a review on Amazon.

My author page is linked below to follow me on Amazon and to leave your review.

https://www.amazon.com/C-C-Carroll/e/B07XJ7QFMG/ref=dp_byline_cont_ebooks_1

Please follow me on Facebook for upcoming announcements and contests.

https://www.facebook.com/C.C.Carroll2019

Made in the USA
Coppell, TX
02 October 2021